The W

John Pritchard wa
NHS career bega
Casualty receptionist in his local hospital, after which eye-opening introduction he worked in administration and patient services. He currently helps to manage the medical unit in a large hospital in the south of England. *The Witching Hour* is his third novel, following the highly successful *Night Sisters* and *Angels of Mourning*.

By the same author

NIGHT SISTERS
ANGELS OF MOURNING

Voyager

JOHN PRITCHARD

The Witching Hour

HarperCollins*Publishers*

Voyager
An imprint of HarperCollins*Publishers*
77–85 Fulham Palace Road,
Hammersmith, London W6 8JB

The *Voyager* World Wide Web site address is
http://www.harpercollins.co.uk/voyager

A Paperback Original 1997
1 3 5 7 9 8 6 4 2

A catalogue record for this book
is available from the British Library

ISBN 0 00 649636 9

Set in Postscript Linotype Sabon by
Rowland Phototypesetting Ltd,
Bury St Edmunds, Suffolk

Printed and bound in Great Britain by
Caledonian International
Book Manufacturing Ltd, Glasgow

To Ennio Morricone

whose brilliant soundtrack for *Il Grande Silenzio*
gave shape to this story
for twenty years of inspirational accompaniment

Acknowledgements

Inspiration for this story comes from sources as disparate as John Webster's *The Duchess of Malfi* (1614) and Gianfranco Parolini's *If You Meet Sartana, Pray for Your Death!* (1968); but its seeds were sown in particular by the work of Giuliano Carmineo, Tonino Cervi, Sergio Corbucci, Giorgio Ferroni, Lucio Fulci, Piers Haggard, Sergio Leone, Ennio Morricone, Bruno Nicolai, Audrey Nohra, Mike Oldfield, Don Powell, Michael Reeve, Julianne Regan, Nello Rosati, Pasquale Squitieri, Duccio Tessari, Tonino Valerii and Luigi Vanzi.

Thanks are also due to Geraint Lloyd Davies; Fabrizio Li Perni; Rene Hogguer of *CineCity*; Lionel G. Woodman of *Soundtrack Deletions*; Iris Fitzgibbon and Viv Care, for their insights and advice; Justine Picrdie, for sharing her Home Thoughts; Sophie Lorge, for her prompt and enthusiastic translations; F.M.E. (as ever was); and to Anton Abril, Luis Enriquez Bacalov, Francesco di Masi, Gianni Ferrio, Nico Fidenco, Benedetto Ghiglia, Marcello Giombini, Michele Lacerenza and Piero Umiliani, for musical refreshment in dry seasons.

St Catherine's Hospice was founded, staffed and populated by my imagination, and Rachel's observations are her own.

1

RESTLESS

The drowning man groped upward, and gripped my hand in his.

The *squeeze* was a surprise, from someone so frail. Fear made his fingers strong. He caught me off guard for that first moment; and then, leaning forward, I was squeezing tightly back.

Across the bed, his daughter had his other hand in just as firm a grip: as if, between us, we could keep him alive by our efforts alone. And like grim death he clung to us both.

Having fought back to the surface, he gasped for air; a fierce determination on his wasted face. His grip relaxed a fraction. The sound of his lungs was laboured and coarse.

'. . . oh, Dad . . .' the woman whispered.

Outside the window, the late October light was thinning out. Details in the room were indistinct already. I could hear the crows, coming home across the farmland.

'Still there, Sister?' he rasped from his pillow.

I smiled through the twilight. 'Still here, Tom.'

He swallowed. 'Do not go gentle; isn't that . . . what they say?'

'It's a good night, Tom,' I murmured. 'No need to fight it. No need to be afraid . . .'

He felt the undertow again, and renewed his grip.

'Susie . . .'

'I'm here, Dad . . .'

'. . . I'm sorry, love . . .'

'Oh, shhh,' she chided, with tearful fondness. 'You've nothing to be sorry for. I *love* you, Dad.'

The pause that followed was filled with his breathing, and the heedless cry of birds. His grasp grew tighter: the fingers dug like iron into mine. And then the strength slipped out of them, as life lost its grip at last. The drowning man went under once more. And this time he sank like a stone.

I sat close and quiet while she finished her drink. Tea mixed with tears: like the bitter cup of hospital bereavement. But the dampness on her cheeks was drying, now; and her smile, though pale, was genuine enough.

'I'm really grateful, Rachel . . . Everyone's been so kind.'

We were back in the Quiet Room, with its soft yellow light and softer chairs. The walls were hung with tasteful pictures: pastoral scenes, where sheep grazed in peace and roads led ever onward. Over the hills and far away . . .

'. . . and I'm sure it helped him: you being with us at the end.'

I gestured. 'Thanks. I hope so. What's important is to know you're not alone . . .'

My hand could testify to that: still gently aching in the ghost of his grip. But what had started in fear had finished as assertion: the bond of human contact. At the end, he'd had two people to hold on to – even though he knew we couldn't come.

Susan took a timid sip of tea. I guessed she was in her late twenties: a little younger than me. I'd known her for a week – ever since her dad had been admitted. He'd gone steadily downhill, as we knew he must, but the team had kept him free of pain and comfortable; and together we'd eased him on towards this final night.

I thought suddenly of my training – being rostered to the labour ward. Birth had been a struggle, too: I'd held the hand of a mother just as tightly. I tried to take some comfort from the parallel. But my heart just wasn't in it.

Sue's silent tears had started up again. Refocusing, I touched her shoulder. 'What?'

'It's just . . . oh . . . there's so much more I could have said.'

'Shhh,' I told her. 'Listen. When it comes down to it, there's just three things you need to say. Thank you; I love you; goodbye. You said them all.'

She sniffed again, and nodded. A little more at ease. I glanced down briefly; before she saw the shadow cross my face.

When Sue had gone, and they'd taken Tom away, I went back to his room with Mel to change the bed.

With the light on full, the sense of emptiness was overwhelming. The room felt bleached and barren. Something inside me seemed to wilt in sympathy; but I set about the task as briskly as I could. God knew, I was used to it by now.

So was Mel; filling the linen sack as matter-of-factly as someone stuffing a chicken, while I stripped the bed. But when I gave her a glance, her shrewd young face was thoughtful.

'You think it would have been better if he'd gone in his sleep? For Sue, I mean.'

I considered it, eyes down. They mostly slipped away in silence, it was true. But some people fought: playing right to the whistle, as my dad might have said. Sometimes, as with Tom, we had to soothe them into stillness.

'No . . . she needed to *know* they'd parted on good

terms.' Looking up again, I marshalled a smile. 'I think they both found peace tonight.'

Not everyone had that chance, of course. I remembered A&E and ITU: people stupefied with grief – as white and incoherent as kebab-shop drunks. Bereaved from out of nowhere, with so many things unsaid . . .

A malignant little ache had bloomed inside me: like the first pangs of food-poisoning. But I knew that it wasn't. As we spread the clean sheet out between us my smile felt as if it had been pinched into place with clamps.

Thank you. I love you. Goodbye.

I'd never had the chance to tell my own parents that. The car-smash had come out of the blue. One minute I'd been reading on the bed in the nurses' home, wondering who that bloody phone was ringing for; and the next . . .

But that was ten years ago now. The scars still itched from time to time, but they had healed.

The wound I'd felt reopening tonight was still raw.

I ignored it for as long as I could: gritting my teeth and working on in silence. The job was quickly and tidily done. The room we left behind us was a slate wiped clean: no trace of him was left. I switched off the light, and quietly shut the door.

Mel went off to dump the linen; I glanced after her, swallowed – and made straight for the loo. The poison was into the deep tissue now. I could feel its pressure in my midriff, like a build-up of suppurating fluid. My heart was a swollen abscess, fit to burst. Shutting myself in a cubicle, I sat down on the closed toilet lid – and burst into a helpless fit of sobs.

I stifled them with my hands as best I could: tears stung my nose, and oozed between my fingers. The purging seemed to last an age; but at length my gulps of grief became dry shudders. Taking a breath, head bowed, I wiped my eyes. In the drained and dripping stillness, a wistful form of words took shape. A fragment of a prayer.

The beauty of death could not contain you. You did not remain in the comfort of the grave.

I'd heard that on the radio once. The boldness of its image was the only consolation I could cling to. But physically, at least, I felt a little better: as if the cry had rid my system of its poison. As if I'd just been sick.

Emerging, I went over to the basin to splash water in my face, drying my cheeks on the roller-towel. A pause then, while I pieced myself together. I'd learned to live with relapses like this. In five minutes' time I'd be a picture of coolness and control again: ready to help the team adjust to losing Tom. I knew I wasn't healed, though. The wound would keep on festering inside me: a depthless well of bitterness and tears.

By nine-fifteen, the car-park was all but empty; the night breeze chilled still further by the bleak white lighting. Still buttoning my coat, I walked over to my solitary car.

Behind me, St Catherine's Hospice lay in silence: dimly-curtained windows standing out against the dark. It could still feel like a hospital sometimes, but of course it wasn't: the outcomes here were not in doubt. A good death was the goal we worked for now. A final, calm acceptance of the things we couldn't change.

I remembered that time in Casualty when I'd barred a mother's way: blocking her off from Resus while we listened to the screaming of her child. I'd been all of twenty-five, a fresh young Sister, but I'd found the cold, hard strength to force her back. *He mustn't see you. Not right now. If he sees you, he'll relax and just let go . . .*

Rage. Rage.

But I had no rage left now. There were times when I thought the blackness, when it came, would be a blessing.

*

Alice was in the kitchen when I got in, washing up her supper dishes. The muted worktop lighting made the narrow room seem cosier – and warmed her smile.

'Hiya. Busy day?'

'Oh God, does it show . . . ?' Still in my coat, I rubbed a hand through my hair. Then managed a tired grin. 'Not too bad.'

'I should have done these earlier, sorry; there was a good film on . . .'

I glanced back down the passageway. 'How's she been?'

'Good as gold. Fast asleep now.'

I felt my smile grow wider, and went on through to look. Easing open the bedroom door, I slipped quietly in. The light behind me spread across the wall, and showed me her shape in the dimness; the silky glimmer of her hair. The sound of her breathing was soft and peaceful.

Cathy.

I sat carefully down on the edge of the bed, and smoothed my gentle hand across her cheek. She didn't stir. Her breathing didn't falter. I can't begin to describe my feelings as I watched her.

Suffice it to say that sometimes she was all that kept me going.

Catherine Frances Nicola slept on: her thumb in her mouth and her panda snuggled up beside her. After a minute I leaned forward, kissed her forehead through her fringe, and tiptoed out.

Alice was waiting in the hall with her flying jacket on. It made her look older than her seventeen years; very cool and grown-up. I felt a nostalgic little twinge.

'Jan was okay?' I asked; thinking of the pleasant terraced house where Cathy stayed and played three working days a week.

'Oh, fine. Sends her love. See you Monday, then?'

'Please. Give my love to your mum and dad . . . Drive carefully.'

She gave me an *as-if-I-wouldn't* sort of grin before closing the door.

The flat was suddenly very quiet. I pulled off my coat, and went wearily through to change, then came back into the kitchen. Silence seemed to follow me in; I flicked on the radio to scare it back out again, and set about making myself a drink. The song of the Piano Man (. . . Billy Joel . . . ?) came on and kept me company: lifting my spirits, despite its melancholy edge.

Taking my Horlicks through into the living room, I slumped down onto the sofa, curling up with the patchwork cats. Cathy loved this throw: a riot of colour, sky-blue and sunset red. The cats rode crescent moons among the stars. I found it quite a comforter myself.

Settling back, I sipped my drink; and wondered how much longer I would need. It was over a year already. The passage of time had smoothed the sharpest edges, like the action of the sea on a fragment of glass. Sudden rushes of grief, like the one I'd had this evening, had grown gradually fewer, and further apart. I was living week by week, now; rather than day by day.

I still felt sore and raw inside, but I knew I wouldn't cry again tonight. So was there a light on the horizon at last? Only one more hill to climb?

Possibly. Perhaps. But I'd believe it when I saw it.

I'd lost too much in the last ten years to take anything on trust again.

*

Cathy asleep was a golden-haired angel. Cathy awake was beginning to get on my nerves.

'Shhh, now. Finish your breakfast,' I told her, going back into the kitchen. Wrapped up in my bathrobe, my bobbed hair in my eyes, I felt a real mess.

'Mum*meet* . . .'

'What?'

'Where are we going?'

'I told you: to see Daddy. Now come on, eat your Ready-Brek . . .' I ruffled her hair as I came back in with my coffee. 'Good girl.'

Cathy scraped dutifully at her bowl; then raised her big blue eyes to me again. 'Can we go to the park after-wards?'

'Oh . . . I expect so.' With a sigh, I cleared a space for *Guardian Woman* and laid it out among the toast crumbs. Taking a sip of coffee, I started to read.

'Finished!'

I glanced up, and sighed again. 'Look at you. Come here . . .' Taking a tissue, I wiped her mouth clean. 'Now go and start getting dressed. I'll be there in a minute. Go on.'

She trotted happily off. I shook my head, and tried to resume my reading. All right, so things were getting easier in one sense: she was three now, and her sleeping and eating schedule was more or less in tune with mine. No more air-raid siren impersonations at four in the morning, or nappies needing changing at inopportune moments. But she was a bundle of life, that girl; and my one pair of hands wasn't always enough to cope.

Still: we have to make do with what we've got.

I wondered what today would mean to her. I'd never taken her before, for fear she'd be upset: at my own reaction, if nothing else. I'd explained it all to her, of course; but who's to say how much a little kid takes in? Now, however, with the first anniversary come and gone, and something there to see, I reckoned she was old enough – and felt that I was ready.

'What am I wearing, Mummy?' came her voice from the bedroom.

'Your best frock, darling,' I called: still attempting to follow the article on men, and what they're good for. Sex and DIY seemed the main conclusion. I wasn't past giving a wry little smile at that.

But time was getting on. Downing the last of my coffee, I went through to help Cathy dress.

'Are we taking a present with us?' she asked, as I straightened her frock.

I raised my eyes as far as her collar, and adjusted that too; then looked on up to her face. 'Mmm?'

'Granny always brings me a present when she visits *us*,' she pointed out seriously.

'Yes . . . she does, doesn't she?' I ploughed back my fringe one-handed, and managed a rueful smile. 'Don't worry, we'll take him a present. A bunch of Mummy's favourite flowers . . .'

I'd always been partial to red carnations; he'd picked up on it soon enough. Many were the times he'd stopped off on his way home to buy me a bunch – undeterred by darkness, rain and rush-hour traffic. Often he'd guess, as if by instinct, the days when I would need them.

So the flowers I held now were like a compliment repaid. Carnations and ferns, still wrapped in flimsy paper. I just stood there for a moment, with my hand on Cathy's shoulder; then knelt, and laid them gently on the grass.

Nicholas Mitchell said the words before me: gold against the grey. They seemed to swell until they filled my vision. Nothing else could get in past them. The rest of the world blurred out around the edges.

Cathy shifted uneasily beside me; I drew her closer, slipping my arm around her. Gradually the carved words sank back into the gravestone, and the cemetery opened out around us. An aching hollow had grown inside my chest; but my eyes were dry.

So was my mouth, when I tried to speak. I swallowed and began again.

'This is where Daddy is now. After he was in the car-crash, he was hurt . . . very badly . . . and the doctors said we had to let him go. So . . .'

I sniffed, and paused for a moment; squeezed her shoulders. She was silent. Her body felt as fragile as a bird's.

'*So*, we turned off the machine that was making him breathe . . . and it was like seeing someone go to sleep. You remember me telling you that when people die, it's like falling asleep and not waking up again?'

Cathy was gazing doubtfully at the grave. 'Mummy . . . what if he wakes up now?'

'He won't, poppet.' I hugged her against me. 'People don't wake up. Not ever.'

Oh, but I hoped that she'd forgive me: if she ever found out what a lie that was. Please God, she never would.

Please, God.

There were more questions coming; I could almost sense them rising to the surface. I cuddled her, and let them come. In a way, they were almost welcome.

'Do people have dreams when they're dead?' she asked me; quite curious, now.

'No . . . When they die, you see, we put their body safe in the ground; but the important part of them goes up to Heaven, for God to look after.'

'Oh . . .' She rubbed at her nose. 'Why are we here, then?'

I smiled faintly, despite myself. 'Well. Sometimes people need to come and visit graves – to help them remember.' I squeezed her shoulders one more time; then eased off and nodded at the flowers. 'Come on . . . let's put these in the vase.'

The carnations were fresh and vivid: life-blood red. Together – me sitting on my heels, she standing – we set about arranging them, pushing the stems into the colander-holes of the vase. Glancing up from time to time, I watched her as she worked: savouring the concentration on her little face. The gilt of her hair, I saw, was growing darker: not the first time that I'd noticed, but it gave my heart a poignant little squeeze. Nick's fair genes were slowly fading out. Another trace of him I'd lose. Soon, perhaps, she'd be as dark as me . . .

The call of a rook scraped the stillness; I heard a rustling through the dry, reddish leaves of the nearest tree. Otherwise the cemetery was silent: hushed. The sky was pale and milky.

Finished, we drew back again, to stare at our patch of scarlet. Cathy tipped her head to study it, then raised her face to me.

'Will he know we've left them?'

I nodded. 'I think he will, somehow. And he'll be glad.'

She mulled that over for a pensive moment; then, with things sorted out to her childish satisfaction, she tugged on my hand. 'Will we be going to the park this afternoon? You promised.'

'Oh, Cathy . . .' I sighed: at once deflated and delighted. Still delicate with grief, I had a sudden urge to hoist her up and hug her. It was the weirdest feeling: like being torn two ways inside.

The bird above us cawed again. Looking round, I could see him perched there, a watchful silhouette against the sky. Our scene was more than literally beneath him. I watched his dark head turning, east and west.

'Is that a blackbird, Mummy?'

I shook my head, half-smiling. 'No . . . that's a rook.

He's got a straight beak, look, so he can dig up grubs and things.'

With that idle little nugget squirrelled carefully away, she pulled on my hand, and we turned back towards the gates. But as we strolled along the path, I couldn't help but glance over my shoulder. It wasn't something I could place, but somehow, subliminally, the rook made me uneasy. Garbed in black, and perched above the graves.

A *digging* bird.

*

When I looked down, there was blood upon the earth: splashed out in all directions; soaking in. Some of it had spattered up the headstone, and was dribbling back down again. The grass was red and matted, the soil beneath becoming mud. And as I stared, the mud began to seethe and pop, like crimson porridge coming to the boil.

Even as I pressed my hands against my mouth, something hidden tried to heave towards the surface – and Nick's voice burst in through my ears. Muffled though it was by slime and darkness, I placed its panic instantly: he'd wake up from a nightmare crying out like that. Once, after coping with a crash-and-burn pile-up on the M25, my tough twenty-five-year-old policeman had been calling for his mother as he struggled up from sleep.

Oh God, he's woken up again – down there . . .

But before my horror at the thought could overcome me, the grave was gone and I'd been dumped on a chair in a bleak, aseptic room. The lighting was as stark as a nuclear dawn; when the woman in black came in, it turned her gaunt face paper-white.

I kicked, convulsed – and came awake.

It took me a bleary moment to get my bearings, and realize I was safe in my bed. With a shudder, I freed myself from the clutches of the duvet, and raised my head.

There was a pallid stain of light against the curtains, but the room was still filled with the greyness of predawn.

I squinted at my bedside clock, and found it was half-past five. 'Oh shit,' I muttered: venting all my upset in the word. 'Oh . . . *shit*.'

I let my head drop back onto the rucked-up pillowcase. My heart was still thudding heavily, but I strained my ears to hear above it – in case it had been some sound from Cathy's room that had roused me. But no; the flat was as silent as the world outside.

Feeling cold and very lonely, I curled up again; but my mind was too clear for sleep to be an option. So I just lay there, on my side, and let memory pick up where the dream had left off.

Recalled in detail, the reality had less style; the mundane noise and bustle of Friday night Casualty put the waiting room in context. The Sister in charge had been wearing navy blue, of course, not black – but I'd been too shocked to register much more than shades of light and darkness. When she came in, I'd instinctively craned my head to peer out past her: down the corridor towards the Resus room. I had just a glimpse of closed wooden doors with blinded windows – and then she'd shut herself in with me.

I remembered feeling desperately confused, as much as frightened. I'd been an A&E Sister myself, in a unit just like this one: part of the healer élite. And all of a sudden, here I was, in mufti – on the outside, looking in. Familiar territory had become forbidden. Sitting here waiting had been intolerable. I'd wanted to get in there, make assessments, start directing operations. They say nurses make the worst patients. As relatives, we're worse still.

But what I wanted was really academic. It felt as if someone had just jumped on my stomach. I wasn't even sure if I could stand.

The pale Sister sat down to face me. The set of her expression drew my heartstrings tight.

'He's all right, isn't he?' I heard myself ask.

'I'm . . . afraid he's not,' she said, with grave gentleness. 'He's not all right at all, Rachel.'

I leaned back against the worktop, waiting for the kettle to boil: my mood as gloomy as the light.

It was often the first moments of wakefulness when I'd feel it the most; when it would hit me hardest. Almost before I'd got my head together, the fact of his absence would come down on me like a cold shower. And after the flow was finished, the world would be left diluted, tepid, tasteless: nothing more than an empty room, an empty bed. An empty place inside me.

He hadn't even been speeding in pursuit of a suspect; just driving along on routine patrol. Some stupid, *stupid* bastard had overtaken on a bend, and come at him head-on. Collided full-tilt. The squad car had been a write-off. And two days later, they wrote Nick off as well.

'All right, Mrs Mitchell . . . we're ready to disconnect the ventilator now . . .'

And sitting there in the relatives' room, I could think no further than: *No, it's Mrs* Young *– not Mitchell. I never changed my name . . .*

The kettle was steaming quietly: it must have boiled. Straightening wearily up, I made myself a coffee.

Nearly six o'clock.

Outside the window, through the blinds, there was a mist over the back field. This early, there would still be rabbits scurrying about. Once upon a time I'd have paused to look – and felt a childish pleasure when I glimpsed one. But not any more.

Thank you. I love you. Goodbye. I'd whispered those things again and again as I sat by his ITU bed; but already it had been too late. He'd been too far gone to hear.

Less than four years we'd had together. Less than *four*.

I felt a trickle of wetness on my cheek, and wiped it off with my dressing-gown sleeve.

We'd come here with such high hopes: glad to put London at arm's length and slacken the pace a bit. We found a lovely house, and settled in; it had seemed like one extended honeymoon at first. And the advent of Cathy had pointed to still brighter days ahead. I'd really thought the past – my past – was well and truly buried.

Except that it was Nick who ended up in the ground.

I'd managed to sell that houseful of stillborn hopes. Home was a ground-floor flat now; and work was the hospice. After all my years of nursing in Casualty and ITU . . . all those lives I'd struggled to save . . . the stone-cold certainties of death were now all that I could cope with.

Walking back down the passageway, sipping miserably from my mug, I found my attention caught by the print on the wall above the phone. It was one of those optical-illusion pieces, where white birds flying west against a dark sky became black birds heading east against a light one. Nick had never been one for modern art, but he'd been quite impressed by that one.

In the half-light, the picture was a patchwork of black and grey. The shadows seemed to have the upper hand. I stopped to stare at it, but the white birds wouldn't register at all. All I could see was a skyful of sombre crows.

Without warning, there was a weight of nausea in my stomach; I felt it take the colour from my cheeks and leave them cold. As if my buried past had wakened in its grave as well. As if all the darkness and dread I'd left behind me was rising at last to claim its due.

*

Our newest staff nurse turned out to be a rather wan and timid-looking girl, so slim she was almost fragile. She was sitting nervously upright in one of Matron's chairs, trying hard to look composed. Her hair pinned up in haste, and wisping loose; her blue eyes watered down behind gold-rimmed glasses.

I took to her at once.

She gave me a shy grin as Matron introduced us, and I returned it with genuine warmth. Maybe there was something waifishly appealing about her that got the mother in me going. Or maybe such fresh-faced expectation struck a different chord again.

Maybe she reminded me of someone I'd seen in the mirror once: a long, long time ago . . .

'If you've any more questions,' Matron was saying, 'I'm sure Rachel will be happy to answer them . . .' I was flattered by her obvious confidence, and concealed the glow behind a modest little smile. Matron stood to shake the new girl's hand again – the gesture eagerly returned – and passed her on to me.

'Nicola, isn't it?' I asked as we walked down the corridor; she nodded back, and moistened her lips to speak. I felt a momentary tightness in my stomach.

Oh please, don't say they call you 'Nicky' . . .

'I'm really looking forward to working here, Sister. Everyone seems so friendly.'

The enthusiasm with which she slotted that in made me smile afresh; but so did the almost physical relief I felt, as the pressure inside me eased.

The admin suite was properly tucked away in a first-floor corner; a staircase took us down towards the body of the building, and the wards. The modern, slatted steps – rebuilt like so much else of the interior – contrasted oddly with the Victorian outer shell. Nicola, looking about her, was obviously intrigued.

'What was this place before?'

'It's been a few things, in its time. Most recently a retirement home . . . but it was empty for a couple of years before the trust bought it. They had to do a load of work on it, of course: basically gut the place and start from scratch . . .' I held the fire-door for her. 'You saw around when you came for interview?'

She nodded. 'I was really impressed. Especially with the wards being so bright and airy. It all looks a bit severe from outside, doesn't it?'

It did, rather. External redecorations were still on hold, and the building – from peeling gables to flaky basement brickwork – looked increasingly the shabbier for it; but it was the age and isolation of the house that really pressed itself upon you. On sombre days it seemed to loom against the open fields behind it. Even when the sun shone, the big bay windows still seemed mournful. Watchful, sometimes, too.

We crossed the hallway, and her gaze strayed to the engraving on the wall. 'And . . . that's St Catherine, is it?'

'Right.'

'Don't think I've heard of her.'

'She lived in medieval Italy – ministering to the sick. This was in the middle of the Black Death and everything. Quite a woman, by all accounts.'

'Is the black and white cross her symbol as well?' It was mounted below the contemplative figure, its dark and light shades alternating by quarter. The same badge we both wore on our uniforms.

'Sort of. She was a Dominican sister; that's one of their crosses.'

Nicola nodded, looking thoughtful.

'Right,' I continued as we came into the ward area. 'You'll be shadowing me today, so we'll just go through some ward policies, and then get on with the drug round. Give you a chance to meet some of our residents.'

She seemed to brighten at the prospect. 'How many beds here?'

'Twelve.' I led the way into my office, which was in its usual state of disarray. 'Have a seat.'

She settled herself comfortably; glanced around. Then: 'What sort of staffing ratio do you . . .' She paused there, looking puzzled; and I felt the grin that had spread across my face.

'Sorry . . .' I half-covered it with my hand; then relaxed, and let her share it. 'I'm so sorry, Nicola . . . You made me think of my daughter, that's all. She's just at that age when she's always asking questions . . .'

'Ooh.' She straightened up with interest and surprise: clearly seeing me in a whole new light. 'I'd never have guessed; you don't look . . . I mean . . .'

'Ah, now that's the sort of flattery your Sister likes to hear.'

Nicola giggled. 'Sorry. How old is she?'

'Three and a bit.'

'I should have realized. That's one of her paintings, is it?'

I followed her gaze to the Technicolor splotch-potch on my pinboard. 'Mmm. I do hope it's the right way up . . .'

She settled back again, still smiling, as I reached for the policies ringbinder. 'But seriously,' I added, leafing through it, 'don't worry about asking questions. Like the advert said, we need enthusiastic staff. People who feel motivated. I'd be interested to know what brought you to us . . . ?'

She shrugged. 'Well . . . Same as anyone, really. I've staffed on surgical wards since I qualified, and we were so stressed-out all the time; no chance of caring for the whole person, you know? Not even the ones who knew that they were dying, and needed us the most . . .'

I drew her on, and was pleased with what I heard.

We'd chosen well. Some people come a bit too glibly into hospice nursing, but young Nicola had both feet firmly on the ground. I moved on to give an overview of our policies and standards; and then it was time to start meeting the people this place was all about.

'Sister . . .' she said, as we were getting up.

'Just Rachel would be fine, Nicola. We're not too formal here.'

'Right . . .' She hesitated for a moment, almost shyly; then took the plunge. 'Actually, my friends all call me Nicky . . .'

'Oh . . .' I said, and smiled again.

But much too widely; it hurt my face.

'Morning, Mike. What sort of night have you had?'

'Not so bad, Sis. How about you?'

I grinned at that quick comeback. 'Oh, fine, thanks.'

'Out on the town, I shouldn't wonder.'

'Hardly. A girl my age needs her full eight hours in bed.' Not that I ever got them, but still . . .

Sitting up in his, he looked exhausted: his bald, stubbled skull resting back against the bolsters. But his eyes still flickered with quirky humour. Cancer was a bastard, but it hadn't ground him down.

'You've got a new helper, I see,' he said appraisingly.

'Yes, this is . . . Nicola. Started with us today.' I paused for his nod, her cheerful smile. 'She's sticking with me while she gets to know you all.'

Retrieving his chart from the bed-end, I opened it out on the shelf of the medicines trolley. Nicola leaned in closer as my voice slipped into a calm professional undertone. 'Michael's got CA pancreas, with liver mets. He's on oral morphine four-hourly.' She watched as I measured out the dose, then took it over to him; supporting him while he swallowed it down. She did it all quite naturally:

unforced and encouraging. My turn to watch, and with approval.

Simon, in the next bed down, was rather younger; newer to us: less resigned. There'd been a bit of a scene yesterday when his parents came to visit: his anger and denial had found a focus, and blistered him and them both. It had taken an hour of quiet talking in the relatives' room to persuade his mum and dad that such a reaction was all too normal – and that he needed them no less.

'Time to take my medicine like a man, eh?' he murmured as we trundled up; but his flattened tone held no resentment. Not right now, at least.

'Diamorphine. It'll keep you comfortable.'

'So what if I won't?' he asked suddenly; quizzical as much as challenging. 'The pain's a part of it, right? Telling my body what's going on. You want me to pretend it's not happening?'

I shook my head. 'There's no pretence about it. We can control pain now, when there's no more need for it. No one has to suffer.'

He regarded me pensively for a moment. 'You're a Christian, aren't you?'

That tasted like bait, but I bit without pausing. 'Yes.'

'Catholic?'

'Allegedly.'

He smiled faintly. 'And you don't think suffering's good for the soul?'

'Not in my book it's not.'

'So what did I do to deserve this?' he asked, his voice drying out: developing an edge. 'I'm thirty-two, you know that? What sort of Divine Plan works out like that?' His gaze flicked to Nicola, and noted only her silence; then returned to me. 'Unless, of course, I brought it on myself, with my *abominable practices . . .*'

I went and sat on the bed, taking firm hold of his hand. 'Simon – don't *ever* let anyone tell you that. All right? It isn't a judgment, it isn't a curse. You caught a virus, that's all. None of my business how. My business is to help you cope – in any way I can.'

He was staring at the window now; but his hand stayed locked with mine. I gave it a gentle squeeze. 'And this is Nicola, by the way.'

His eyes came slowly round again. His wry smile touched them, just. 'Hello, Nicola.'

'Ready for your medicine?' I asked after a pause, and he nodded. I passed him his dose, and was about to move on when his gaze eased down to the badge on my lapel. 'What's that particular cross represent? I've been meaning to ask.'

'It's Dominican. You know . . . the Blackfriars.'

He raised an ironic eyebrow. 'So you're one of the Black Sisters, are you?'

For a moment I must have looked as if he'd just slapped me in the face; I felt a surge of emptiness inside me, like a bottomless pit. Then I had control again, and was squeezing my expression into stillness. Perhaps he hadn't noticed. And if he had, he – surely – hadn't guessed.

My mouth formed a plastic smile, and I wheeled the trolley onward; but the thumping in my chest kept up for several minutes. Like the knocking of somebody buried alive, who's finally awakened in the darkness.

Stifled at length, it stopped. I drew a shallow breath while Nicola talked with a patient. Thin, cold sweat soaked in beneath my dress. God, but he'd brought it out of nowhere – with just that gentle joke. My reaction unsettled me as much as the memories themselves. The jolt of finding, after all time's healing, that they were still so close beneath the surface. Scarcely covered by a tissue-paper skin.

*

'Rachel . . .' Nicola asked as we ate our lunch together; 'there was something else I was wondering . . .' Her eyes stayed on her plate as she said it; then flicked up to meet mine. There was a trepidation there to match her tone.

'Fire away,' I prompted gently: wondering myself.

'I didn't raise it at interview, but . . . this place has a religious foundation, doesn't it?'

I nodded.

'Does it matter that I'm not? Religious, I mean.'

'Good God, no.' She blinked at that, which almost made me giggle. 'It really doesn't, Nicola. A lot of the nurses here aren't. What matters to us is how good you are at *caring*. There are plenty of people here that patients and relatives can talk to about the spiritual side if they want to – but only if. Our first aim's to give good care to the dying: whichever way they want it.'

She gave a soft sigh of relief; and beamed at my encouraging little wink.

With a few minutes left of lunchbreak, we adjourned to the corner by the window, where a couple of the others were chatting. Mel she'd met already; I introduced her to Diane. There were polite exchanges; pauses. Then Diane turned back to Mel, and leaned across.

'I hear Granny Grey's been seen again.'

I wasn't quite sure if she meant to exclude the new girl – or intrigue her. Either way, mousy Mel's face lit up with interest. I felt my own grow stiff, and glanced away.

'What – last night?' Mel asked.

Diane nodded. Her short fair hair gave her smile an impish cast, but she sounded earnest enough. 'One of the girls was saying . . .'

Mel pursed her lips and nodded sagely, like someone old beyond her years. 'So who's she come for this time?'

'Has this a place got a ghost, then?' Nicola ventured, before I could commandeer the conversation.

They both looked round at her: making a show of

deciding whether to share their inside knowledge. Then Diane nodded. 'We think so. People see this old woman around the place from time to time – usually when someone's about to go . . .'

'Sometimes she appears at the foot of the bed,' Mel volunteered. 'And sometimes . . .'

'I think Nicola can do without this,' I broke in: trying to sound briskly dismissive, but it came out curt and snappy. 'It's just night-shift gossip, and you both know better than to spread it around.'

Poor Mel looked quite put out by that; Diane took it more coolly. I guessed she was intrigued at my reaction: superstition in nurses is second nature, we both knew that. I felt the dry appraisal in her stare, and didn't like it. Discomfited, I got quickly to my feet.

'Well . . . I've got some paperwork to catch up on, Nicola. I'll see you later.'

Making for the door, I could almost hear them huddle up to talk behind my back: Nicola invited in now, and me left out in the cold. Diane – who was a real stirrer when she put her mind to it – would doubtless be remarking on my touchiness today. Mel might feel sufficiently stung from her natural quiet to do likewise. And what contribution might Nicola make, in the security of her new peers? *I said for her to call me Nicky, but she'd have none of it. Bit hoity-toity, isn't she . . . ?*

And then Diane would lean conspiratorially close and say, *It's not really for me to tell you this . . . but Rachel lost her husband a year ago. So we sometimes need to give her room, you know . . . ?*

I gritted my teeth against a surge of anger: unwarranted, for all I knew – but I wouldn't put it past her. And what other conclusion could she come to, after all? I wasn't usually so snappy on the subject of ghosts.

Not that I'd ever liked to talk about our own grey lady. The very idea brought back some most unpleasant memories; but even taken on their own, the tales were eerie and upsetting. They painted sombre pictures of a shadowy recluse, who sometimes quit the isolation of the attic to stalk in silence through the wards. Grey lady was the time-honoured hospital term; but I reckoned this was much more *it* than she.

We called it Granny Grey in an attempt to keep it at a safe, domestic distance; close up, it wasn't so cosy. I'd heard only one account of a face-to-face meeting: the nurse involved had needed several medicinal gulps of brandy before she got her story out. Where others had glimpsed just a husk of movement in the dimness, she'd found herself three feet away from a face like a withered grey mask, its eye-holes empty. Even as she'd recoiled in fright, it disappeared – leaving a chilly aftersmell of foulness that lingered on into the morning.

I supposed it was some strange relic of the building's past – perhaps unaware of its own existence. But that it existed, I didn't doubt. My experience of phantoms didn't mean I understood them; but I was all too sure we shared this building with the shadow of an old, forgotten woman. Trapped here somehow. Unfaded by the passage of the years.

And, for whatever reason, restless still.

Just after three, there was a gentle tap on my office door. Nicola again, just about to go off duty.

She'd been getting to know a few more patients this afternoon: I'd last seen her in the dayroom, deep in conversation with one of the ladies. 'So how's your first day been, then?' I asked her, sitting back.

'Really good, thanks,' she said, with a grin that showed she meant it. 'I think I'm going to like it here.'

We talked briefly about what else her orientation week had in store; and then, after a moment's hesitation, she took me by surprise. 'Rachel . . . I was really sorry to hear about your husband.'

It wasn't the fact of her finding out that threw me – I'd half-expected that already. What I hadn't foreseen was her readiness to be upfront about it. Most people left that subject well alone.

And me alone with it.

'Thank you.' I made an awkward gesture.

'I wasn't sure if I should say anything,' she went on – still sounding not quite certain. ' But knowing, and not saying . . . It sort of felt like a barrier between us, do you know what I mean?'

That last bit wasn't rhetorical; I nodded slowly.

'Anyway . . . I'm sorry if that was out of turn.'

'It wasn't, Nicola. Thanks. I mean that.'

She grinned again, and began to close the door.

'Nicky,' I called suddenly.

She put her head back in again. Her turn to look surprised.

My throat had drawn tight as I spoke the word; its very taste was dusty with disuse. I had to swallow before continuing; but with it said, the rest came so much easier.

'I think we're going to like having you here as well,' I said.

*

Driving away from the house that afternoon, I glanced up, saw its grey bulk receding in the mirror – and wondered where Granny Grey was lurking now.

It was never seen – and rarely heard – in daylight. Perhaps it crept away into the darkest corner, like a spider, until night filled the house. Or perhaps (I thought unwillingly) it was ever-present, like the stars overhead: following its cold course around and around, but not becoming visible until after the sun was down.

If so, I hadn't felt it; my sharper instincts – blunted now – had picked up no such stirrings. The hospice had always been a peaceful place for me; its souls being soothed towards their final rest. Tales of a ghost had unsettled me at first; but after a while, with only hearsay to go on, I'd found I could ignore them.

But not today.

Val Thomas had the ward this evening; and Janet Kerr would be in charge tonight. As their faces came to mind, I felt a growth of tightness in my stomach. While I was safe and sleeping in my bed, they'd be sitting up through the small hours: marooned on islands of light amid lagoons of grainy darkness. Trying not to listen to the night-sounds from upstairs.

There was still an hour or two of autumn daylight left; but I could imagine that eyeless face taking form in the attic, like a grey moon rising from the gathering dusk.

Picking Cathy up from nursery was a pick-me-up itself; my mind unhooked from the hospice and twanged back to the here and now. She'd had a fine time slopping paint around, and told me about it all the way home. Listening to her burbling away in her back-seat harness, I couldn't stop a smile setting in.

The car ate up the leaf-scattered road, cruising smoothly through the westering sunlight. I was half-inclined to put a tape on: something aptly rolling and autumnal, like Michael Nyman's *Piano* piece. But no; I wanted to listen to her every word – and not just so I could make the right noises in all the right places.

After we'd got home and I'd made her tea, I took a bath – leaving the door open so she could wander in and out. Up to my chest in Radox bubbles, I put my head back, closed my eyes, and let the warmth soak in. The chill I'd felt this afternoon seemed a secondhand experience now: something distant and unreal.

'Mummy, when will you read Panda his bedtime story?' came Cathy's voice at my elbow.

'Shh, darling. Mummy's relaxing.'

I could have sworn – without even opening my eyes – that there was a miffed hint of haughtiness in her withdrawal: she could be quite a little madam sometimes. I grinned to myself . . . and reality slipped briefly out of joint. Suddenly – as so often before – being a mother felt so strange.

I'd begun my nursing training at eighteen; it seemed like yesterday. Still my own mum's little girl, as she lovingly insisted – though we'd both known I had to break free. The future had been wide open then, without a hint of what would come. Motherhood was something well over the horizon: a prospect as distant as old age.

Yet here I was with the three-year-old I'd borne inside me: a separate life that had kicked to be let out. Every perspective was different now. When I'd had Cathy, the universe had changed.

I'd adapted, as everyone does. Waiting for Cathy to emerge this afternoon, I'd been chatting to Pat, a mum in her twenties who I'd met at our Catholic Women's group (the liberated sort, where we swapped contraceptive advice over coffee). Her little boy was nearly four now. Her joys and tribulations sounded much the same as mine.

But there were other things I hadn't known at eighteen. Undreamed-of things – too dark for me to see them up ahead. Like losing my parents. Like having a husband taken from me.

Like being ensnared by a practising witch: as bait in her quest for rapture and revenge . . .

I'd settled deeper in the bath by now, almost up to my neck; but that last, unbidden thought sent a spasm of cold right through me. All at once, I might just as well have been immersed in dishwater, for all the comfort I had left. Grimacing, I opened my eyes, and lay there staring glumly at the ceiling.

It was over. Years ago. But I'd seen how evil walked the real world. Nothing from all my childhood had frightened me as much. Nothing I'd seen in nursing had brought such horror and despair.

And yet, in some strange way, I'd adapted to that piece of past as well. The memories might linger, but the worst was well behind me. I'd come through blessing and bereavement, and pulled my life together after both. I was almost proud of myself, some sunny days.

I still missed her sometimes, though: the girl from fifteen years ago I'd never meet again.

Two minutes later, Cathy was back, her panda trailing behind her by its arm. 'Are you still relaxing, Mummy?'

I rolled my head towards her, and summoned back my smile.

'Not any more, poppet. Go and get yourself tucked in. I'll be there in just a minute.'

With her safely in bed, I just flopped around in my cotton Oxfam kaftan for a while; aware – though I searched for a distraction – of the pink day dying all around the house. The air in the living room grew greyer; the birdsong from the woods thinned out to nothing. And at last I knew that I could put this off no longer.

Going through to the spare room, I was still trying to reason it out. Perhaps by facing up to this final relic, one more time, I could reassure myself that it was truly finished. The rampage of evil reduced to a coldness I could hold in the palm of my hand.

I closed the door behind me and leaned silently against it – as if listening to the settling dust. The last mote must have landed by the time I took the next step forward, over to the peeling chest of drawers. Kneeling breathlessly before it, I pulled out the bottom drawer and began to delve. Odd socks, old sweaters – and as I dug beneath them, my mind flickered back to a different place: showed me ever-clearer glimpses of my own mittened hands as they scrabbled through cinders. The sooty daylight of a burnt-out warehouse all about me; my heavy heartbeat thudding in my throat. And then, just as my nerve had been about to fail me, I'd seen it, gleaming dully in the ashy dust –

– and my fingers touched it now: the silver case still as cold as if I'd stored it in the fridge. I swallowed, and brought it out into the last of the light, cupped there like an offering in my two pale hands.

With its lid shut tight, it looked like an old pocket watch, its bright sheen scorched and tarnished. I knew it wasn't, of course; but nothing on earth would have induced me to prise it open and verify the fact.

I'd scarcely set eyes on the thing since the day I retrieved it. Its weight in my palms was almost more than I could bear. But I gritted my teeth, and forced myself to turn it over in my fingers: a reminder it was real, and dead, and in my power. And as I meditated, unwilling, on its icy silence, my head filled up again with thoughts of grey ladies.

And Black Sisters.

2

SEASONS

Autumn wears down Nature like a wasting disease. The patient grows corpulent and florid in the early stages – then withers and fades to death and black decay. Not surprising that it touches me so deeply.

But strange that I should like it quite so much.

Standing with Cathy in the back field, watching Mr Wheeler tend his bonfire, I found the season hadn't lost its savour. The warm tang of smoke took me back to my teens: recalled waning golden evenings which bulged with homework, but pointed the way towards Christmas. The scent blended in my nostrils with the leaf-mould we'd smelled on our walk. The wood had been a riot of colour – but nothing so bright as the flames now licking up against the hazy afternoon.

'Been far?' Mr Wheeler asked, pausing for a breather on the prop of his rake. He lived a couple of doors down from us; retired, but always busy in his garden. He was wearing his gardening clothes today: that old tweed jacket and worn cloth cap. Still flushed with rude health, he looked like a well-fed farmer.

'Just down to the brook,' I said; gently rubbing Cathy's shoulders. She was leaning back against me, snug in her little coat; her shiny new wellingtons smeared with mulch.

'Did you see any fish?' he asked her solemnly. She

shook her head, still too shy of him to answer; then craned back to look at me. 'Mummy . . .'

I hunkered down behind her. 'What?' I murmured in her ear.

'Why does he have to burn the leafs?' She sounded quite upset.

'Because they're dead, poppet. He has to clean them up.'

'They're pretty colours, though.'

'So they are. But once it's rained a few times, they'll be all black and gooey. You wouldn't like that, would you?'

She considered it, and shook her head once more; then looked back at Mr Wheeler. He winked at her through the smoke.

'Your mother's right, you know. We can't keep these old colours. Better to burn them up: give them back to the air. Nature gives us new ones soon enough.'

She seemed reassured by that; it gave me food for thought as well. Cuddling her against me, I pictured my rotted mass of memories being fed into the flames: the last unhappy decade set ablaze.

So light up the fire, and let the leaves burn . . .

Would that it were so easy.

'No more problems with the cistern?' Mr Wheeler asked me; I pulled my thoughts together and shook my head. He was always happy to help me out with jobs around the flat, be it a loose connection or a leaky pipe. And proud though I was of my independence, it felt good to have someone I could call on when I needed to. I valued the contact, as much as the convenience.

What had that piece in the paper said? Just sex and DIY? An unfair judgment, really; but one out of two wasn't bad.

'If you'd like a cup of tea or something when you're done, just give me a knock,' I offered; straightened up, and reached for Cathy's hand. 'Say goodbye, now,' I told her, and she waved politely. Mr Wheeler nodded gravely in return.

Only when Cathy was bathed, pyjamaed and plonked in front of the TV screen did I at last feel able to withdraw into a space of my own – and reflect on what I'd rooted out last night.

Not a watch; a witch's compass. Something which turned on unnatural polarities, and told the future.

I'd first met its owner seven years ago – and survived by the skin of my teeth. She'd not been as fortunate, or so it had seemed: sucked down into the Hell she'd cheated for three centuries. I'd gone on my way, rejoicing – and she'd crawled out and caught me up again. Our second encounter had been even more horrific: filling up mortuaries all over London as she'd searched for self-redemption. And at the end her quest had been her downfall. She'd trapped herself into confronting an old, ferocious spirit from under the City. A duel to the death. I doubted if even Razoxane could have walked away from that.

Razoxane. Simply thinking the name sent an icy reflex through me. But this time it was over. This time I had proof.

We'd had our final face-off in a deserted King's Cross warehouse; and just before dawn (long after I'd broken free and fled), that building had burned down. I'd learned of this a day later – and scoured the news reports for details. Police suspicions of a fire-bomb tied in with the terrorist device she'd used to lure me there; but what I needed to see was evidence of *her* – and her destruction.

At length – at last – I'd found it. Human remains had been discovered in the debris. Too badly burned to be identified, even by sex. Some hapless dosser, so the theories went. Not even dental records would have helped.

Razoxane. Her dark shape stirred in the shadows of my mind, and drifted closer to the light. A sinister figure, wrapped up in scruffy black. The glimmer of memory touched the paleness of her face: hauntingly young – and horribly good-humoured. Dark glasses masking her pitiless eyes.

The image was too insidious: I jerked my head aside to jar it free.

I'd had to be sure: so after two whole days of gnawing indecision, I'd ventured down to look. The ruins had been taped off, but I managed to slip inside. Even with the sun up, the place had spooked me; an echoing hulk, still thick with the smell of wet ashes. But I'd persevered: scuffing through the clinker for something they'd missed. A piece of cloth; a fragment of bone. Anything to prove that I'd survived her.

Somehow they'd overlooked the arcane compass; but finally, on hands and knees, I'd found it. Its silver casing blackened by the fire; the lid fused shut. I remembered the minute's hesitation before I picked it up: wondering whether or not to let it lie. But in the end I knew I had to have it. As if, by taking possession of this last remnant, I could have the past in my power – and thrust it, with the compass, to the back of the darkest drawer.

I'd just finished putting Cathy to bed when the telephone rang. Walking through into the living room, I scooped up the cordless handset from the sofa, punched the button, and found Nick's mother on the end of the line.

'Is that you, Rachel?'

'Ellen. Er . . . hi.' I pulled a face, but tried to sound congenial. 'How are you both?'

'Oh, we're keeping well, thank you. Yourself . . . ?'

'I'm fine.'

'That's good. And how's little Cathy?'

'She's fine too.'

'I was wondering . . . if it was too late to have a word with her . . .'

'Sorry, Ellen, I've just put her to bed.'

'Just a very quick word . . .'

'I really don't want to disturb her,' I said, with flat politeness.

In the stand-off pause that followed, I sensed her hurt – like someone who's found a door shut in her face, and has to speak through the letterbox. A part of me stirred in sympathy; but my stubborn will was clenched too tight to budge.

'Can we expect you here for Christmas, pet?'

'I don't know, yet. Depends how busy we are at work.' I hedged without thinking; a bloody-minded streak had me in thrall.

'It's been a while since we've seen her . . .'

'I know. I'll let you know nearer the time, all right?'

'All right, pet. I'll speak to you soon . . . Goodnight.'

The receiver clicked and buzzed against my ear – and suddenly the bitchy spell was broken: I could have screamed at myself. I lowered the handset, and stared at the keypad for a moment, composing her number in my head; then sighed, and dropped it back onto the cushion.

No use. Unfair though I'd certainly been, I didn't feel up to saying sorry. Not tonight.

I didn't really think she'd been surprised. Oh, we got on: but not too famously. She'd been wary of me from the first: a girl too snotty for her precious son. The trauma of Nick's death had only widened the gulf between us; harsh things had been said while we were none of us in control. For the past year we'd been piecing a relationship back together again.

Progress was still in fits and starts. She and her husband doted on Cathy, which always put me back on the defensive. Whenever we drove up, or they came down, they spoiled her rotten. There was something genuinely spiteful in the way I blocked their access sometimes; made excuses. Or was blandly non-committal – like I'd been just now.

Leave her alone, she's mine.

The exchange had left me soured inside; too restless to sit still and listen to soothing music. I made myself a hot milk drink, and sipped it slowly in the kitchen: watching the dusk slip through the window and soak into the walls. The woods beyond the field were lost in it already, blurred and indistinct. Here and there above them, the first stars pricked the haze. I was just about to go back and check the TV listings when Cathy's screaming, thin and high, came at me from her bedroom.

She was sitting up in bed when I rushed in – her small face flushed and tearful, disfigured by distress. Her screams had lapsed into a single helpless bawl. I sat on the bed and hugged her to me, muffling her sobs against my shoulder: whispering softly; stroking her hair.

'Oh, *Cathy* . . . Shhhh . . . What is it?'

'Bad *dream*,' she wailed: a fresh miserable outburst.

I nodded – to myself, relieved – and squeezed her closer. 'All right. All over now. Shhhh.'

'The *Ragman* was coming to get me.'

'No he's not. I'm here, and you're safe. Quite safe.'

Her outpouring of grief had dried to sniffles, but she still found it hard to get the words out. 'He was horrid, Mummy . . . all made of old clothes, with *stuff* growing on them . . . and his *eyes* . . .'

'Shhh,' I insisted, before she could elaborate. The image was quite unnerving enough as it was. I rocked her gently. 'Your mind just made him up. He isn't real.'

She sniffed again; and I drew back, tugged a hankie

from up my sleeve and wiped her face. 'Going to give Mummy a smile? Come on . . .'

She hesitated for a moment, reluctant to imply she no longer needed comforting; then managed a damp one. I touched my nose to hers, and lowered her back down. 'That's a good girl. No one's going to hurt my little angel.'

Her tremulous smile had gone again. Staring up, she looked ever so serious. 'Mummy, I'm scared to sleep.'

'In case you dream of him again?'

She nodded slowly, mouth pinched closed.

I smiled, and smoothed the fair hair off her forehead. 'Don't think about him, poppet. Listen . . .' And softly I began to sing – a lullaby which, brunette though I'd been, my own mum used to croon above my bed.

I know a girl with golden hair
Waiting by the window, all alone.
I know my girl knows how I care:
Won't be long my darling, soon be home . . .

She quietened, and finally drifted off. I finished the last verse in a whisper, kissed her forehead and silently crept out.

We had a music box which played that tune: a pretty little cottage with a thatched-roof lid. She'd been listening to it this morning, and it was still on the living-room carpet. Picking it up, I wound the spring (the mechanism rasping like a rook) and put it on the table; then folded myself up on the sofa as the soft chimes played. They took me out of myself, and back to safer times. They pricked my tear-glands, too. I didn't move again for a long while after they'd finally run down.

There was nothing much on TV. A documentary I latched onto seemed the most diverting bet. Tucking a scatter cushion behind me, I laid the remote aside . . . and after a minute it slipped to the floor. I couldn't be bothered to pick it up.

The programme was mainly a series of interviews: ageing people remembering the war, interspersed with bleak and flickering archive footage. I realized we were following the progress of two pilots, visiting the German cities they'd once flown against. Meeting with the people who'd been under their bombs. The image of reconciliation was a pleasing one; I began to pay attention. It left me wide open for the horror that came next.

A motherly German woman was giving them an account of what the wrong end of a fire-raid had been like. I shifted uncomfortably as she began to paint her picture; decided that I didn't want to hear the worst. I groped for the remote – and couldn't find it.

'. . . *the surface of the road was melted, and I remember . . . a little child was stuck to it. Stuck to the road, and crying for his mother . . .*'

I leaned down to feel beneath the sofa, trying not to listen. Just a few more seconds, a touch of a button, and the room would be filled with something vacuous, like sport . . .

'. . . *So his mother went to help him, and she got stuck as well . . .*'

Oh *Jesus*, I thought, still searching: almost scrabbling now.

'. . . *And the fire came over them both.*'

I made a small sound of disgust – and touched smooth plastic. Scooping up the remote, I thumbed a button at random and found myself watching a quiz show. But not before I'd been hit by a worse image still. A baby torn from its mother's arms by the fire-storm wind, and sucked into the flames . . .

I zapped the television altogether, and sat back, feeling sick. With its bubble of light burst, the living room was dim and quiet again. I took a shaky breath, and realized my eyes were smarting: stung by helpless sympathy for people who'd died long before I was even born.

Two mothers, horribly bereaved. And hadn't *they* sung lullabies to their children? Hadn't they too promised the infallible protection of their love?

Oh God: how could you let that happen . . . ?

I'd had a big row with God when Nick died: a really . . . mega row. Losing Mum and Dad was bad enough, but the death of my darling was the end of the world – or so it had seemed. Just night and rain forever. After all I'd been through; all that I'd believed. In the end I'd found my way to a washed-out morning – but with my faith stripped down to bone and bare essentials. No more flannel or fancy language. I just called him God now.

Sometimes – against all expectations – I even felt the closer to him for it. But maybe that was just my wistful thinking.

Still nursing a bellyful of bile, I slipped back into Cathy's room and bent over the bed. She was well asleep now, her breathing deep and even. Listening, I could hear the chimes again, their echoes faint and fitful in my head. Like a requiem for hopes turned to ashes; dreams into dust.

I didn't want to wake her; but I couldn't stop myself from reaching down to finger her silky hair.

Listen, God, I thought. *Just listen. If you take my girl from me as well, I'll never speak to you again. Not ever.*

I meant it, too; but it made me feel no better. Because words cut no ice with the way of the world. Of course, the two of us were special: we were charmed. But so was every mother; every child.

Yet innocent kids had suffered before. They were suffering now.

And I knew that they would suffer again.

That night I dreamed as well. Not of burning cities,

though I'd half-expected to. Instead I found myself fleeing through a skeletal forest in a blurred, confusing rush: snow skidding underfoot, murky sky overhead, and something pounding up behind me, panting and huge.

At which point I woke with a start.

In the dismal hour of restlessness that followed, an ugly thought crept up on me, and squatted in my skull. The moment it came clear, I felt a cold flush spread beneath my nightshirt.

I'd once possessed an intuition so acute, it sometimes gave me glimpses of the future. Dreams of nightmares yet to come. A natural talent, so I'd been told: I'd ruthlessly suppressed it in the years since it emerged.

But what if Cathy had inherited it in turn?

I tried not to think it any further through – but the idea had sprung too far ahead already. What if her sleeping mind had picked up signals from the darkness? What if her scary dream had been a warning?

Even as I refused – point blank – to accept that awful prospect, a part of me was wondering what my own dream might have had to tell me. Its phantom trace still lingered on my skin – and in my nostrils. The smell of a snorting, sweating beast behind me . . . and a foretaste of the fires up ahead.

*

The first time I saw him was from the corner of my eye, as I walked past the side-room's open door. A motionless figure in the visitor's chair, silhouetted against the window and the afternoon light. For a stomach-chilling moment, as I stumbled to a halt, I thought that Granny Grey had started walking in the daytime.

Then I realized it was a man in there: hunched forward in an attitude of watchful patience, his elbows on his knees. All his attention focused on the figure in the bed.

Mr Jackson. I couldn't think of him less formally, because we'd never spoken: never really met. Oh, I'd turned and changed him often enough – but he'd been unconscious more or less since he arrived here. He was practically comatose now.

And nobody had visited before. No family were mentioned in the notes. Puzzled, I pulled myself together, went over to the doorway and gave a polite, enquiring cough.

The visitor looked round: his pensive profile giving way to a lean and solemn face. He had longish hair, brushed back from the temples. I put him down as late twenties, early thirties – yet with an openness in his expression that made him seem much younger.

'Sorry . . .' I said tentatively. 'Are you a relative?'

He tightened his lips to the ghost of a smile, and nodded. 'He's my father.'

The statement was so simple that it threw me for a moment. Mr Jackson lived alone, we'd established that much; when they'd transferred him from the General, the referral form had mentioned *Wife Deceased*; the next of kin not known.

The young man seemed to sense my bafflement – and sympathize. 'I've only just found out,' he murmured, looking back towards the bed. 'We're not that close. I haven't seen him for . . . a while.'

God, he must be feeling guilty. I walked slowly round to the foot of the bed; made a show of checking the charts.

'What is it?' he asked calmly: clearly meaning what disease.

'Malignant tumour of the brain.' I hesitated then, as inbred reticence caught up – but tried to get the next bit off as lightly as I could. 'Who did you speak to, at the hospital?'

'Dr McKay. He said my father been transferred here. To die, obviously.'

I nodded, and relaxed a little. 'He's comfortable, and that's what counts. It shouldn't be long, now.'

He hadn't returned his gaze from the patient's faded face. I took the opportunity to look him over. He was thin to the point of emaciation, his jersey and jeans ill-fitting. I was reminded of a newly-discharged psychie patient: uprooted, out of step. I could well imagine him out on the margins – living in some damp and dingy bedsit.

'Has he asked for me at all?' Whatever his looks, he sounded rational enough: his voice the more compelling for its very quietness.

'Not that I'm aware. He's been unconscious for most of his time here.' I paused, then: 'Sorry, I should have introduced myself . . . Sister Rachel Young.'

He got rather awkwardly to his feet – once more I thought of a lad whose mind hasn't fully matured – and shook my hand. His grip was cool and dry.

'Christopher Jackson.'

Close up, I saw, his eyes were almost amber. They searched mine for a moment: soulful and sincere. His whole unguarded face seemed exquisitely tender, like a barely-healed wound. Something about the way he was keeping it blank sent a small twinge through my chest.

'If you like . . .' I said, 'when you're ready . . . you can come down to my office, and I can explain things in more detail.'

He nodded. 'I'd be grateful.' And with that agreed, I prudently withdrew. My last backward glance found him easing down onto the chair again, to resume his solitary vigil.

'I never knew Mr Jackson had a son,' I said to Diane, as I joined her at the desk.

'Me neither. Maybe they didn't get on. He's a bit strange, isn't he?'

'Is he?' I asked, although half-knowing what she meant.

'Well . . . I was talking to him when he arrived, and he was very polite and quiet . . . but do you get the feeling that he's not on quite the same wavelength?'

I reappraised my first impressions – and nodded. Nothing I could actually pin down; but there was something slightly *creepy* in his calmness. Then again, the poor bloke was probably still shocked.

'Fancy a read?' Diane asked, and passed the *News of the World* across. Not a paper I usually bought, unless I felt like spoiling myself; but I could rarely resist the ward's communal copy. I helped myself to a chocolate, settled back, and was half-way through this week's column by The Voice of Naked Prejudice when I became aware of someone standing over me.

I looked up, startled, to find Christopher Jackson standing there.

My hand went instinctively to my mouth, while I swallowed down the toffee I'd been chewing. Acutely aware of how unprofessional I must have looked, I quickly folded the paper and got to my feet. 'Sorry. Shall we go into my office . . . ?'

He followed me over, with a hint of faint amusement on his face; I was heartened by that, at least. Once inside, I invited him to sit, swivelled my own chair away from my desk to face him, and brought him fully up to date with his father's condition.

He absorbed it gravely, nodding me on from pause to pause: he had no questions. When I'd finished, he looked away, towards the window; the discs of his eyes translucent in the light.

'So long as he's not suffering, that's the main thing.' He seemed to meditate on the words for fully half a minute; then turned back to me. 'And I'm glad he's in good hands now. I mean that, Sister.'

I gestured modestly. 'Please, call me Rachel.'

He acknowledged that with a grateful nod. 'How long is he likely to live?'

'I couldn't say exactly. But days, no more than that.'

He looked towards the floor.

'Had you been away?' I ventured; wondering if his apparent guilt would benefit from being talked out.

He glanced up again, and held my gaze. 'Too far away, Rachel,' he said softly.

I got the impression he'd prefer it left at that. A silence set in between us; I found I was fiddling with my fingers in my lap. My counselling skills seemed to have deserted me today; the comforting words just wouldn't come.

'You have a daughter?' he asked suddenly, out of nowhere.

I stared at him in surprise for a moment; then followed his gaze to the photo of Cathy on my desk. When I looked back, I saw the thin end of his smile once more.

'She looks very pretty. What's her name?'

'Catherine,' I said – and then clammed up, as mother's pride gave way to much warier maternal instinct. Gazing at this strangely detached young man, with his scruffy clothes and enigmatic smile, I was suddenly jealous of my treasure: jealous and on my guard.

He sensed it at once, and spread his hands. 'Forgive me; you don't want a stranger prying into your affairs. And anyhow . . . it's time that I was going.'

I couldn't properly classify the sinking feeling I felt as he got to his feet – but put it down to fear that I'd pushed him away in his hour of need. 'Listen, there's no rush. If you want to talk, I'm more than happy to listen . . .'

He smiled again, but shook his head. 'Thank you; but I need some time to myself now. Will you be working tomorrow?' I nodded. 'I'll see you then. Thank you, Rachel, for all you've done.'

I saw him off the ward, then walked thoughtfully back

towards my office. Diane's analysis still held good: a rather strange young man. But polite and personable for all that – with a gravity I found curiously touching. And a reticence I really rather liked.

*

He was back again the next day, right enough: holding his father's trailing hand for an hour or more. As ever, there was no response. But Christopher and I had quite a chat.

Wherever he normally lived, I gathered he was staying at the house while he was down here, and coming in on the bus. It seemed he didn't have a job. I probed and prompted as gently as I could; and one by one, he volunteered more details. Slowly I began to coax him from his shell.

'Dad was a slaughterman, you know?' he said at one point: as if the thought amused him, in a bitter sort of way. 'The farmers used to hire him to put their animals down. Out in the open: a quick, clean shot. But none of us can do the same for him . . .'

It was clear that he would only come so far. By the time he left, I wasn't that much wiser. But he seemed more at ease today, his gestures less uncertain. I reckoned I could count that a success.

It wasn't until I was back at home, curled up and reading on the sofa, that I started to reflect on what I'd felt that afternoon. The sensations had been faint enough, and fleeting; mixed in with the emotions of a busy hospice day. But I remembered being genuinely pleased to see him again. And reluctant to draw our conversation to a close.

I re-read the same paragraph a second time. A third. It still hadn't sunk in.

Was he attractive? Yes, in his callow way. His face was haunting as much as haunted. And those almost-amber, wise-child eyes . . . So, yes, he was attractive.

Was he attracting me?

I rested my head against the sofa-back, and gave it some serious thought. I felt ambiguous about concluding that the answer might again be yes.

Not that my thoughts had stayed entirely chaste since Nick's death. Convinced though I was that love was something I could never feel again (except for Cathy), my physical self still craved from time to time, as if divorced from heart and mind. Such feelings had shocked and even shamed me to begin with; but they were natural enough. My body was as healthy as ever. Only my soul was maimed.

So did I fancy Mr Christopher Jackson? I breathed out softly through my nose, and thought about sex.

'Oh, sex . . .*' Nick murmured, looking thoughtful. Then: 'I remember that.'*

'Sod off,' I giggled, punching his shoulder. 'I was knackered last night, you know *I was . . .'*

The memory was so vivid it was almost a vision; I closed my eyes and let it come. We'd been together on a sofa just like this one, Nick with his legs stretched out, and me curled up like a kitten beside him, playing with his collar, with his hair . . .

'You know, Raitch . . .' he went on, dryly dreamy. 'When we first started going out together, I thought you were quite strait-laced, it has to be said . . .'

'Little did you know.'

'Mmmm. I've seen the light now, all right . . .'

I gently tasted his ear, then drew back as he turned his head. 'Your mum still thinks I'm a proper little madam, though, doesn't she?'

He shrugged against me. 'She's just being protective, that's all. She always was. Just give her time . . .'

I smiled, and took his chin in my hand. 'Time, Nicky boy, is just what you don't have.' I licked my lips, leaned forward . . .

'Mummy . . .'

Someone tugging at my sleeve. I opened my sticky eyes to find Cathy standing there, her small face solemn.

'Why are you crying, Mummy?'

'Oh . . .' I sniffed, and wiped my eyes with the heel of my hand. 'Don't worry, poppet. Mummy's just tired . . . that's all.' I sniffed again, and managed a wet smile. 'Let's get you put to bed.'

*

I came into work on my next day on to find someone else in Mr Jackson's bed. The once-bare corkboard was covered with cards, as though a swarm of butterflies had settled there. Fresh flowers adorned the window sill, and added their colours. It might have been a different room entirely.

Fearing the worst, I went on to the desk, where Nicola confirmed it. Mr Jackson had slipped away the previous afternoon. They'd tried contacting his son, without success. He'd missed him by an hour.

I almost winced. 'How did he take it?'

She shrugged. 'Well . . . obviously he was shaken, but he took it well enough. Very calm, like always. He thanked us, and said he'd be making the necessary arrangements. And that was it.'

I found myself wondering if it really was; if I wouldn't see him again. It had taken that long to recognize my first impression: dismay at the prospect of Mr Jackson's death. It wasn't what I usually felt when a patient passed away.

Not that I even knew that much about him. A couple of days' acquaintance wasn't anything to go on. Whatever I felt had its roots in the shallowest soil. The realities of a hospice Christmas would see it wither soon enough.

*

Waiting in my car for Cathy, that sombre afternoon, I didn't immediately notice what was going on behind me. My eyes were fixed on the nursery's bright windows, with their paint and decorations: aglow beneath the glowering sky. The shapes of the children moved to and fro behind them, elusive as elves.

I was a little early today; but even if there'd been other mothers waiting, I doubted if we'd have given up the shelter of our cars to say hello. There was an edge in the wind, and a dandruff scattering of snowflakes: an early sign which didn't augur well. I wondered gloomily if Cathy would get her current dearest wish and see a real white Christmas.

Last nursery class before the holidays. More of her time on my hands for the next two weeks. My child-minder would be away – and Alice would be too busy to do much babysitting: enjoying herself with family and friends, as a seventeen-year-old should. The thought made my stomach shift and sink, a reaction midway between envy and resentment. Brief though it was, it did worse than make me feel selfish. It made me feel *old*.

Beyond the warm windows, the elfin shapes danced round and round.

I stretched myself between steering wheel and seatback; drummed my fingers on the rim . . . and a glimpse of movement in the mirror drew my idling attention. I saw a skewed and blurry image of men in a group – heads cut off like a bad photograph. They seemed to be arguing, their movements jerky and aggressive. Then one of them fell, and the group closed in around him and began to kick.

I twisted round to look. There were five blokes on their feet: beefed up by anoraks, but already hefty enough. From the faces I could see, they were mostly in their thirties. Almost old enough to know better – except that no one ever is.

I swung round to face front again, and bit my lip. The street ahead was empty: no sign of someone who could intervene, or run for help. Which was all the excuse I needed to sit tight where I was. *Make a note of all the details; pass them on to the police.* I tried to tell myself as much – to no avail. The pressure to act constrained me like a clamp around my chest. It magnified my heartbeat in my ears, and squeezed my throat dry. I swallowed hard, and began to move: pushing open my door and climbing out into the cold before my doubts had time to get themselves together.

'Oi!'

The sound of my voice surprised me – much louder than expected; I almost put my hand to my mouth. Their heads all turned, and for a moment I just stood there, lost for words; then gathered my face into a scowl, and started forward.

'Pack it in,' I called, as assertively as I could.

The nearest man had receding hair and a handlebar moustache. The look he gave me was rank with patronizing smugness. 'Piss off, love . . . just keep your nose out of it, all right?'

My courage, which had been dwindling with each step, was rekindled in an instant: blazing hot. My mum had done her best to bring me up nicely – but now a bluntness engendered by years of nursing came steaming to the fore.

'Don't tell *me* to piss off, mate.'

He blinked, but seemed otherwise unfazed. 'Well don't be a silly bitch, then. No business of yours, this isn't.'

I closed with him, incensed. 'There'll be *kids* out here in a minute.'

'Yours, are they?' a bearded man asked dryly.

I turned my glare on him. 'Yes . . . one of them – what's that got to do with it?'

'You should be bloody thanking us, girl. We caught this pervert hanging around . . .' He gave the bloke on the road a deliberate kick. 'Looking to pick one of those poor kids up, I shouldn't wonder . . .'

I peered down through the thicket of jean-clad legs. The subject, curled up in a foetal ball, wasn't even wearing a coat over his threadbare jersey. His longish brown hair was dragging in the dirt. Suddenly, in the moment before he'd even raised his face, I realized it was Christopher Jackson.

A man across the circle was raising his boot.

'Stop . . .'

'. . . wanker . . .'

'Look, just leave him *alone*, will you?' I blurted, and shoved my way through to crouch beside him. The five aggressors seemed to tower over us. I glanced upward and around at them. 'Just . . . go away.'

The man with the clipped, dark beard gave a sneer of contempt. 'Fuck you then, you stupid cow . . .'

Equality of treatment was all very well, but I still found it scary to be sworn at. Not so much from the words themselves as the viciousness that fuelled them. My eyes had started smarting. Suddenly I had to grit my teeth against the tears.

But the knot of angry bodies was coming undone. Frustrated, they were backing off and giving us some air.

'Lefty do-gooder cow . . .'

I snapped again at that – and my voice almost broke as well. 'And if *you* don't fuck off out of here, right now, I'm calling the police. All right?'

I got some tiny satisfaction from spitting his own medicine back at him; but he just leered contemptuously, and turned away.

Christopher was wiping his bloodied mouth, his eyes on the dispersing group; his face as calm as ever. There was something not quite natural about that solemn self-control. I hesitated before speaking: half-afraid that I'd disrupt it. And what mightn't be running deep, beneath those still, still waters? I had the briefest inkling from his eyes. For just a moment, as they followed the bearded leader, they seemed to have glazed with ice.

Then he spat into the gutter, and turned those eyes on me. They were as clear and vulnerable as they'd been before.

'Rachel . . . Ow.' He rubbed his jaw, and shaped a tentative smile. 'Thank you. So very much.'

Heart thumping with reaction, I helped him up, and set about examining his bruises: assessing a casualty as I hadn't done for years. 'What happened?' I asked, sponging blood from his cut lip with my handkerchief.

'I couldn't really say,' he murmured slowly. 'I've just been walking . . . letting it sink in, I suppose. Those . . . gentlemen took exception. The one with the beard decided I looked like a shirt-lifter – as he put it. And so they decided to clean me off the street.' The matter-of-factness of his tone made the injustice seem more glaring.

Nothing appeared to be broken, at any rate. I finished dyeing my hanky crimson, and looked down at it without enthusiasm. A coldly professional part of me was saying I should have put gloves on first. *He might have used drugs, you know . . .*

'So that's a school, is it?' he asked, nodding.

I glanced over my shoulder. The doors still hadn't opened. 'Yeah.'

'Your daughter's?'

'Mm.' I looked him over, not disguising my concern. 'You shouldn't be out without a coat, you know: not in weather like this. Come and sit in the car.'

He smiled faintly, shaking his head. 'It's all right. Don't trouble yourself. I'd really . . . prefer to be alone.'

'It sometimes helps to talk, you know. And I'm happy to listen.'

His smile grew wider, but in a noncommittal way.

Other cars had started drawing up; the doors were opening. I could hear the first outspill of childish chatter in the background.

'Listen . . . let me at least drop you off somewhere.'

'Thanks, but no. I've got a way to walk yet.'

I looked back to see if Cathy had emerged yet, then returned my gaze to him: loath to just leave him to this bitter afternoon. Though he was managing to keep discomfort out of his expression, his thin shoulders had hunched up against the cold.

'I'll manage, Rachel. Don't worry.'

Another backward glance – and I moistened my dry lips. 'So . . . will we be seeing you again, or . . . sorry, there's no reason for you to come back to St Catherine's, is there . . . ?' *Sod it. Screwed it up.*

He shrugged. 'I might pay a visit to thank you properly . . . once I've got myself together.'

'I hope you can. Take care you don't catch cold, now.' Taking a step back, I gave him a small wave. ' 'Bye.'

I walked over to the growing group of parents with a feeling of churned-up warmth in my stomach. It might just have been the aftershock of confrontation; but I wasn't entirely certain that it was.

Cathy came bouncing out a short while later, full of beans: putting the past five minutes into context. I had a fleeting sense of guilt at having sworn in the street, with her tender ears so close. The fact that I'd risked getting slapped around came down quite heavily as well.

Leading her over to the car, I looked for Christopher again: but he was already in the distance, trudging steadily away. A lean and lonely figure on the bleak, grey street.

*

'How's your little horror, then?' Steve asked.

I smiled against the mouthpiece of the phone. 'I don't know *who* you mean.'

'*Dulux emulsion* ring any bells?'

'Um . . . yes, all right, she's fine. Fast asleep, thank God.'

Steve was helping me redecorate – fitting it in around his full-time job. The first afternoon he'd brought his paint pots round, Cathy had found them unattended and proceeded to experiment, leaving a trail of splotches and strange designs by which we'd finally tracked her to the locked bathroom door. It had taken delicate negotiation (and plain bribery) to get her out again, upon which I'd given her an earful – mortified as much as angry. It took Steve quite a while to make me see the funny side.

'You're sure this Sunday'll be all right?' I asked again, pacing back across the kitchen. I'd rung him this evening, just to check. The work was coming on well: the old, drab wallpaper and paint giving way to clean new whiteness, room by room. I wanted to be sure I wasn't taking advantage; he was giving me preferential rates already. We'd met at the hospice, when I'd been nursing his mother. It gave me a twinge of guilt to think I'd indebted him just by doing my job.

'No problem,' he said cheerfully. 'Really.'

I could visualize his grey-eyed grin. He was a good-looking bloke, only midway through his twenties – and married. Happily, I assumed. If he hadn't been . . . well, who knew?

'I'll see you after lunch, then. And thanks, Steve. I mean that.'

Disconnecting, I walked back through to the living room and settled down on the sofa, tossing the cordless handset onto the adjacent easy chair. The practical part of my mind warned that I was bound to sit on it if I left it there, but right now I felt too floppy to care. Drawing up my legs, I flicked the television on.

Cathy wailed aloud.

Oh God, now what? I clambered up and hurried through to her room. She wasn't sitting up in bed this time, however, but cowering under the covers. The sleepy rabbits on her bedspread contrasted sharply with the misery of the face beneath them.

'*Mummy* . . .'

'Shhh, now,' I urged her, holding tight. Her body felt hot and shaky. 'Mummy's here, poppet. Just another bad dream, that's all . . .'

'The Ragman was here, Mummy . . . looking in through the window.'

'No he wasn't. It's all right . . .'

'The Ragman was *here*.'

The tearful strength of her insistence made me hesitate. I recalled her description of the grisly creature in her dream. Almost despite myself, still hugging her, I turned my head towards the window.

The curtains hung just apart; but the glass beyond was black – the dusk outside had turned to darkness as soon as I switched on the light.

Cathy, her face pressed to my shoulder, was peeping too. 'He was looking *in* at me, Mummy,' she whimpered.

And what if someone had been?

The thought sank into my stomach like a cold, tight fist. Anger and fright put their force behind the blow. The idea of some man scaring my daughter turned me livid; but with just the two of us here alone, and that void outside the window, I felt an ugly twinge of fear as well.

Easing Cathy back down against the pillows, I began to straighten up – still staring at the blank, reflecting glass. At once she snatched at my cardigan sleeve.

'No, Mummy, don't go near him . . .'

'Shhh. It's all right, we're quite safe.' But the thudding in my chest gave the lie to my conviction as I crossed the room to look. Bending forward, I cupped my hand around my eyes and peered out into the darkness.

The back field and the trees beyond it were a single mass of shadow; the last, ghostly afterglow just offsetting the sky. I could see no trace of movement. But anyone out there would be seeing me clearly enough. They could be standing only yards away – and smiling at my blindness. I drew back quickly, and pulled the curtains closed.

'No, there's nobody there.' I turned my back firmly on the window, and came over to the bed. Poor Cathy was hugging herself as if she had tummy-ache, her lip still trembling. I sat down beside her, and put on my sunniest smile.

'Off you go to sleep, now. Brave girl.'

Her tears began again, and this time my cuddles couldn't stifle them. She grizzled at my whispers; rubbed her wet and streaming face against my breasts. At last, having run out of cajolements, I tried a different tack. 'Would you like to come and watch the telly for a bit? Special treat . . .'

She sniffed, and nodded, so I carried her through and made her comfy on the sofa. She promptly sent me back to fetch her panda; and as I left the bedroom a second time, and switched the light off, I looked back towards the window. With the room in darkness, the day's last gasp seeped greyly through the curtains. I had a fleeting urge to go over, pull them open and face the dusk on equal terms – able to glimpse what had previously lurked in shadow. Just an empty field, most likely; and the harmless, timid creatures of an English night. But I didn't have the nerve to see for sure.

The glowing TV screen dried Cathy's tears like sunlight on wet pavements. No doubt the subject of the talk-show went over her head, but she watched as if deeply absorbed. Snuggled up against me in the flickering gloom, she gradually sank into sleep.

Absently I fingered her hair, and wondered if I could get her back to her room without waking her. Apart from anything else, she was getting to be quite a heavy little girl. But even if I did rouse her, she'd probably drowse off again a minute later: catching up on lost sleep with all the resilience of the young.

I heard an engine changing down behind me, as a car reached the junction in front of the house. Its headlights briefly swept the room, projecting magnified shadows across the wall in a weird kaleidoscope effect. I listened to it accelerate away. Our quiet street seemed quieter still when it had gone.

The talk-show gave way to trailers; it was almost time for the news. I gave Cathy a speculative glance. Now seemed as good a time as any. I heard another car coming up towards the junction as I gently began to disengage.

Again the flare of headlamps washed the wall; but this time they cast a monstrous human shadow, ragged and blurred, that loomed up and *up* and over us, ready to swoop – before fading with the passing of the car.

I cringed from it in horror: pressed my fist against my mouth for fear of crying out. Then the car was gone; the corners of the room receded back into the dark. On the TV screen, two people talked regardless.

Someone was standing right outside our window.

Screened though I already was by the back of the sofa, I sank down lower, and closer still to Cathy – thanking God she was still asleep. Tense, every fine hair tingling, I listened.

Not a whisper of movement from outside.

The Ragman was here, Mummy.

With a sudden rush of adrenaline, I reached across and grabbed the cordless handset . . . then wondered who the hell I could call. My mind was a blank, wiped clean by fright. I couldn't remember a single number.

Then inspiration struck, and I punched the redial button. The clack and whir of the connections sounded much louder than the television's murmur. The phone at the other end gave eight interminable rings before a click gave way to Steve's crisp voice. 'Hello?'

'Steve . . .' I almost croaked.

He recognized my voice at once – and picked up its distress. 'Rachel? What's wrong?'

'Could you . . . come over here very quick, please?' It was all I could do to keep my whispered voice from wavering.

'What's happened?'

'There's someone creeping round outside the house.'

'Shit. Hold on, I'll be right there.'

He would be, too: living not five minutes' drive away. A sudden chill went through me. 'Steve . . .' I blurted quickly, before he could hang up.

'I'm here, Rachel.'

'Please . . . be careful.'

'See you in a minute,' he said firmly, and the connection was broken.

I lowered the handset – and belatedly wondered if I should have called the police. But if this was just some common or back-garden prowler, I'd probably be wasting their time.

And that had to be case, of course. Because if it wasn't . . .

Oh Steve, I thought, too late: *what have I let you in for?*

Cathy was snoring softly at my side, her face a blessed blank. I laid a hand on her cool forehead, and waited for the hammer of my heart to wake her up. She'd surely hear it. And so must the watcher at the window.

Ignorance of what was happening might be bliss for

Cathy, but for me it was the worst thing of all. Was he still there, staring – or had he moved, in search of some way in? I didn't dare raise my head above the sofa-back to look.

The minutes slithered by. The bright bubble of the TV screen was like an intrusion from another world: a place quite heedless of my plight. I cowered in its fitful glow, my arm round Cathy; straining my ears for the first, faint rattle of door or window . . .

At last I heard the engine of another car, approaching quickly; I hoped to God that it was Steve. The lights came streaming through the window, and tracked across. Apart from the shadows of hedge-twigs, the wall above the TV set showed blank and white.

I felt the decompression of relief inside my stomach, even as he came scrunching to a stop against the kerb. The slam of his door, the click of his footsteps on the pavement, were sounds like sweetest music. I was already up and moving on wobbly legs as he rang the doorbell.

'Are you all right?' he asked, as soon as I opened up. His face was serious with concern.

I nodded quickly. 'I think he's gone. You probably scared him off. Come in . . .'

He insisted on checking front and back, borrowing the kitchen torch to flash into the darkest corners and off across the field. I concentrated on putting Cathy to bed; she murmured sleepily as I tucked her in, and then was quiet again.

Steve rejoined me, slapping the torch thoughtfully against his palm. 'No sign of anyone now. Do you want to give the cop shop a ring?'

I shook my head. 'It's probably not worth bothering them. If it happens again, maybe . . .' But I was already fiercely telling myself that this had just been a one-off. Some sad voyeur who'd been frightened back into the night.

'Okay, then . . .' He politely declined my offer of a coffee or something, and I saw him to the door.

'Thanks ever so much for coming round.'

'No problem. Just call me if you've ever got a problem like that. I'll see you Sunday, then.'

I said goodnight, and was still smiling when the door was shut and chained between us. It was good to find that people still looked out for one another – and not just for selfish reasons. It made me feel a little warmer, deep inside.

I went round checking the window locks, just to be safe; then went into the darkened kitchen to bolt the back door. In doing so, peering out into the murk, I glimpsed a movement.

A sweaty chill spread down my back. I stood there, staring – and saw it again. An indistinct displacement of the darkness.

Someone was moving about in the back field.

For a moment I was too petrified to stir; and then a spasm of anger gripped me. Goaded by the image of Cathy's terrified face, I wrenched back the bolt and yanked the door open.

'Just piss off, will you! Leave us alone!'

My words thinned and faded towards the unseen edges of the field; the frosty evening air flowed back in answer. I shivered, and hugged myself; my courage abruptly left me in the lurch.

Once more I sensed the movement: further out than I'd first thought, maybe twenty yards or so. I squinted, trying to see. And then, for no clear reason, another possibility occurred to me; so strongly that my hand went to my mouth.

'Christopher . . . ?' I almost whispered.

A tiny spark flared yellow, out there in the night; I heard the rasp of a match. It wavered like a firefly for a moment – then plummeted downward, and went out.

My nerve went with it. I ducked back inside, shut the door and bolted it tight; then retreated to the far end of the kitchen. As I stared towards the window, and listened to the throbbing in my chest, another sound crept up to tease my ears.

At first I couldn't place it as external noise at all; then I realized it was coming from somewhere else inside the flat. A faint and stifled whirring that was almost insect-like. It nagged and puzzled me. At length, dragging my gaze away from the night beyond the glass, I began to look around for the cause.

By an increasingly jittery process of elimination, switching lights on at every turn, I finally traced it back to the closed spare room.

I hesitated for a long time with my fingers round the handle. Behind the door, the buzzing noise seemed louder. Drawing a breath, I pushed my way in and fumbled for the light-switch. The glare of the naked bulb wiped out the shadows, but made the stale and jumbled room look all the bleaker.

The noise was coming from the old chest of drawers.

I chewed my lip in wretched indecision; then crossed the room in a stride, dragged the bottom drawer open, delved into the mothballed clothes – and came up with the silver compass. It was whirring like a rattlesnake, its chilly case vibrating; and as I took it in my hands, the lid flipped open – I gasped with shock – and its black face was revealed, the five-pointed needle spinning round, so fast it was a blur.

3

STIRRINGS

'I hope you're not expecting a death-bed conversion,' Simon murmured from the pillow.

I smiled faintly, and shook my head. A weary narrowing of his eyes was the closest he could come to smiling back. With the pain now burrowed deep, and chewing, we'd increased his analgesia: he was sluggish with the morphine in his system. But even on the brink of easeful sleep, there were things he'd had to say.

I'd settled down to hear them in his bedside chair. The hooded glow of the bedhead light was intimate and homely: holding us together in the dimness; softening the lines on his dried young face.

'Isn't it past your home-time?' he asked after a pause.

'Your parents said they'd be here as soon as they could; I'll wait until they come. If you don't mind . . . ?'

'No need . . . to trouble yourself . . .'

'Shh, now. You don't have to be alone tonight. Not for one minute.'

I already had his hand between my own; had held it all the time that we'd been talking. I rubbed it gently with my thumb.

His eyes fluttered closed. There was silence, except for his slow and heavy breathing.

And who would hold *my* hand tonight?

The unbidden thought made me purse my lips. The stress of helping him shed his burden had kept me fully occupied this evening; but with the first lapse of concentration, the tapeworm in my belly reawakened, and began to bite.

That whirring, spinning compass had scared me out of my wits; I'd flung it away, like something alive I'd inadvertently picked up, and scrambled back into the corner. Not having seen it land, I could only crouch there, listening to it buzzing from somewhere amid the clutter of the room: as insidious as an angry wasp. But gradually the noise had faded, like something clockwork running down, until at last the silence was as thick as in the rest of the flat. Only then had I climbed hastily to my feet again, backed out and shut the door.

Cathy had slept in my bed last night: I'd carried her through, still snoring, and settled her beside me. She'd slept like a log, of course. I was the one who scarcely closed my eyes.

And in the morning's misty light, the back field lay quite empty. No trace of any prowler to be seen. I peered warily out through the kitchen window; looked over towards the trees. Not even a rabbit caught my eye.

I hadn't imagined the match flame, though: had I? Even if I ventured out to look for the blackened stick, and failed to find it, I couldn't kid myself on that score. And whoever it was who'd been lurking in the darkness, their very presence had reactivated the dormant compass – and sent it haywire.

Whoever: whatever.

'Rachel . . . are you okay?'

I blinked my way back to the here and now. Simon's head hadn't moved from the pillow, but I saw the shadow of concern on his slack face.

'How do you mean?' I hedged, as casually as I could: renewing my clasp round his limp hand.

'You looked so worried just then . . .'

'Oh . . . it's nothing.' My smile was almost guilty; the

last thing I wanted was to perplex his last few waking minutes. 'Nothing for you to worry about . . .'

'Are Mum and Dad here yet?'

'Not yet, no.'

'Only . . . I can't hold on much longer . . .'

'Don't fight if you don't want to, Simon. You can just let go, whenever you're ready . . .'

'*Not* . . . until I've said goodbye.' His own grip strengthened briefly as he said it. I just nodded – and wondered if he'd guessed. His own peace was my first priority, of course; but our conversation had kept him conscious. And even as we talked, I'd been willing him to live a little longer. For his parents' sake.

Thank you. I love you . . .

'You're a brave man, Simon,' I told him softly. 'I'm glad I met you.'

His skin tightened over his cheekbones in a shadow-smile. 'Mutual,' he murmured. 'You're really someone special, Rachel Young.'

He slipped out of consciousness soon after; and died just seven minutes before his mum and dad arrived.

I drove home feeling pretty down. Yes, he'd had a good death: peaceful and pain-free. But the final lack of symmetry seemed to spoil it all somehow. His parents had been distraught, of course. I'd ushered them into the light behind drawn curtains so they could see his calm, blank face, and touch it. Tearful farewells were said, and meant. But it wasn't the same.

Hovering there behind them, half in light, half-shadow, I'd tasted the bitter tang of disappointment on their behalf. *Couldn't you have waited, God? Just a few minutes more?*

But when did death ever listen to reason? When your hour comes, it comes. And with the care of the patient over, the care of the relatives went on. I stayed with them for as long as I could, trying not to think how restive poor Alice must be getting.

I apologized profusely when I finally got back. She assured me it had been no trouble, but I could tell that she was itching to be gone.

'Could you give me a call tomorrow sometime?' I asked, as she pulled her jacket on. 'Let me know when you'll be free over Christmas . . .'

'I might not have much time to spare for a while,' she murmured, sounding a little apologetic herself. 'I've got my mocks coming up in January, and I need to do a fair bit of revision . . .'

'Of course, don't worry. It's better I know in good time, so I can make arrangements . . .' I hesitated. 'Everything's been all right, this evening?'

I'd mentioned it when I'd phoned her up this morning: reports of a peeping tom behind the houses. 'Best make sure the curtains are drawn before putting the lights on – just in case,' I'd told her; trying not to make it sound like an instruction.

All through the working day, I'd had Cathy on my mind. The afternoon had been windy autumn gold, and Jan had taken her charges to play in the park; but once Alice had brought her home, and the evening had closed in, who knew what might have crept towards the windows? It was only Simon's deterioration that had kept the worry from really digging in.

Could it really have been Chris Jackson, out there in the cold? Too awkward and ashamed to speak when challenged? In a way I really hoped so: whatever his motives, they were unlikely to be threatening. But I'd no reason to believe it had been. He wouldn't even know where we lived . . .

'No problems,' Alice said. 'We've been nice and snug. I let her stay up for a bit; she didn't want to go to bed without you here. But I got her off to sleep in the end.'

'Thanks,' I said; just managing to keep my face from falling. It wasn't the first time I'd felt guilty about not being there for Cathy. But after the fright she'd had last night, I could guess how upsetting it must have been: the sight of the grey dusk slinking back while I was still out working.

Won't be long, my darling: I'd promised her that. Perhaps she really had been watching from the window, waiting for my car to turn the corner. But her hopeful patience hadn't been rewarded; bedtime had come with the road still empty. And the night had got here first.

I looked in on her as soon as Alice had left, but she was fast asleep now. Was it my imagination, or was she hugging her panda a little tighter than usual? I slipped glumly back out to make myself some supper.

With the scraped but unwashed plates left standing in the sink, I settled down in front of the TV (after making sure the curtains were tightly closed behind me). These days – and darkening evenings – it seemed I hadn't the stamina for anything more demanding than a soap opera. The radio couldn't hold my restless attention; favourite music failed to move me. The book I currently had on the go was still lying where I'd left it last weekend, its bookmark wilting and forlorn.

With the light switched off, I'd hoped that the glow and flicker of the screen would at least bring a cosiness of sorts: the modern equivalent of a fireside tale. But then a movement on the carpet caught the corner of my eye: the briefest impression of something scuttling across.

Spider.

I hastily drew up my knees and peered about me, feeling a surge of gooseflesh at the very idea. It must have been quite big, to register like that; but I lost track of it at once in the shifting layers of light and dimness round the set. Perhaps it had taken refuge under the video, and was lurking there now. Or maybe it had just stopped moving: much closer than I thought . . .

In a way, of course, it was absurd: letting such a harmless little thing take control of a room and maroon me in the middle. After everything I'd been through: all the real horrors that I'd faced. Yet my reaction was still one of visceral fright. As I huddled up on the sofa, the prickling of my neck made me think, for one lurching moment, that it had crawled up there already: about to creep into my hair . . .

'Nick! There's a spider in the bathroom . . .'

'Say hello to it from me.'

I remembered the moment so well: hovering on the landing in my nightshirt, feeling abjectly embarrassed. 'Could you . . . come and get rid of it, please?'

'Rachel. You're a big girl now.'

I leaned over the banisters, pouting. 'No nookie until you come and get rid of it.'

That got him upstairs smartly enough. I watched nervously as he went on in. 'Don't hurt it,' I called suddenly.

His shoulders slumped with mock exasperation. 'I thought you couldn't *stand* the bloody things.'

'I can't. But it seems unfair to kill them just for that.'

Shaking his head, he returned his attention to the washbasin, and came back out a minute later with his right hand loosely closed.

'Want to check it's still breathing?' he grinned.

Unfazed by the face I pulled in answer, he walked by me – and as soon as he was past, his left hand landed on my neck, his fingers scrabbling: 'Look out, he's *loose*!' – and I shrieked and went up in the air.

Even with my sinuses beginning to sting, I couldn't help smiling at the memory. It was a pinched expression, though: I wasn't sure if the growing pressure in my throat bespoke giggles or tears. Sniffing, I let myself sag back.

Oh, Nick.

Something scampered up the nape of my neck and fluttered in my hair.

With a squeal I started upright, tossing my head: the spidery threat around my feet forgotten. It took me a moment to find my balance – and realize those were fingertips I'd felt. Someone's hand had just scurried across my shoulder. Somebody was behind me in the room.

Drenched with dread, I swung around to see – but apart from my own jumpy shadow, projected by the television's light, there was nobody there.

I clapped my hands to my mouth: made a small, scared sound behind them. The coolness was still fading from the skin behind my ears: the fingerprints of a touch as mischievous as Nick's. But this time the fingers had been *real.*

And there was *nobody there.*

Timidly, heart thumping, I edged round to look behind the sofa; resigned to knowing the worst – whatever that might be. But nothing was crouching in the dimness there. Backing away towards the door, I switched the light on: bleaching back the shadows. Apart from me, the room was plainly empty.

Something psychological, then: it had to be. A mean trick played by memory on my mind. I hugged myself and mulled it miserably over: still too shocked to shed tears. No other explanation presented itself. At last I went and sat down again, trying to make myself as comfortable as I could. But the cosiness of the room was long lost. In cleaning out the darkest corners, the light overhead had emptied it of life, and left me in a bleak and charmless shell.

Sleep came late that night. The dream came later still. It was during the last and lowest part of the night that the confusion in my head sprang into focus.

Before I knew where I was, that frozen wood was closing in around me and I was fleeing through it. The ground underfoot was searing hot, breaking up my frantic strides with hops and skips of pain; and then I realized that my feet were bare and I was running on snow. The full weight of winter registered at once: clawing in through the loose white dress I wore. It was ankle-length, and snagged on every thorn. I had nothing on beneath it.

I risked a fast glance backwards, and just glimpsed the shadow in pursuit: crashing through the frost-stripped undergrowth behind me. With a gasp of panic I looked ahead, and saw we were coming to the edge of the trees. A snowfield stretched beyond it – with dark figures waiting in the whiteness. I saw scaffolds of wood rearing up against the leaden sky, and vivid yellow flames . . .

'*Rachel* . . .'

Nick's urgent voice: I knew it at once, and my heart surged with relief. The bitter vision fell apart as I shook myself awake, reached gratefully out for him –

And found myself alone in my widow's bed.

The come-down was vertical and sickening. I slumped back onto the pillow, releasing my breath in a single, broken sob. The bedroom around me felt dim and cold and very empty. I drew my knees up tight into my stomach.

How could my own mind be so cruel? How *could* it?

And why dredge up the same weird dream again? Chewing my lip . . . feeling wetness on my cheek and on the pillow . . . I couldn't stop myself from wondering. The same breathless chase through a forest. But a little clearer, this time: as if my hateful talent, grown rusty from disuse, was slowly coming up to speed once more.

*

'And how are things at home?' asked Matron, beaming.

'Oh. Fine, thanks.' Hoping she'd leave it at that, I allowed myself another sip of coffee. The delicate china cup was quite a change from my working office mug; I'd had to remind myself to hold it politely by two fingers, rather than wrap my hand around and take a swig.

Matron nodded; drank herself. But her calm, apprais-ing eyes remained on me.

I let my own gaze flick off around the office; hoping I didn't look too shifty. Coffee with Matron was a common privilege: she'd use the opportunity to discuss current policies, or future plans – and sometimes we just chatted. The mid-morning summons had been a daunting thing at first; but now I took it as an invitation – and was more concerned about being seen as Matron's Pet.

Matron. I still had to shift the mental gears to think of her as Mrs Lambert – let alone by her first name, though she encouraged us to use it. Yet she wasn't much older than me; a well-built, cheerful woman in her middle thir-ties. Someone easy to relate to – but with a keen nursing mind behind her affable smile. I knew it was assessing me now.

'I see young Nicola's settling in nicely,' she observed.

She was; but this was beginning to sound like small-talk – circling round a larger but unseen subject.

'Yes, I think we chose well there,' I agreed: playing along. Hoping to resist the gravitational pull.

'I know she's grateful for all the support you've given her. One more job I've unloaded on you. You're not . . . feeling too pressurized, I hope?'

'No, no . . .' I jumped in hastily. Perish the thought.

'Only, I think you rather upset Diane the other day.'

So that was it. She'd spoken almost idly; but a pang in my stomach warned that this time I'd been summoned for a scolding.

It must have shown on my face, for she followed

quickly on. 'Not that she's been carrying tales. I noticed, and I asked her. Nor do I doubt that our Diane can give as good as she gets. It's you I'm concerned about, Rachel.'

I glanced down at my coffee.

This last time with Diane, I'd been really rather sharp. She'd been probing, in a casual way: piqued by my rejection of her ghost stories. Her musings on uncanny happenings at her previous hospital just happened to coincide with the latest onset of my nagging inner fears. In overreacting, I'd slagged her work off: found faults where few existed. In front of other staff as well, which must have hurt. Apart from where our duties required it, we hadn't spoken for two days.

'You're sure things are all right?' prompted Matron gently.

'Well . . .' I paused; gestured. Then gave in. 'It's just, it's been a year since . . . my husband's death, but it feels like forever. The anniversary of that's . . . just come and gone.' I heard my own voice wavering, and paused, eyes down; my knuckle pressing tight against my lips. Silence, while I got myself together. I sensed her waiting, patient and concerned.

That would explain the dream, of course: my mind still readjusting. The same with the sound of his voice . . .

I breathed in through my nose, and raised my eyes again. 'Sorry. And coming up to Christmas doesn't help. But I did snap at her, and she didn't deserve it. I'll apologize.'

'Christmas this year will be a challenge, won't it?' she murmured after a moment.

'I'll be happier when it's past,' I admitted frankly. Which was putting it in a nutshell. My favourite time of year had become its lowest point: the darkest depth of winter. The childhood magic had long since dwindled, but my parents' deaths wiped the goodwill out as well. And in the run-up to last Christmas, I'd lost *love*. Now, more than ever, I wanted to avoid the season – but it was always there waiting at the end of the year, and I hadn't any choice. No more than a wandering comet, drawn home by a cold black sun.

'I'm still glad I managed to persuade you to take a break,' said Matron, equally direct. 'You've earned it, Rachel.'

I didn't reply. Originally I'd planned for my pattern of work to stay as normal as possible; needing to keep myself busy. But it would mean asking favours of so many friends – and in the end, she'd won me over. I'd accepted the whole of Christmas week off. Instead of the pressures of clinical care, I'd have a Christmas Eve party to occupy me. A few of us from the Women's Group were organizing one for our collective offspring; Pat and I were in charge of the cooking. Cathy was looking forward to it already.

At least my little angel felt the magic. Who knew, maybe some of it could still rub off . . .

'Will you be going away?' asked Matron.

I made a noncommittal face. 'Maybe to my in-laws. I haven't decided.'

'Just so long as you have yourself a good rest.'

'With a *three-year-old*?' I came back, mock-incredulous; and we both laughed.

With the day's shift ended, I emerged into a gusty afternoon. The clouds flowed overhead in filthy currents, sucking leaves along beneath them. I glanced up apprehensively; then round to where St Catherine's loomed behind me, like a black rock braced against the tide; its windows warmly lit. Shelter from the oncoming storm.

Tugging up my raincoat collar, I turned away and walked towards the car.

Christopher Jackson was waiting beside it.

I'd been delving for the car keys in my bag, and didn't

notice until I got up close. He startled me so much, I almost dropped them. A rueful smile crossed his face as my hand went to my mouth.

'I'm sorry, Rachel. You didn't expect to see me again, did you?'

'Well . . .' I began; and found no words to follow on with. He was right: I hadn't. Part of me, remembering that presence in the blackness of the back field, wasn't sure if I'd wanted to, either.

At least he was wearing an anorak today: albeit a threadbare and unzipped one. The collar of the shirt beneath was buttoned up – looking curious in the absence of a tie. His hesitant manner only emphasized the awkwardness of his appearance.

'Here . . .' He proffered a small box, carefully wrapped. 'For the ward. It's the least I can do, after your kindness.'

'Oh . . . thanks.' Surprised and gratified, I took it; then gave him a searching look. 'Why on earth didn't you come in? We'd have made you a cup of tea, no trouble . . .'

He just gave a faint – increasingly familiar – smile, and shook his head. 'No: I didn't want a fuss made. Better to wait out here . . .'

'*Christopher*. It's such a miserable day.' I said it with genuine concern. The thought of him kept out in the cold by his shyness was quite upsetting.

The damp wind blew his hair across his face; he shook it back. 'And thanks again for what *you* did, Rachel. Defending me from those *good citizens* . . .' I couldn't help but smile at the sardonic slant he gave those words; it made a pleasing contrast to his passive demeanour.

'It was nothing. Really.' It didn't even feel that odd: being thanked by a bloke for rescuing him from his attackers. The sense of equality put us further at our ease; and drew us closer.

He cleared his throat. 'I wonder . . . could I buy you a drink or something . . . sometime?'

My turn to hesitate; glancing down at the parcel in my hands. 'Um ... It would be difficult, really. What with my daughter and all ...'

He shrewdly picked up on the bit I'd left unsaid. 'You live alone with her, then?'

Not really the sort of thing you should admit to; but I knew I had to place myself in context – here and now. Meeting his eye again, I nodded, once. 'Yeah. My ... husband died a year ago.'

His face grew tighter. 'Rachel. I'm sorry.'

'No, don't be ...'

'I shouldn't have asked.'

'It's all right.' I glanced up as the first spots of rain arrived – a welcome distraction from the discomfort of the moment. But I found I didn't want to disengage completely. 'Listen, how are you getting back?'

He gave an unconcerned shrug. 'Walk.'

'You'll be soaked. Let me drop you off. It's no trouble.'

'Really ...'

'You're not talking your way out of it this time, Chris,' I smiled. 'Get in.'

We didn't say much on the way to his father's old house, but the silence was comfortable enough; made more so by the car's warm interior, sealed off from the rain and spray and streaming streets outside. I concentrated on my driving, but was aware of him taking details in: the rosary beads that dangled from the mirror; the cassette boxes scattered in the footwell. Cathy's empty seat behind us ...

The house to which I followed his quiet directions was right at the edge of town: a dour, two-storey cottage. Pulling up, I noticed how the paint was peeling from the window frames, revealing dark wet wood beneath. The rest of the exterior looked similarly the worse for wear. A misaligned gutter drooled dirty water. The small front garden was overgrown and weedy. An unlovely-looking place in the best of lights, I guessed; but the steady rain cast a dull grey pall across it. Imagine coming home alone to those unlit windows. I felt my spirits sink in sympathy.

He unlatched his seatbelt with deliberate care; and glanced at me. 'Are you sure I can't offer you a coffee or something?'

And we're not even coming back from a date.

An idle thought; it turned my mouth bone dry. Caught unawares, I swallowed, breathless: staring forward. He'd surely take the pause as an open door to push against – but I was suddenly a prisoner of my instincts. And my painful indecision.

'I'd like to . . .' I allowed at last. 'But I'm due back home.'

'Some other time, then?' I could sense him beside me, looking out through the rainswept windscreen too.

'I don't know.' I paused, and took the plunge: that's how it felt, inside my stomach. 'I might be able to get someone to babysit on Thursday night . . .'

'Shall I ring you?' Pressing his advantage cautiously home.

'Uh . . . Can I ring *you*?'

He accepted my reticence with a sidelong smile, and told me the number. I scribbled it down on a scrap of paper with a pen from my uniform pocket.

'Will you be in tomorrow?'

'Oh, I expect so. There's not a lot else to tempt me out.'

'Right. I'll talk to you then.' I watched as he climbed out, bowing his head beneath the weight of rain; then leaned across. 'Take care.'

He waved, looked left and right and ducked across the road. I waited until he was in through the door – half-hoping he'd look back – then got going again myself.

The house's gloomy image slid sideways off the rear-view mirror, and was gone.

Reaction to what we'd just agreed made my spirits swell inside me – like a helium balloon trying to force its way up through my chest. Its slow deflation left me feeling weak and shaky. Whatever my previous feelings, they hadn't prepared me for the moment. Perhaps he himself had been taken by surprise.

From out of nowhere. We'd just been talking, passing time – and suddenly we were going out together. Outstripped by our own instincts. Out of *nowhere.*

I'd bought myself some time to reflect on it now; a chance for second thoughts. But even now, still driving home, I knew they wouldn't sway me.

I'm being taken out, I thought again; and felt my chest close tighter round my heart.

*

The second thoughts assailed me, sure enough. Washing up our supper things that evening, I faced them one after another. Should I be going out with a patient's relative? What if it really had been him sneaking round behind the house?

Would Nick mind?

That last was the hardest one of all, of course. I put it to myself that he surely wouldn't resent me getting on with my life. If he could see me somehow (and I was sure that he could), the loneliness I often felt must hurt him. And this would only be a meeting, after all: no strings attached. Just two bereaved young people drawn together.I hadn't yet allowed myself to think where it might lead.

Perhaps to nowhere. Would that be for the best? Or worst of all?

Alice wasn't free on Thursday night. I felt my stomach

sinking as she said so. That had been earlier in the evening. I'd hung up the phone, and paced unhappily round the kitchen. The smell of supper cooking left my appetite unmoved.

'Mummy,' piped up Cathy from the doorway. 'I've found a new toy to play with . . .'

'Go and play with it, then, darling,' I told her absently. 'Mummy's little angel.'

She'd done as she was told; and I hit upon the thought of phoning Pat.

She'd sounded bright and breezy when she answered, despite the childish racket I could hear in the background. Yes, of course she could spare an hour or two on Thursday evening; husband Mark could hold the fort. I tried to stem the gush of my gratitude, but she seemed to take the favour in her stride. She had some studying for her evening class to do, she told me; away from the demands of her family, she might just get some peace.

Her little son and Cathy got on quite well. They even played together. I couldn't get my head round the change that had to come: the distant day when the thought of a boy would tie her stomach up in knots – just the way that mine felt now.

But with that last piece fitted neatly into place, I could let myself look forward. To an evening out: my first in far too long. What would I wear? (What would *he* wear?) Where would we go?

What would we talk about?

Hopes and doubts blew hot and cold. Back at the sink, wrist-deep in soapy water, I told myself not to get too excited. We'd both be nervous; wary with it. His hermit-crab exterior might be difficult to crack – even though I'd seen the tenderness beneath. With an effort of will, I calmed my spirits; stilled my expectations. And then, just as I was rinsing down the plates, the radio news cast a stone into the pond.

I hadn't really been listening; a song I rather liked was coming up, and my mind was rehearsing it already. But my unfocused attention latched onto the pause between one item and the next, and it seemed I heard what followed with fresh ears.

'Police say the woman whose body was found at Elm Hill weir earlier today, was *murdered*. Her wrists and ankles had apparently been *bound*, before she was put into the water. A post-mortem examination confirmed the cause of death as *drowning* . . .'

The earnest emphasis placed on each key word only served to rub it in. I slotted a dripping plate into the rack, and pinched my lips together. I'd never been to Elm Hill, but I knew the name; it featured on many of our road-signs. That was close enough to home to make it local.

God, that poor woman.

I'd almost been drowned myself once. Deliberately, cold-bloodedly drowned. A mild but persistent phobia had lingered ever since. I could all too well imagine being dropped into a river, unable to swim or even struggle. Helpless to do anything but squirm, and sink into the darkness . . .

The idea laid a sympathetic chill across the small of my back. Almost instinctively I raised my eyes to the window. My own dim reflection peered shortsightedly back at me. A black gulf lay beyond it – only inches from my nose. With sudden, spooked unease I reached for the pull-cord: drew the blind. And stood there staring at its pretty floral pattern, while the song I'd so looked forward to leaked uselessly away.

Whoever had done it was still out there somewhere, behind the fabric. Perhaps ten miles away.

Perhaps ten feet.

Just who *had* been creeping round the field, the other night?

Unwilling to work at that indigestible thought, I busied

myself with drying my hands, and hoped it would dissolve. This was the far side of the borough we were talking about, after all. And one unfortunate woman. Even working at random, he had a hundred thousand more to choose from. So what chance he'd choose me?

I didn't doubt some man had done it. Most likely a man she knew. But maybe he'd been a stranger to her. Someone she knew no better than I knew Chris Jackson . . .

A rogue thought: it surprised me. But even as I tried to concentrate on putting the plates away, I felt its seed beginning to take root. Very different questions were arising now – and they brought their answers with them. How well did I really know him? Hardly at all. What did others think about him? *Not quite on the same wavelength*. From an integrated background? No: a calm, laconic loner.

The seed in my stomach kept on growing. By bedtime, it had sprouted to a thorn-bush. It was well past midnight before my restless turnings tired me out, and tipped me over into sleep.

Suddenly, before I knew it, I was wide awake again. Convinced, as soon as I opened my eyes, that someone else was with me in the darkness.

My worry-pangs had faded while I slept; but with that thought, they came again – in painful, cold contractions.

The hush was deep and thick, like undisturbed dust. There wasn't a sound of breath; no trace of movement. I lay quite still, curled up beneath the covers; but they offered no comfort. The warmth I'd burrowed into was now more stifling than a shroud.

I hadn't been dreaming this time, I was sure of that. Some outside presence had called me to the surface.

Cathy? Cathy can't sleep? I moistened my lips . . . but didn't dare to raise my head.

Minutes passed. Still nothing stirred. At last I

summoned up the nerve to risk a look. And of course my room was empty.

I switched on the bedside light and sat there, hugging myself. The waves of my fear were still subsiding, gurgling down into my stomach – leaving me bathed in chilly sweat.

The bedroom door was firmly closed; the curtains drawn. I listened hard, but no sound came from beyond them. Which left my imagination as prime suspect once again – its mud stirred up by my concerns, and giving sight of things sunk deeper in the ooze. For the first time I wondered if I might need psychiatric help to dredge them up and dump them.

Now *there* was a thought to freeze the blood.

With my mind thus absorbed, it took a moment for the ambience to register; but when it did, I almost gasped against my hand. The feeling was no longer one of presence, but a subtler sensation: an awareness of someone having been and gone. Someone as familiar as myself.

It took years of intimacy to pick up such a trace. It wasn't a thing that could be touched, or smelled. But suddenly, enthralled by shock, I knew that Nick had been here. I could almost taste his memory in my mouth.

*

What's he trying to tell me? What does he *want*? The question pulsed inside me like the throb of an infected wound. Consumed by its fever, I trudged dejectedly onward.

'Wait for me,' wheezed Cathy. 'Wait for *meee*.'

I reined the trolley in, and threw an irritable glance over my shoulder: slowing but not stopping as she panted after me down the aisle. Her little face was flushed and hurt, but that cut no ice with me. She'd been snivelling all morning, and I'd really had enough.

'Look,' I muttered sourly as she caught up, 'do you want to ride in the bloody seat or don't you?'

She shook her head, peering miserably up at me: not far from tears now. I turned huffily away from her bewildered expression, and pushed on towards the in-store bakery.

Oh Nick: what did you come back for? And an answer followed close on the question's heels. *To make sure I stay faithful.*

My reaction to the thought was quite unsettling: a defensiveness that bordered on resentment. After all the months of weepiness and longing, it left me feeling guiltily surprised. But wasn't it just a reflection of the relationship we'd had? He'd sometimes been too possessive for my liking; I'd bridled at it more than once.

I'm only going out for the company, Nick. You can't begrudge me that.

'Mummy . . . can we have a gingybread man?'

'No, we can't. Put it back.' Forlornly she did so, while I selected the obligatory white sliced loaf. 'It's high time you started eating brown bread, you know. Much better for you than this stuff . . .'

'Don't like brown . . .' she whined.

Drawing a sharp breath through my teeth, I steered the trolley round into the next aisle. She hurried to keep up, almost getting underfoot. Having forgotten my shopping list (as usual) I ran my gaze along the shelves, hoping that something would jog my memory. Cathy's own attention was caught by the bright packaging of the soap powders, and she fell behind once more.

'Come on,' I snapped, when I noticed; and leaned down to scold as she scurried up. 'I don't know what's *wrong* with you today.' My angry whisper was loud enough for half the aisle to hear. A few half-interested shoppers turned their heads as we moved on past them.

'Mummy, don't be cross . . .' she whimpered.

'Shhh. People are staring at you, look . . .'

'I want to go home.' The tears she'd threatened were starting at last. She rubbed ineffectually at her eyes.

'Not yet. We've nearly finished.'

'I want to go home *now*,' she insisted, suddenly loud.

I could feel my patience fraying like an overstretched rope. 'Catherine! You're going to get a *smack* in a minute.'

She lapsed into silence; we turned back towards the checkouts. Plodding moodily behind the laden trolley, I tried persuading Nick – or myself – once more.

It doesn't change a single thing. You know I'll always love you.

My thoughts were interrupted by an avalanche of scattered thuds. Cathy, trailing behind me, had paused to investigate a pile of biscuit packets, and managed to upset the lot.

'Right!' I stooped, tugged up her skirt to bare her leg, and slapped her hard.

At once she exploded into howls: a siren wail of misery and grief. I could only stand there, helpless, while *everyone* around us turned to see. I could feel the weight of their silent disapproval, bearing down on me from all sides. I wanted to crawl away and hide. And as I stared into Cathy's scarlet, streaming face, the blockage inside me broke at last, and tides of shame and pity flooded through me. Heaving her up into my arms, I held her to my shoulder, as if my coat could absorb her sea of tears. When she kept on crying – an awful, *desolated* sound – I simply abandoned the trolley, and carried her out into the car-park. It felt like walking a gauntlet of reproach.

That poor child. That hard-faced bitch.

By the time we were back in the car, with her sitting on my knee, her sobs had become sniffles; but she clung on tight, her face still buried. I was rubbing my fingers through her hair when somebody tapped sharply on the window.

I looked round to find a middle-aged woman peering in. From her set expression, I knew at once she'd come to tell me off. No doubt she was a mother herself: concerned to see a little one mistreated. And ready to take action, too, rather than just mutter and do nothing. She'd followed me out here to give me a piece of her mind.

Perhaps it was the sight of the tears now rolling down my own cheeks that caused her face to fall, and turn away.

Cathy sulked all afternoon. My apologies and cajolements failed to lighten her mood. Sitting in a corner with her panda and her toys, she'd built a stony wall around herself. I couldn't break it down.

'Didn't you say you'd found a new toy?' was my umpteenth attempt – almost glowing with forced brightness. 'Can I see it, then?'

She shook her head, not even bothering to look. I sat beside her on the carpet, and tried stroking her hair – but she ducked as if avoiding a wasp.

I felt a choking tightness in my throat. 'Oh Cathy, love, I'm sorry. Can't you give Mummy a teeny little smile?'

Again I was ignored. She busied herself with her panda. Maybe it was no more than I deserved. With a sniff, I climbed to my feet and went back into the kitchen.

The washing machine had finished, and sat waiting to be emptied. Time to lug the soggy basketload outside and peg it up on the line – even though the grey, windless day would dry it scarcely at all. And there was still the floor to be scrubbed. The toilet to be cleaned . . .

The phone call to be made.

I stood staring at the wall-mounted handset, chewing pensively on my thumbnail; becoming more aware of my heartbeat by the moment. The piece of paper with Christopher's number was still pinned to the corkboard beside it.

I'd put this off as long as I could: the moment when mere anticipation would be turned into commitment. But it wasn't fair to keep him waiting any longer. Especially since the answer was the one we both wanted.

Sorry, Nick. You're just going to have to trust me on this one.

Taking a deep breath, I lifted the receiver and began to dial.

*

I showed Pat where everything was: the loo, and Cathy's bedroom, and the coffee-making things and biscuits laid out ready in the kitchen. 'Just help yourself,' I smiled.

'Going anywhere exciting?' she asked.

'Just out for a meal,' I told her carelessly. 'With a friend.'

She nodded, but couldn't quite hide the quizzical flicker that crossed her face. I guessed that she suspected – and wasn't sure if she should probe further.

'Oh, all right,' I added, mock-resigned. 'It's with a bloke. A very nice young man. But we're just going out as friends . . .'

The offer of a meal had come as rather a surprise, in fact; I'd not been thinking further than a drink. But the prospect of a longer, more luxurious evening out was quite appealing: a chance to relax, and leave my cares at home. With Christmas almost at the doors, it might even help to insulate me from the merriment around. So I'd said yes.

Pat was nodding sagely.

'No, really,' I insisted, all injured innocence. 'It's someone I met at work, that's all. We decided we could both do with a bit of company.'

'Raitch, you don't need to convince me either way,' was her gentle rejoinder. 'I'm glad to see you going out. There's nothing wrong in it.'

I shrugged; and gave her a slightly anxious smile. 'I've been worrying, you know? About ... what he'll think.'

'He won't mind,' she said firmly; not needing to be told that I meant Nick. 'Does this bloke know?'

I nodded. 'He's recently lost somebody as well. We've got a lot in common.'

'Well make sure you don't get too gloomy. Have yourselves a good time out tonight.' She put her hand on my shoulder. 'And don't *worry*. All right?'

'All right.' I nodded gratefully – and reached up to cover her hand with mine. 'Thanks.' It felt strange to be taking such down-to-earth advice from someone younger than myself.

Cathy was tucked up nicely in the Land of Nod, and unlikely to give her any trouble. Looking down at her untroubled face against the pillow, just before Pat's punctual arrival, I'd found myself wondering what bad dreams might be brewing beneath that tranquil surface – ready to bubble up once I'd left the house. What if she woke, in tearful terror, only to find someone else's mother by the bedside?

A fresh needle-stick from my conscience; but I'd made myself ignore it. There had been no further nightmares: not since the prowler at our window. No sound from the witch's compass, either – even after I'd retrieved it from the dusty corner and dropped it back into its drawer (while *spider* signals thrilled along my nerves). In the absence of evidence to the contrary, I'd more or less convinced myself that it had picked up the psychic equivalent of a pirate signal: something fading in and out across the ether. Now it was gone, without a trace, and the compass was as lifeless as before.

'When do you think you'll be back?' Pat asked.

'Probably about nine-ish.'

I'd decided not to get dressed up for this; opting for

the casual comfort of an oatmeal jumper over my blouse, and a long quiet skirt. A wooden bead necklace from the Oxfam shop completed the picture; my earrings were concealed beneath the wings of my hair.

I rubbed my hands nervously together – and looked down as if to check I was still wearing my wedding ring. It was in its accustomed place, of course: the gold bleached white by a mercury spill two years ago. I'd been quite upset at first; then come to like it – an alchemy of hospitals, and healing hands. Besides, it matched the silver rings I wore.

'You look fine,' she said encouragingly. 'Really. Now out you go and . . . um . . .'

'Knock him dead?' I asked dryly.

'Sorry, Raitch.' She sounded so mortified, I had to smile. Going over, I kissed her lightly on the cheek.

'It doesn't matter,' I assured her. 'Don't *you* worry. I'll be all right.'

As arranged, I picked him up from home and drove into the centre of town. Like me, he was dressed for comfort – jeans and sweater beneath his anorak. Then again, he probably hadn't much choice. I guessed he was a little unsure of himself: his manner pensively polite. I felt a bit reserved as well. After initial greetings, we neither of us spoke until I'd found a parking place.

'Would you like a quick drink before we eat?' he asked as I locked the car.

I slung my shoulderbag, and spread my hands. 'Fine. Don't mind at all.'

The pub he selected had a warm and friendly feel to it: dark cosy corners, and fairy-lights sparkling in sequence above the bar. I took a seat at a table near the window, while he got the drinks. Orange juice, I'd assured him, would be quite all right for me.

'Were you at work today?' he asked, when he'd settled down.

I nodded.

'Busy?'

'Not too bad.'

That sparing smile again. 'Sorry: you didn't come out to talk about work, did you?'

'No, it's all right . . .' I rubbed my forehead, as if to stimulate my thoughts. 'It's a job I like doing. It can get you down sometimes, as you can imagine. But if I can just . . . make things *easier* for someone, at the end, then it all seems worth it. You feel you've been of use.'

'I hope you never doubt that,' he said seriously.

'I try not to.'

He sipped at the beer he'd bought himself; kept his hooded eyes upon it as he lowered it again. 'You said you'd lost your husband . . . Does it help you: working with the dying?'

No doubt it was our mutual bereavement that had cut through the small-talk to get us here so quickly. It also made it easier to stay with the subject. I breathed in slowly, studying my own glass.

'Help me to cope, you mean? Yes . . . I think it does. You see how ready people are to rest. They can see the light at the end of the tunnel, and it's a promise of freedom. I tell my little girl that dying's like going to sleep, and in a way that's true. I *do* believe your soul keeps going onward.' I hesitated for just a moment, before putting my wistful conclusion into words. 'Like a dream that lasts forever.'

'Good or bad?' he asked quietly.

I shrugged. 'Maybe that depends on the person.'

He absorbed the idea thoughtfully. Sipping my drink, I felt surer still that there was more to him than met the eye. His early awkwardness seemed smoothed away now; his probings had been gentle and precise. His mind, I guessed, was keener than his manner might suggest.

A deeper character to fathom. The prospect pleased me.

'Gordon Bennett, look who's here. It's the shirt-lifter.'

I looked round sharply – and turned cold to see them sauntering through. The gang of blokes who'd attacked him in the street: all five of them. The one with the beard was leading. The mocking exclamation had been his.

'*And* his lefty girlfriend,' the man behind chipped in, with a gruesome smirk at me.

Oh, God. We had to choose *their* local.

They lined the bar to get their orders in; and while they bantered with the bar-staff, I let myself hope that they'd leave us with those insults, and find somewhere to drink at the far end of the pub. But having bought their pints, they turned again towards our table: picking up their conversation with exaggerated volume.

'So if he's a poofter, then . . . how come he's got a girlfriend?' This from a lean-faced bloke with a shock of fair hair.

'Dunno,' another answered. 'Perhaps she's a lesbo.'

'I don't mind, Chris,' I whispered urgently across the table. 'They're trying to wind you up. Don't let them.'

He was gazing downward, and didn't respond. There was a look of unearthly calm on his motionless face.

'You know that woman who got murdered the other night?' another pointed voice put in. 'Bet it was a queer done that. Wasn't able to give her what she wanted, so he wasted her instead . . .'

'Reckon she knows that?'

'Perhaps we'd better warn her.'

'Excuse me, darling . . .'

'Shove off,' I snapped abruptly, forgetting my own advice.

The man with the moustache made a show of cupping

his hand to his ear. 'Come again, love? I didn't catch that.'

The gesture infuriated me beyond words, but the ones I found were vehement enough. 'I bet she was killed by someone just like *you*.'

He just beamed smugly: glad to see me bite.

Chris laid his hand across mine where it lay on the tabletop: his turn to urge restraint. I glanced back towards his calming eyes – and glimpsed amusement there. A quiet, cold amusement: as if this was just some minor irritation, beneath us both.

Our tormentors had started moving; were beginning to close in. 'I wouldn't talk to Len like that, darling,' one of them advised tartly. 'He was with the paras in Ireland . . .'

'Yeah? No wonder the bloody Troubles lasted twenty-five years.'

A warning squeeze from Chris' hand; and then, at last, he turned his head to look. The cool disdain in his expression seemed to reach them right away: cutting through where angry words had just bounced off. I sensed the atmosphere beginning to charge up.

'What you staring at, mate?'

No reply from Chris; but his stare didn't waver. His fingers gently massaged mine.

Silence in the room. My heartbeat thudded through it.

The bearded man had been content to lean back and let his cronies do the baiting; but now he took command of things once more. As I stared up, furious and upset, he came over to our table. He was built like a rugby forward; his short black hair gave him an even tougher aspect. Yet his face could have been jovial, the wide wolf-grin infectious; if only there hadn't been *hate* behind its humour.

'This is a decent family pub,' he told us quietly. 'I'd finish your drinks and leave, if I were you.'

Everything inside me cried out against complying; but

Chris nodded almost imperceptibly to me, and I knew that he was right. No sense in staying. I downed the last of my drink with a long, deliberate swallow – but couldn't keep the flush of humiliation out of my cheeks as we gathered our coats and went on out. Every pair of eyes in the pub had turned to watch us. But nobody had tried to intervene.

Outside in the damp night air, I took a shuddery breath and ground my teeth together.

Chris touched my shoulder. 'Forget them, Rachel. They're less than nothing.'

I was so het up, I almost shrugged him off – but stopped myself in time. My surging rage went off the boil, and slowly faded . . . leaving me dazed and perplexed by the strength of my feelings. I hadn't been quite as angry for a very long time. The urge to spit back poison still persisted, like a sour taste in my mouth: giving the lie to piety and principles. It frightened me a bit.

'Would you have preferred me to take them on?' he asked softly.

I breathed out again – clearing the weight from my stifled chest like smoke – and shook my head. 'No. I'm glad you didn't.' Another, looser breath; I gave him a sidelong glance. 'Nick would have. My husband . . . would have. We'd sometimes be out, and a gang of blokes would start picking on him, and he'd feel obliged to give as good as he got. But that's just playing their game. You broke the rules – and got them rattled. Didn't you?'

He just made a noncommittal gesture. 'Maybe; what matters is they haven't spoiled our evening.' His sudden smile surprised and rather charmed me. 'Come on: it's time to eat.'

We chose a quiet little bistro, and thoroughly enjoyed our meal. I even let him talk me into sharing a bottle of house wine. With a candle flickering between us, and soft music in the background, it seemed the outside world – with all its pain and prejudice – had melted back into the darkness.

I couldn't quite relax, though. The very cosiness of the place had a poignant sting to it. As we chatted together, leaning close, a gesture or word would strike echoes from the past: sometimes so resonant that they caught in my throat, and almost choked me.

He seemed to sense those moments, and helped to guide me through them: prompting or pausing as the need arose. It was a pleasure to be so gently put at ease. By the time we'd finished eating, the prickly foretaste of tears had been swallowed back down inside me, along with the food.

'I know we're going halves on this . . .' he murmured, when our plates had been collected, 'but can I offer you dessert?'

I hesitated. 'Um. I'd better not. Eating a sundae just makes a girl feel guilty and fat.'

'I don't think you need to worry,' he said – more matter-of-fact than flattering.

I smiled modestly, and took another sip of wine. Not about feeling fat, perhaps. But as for feeling guilty . . . well.

'Come on,' he cajoled; and my half-hearted resistance crumbled and gave way.

'All right.' I glanced down the menu again, and grinned. 'Able was I, ere I saw melba.'

'Pardon?'

'Sorry,' I said, with a sheepish smile. 'Just me being show-offy.'

We placed our orders; the waitress asked if we'd like coffee. Chris and I just stared at each other for a moment, undecided – and then I said: 'You can come back to my place for a coffee, if you like.'

He accepted gratefully, and I sat back, the fullness in

my stomach replaced by a nervous flutter of reaction. It quickly faded as we picked up our conversation. The background music had changed to a compilation of eighties hits, the songs of my growing-up years, which brought a warm swell of nostalgia – without the maudlin effect it might have had if I'd been listening alone. Glowing inside, I blushed at a friendly compliment; giggled at a joke. Then the desserts came, piled with cream, and I pigged myself with a clear conscience.

'Thanks,' I said, when I was finished. 'That was a really lovely meal.'

He steepled his fingers, amiably solemn. 'I'm glad. Nice to watch you relax, after all your hard work.'

Beaming despite myself, I finished my wine. The next song on the tape began to play.

And suddenly I was in tears.

Chris gave an anxious little frown. 'Are you all right . . . ?'

I nodded, eyes still streaming. 'Yeah . . . Sorry. This one always gets to me.'

New Order. *True Faith*. It took me straight back to the discos of my final year as a student nurse – when everything really did seem rosy as tomorrow's sunrise . . .

He took it in his stride. Finding a clean part of his napkin, he leaned across and carefully dried my dripping cheeks; then dabbed at my eyes until the tears stopped flowing. I sniffed, and managed a grateful smile.

'. . . thanks . . .'

'Shh. Don't worry.' He sat back, calm as ever, as I dug out a hankie to blow my nose. 'Do you still want me to come back?'

I nodded urgently. 'Yeah . . . Don't let me put you off. I get like this from time to time . . .' I fixed a brighter smile to my fresh-scrubbed face. 'But it's all right now.'

*

'Had a nice time?' Pat asked; then noticed Chris behind me in the hallway, and nodded with intrigued politeness.

'Very nice, thanks,' I told her. 'This is Christopher . . . Chris, this is Pat . . .'

'Pleased to meet you,' he said quietly.

'Any problems?' I went on, with a nod towards Cathy's room.

'None at all. Sleeping like a little log . . .'

'That's great,' I pushed in cheerfully. 'Thanks ever so much.' *Don't want to rush you, but . . .*

Perceptive as ever, she picked up on my slightly breathless tone, and began to clear her study things away. I hovered attentively while she got her books together; then realized I must look like a shop assistant at closing time, and went into the kitchen to start making the coffee. Chris stayed standing in the hall. We'd neither of us taken off our coats.

'Go and sit down,' I urged him. 'I won't be a minute.'

Pat put her head in as I got the coffee-maker going. 'Goodnight then, Raitch . . .'

'Thanks again,' I told her, seriously: as grateful for her tactful withdrawal now as for her care of Cathy. 'I'll call you tomorrow, okay?'

'Okay.' She winked. 'Be good.'

I pulled an amiable face at her; we both giggled. I saw her to the door.

A warm ache grew inside me once I'd closed it behind her.

Dry-mouthed, I shrugged out of my coat and went back to pour the coffee. Carrying the mugs through, I found Chris sitting on the sofa, his anorak draped over the back.

'Sugar?'

He shook his head. I handed him his mug, and retreated to the easy chair, drawing my legs up under me.

It seemed we talked for hours; I lost all sense of time. Idle chat turned to earnest conversation – and back again, with the introduction of some frivolous subject. I told him of the hospitals I'd worked in. He traded in some glimpses of his own amorphous past. A nomadic, jobbing lifestyle, as far as my promptings could reveal; but I was struck by his feel for the countryside he'd moved through. It came over warmly in his words.

Perhaps it was our comfort that began to get me down. I hadn't enjoyed an evening like this for longer than I dared remember – and soon, I knew, it was going to have to end. Or perhaps it was the pull of my darker past; the things I'd skirted widely round in my lazy recollections. Those bottomless black potholes in the road.

Either way, I felt the melancholy brewing. I grew pensive; introspective: less talkative than him, now. I tried to fight, but it was no use. My sunny mood had gone down in a blaze of glory, but now there was only afterglow and clouds.

He'd surely notice – and make his excuses soon enough. The bond would be broken, leaving me to this empty room, the reproving ghosts of memory . . . and my unwarmed bed.

'You're sure you're all right?' he murmured. I nodded vigorously.

'Then I think perhaps it's time I made a move . . .'

I swallowed; tried to smile. 'Okay, then . . . If you want to.' I clambered up to see him to the door, and for a moment we just stood facing each other, as if we'd both lost our way.

Then, very gently, he reached out and stroked my cheek.

His fingertips woke tingles on my skin – and down my spine. All I could do was gaze at him. His eyes were so, so solemn.

'Rachel,' he said softly.

A wave of warmth broke through me: almost took my breath away. My inhibitions struggled, sank and drowned. I lifted my face to meet him as he kissed me on the mouth. My arms slid up around him. Held him close.

'Listen, Chris,' I whispered, when he finally drew back. 'I don't want to be alone tonight. I really don't.'

The amber eyes stared into mine. 'You're sure . . . ?'

'Yes,' I said; took both his hands, and led him to my bedroom. My heartbeat seemed to echo in my chest, but otherwise I felt quite calm. I'd stepped off the cliff of my own free will; now all I could do was fall.

One hiatus; the sort of thing a nurse will always think of. Already down to my undies, one bra-strap hanging off, I pushed my fingertips against his chest: embarrassed, but I knew I had to ask. 'Sorry . . . but have you brought . . . um . . . ?'

'Shh,' he said. 'Of course. Don't worry.' He kissed me again, and sat up. 'In my jacket.' A look of mock confession lit his face. 'I actually went into the chemist to buy some *mouthwash*, but was just too embarrassed to ask . . .'

I giggled nervously, and lay back on the rumpled duvet. The pause while he went to fetch them was like the still eye of a storm. *Last chance to change your mind*. Feeling flushed and breathless, I sat up again. My mouth tasted dry, metallic. I glanced towards the half-closed door – then down at my breasts. My crucifix gleamed piously between them.

A moment's hesitation; then I swallowed. *Sorry, God*. With the decision made, my doubts were swept away. I shrugged out of my bra, and slipped my knickers down. Being nude hadn't felt this good for bloody ages. When Chris came back in, I was ready and waiting.

*

'Mummy . . .'

Peeling back my bleary eyelids, I found Cathy's earnest face a foot away. I yawned; half-raised myself. Brushed the lank hair from my eyes. 'Hello, poppet . . .'

'Who's him, Mummy?'

Oh, *God*. With a fleeting glance behind me – his own hair masked his face against the pillow – I scrambled up, and shooed her out before me: grabbing my dressing-gown en route. I wasn't usually fussed if she saw me naked; but this morning I felt shamed, as if I'd something to hide.

Chris didn't stir.

The passage outside was still full of half-diluted darkness. 'Cathy. What time is it?' I complained softly, following her back into her room. Not that she could have told me yet; but I guessed it was well before seven.

'A big bird woke me up,' she announced. 'He knocked at the window. I came to tell you.'

'Probably on his way to catch a worm.' I managed to dredge a smile from the turmoil inside me, and set about tucking her in. 'Did he frighten you?'

She shook her head bravely.

'That's a good girl. You go back to sleep, now. Not getting-up time yet . . .'

'Who was in your bed, Mummy?'

'Oh . . . that's one of my friends, poppet. He . . . was very tired last night, so I said he could sleep here.'

She accepted that economy-sized untruth at face value, and snuggled up with Panda. I stroked her forehead – and glanced towards the window. The curtains were fully drawn, with pallid light against them. I frowned.

'Cathy, love . . . how did you know it was a bird at your window?'

'I saw his shadow, Mummy,' she murmured. 'His big black shadow on the curtain.'

At which point I realized how chilly it was, this early

in the morning: a cool draught had crept up beneath my gown. I shivered and drew the garment closer round me, hugging it in place. 'All right,' I whispered. 'You just lie there quiet, now. Nice and snug.'

I stole to the door, closed it gently behind me – and let my breath out in a sigh. Deep though it was, it didn't shift the pressure on my chest. I stayed there, downcast, for perhaps a minute longer; then looked towards my open bedroom door.

Oh, Rachel Young: what have you done?

My churned-up stomach was settling again; but it still felt overfull. An indigestible weight of doubt and guilt now rested in my belly. Worst of all was the sense of something spoiled. Something that could never be replaced . . .

'I'm sorry, Nick,' I murmured, to the disapproving silence. 'I didn't mean to.'

And back my inner voice came: *Yes you did.*

Chastened, I went on into the kitchen and put some coffee on to brew – hoping to distract my head by busying my hands. But it was useless; I'd pause to reflect for moments at a time, with the powder half spooned out, the measured jug unpoured. I'd let my long-lost darling down. I'd been *unfaithful* . . .

But I'd enjoyed myself last night. Dishonest to deny it. Making love again had been a joy and liberation: an oasis in the wilderness of grief.

Once more I felt defences raised inside me. *It's only natural, Nick. Don't envy me my* life.

A sudden sense of presence at my shoulder made me turn, heart leaping – but it was only Chris. He'd pulled his jeans on, but his chest and feet were bare. No wonder he'd crept up on me so quietly.

I gasped, and let my shoulders sag. Giving him a pinched little smile, I turned back towards the work-top.

'Sorry,' he said. 'I didn't mean to make you jump.' He gently slid his arms around my waist.

I wriggled loose.

'Listen . . .' I muttered, as he hesitated. 'I need some room. Some space to myself, now . . . please . . .'

'Have I hurt you, Rachel?' he asked softly.

'No. No, you haven't . . .'

'All those tears last night . . .'

And not just the ones before bedtime. His face and chest had been wet with my weeping. Even in the throes of sex, I'd sobbed. And more were threatening now. I sniffed them back.

'Your husband . . . ?' he ventured, and I nodded.

'Don't blame yourself. Blame me. I shouldn't have stayed.'

'Not your fault, Chris.' I turned to face him. 'I wanted you to. I'm glad you did. But I have to think about this . . .'

'Do you want me to go?'

I swallowed. 'Please. But I'll ring you. In a couple of days . . .'

He reached up and lightly brushed my cheek. 'All right, Rachel. I'll wait to hear from you.'

'Chris,' I said, as he reached the doorway. He looked back.

'I don't normally . . . I mean, you're only the second man I've ever slept with.'

Chris absorbed that in a moment's silence; then smiled with what seemed genuine affection.

'I'd say that's quite a compliment,' he said.

That afternoon, I went to make my peace with Nick.

I'd telephoned Alice, hoping against hope that she could help me out. Just for a couple of hours, promise. Something's come up. She'd hummed and hawed – then said that she could manage it. Perhaps the urgency in my voice had run too deep to be disguised.

The afternoon was mild and breezy, with a damp smudge of sun. Walking down the central roadway between the graves, I saw that the trees were mostly bare, now: their fiery autumn foliage boiled down to the gnarled, black dregs being swept up by a groundsman as I passed. The year's decay was well advanced. Love turned to winter, and gold into rain . . .

I came to his gravestone, and stood staring down at the inscription.

It was impossible to imagine our life together – everything we'd shared – compressed between those dates of birth and death. No hope of packaging things so neatly. Besides, as I'd told Cathy, the living soul went on beyond the body. And sometimes it came home to haunt its loved ones.

The grave was just a focus: I knew he wasn't in there. Not in any way that mattered.

'Hello, Nick,' I began lamely.

Silence, apart from a rustle of wind through the branches overhead: the sound quite lifeless.

'You know why I'm here . . .' I faltered on. 'I want to explain – about last night.'

He certainly wasn't making it easy for me. There wasn't so much as a whisper of attentive presence. I shifted uncomfortably. This was a scene I'd never had to play while he'd been alive. I didn't know the words.

Hunkering down before the grim grey stone, I clasped my hands together and rubbed my wedding ring: turning it slowly on my finger.

'Remember what we promised?' I asked him softly, gazing down at the whitened gold. 'Till death us do part? But death never parted us, Nick. You're still inside me. And I still love you so much . . .' My voice brimmed over with sudden tears, and I had to pause until the spasm of grief was past.

'But I have to go on, my darling,' I whispered, at length. 'I can't spend my life regretting.'

He was silent.

With a sigh, I raised my stinging eyes – and glimpsed movement beyond the gravestone. There, against the tree. Its knurled bark seemed to bulge and split, distorted by the lenses of my tears. I blinked: and found a shape had detached completely from the darkness of the trunk. A figure as dismal as the old, damp wood.

And it was *Razoxane*.

I sucked air with a sob of fright, recoiling so violently I went over on my back. It was her to the last detail: from grave-digger greatcoat to battered black hat. The hand she extended wore a glove with missing fingers; her long, tatty scarf was slung back over one shoulder. The lenses of dark glasses stared like unseeing eyes.

She parted her smiling lips – and vanished.

I muffled a wail with the palm of my hand; but she had definitely gone. Into thin air, as if she'd never existed. The turf around was empty and untrodden. The dark tree stood abandoned. I was alone.

Feeling faint and nauseous with shock, I crouched where I was for a moment longer; then clambered quickly to my feet and looked around me. Nothing to see but grass and graves. The onset of reaction made me pant to get my breath.

God help me. Going mad.

I shied from that thought as violently as I'd recoiled from the vision. Just a twisted grief-reaction: *nothing more*. No wonder, considering the state that I was in. Why . . .

And there the voice of reason dried completely. Because suddenly I *knew* that Cathy was in danger. Now. This very instant.

It was an awful interruption: like an icicle being thrust into my stomach. I almost groaned aloud. The sweat beneath my clothes chilled out in sympathy.

Cathy. Crying out. I felt her in my bowels and my bones. As if maternal instinct had married with my weird talent, and multiplied a million times.

Please God. My little angel.

No time to say goodbye: not even to Nick. With a whimper of fear, I began to run towards the gates.

Somehow I managed to drive home without writing off the car. The journey was a nightmare on wheels. Every wait at a busy junction seemed to burn up breath. My heart was loose: galumphing through my chest.

Memory showed no mercy. It brought back one of those ghastly Public Information Films they used to show when I'd been a wide-eyed child. Keep Matches Away From Children, or some such. The grim voice of the narrator kept coming through in snatches.

When she got to the corner of the road, she saw the smoke . . .

I almost shunted a police car as it stopped for a red light. Pulling up short, I waited for the gory glow to change; alternately praying and swearing under my breath.

When she came in sight of the house, there were flames . . .

Please God. Don't take it out on Cathy. *I'm* the one you want.

'Mum! MUM!'

Coming up to our road, I gripped the wheel tighter, in dread of what I'd find; but the building, when I saw it, looked undamaged. No fire engines blocked the way. No bystanders were staring. I screeched to a halt against the kerb, and struggled out.

It's all right. Mummy's here, now. Mummy's home.

Gasping with the anticipation of relief, I came to the front door, unlocked it, pushed it open . . .

And an awful, pent-up smell surged out to meet me; I grimaced and choked upon the threshold. It was as if I'd breached a hospital ward where the patients had been locked up and left to die. Months of unmopped stools and sputum. Death. Decay. Exhaled in my face like a body's final breath.

Only lifeless stillness followed.

I stood there, reeling: unable to take another step. Nothing I could see from here seemed out of place – yet our cosy flat, fresh-perfumed with pot pourri, now sweated the stench of a charnel house. Its character had been gouged out, its sense of peace excised. Somebody had disembowelled our home . . .

And then a small, despairing sound invaded the hush. A whimper . . . and a hoarse, raw retching noise.

'Cathy . . . ?' I quavered; struggled clear of the spell, and stumbled forward. On through the flat, and deep into the stink. The sounds were coming from the bathroom. I swung into the doorway – and found Alice crouching down before the toilet bowl. Still trying, with all her stomach, to be sick.

'Oh Jesus God, what's happened?'

She twisted her tear-streaked face around to see me. Her skin was waxy white. Her eyes were staring.

'*Alice!*'

'Oh Rachel . . . God . . .'

I dropped to my knees beside her: grasped her shoulders and dug my fingers in hard. 'Where's Cathy?' I demanded in her face, aware of the peaking pitch in my own voice. 'What's bloody *happened*?'

'She was playing,' Alice whimpered stupidly. 'Playing with her new little top. And then she started crying . . . said she'd seen "the Ragman" outside, and he was coming to get her. So I said, shush, there's nobody there . . . And then . . . oh, Rachel . . . the Ragman *came*.'

I stared into her eyes, appalled. There was living terror there.

'He came in from the back . . .' she went on, between gulping sobs. 'He came in through the door. His coat was all rotting. There was a hood over his head . . . but I could still see his eyes through the holes . . .'

'Alice, listen –'

'I saw his *eyes*, Rachel,' she insisted. 'They were horrid. All white, like they'd been boiled . . .'

'What about *Cathy*?' I ground out; clenching my teeth against the surge of my panic.

She shook her head helplessly, scattering tears. 'I don't ***know***. I just curled up in the corner until he was gone. Oh God, I'm sorry, but I was so fucking *scared* . . .'

I left her and went rushing through the rest of the flat: buoyed up by the vain, betraying hope that my angel had been somehow overlooked. But apart from the thick, necrotic smell, the place was empty.

He'd come through the kitchen door: it stood ajar. The back field opened sullenly beyond it. I could clearly picture a tall, tattered shape striding off towards the trees, a mewling bundle wrapped up in his arms. But the field was empty now; the wood a mass of shadow. I had a frantic urge to run towards it. But a cold conviction said I'd never catch them.

Oh God. Oh God.

There was a ripped-out, raw sensation in my belly – as if she'd been wrenched not only from my arms but from my womb. A plunge of nausea almost brought me to my knees. Gathering my feeble strength, I tottered back towards the bathroom.

I almost overlooked the thing on the dining table. It hadn't registered the first time I came through. But suddenly it caught my eye – and jerked my head round.

A mouldy wad of paper, pocket-sized: compressed between covers as brittle and black as the husks of dead flies. It took me a moment to see it was a book.

Heart in my mouth, I crept up close to look. The thing looked as if it had been dug out of somebody's damp attic and brought straight here; strands of cobweb still clung to the mildewed leather. The words embossed on the spine were illegible with age.

I didn't dare to touch it, let alone to read the title page. But the sense of antiquity alone made horrible connections in my head.

The Ragman. Coat all rotting . . .

Pressing my fist to my mouth, I backed away, and returned to Alice.

'Did he say anything?' I asked plaintively. 'What did he say?'

She shook her head again, as if rejecting memory itself.

'What did he *want* . . . ?'

'I'm supposed to be revising,' Alice mumbled. 'How am I ever going to study again? I'm going to fail *everything* . . .'

I was sufficiently with it to realize she was still in shock, and made allowances accordingly. 'Alice, shhh . . .'

'Why didn't he kill me?' she burst out wretchedly. 'So I wouldn't have to remember . . .'

'Alice!'

She blinked: seizing up as if the word had been a slap. It saved me from giving her a real one.

'Now listen,' I went on, my voice strung taut and trembling. 'I want you to go home now. Go home and get to bed. Tell your mum you've seen a car-crash, you've got food poisoning, *anything*. Just . . . please . . . don't say a word about what's happened here.'

'But . . . the police . . .'

'*We can't tell the police*. He might hurt Cathy if we do. I've got to wait . . . wait for him to get in touch.'

'Oh Jesus, Rachel . . .'

'It's not your fault, Alice. Believe me, it's not. You get home now: get safe. This is down to me now.'

'But what if he's not a kidnapper . . . ?'

She tried to clam up on that dreadful thought; but I couldn't encompass any other reason. Why else had he left that grisly calling-card, if not to promise future confrontation? And to meet him face to face would mean a chance to beg, and bargain . . .

Unless it had been no more than a memento: setting the seal on the worst already done.

Fighting down the spasm in my throat, I helped poor Alice to her feet and hugged her; she held on tight. 'I'll manage,' I insisted grimly against her hair. 'I'll phone you . . . soon as I can. All right?'

She nodded, still shaky; and when she was ready I went out with her to her car. Strapped in, she gave me a bleached and tearful look; then started up, moved out and drove away.

I stood there staring down the road, long after her car had turned the corner. My heavy heart had slowed, as if exhausted. It beat like a funeral drum.

Turning away at last, I trudged back into the flat. The deathly stench was beginning to settle. I went round like a robot, opening all the windows: diluting it with damp December air. Then I walked back into the living room, and slumped down in the easy chair. Still wearing my coat and mucky boots. Still clammy with the cold sweat of despair.

The ancient book lay brooding on the table like something alive. I sat and stared at it, while silent tears leaked down my face. I couldn't look away. Reaction had clamped down on me like spinal shock, and the paralysis was total.

Oh God. Oh please. I know I shouldn't have . . . but this. *You can't do* this . . .

The grey day died by inches. Shadows deepened in the room. They swallowed the extinct TV; devoured the Christmas tree and decorations. The air grew dense and chilly.

And something stirred.

A jolt of fright made my heart cringe in my chest. The movement had come from a chair by the table, barely visible in the dusk. A chair I'd been gazing at for hours, now. A chair I knew was empty.

The shapeless shift of shadow came again. I felt my finest hairs rise up in horror. And then a sudden rasping sound gave birth to living flame: a single match. Its pale light glinting on Razoxane's shades, and on her icy smile.

4

SISTERS

'I hope I didn't startle you,' she said.

I just gawped at her from where I'd finished up: crumpled and cowering in the shelter of the corner.

For that first, appalling moment, I'd been stupefied with shock. Then fear had bolted through me like a power surge, tipping me out of my chair and down onto the carpet. Stunned, I'd scrambled clear of her dying halo – and found nowhere to go beyond the angle of the wall.

Huddled against the skirting board, I'd tried to get a grip. My swimming thoughts were slippery with terror – but hadn't I already been through this once today? And for a mirage? With a tearful gasp, I glanced around.

The match had gone out; the room was still and shadowy again. But then I'd glimpsed her rising from the chair. She moved towards the doorway like a phantom – a shapeless figure, darker than the dusk; yet the sound of her creaking boots was all too real. Reaching through into the hall, she'd found the light-switch, and flicked it on.

Oh Jesus, Lord. It's her. *It really is.*

The glow spilling in failed to wipe her away. Her mock-apologetic grin remained in place. Pacing back towards the table, she'd resumed her seat: there in the half-light, by the black shape of the book.

The book.

The sight of them together – each as dark and dusty

as the other – brought it all into perspective. I swallowed painfully, and raised myself.

'What have you done with her?' I whispered.

She settled back, unsmiling now. 'Your daughter?'

A spasm of frightened rage surged up my throat. 'Of course, my bloody daughter.'

'I haven't touched her, Rachel.'

'*Razoxane* . . .'

'I hoped I could *prevent* this,' she cut in. 'They've moved at night before. I didn't think they'd dare to come by day.'

I hesitated, open-mouthed. Then: 'Who?'

Razoxane breathed slowly out, and took her hat off; its tarnished silver fillet caught the light. She gazed into the crown for a moment, as if to read the answer there; then laid it on the tabletop before her.

'I don't know,' she admitted.

'Why not?' I demanded, outraged.

She shrugged. 'They're putting down chaff. The signatures aren't clear.'

Her tone was matter-of-fact; the words meant nothing. A brick wall with my darling trapped behind it. But I'd bash my head against that until it bled.

'Who's *they*, then?' I insisted, rising to my knees.

'Enemies,' she said.

A pause. I swallowed stiffly. 'Yours or mine?'

'Ours.'

Helplessly I searched her calm, pale face; then tried a different tack. 'You said they'd . . . tried before?'

She nodded.

Realization thumped my stomach. 'God, that man at the window . . .'

'One of them, I think. I scared it off.'

'That was *you* in the back field, wasn't it?' I remembered the falling firefly of her match. No wonder her compass had awakened, with its owner so close.

And now she'd come right in from the cold. It must be going wild: rattling away inside its drawer.

'Oh please tell me what's happening,' I breathed.

'I can only tell you what I know,' she came back evenly: looking down at the closed book.

'They've taken my *daughter*, Razoxane! You know that much!'

She inclined her head, unperturbed by my outburst.

I wavered: still afraid to delve into the darkness. The circles in which she moved were magic ones – hedged round with hideous things. She'd shown me witches and demons in the workaday world. God knew what *enemies* she meant this time.

But I hadn't any choice. Bracing myself, I began to scratch. 'Do you know . . . I mean, are they . . . human?'

'Yes.'

I let out my breath in a small sigh.

'But not alive,' she added.

Oh, my angel. I pressed both hands against my mouth.

'I think they're quite old,' she went on calmly. 'Centuries, probably.'

I swallowed – and put the question that Alice's words had planted in my mind. 'Are they . . . Clinicians?'

The order of demon doctors from which Razoxane herself had risen; but tapping the book's black cover, she shook her head. 'Clinicians don't pray.'

I clambered slowly to my feet, and came across. 'What *is* that?'

'I rather think . . .' she murmured, opening the cover, 'that it's a devotional copy of the *Actes and Monuments*.'

The stench of violation had almost faded from the flat; but now it bloomed again, like a rotting flower rooted in the pages. She blew its pollen outward in a cloud.

'Acts and monuments of what?' I asked, grimacing.

'A *millennium* of atrocities,' was her dry answer. 'Perhaps you'd know it better as Foxe's Book of Martyrs.'

I'd heard the name – and accounts of its catalogue of tortures. Numbed, I drew out a chair across from her and slumped wearily down.

'So what did he mean . . . by leaving it?'

She shrugged, still turning pages. 'I imagine it's a message of some kind.'

My cheeks were wet again. I wiped them with my sleeve. 'But if I can't understand it . . .'

'Perhaps it was meant for me,' she said.

I stared at her in silence for a moment; then let all my frustrated rage come blurting out.

'Is this your fault? *Again*? Why aren't you bloody *dead*?'

Unfazed, she gave the shadow of a smile. 'How shall we describe the Judgment of God – Sergeant?' And grinning, she raised her gloved left hand, palm forward. 'Firm but fair . . . Inspector.'

Her right-hand glove was fingerless wool, but this one was scorched, black leather. A couple of its fingers were missing too: revealing her silver rings.

I knew at once whose glove it was – or had been. My mouth became an O of disbelief.

'You *beat* him?'

She hesitated. 'Not exactly.'

I could feel the chill of that final confrontation; the anger of the demon she'd invoked. The two of them trapped in her magic circle – like dogs with no way out except survival. I didn't doubt she'd be destroyed this time. I'd left her for *damned.*

'After you ran out on me . . .' she said, with pointed emphasis, 'I had to try communing with it. I used every artifice I knew. Every gasp of power I had. And in the end I struck a bargain . . .'

'There were *bones* in the ashes,' I insisted, almost petulant.

She nodded once. 'I know.'

'His?'

A slow, sardonic shake. 'Its material form was totally consumed.'

'Then . . .' I began; but no third alternative existed. And as I stared into her bottomless black shades, I recalled how she had vanished in the cemetery – and risen from the shadows of this room.

I fled from the conclusion – and found it still blocking my way.

'Oh Jesus help me . . .' I whispered.

'No need to be afraid,' she murmured back. 'Haven't you always believed in ghosts?'

Robbed of my breath, I sat there frozen – and then my hand flashed out and grasped her wrist. It didn't dissolve between my fingers. The bone was firm beneath the clammy skin.

'You're real,' I gritted, squeezing. '*Look*: you're flesh and blood. It's just your *madness* talking . . .'

She made no move to disengage. Her voice was soft and steady. 'So how did I sit down here, without you seeing?'

Panting, I released my grip. 'But I can *feel* you . . .'

Mock-solemn, she reached up and tapped her temple. 'You know your problem, Rachel? You've got *fixed ideas*.'

'So how *did* you get in here?' I asked, forlornly.

In answering, she made an off-hand shrug; but I sensed her voice grow tighter.

'It's difficult . . . but one can do it. Once the mass of the darkness is great enough. Black enough. You get a criticality, of sorts . . .'

'It wasn't dark by the grave, though . . .' I protested.

'I wasn't substantial then.'

'But now you are?'

She spread her gloved palms in ironic answer. *Touch and believe.*

I swallowed. 'And you can . . . come and go at will?'

'It isn't that easy. Not any more.'

I wasn't inclined to ask why not; there were far more pressing questions queuing up.

'So why have they taken Cathy?'

'I don't know.'

'Why do you *think*?' I persisted, near despair.

She dipped her head, running a hand back through her cropped dark hair; then raised her shades to me.

'I need more gleanings: clues to what they are. We have to wait.'

The prospect was unbearable. Counting the minutes my angel was in the Ragman's hands would be like dying by a thousand cuts.

Full of myself at the prospect of going out with Chris, I'd tucked her in last night with extra fondness: called her Cathykins, and Peaches Puss. My girl with the golden hair.

What if I'd kissed her sleepy forehead for the very last time?

The thought made me burst out sobbing.

'Rachel. Listen . . .'

She must have screamed for me to save her from the Ragman. But Mummy hadn't come . . .

Razoxane's hand slammed down upon the tabletop; the Book of Martyrs jumped an inch into the air. I jumped with it – and almost cringed as she leaned forward.

'Be quiet for a minute and listen to me. An evil has taken your daughter. I don't know what, or why. But they've left us a book that looks as if it's been in a grave since God knows when; and they're using a type of chaff-drag that's at least three centuries old.'

'So . . . what do we do?' I sniffed; not wasting time to wonder what a *chaff-drag* was.

'What I said before: we wait. Until they make a move.'

I just stared at her; then shook my head in vacant disbelief.

'What?'

'It can't be you. It *can't* be.'

She glanced over her shoulder, towards the kitchen; then back at me.

'Have ye anything to eat?' she asked slyly.

It was perhaps the sheer audacity of that Resurrection reference that convinced me it was Razoxane all right.

'There's no need to get blasphemous about it,' I muttered.

'That's a little bit more like it.' Her fleeting grin became a sombre smile. 'But now you'd better make yourself a meal. You may not feel like eating; but you're going to need every ounce of your strength for the road that lies ahead.'

I reckoned some soup and bread was the most that I could stomach. Having hung up my coat at last, I stood over the saucepan, stirring listlessly. Razoxane still lingered on the threshold, her hat pulled low – as if unwilling to come fully to the light.

'Have you been keeping watch on us?' I asked dully, and glimpsed her nodding. I turned my head to look at her direct.

'So you *knew* that this would happen?'

She gestured. 'I sensed the gathering of shadows. I knew there was a threat.'

Fear made me hesitate before following through. Fear of whatever answer I might get. 'So . . . what are you up to this time?'

'Protecting my sister,' was her calm response. 'I owe her that much, don't I?'

Disbelief surged up again. I felt my mouth drop open. 'Razoxane. You tried to *kill* me.'

'It was nothing personal,' she said dryly. 'You know that.'

'*And* before,' I pointed out, with growing heat.

Razoxane shrugged.

I was her sister in spirit: that's what she'd told me last time. The two of us like faces of the moon. I'd been her pawn and plaything nonetheless. She'd nearly sacrificed me more than once.

And all of it to save her soul: that part of her she believed had been an angel – lurking inside her like the remnant of a burnt-out star. In seeking to rekindle it to its former glory, she'd lost herself in darkness, and done her worst. Sorcery. Butchery. *Grave-robbing* . . .

Yet all in vain. She still hadn't found a resting-place.

The soup was sprouting slow, thick bubbles. Mechanically I turned down the gas, and glanced at her again. Her head was bowed, as if in thought – or to keep her face in shadow.

Oh why had she returned to haunt *me*? Now, of all times. Like a ghastly, mocking answer to my prayers.

'I mean it, Rachel,' she murmured. 'I'm going to help you save your daughter. Think of it as payment of a debt . . .'

It was surely the Devil's soft voice: floating me that straw to clutch at. I gritted my teeth, and shook my head.

'I don't believe you. Not any more.'

'I can understand that,' she came back mildly. 'But right now you haven't really any choice.'

'No, *listen*,' I said, and stepped away: pointing the wooden spoon as if it had power to drive her back. 'You *use* me, Razoxane. You always do. So don't come here and say you're on my side.' My voice almost quavered out of control. I swallowed down a sob.

'It's more than taking sides,' she said, as I wiped my

mouth. 'It's joining souls. We both belong together, you and me.'

The image made me shudder – like the taste of something horrid. Two sisters, as inseparable as lovers. So close that even death could not divide us . . .

Was she still convinced that her sins could bring salvation? Not just for herself, but Cathy too? If so, I knew, I'd have to go along. Whatever she was planning. Whatever the cost.

I forced my attention back to the soup, as it started to sizzle. The contents of my stomach were simmering too, with acrid little bubbles of unease. Nothing in life was free, I'd learned that much; least of all her sinister protection.

With Razoxane, there'd always be a price.

The idea of food had been indigestible enough; the prospect of sleep made my every nerve rebel. But at length her grim persuasion wore me down. 'You need to be at work tomorrow,' she said flatly. 'You have to act as normal. There's a stratagem at work, be sure of it; but we can't make a move until they've shown their hand.'

She was stretched out on the sofa like a queen of the cats: mangy and lean amid their well-fed cotton smiles. Still as wary of the light as something rabid – the glow of the hallway bulb could barely reach her. She hadn't removed her greatcoat or her gloves, I noticed. As if, even now, she felt the cold.

I watched from the doorway, absently hugging Cathy's panda: holding it close, although it still smelled of the monster that had carried her away. I was taking it to bed tonight: the only crumb of comfort I could find.

Her music box was missing, too – no longer on the sideboard where I'd left it. God knew what else had gone. I couldn't bear to look into her room . . .

'Think you can manage that?' asked Razoxane.

I bit my lip and nodded. Just one more day, and then I'd be on leave. Minute by minute, I'd make it somehow.

But that was assuming I ever saw the dawn. 'What if it comes back?' I whispered.

'It'll find me waiting,' she answered softly. 'Some of us don't need sleep.'

If that was meant to reassure, it had the opposite effect: made me wonder what else might be creeping round outside, while the living world slept . . .

'Razoxane . . . ?' I ventured: hugging the panda tighter.

'What?'

'The thing from London. It's not going to follow you, is it?'

She shook her head. 'It went back under the City. Back to its anchorhold. It'll sleep for a hundred years and more.'

'So what did you give up – your soul?' I asked warily; wondering if the Devil might yet be here to claim his due.

She shook her head. 'Only my flesh: fair bargain.'

I swallowed. 'So you could go on as a ghost?'

'I sell my skin dearly,' she agreed, and settled her hat over her face.

I looked away: my own skin turning cold beneath my nightshirt. A tearful spasm was rising up inside me. I pinched my lips tight shut, but couldn't hold it. Out it came, becoming words: as bitter as hot bile.

'Why me? Why always me? What did *I* ever do to deserve this?'

She lay there like a corpse for a moment; then raised her hat again. The look on her face was almost sympathetic.

'Do the people in your hospice deserve their disease? You know they don't. Life doesn't work like that.'

She was right, of course: I knew that well enough.

But how I wished it bloody would, sometimes.

5

CROWS

Something had died, out there by the edge of the wood. Crows were gathering above it, like cinders in the updraught of a bonfire.

I stood at the window of the dayroom, watching them flutter and fall. Scavengers. Carrion-birds.

Something had died.

An animal's remains, of course: perhaps a rabbit, maybe even a fox. But not a person. Not a child . . .

'It's a little early to be looking out for Santa,' Kate Thompson murmured gently from beside me. 'He's not coming till next week.'

I came back to myself with a start, and turned towards her; dragging my gaze from the hungry downward spiral. I'd only come over in the first place to check if she was comfortable; the birds had caught my eye as I'd straightened up.

It was warm in here, the window slightly clouded. The lights made the air outside look dense and grey.

'I remember my daughter waiting up,' Kate murmured. 'We'd come upstairs on Christmas Eve and find her kneeling on her bed, with her head under the curtains – watching for a gap in the clouds . . .' The thought brought a smile to her gaunt, tired face.

I swallowed before nodding; she didn't seem to notice. Putting my back to the window, and the world outside it, I made an effort to fix my haunted thoughts on her. 'How old is she now?' I asked, deliberately.

'Twenty-two. She graduated from university last year. I'm . . . glad I was there to see that.'

She was reclined and resting in a high-backed chair, with cushions and sheepskin pad to keep her comfy. The cancer she'd held at bay so long was in its end-stage now. Surgery had failed to stop it; they'd cut and cauterized in vain. The hydra had too many heads.

Evil on the march again, triumphant . . .

'You have a daughter, don't you, Rachel?'

'Yes,' I said.

'Bet she's looking forward to Christmas. Still magic for the young ones, isn't it?'

Pursing my lips, I could only nod.

The room around us looked quite homely. We'd put a tree up in the corner, festooned with tinsel, and pinned homemade paper chains across the ceiling. Only three days ago, I'd been directing operations: enjoying a giggle with the girls, while our indulgent residents looked on. The ritual seemed dim with distance now.

Despite myself, I glanced behind me. The pall of crows seemed thicker, as if a summons was going out across the fields and hedgerows. Raw meat. Dead meat. Come and feed . . .

'I'm off next week,' I told her, turning back; praying the poison in my stomach wouldn't sour my smile. 'This is my last day. But I'll say goodbye before I go.'

Even if things had been normal, the promise would have given me pause. We could lose so many faces over just a long weekend. Perhaps I'd never see her again.

Or maybe she'd never see me.

A daunting prospect; but it didn't really scare me any more. Walking back across the room, I felt resigned to my fate – whichever way it went. If Razoxane's road led only to oblivion, then that would be a merciful release.

Oh Cathy, love, I'm coming. Wait just a little longer.

Nicola was over by the doorway, looking down in the mouth; she'd been moping around all day. Whatever the cause of her dejection, it made her seem still younger, and more frail.

'Nicky, when you've finished, could you help Mel bag up some linen?' I smiled as briskly as I'd spoken. She blinked back at me, forlorn; then nodded.

'Everything all right?' I asked belatedly – against my better judgment. Again she nodded, quickly. I sensed at once, from the way her lips grew tighter, that her natural shyness had wrong-footed her: fending me off when she'd wanted to talk. But it was my way out: wide open. *I'll leave you to it, then ...*

'Make sure you get off on time,' I added, as a sop for my own conscience. 'And have a good Christmas, if I don't see you ...'

She mumbled something in reply, and I went on down the corridor. Once out of sight, she was promptly out of mind. That brewing cloud of crows came back to haunt me, reclaiming my attention beak and claw. There had to be a *feast* of flesh out there, to muster so many. No smoke without a fire ...

A sickened chill spread outwards from my stomach: I had to pause and wipe my clammy brow. There might be a little shoe among the leaf-mulch; a tattered piece of frock snagged on a twig. And deeper, in the ditch or dusky treeline, something else. A small, misshapen bundle, found by hopping, pecking birds.

Thank God there was no one to see me slump against the wall and sob for breath: stifling the sound in both cupped hands until the spasm had passed. Eventually, stiffening my back, I made it the rest of the way to my office and shut myself in.

Oh Cathy, Cathy, Cathy ...

I'd have to go and look. I needed to see and know the

worst. As soon as the shift was finished. A glance at my watch made my shoulders sag. Another hour to wait. It might as well have been a day.

Sitting back in my chair, I found a phrase from Kate's notes had trapped itself inside my head. *Malignant neoplasms.* Familiar enough as a term for cancer, it came home to me now with crushing weight: put me forcibly in mind of what had happened while I lived in London. The things that had grown beneath the City had been cancerous, all right: unspeakably malign. Excising them had done no lasting good. The whole world was diseased, I realized bleakly; festering with evil. Even as you gouged at a tumour, its secondaries were sprouting somewhere else.

My name is Lesion . . . *and we are many.*

But what kind of hydra had reared its head this time?

Someone knocked timidly on my door. I swore under my breath, and said come in.

It was Nicola, pale and unhappy. 'Rachel . . . have you got a minute?'

A minute? I had sixty. They stretched into the future, long and slow. Perhaps a share in her problems would help a few of them to pass. 'Sure,' I said.

It turned out that her boyfriend had given her the push. I sat there, making sympathetic noises, while she got it off her chest. She managed not to cry in front of me, but her rising tone was wet with pent-up tears.

'He said I was getting too serious. I mean, how *can* you get too serious? Either you love someone or you don't . . .'

I glanced downward at my desktop; then up, as someone else tapped on the door.

'Sorry . . .' Nicola sniffed, as I rose to answer it; but I waved the apology aside. It was Diane at the door. 'Can you give me a minute?' I asked.

She'd noticed my disconsolate visitor, and frowned with concern. 'Everything all right?'

'Yeah . . . Nicky's just been dumped by her boyfriend, she needed to talk.' I instinctively knew it was right to draw her in: there was sympathy in numbers, as well as strength.

Diane squeezed past me, seeming genuinely affronted on her friend's behalf. 'This close to Christmas? What a bastard.'

'No, don't worry,' said Nicola dolefully, peering up: 'I'm glad he told me now; at least I know where I stand . . .'

'You're too forgiving, Nic. He is a *bastard* . . .'

Gradually I got myself untangled: answered Diane's passing query, and cheered Nicola up a bit. Trying all the while not to think of the crows. The closer it got to home-time, the faster the minutes ticked by – until I felt trapped on a downhill slope, and wished they'd pass more slowly.

'Thanks ever so much for sparing the time,' said Nicola at the door. 'I really needed that talk.'

'You're welcome,' I smiled. 'Anything like that. Don't ever be shy of asking.' I was itching to look at my watch.

'Have a lovely Christmas.'

'I will. You too.' My smile, skin-deep, peeled away as the door closed behind her. I let out a sigh, and rested my head in my hands.

After a pause, I turned my watch towards me.

The moment of truth had finally arrived.

By the time I got outside, the sky had thickened: the light was the colour of mushroom soup. I went and put my bag in the car – feeling my spirits drop as the multiple bolts thunked down again and locked me out in the cold. Shrugging deep into my coat, I walked across to the edge of the car-park.

The swarming crows (wasn't *murder* the collective

term . . . ?) had disappeared. The lumpy field between St Catherine's and the wood lay empty. No croaking calls came drifting from the mass of naked trees.

I looked back towards the near wing of the house. A couple of the windows facing me were lit, their bright panes fogged with condensation. Matron's was one of them, up under the eaves. The others were blind and dark. A cloud of laundry-smelling steam rose palely skyward.

Now or never: before someone saw, and started wondering. Turning away, I followed the low wire fence to the stile at the corner. A *Public Footpath* sign pointed off along the boundary of the field. Climbing over, I started down the narrow, trodden path towards the treeline.

As the bulk of the hospice fell behind me, a sense of emptiness encroached. The fallow field got bleaker and more desolate with every step. I found myself glancing back towards those welcoming lit windows, imagining the warmth and company behind them; but such comforts were closed off to me now. I had to walk this way alone.

My heart felt hot and swollen in my chest. My mouth was dry. Reaching the edge of the wood, I turned left along a shallow ditch: wading ankle-deep through loam and leaves. The dark shape of the hospice seemed a long way off now. The dayroom's bright bay-window shifted slowly into line.

Here. They'd been gathered over something round here. Moistening my lips, I began to peer around: my stomach poised to clench at the first glimpse of clothing. The sound of my heart was thick and muffled, like a beater on a carpet.

There were no birds at all now. The branches overhead shifted faintly in the breeze: but apart from their dry scraping, there was silence.

Steeling myself, I crept in a little deeper. There was a dusty greyness to the air between the trees, foreshadowing the dusk.

Of course, I told myself fiercely, there'd be nothing to find. They couldn't just have . . . left her. My baby had been snatched for a reason. The cryptic message of the book was surely only the beginning.

But if I was wrong . . . at least it would be me who found her . . . and carried her little body home . . .

I stumbled and clutched at a tree-trunk, panting with dry, bilious breaths. After a minute resting my forehead against the damp bark, I forced myself to straighten and resume my search.

The atmosphere grew denser as the light began to fail; I started seeing contorted shapes where none existed. Each glimpse was like a poker being thrust into my stomach. Realization wrenched it out again . . . but left my innards black with phantom bruising.

There was nothing here: I accepted it at last. The crows had gathered for their own good reasons . . . and drifted off again. Feeling suddenly weak and light-headed, I put my back against another trunk, breathed shakily out, and waited for my heartbeat to slow down.

As the thumping in my ears diminished, the stillness of the wood pressed in – and something odd began to register. The sense of *absence*. Not just hush, but hollowness. Frowning, I raised my head and glanced about me.

The wood had the feel of a place abandoned: a rookery of ghosts. I was suddenly reminded of that old superstition – how even the birds of ill-omen will flee before approaching disaster . . .

A flurry of wings erupted without warning: the suddenness made me jump. Swinging round, off-balance, I saw a black shape swooping down through the treetops, to settle on a nearby branch.

Not all the birds had flown.

This straggler was a haggard-looking specimen: an outcast from its colony, perhaps. I could tell it was a rook from the shape of its beak. It sat above me, brooding like a chess-piece. Peeved by the fright it had given me, I gathered myself, and glowered back – then jumped a second time as the stillness stirred again.

Something on the ground this time: twigs snapped and crackled underfoot. The noises came from deeper in the wood – where the thorny gloom was thickest. I looked between the trees, but brambles blocked my sight-line. Some of them moved vaguely in the dimness.

Even as my heart picked up the pace again, my hopeful mind suggested that this was just a rambler . . . maybe someone walking his dog. He'd emerge in another minute, zipped comfortably into a Barbour, and give me a friendly nod of greeting as he passed. But then the sounds began to take on shape. Something tentative and large. Too large to be a dog – or a person.

I glanced at the rook again, in nervous reflex.

It rasped at me.

The cry was as abrasive as rusty nails: I flinched away. But what cut me to the quick was the sensation that came with it. A sudden, stabbing chill behind my eyes. It felt, for one horrid moment, as if that digging beak had pecked into my brain.

The bulk in the bushes paused, like a wary animal; then came rustling closer.

I stumbled back, still staring at the rook. It skewed its head to follow me. There was something unnervingly *aware* about the way it looked me over; or perhaps it was my shock that made me think so. The flash of pain had faded from my head, but left an ache behind it. A tide of nausea rose inside my stomach.

Another rasping croak made me duck my head, as if in fear of a blow; but the ice-pain came again. The thing was defending its territory – its cries so sharply pitched that they were somehow sparking migraines in my head. I hadn't time to wonder how; the noises from the depths were coming steadily towards me. A sudden crush of panic squeezed my chest. Breathless, I beat a retreat to the edge of the trees, and broke from cover: cutting the corner of the field to get back onto the footpath. The earth was indistinct and boggy; I almost tripped. Not until I was back on firmer ground, and half-way to the hospice, did I dare to glance behind me.

The wood lay deserted in the gathering dusk. Nothing and no one had emerged in my wake. I stared back, panting, for a moment longer, straining my eyes in search of movement; then pushed on towards the lights of the building.

Just before reaching the stile, I had a stomach-churning urge to look back again. The body of trees seemed darker with the distance between us: an ominous huddled mass against the skyline. But once more there was no movement to be seen.

*

My nightmare came again as I headed for home. The trouble was, I was still awake and driving at the time.

The seizure came from nowhere. Slowing down for a bend, I was suddenly out of myself and floundering in snow. Hands like bony claws were clutching me, tearing the flimsy dress I wore. The white carpet *burned* at my bare skin; the harsh air rubbed it raw. Struggling in panic, I smelled fire and blistered flesh. Not really mine – not yet; but as my captors hauled me upright, I glimpsed a great, cold pyre before us, waiting to be lit.

And then the road again: the verge approaching. I sensed the shell of the car around me, I knew where I really was – but I couldn't move a muscle. It was as if I'd succumbed to sleep paralysis: that moment when the mind wakes from a dream to find the body still asleep.

Men draped in mangy furs. I smelled them; felt their *fingers*. If movement had returned, I'd have tried slapping them off before ever I tried fighting the wheel . . .

Then we mounted the bank, came jouncing to a bruising stop, and stalled.

I sagged against the seatbelt, gulping for breath; and pushed my hair back from my eyes. My body was my own again, though numb with shock. I knew it would start aching soon enough.

Yellow eyes.

I looked up quickly, through the windscreen. Beyond the blank spill of the headlights, there was only darkness.

The vision had been fast and confused, just a jumble of images . . . but the eyes stood out like beacons in the blur. Someone looking on while I was dragged towards my fate. No other detail of his face had registered; just two eyes, yellow-green, like pools of pus.

The road was silent: industrial warehouses on one side; trees and open fields on the other. The nearest streetlamp seemed to flicker as the wind tapped overhanging twigs against it. Peering upward, I watched them move as if of their own volition . . . and thought of spindly fingers, grasping blindly at the light.

Swallowing, I turned the ignition. The engine restarted on the third attempt. Glancing round once more at the orange-stained emptiness, I moved back into the road and put my foot down: bracing my arms against the wheel as the quivering began.

Razoxane was sitting at the kitchen table, her chin in her hand: staring down at the open compass.

I hesitated on the threshold, pursing my lips with apprehension and distaste. She must have rooted it out while I'd been working; perhaps it had started whirring again, like a mechanical insect, to catch her cold attention. But it sat quite motionless now, its silver carapace peeled open; the pentagram needle frozen into place. She looked as if she'd been watching it for hours.

With a flicker of vindictive self-assertion, I switched the light on; but she scarcely flinched. Maybe she was getting acclimatized. Sullenly, I came on in – stepping wide around the table; giving the compass a sidelong look. Even isolated in the middle, with bare wood all around it, the thing stirred my anachrophobic instincts.

'Nice day at work?' murmured Razoxane dryly, scarcely bothering to raise her head.

'Nobody died, if that's what you mean.'

'Somebody came close, though.'

I hesitated: her tone was so soft that the words took a moment to sink in. 'What's that supposed to mean, then?'

'Just that I'd stick to the beaten track, if I were you.'

I stared at her – and felt a glacial chill spread through me. It took me back in spirit to the gloom of the wood; I could *feel* the approach of that heavy, crunching shape. With an effort, I broke back into the present.

'You were there?' I whispered.

'No need,' she countered calmly. 'My intelligencer brought me word.'

I blinked at her, blank-faced. 'Your what?'

'Intelligencer. A familiar spirit, given flesh. The eyes in the back of my head.'

Comprehension caught up with a jolt. 'The *rook*?'

'Her name is Vedova,' she said mildly.

Memory of the bird made me wrinkle my nose – then grimace in disgust as I absorbed what she'd just told me. Even the name had an ominous taste: a hint of desolation and despair.

Vedova,' she repeated, stressing it; the O-sound like a long, soft moan. 'She was conjured by a Florentine magician, three centuries ago. That was the secret name he bound her with.'

A big black bird at the window, Mummy.

Cathy's voice piped clearly through my head. I felt my eyes grow wider.

'This thing's been watching us?'

Razoxane nodded. 'And searching for them. She flies where I can't follow; seeks out the cracks and crannies. Looking for gleanings. Looking for clues. Even from the minds of men, she digs up *worms*.'

I realized I was rubbing my forehead, and quickly dropped my hand. There was a pause. Then I moistened my dry mouth.

'And one of them . . . was in the wood?'

'We think so, yes.'

'So what *was* it?'

She shrugged. 'Its mind was encrypted. Just gibberings. She couldn't read it.'

'Well couldn't she have followed it, or something?'

Razoxane shook her head. 'She'd have lost it in the dusk. I told you – there's too much chaff in the air.'

'What do you mean, *chaff*?'

'Something that blocks and scatters psychic signals. Usually generated from dead or desecrated matter. You can cloak yourself against witches with it; cover your tracks. Even though it's witchcraft in itself.'

Chaff. I thought of the Biblical version: sifted out from the wheat, and cast into the fire.

'So.' I swallowed. 'Witches, then.'

'Perhaps.' She seemed to lapse into thought, her opaque glasses resting on the compass before her.

'No?'

'Chaff can be used in a number of ways. Pieces of flesh scattered around; decoy organs buried. But these are using a drag to cover their tracks. Like I said before, that places them in time.

'The last time I saw a chaff-drag, I was new to this life . . . maybe three or four years old. I remember them passing our cottage: men riding and on foot. Soldiers. One of the ones on foot was dragging an old coffin at the end of a rope. I remember, I asked my mother what it was.'

I listened, chewing my lip. By now it was almost easy to believe: that she'd been around for centuries, ageless and watchful. The latest incarnation of that long-lost angel . . .

'. . . It would had been dug up from a graveyard, so she told me. There'd be a body still inside. Prepared in sorcerous ways, so that the flesh gave out energy as it decayed, and clouded the all-seeing eye . . .'

And her mother would have known. A witch herself, so Razoxane had told me; a white witch, so she'd claimed. Had the woman ever dreamed how black her daughter would turn out . . . ?

'Razoxane. Listen. How are we going to find *out*?'

'Just sit down, and have a little patience. The compass should register their movements – even if it can't get a bearing. And as soon as it does, we can start to track them down.'

'Cathy . . .' I felt a spasm in my throat. 'How can she stand this? She'll be out of her little head.'

'Rachel. Try not to *worry*. My guess is, they've put her to sleep somehow; used a spell or soporific. Otherwise the waves of her fear would just give them away . . .'

'She's . . . still alive, though. Isn't she.' It was a statement of blind faith, rather than a question.

'Yes,' she said. 'You'd feel it if she wasn't.'

For a moment I was scared to search my feelings: in case, deep down, I knew the worst, and simply couldn't face it. But no; the light inside me was still burning. A pale, blue candle-spark of hope.

'You'll be a wanderer this Christmas,' promised Razoxane bleakly, as I let the nearest cupboard take my weight. 'Ready to up and leave at a moment's notice. From now on, you sleep in your clothes. They're more than likely to move at night.'

I could only nod in miserable acceptance.

'So listen: would you be missed, if you left without saying?'

I shrugged – but knew I might be.

'You'd better make some phone calls, then,' she said.

'I don't think Cathy and I will be coming to the party,' I told Pat. 'She's come down with something. Feeling . . . very sorry for herself, she is . . .'

I listened, and bit back sobs, while she commiserated from her end of the line. The words buzzed in my ear like the meaningless complaint of an insect. I nodded woodenly; grunted in response. Staring all the time at Razoxane. She'd linked her hands palm downward on the tabletop and rested her chin upon them, still gazing at the black face of the compass.

'Mr Wheeler . . . ? Richard, yes, sorry . . . I'm taking Cathy to see her grandparents for Christmas, could you just keep an eye on the place for me? . . . Thanks ever so . . .'

Had the needle moved just then? No, of course it hadn't: not a hairsbreadth.

'Steve? We're off to see the in-laws, so I just thought I'd wish you . . . a happy Christmas. Talk to you in the New Year . . .'

It looked so dark outside: black against the windows. Night pushed up against the panes.

'Christopher.'

'Rachel?' he came back calmly.

Twisting the telephone cord around my finger, I moistened my lips. 'How are you?'

'Well, thanks. Glad to hear your voice again.'

It was reciprocal; I felt a crushing sense of yearning

rise inside me as I pictured his face. If only I could reach out to him across the ether: convey my dreadful predicament – and cling to the rock of his composure. He'd get this sorted somehow: bring Cathy safely home. The Christian optimism still glimmering inside me sprang up at the thought: inclined to trust his honest simplicity more than all of Razoxane's twisted guile.

The fleeting moment duly fled – leaving me stuck in my kitchen with her sinister ghost. Turning my face away from her half-smile, I swallowed dryly.

'Listen . . . I'm going away for a few days. Me and Cathy. I'll call you – when I . . . when we get back.'

Perhaps he thought I was just playing for time; but if so, he didn't contest it. 'That's fine by me, Rachel. I'll talk to you then.'

'Who was that, then?' Razoxane asked as, our farewells coyly made, I broke the connection with a firm finger.

'Just a friend,' I said defensively, looking back over my shoulder.

She stared at me for a moment, almost quizzical; then returned her attention to the motionless compass.

The hardest call of all, I'd left till last. I knew that there'd be ructions. I was right.

'Rachel,' Ellen said, her petulance spiked with real hurt. 'You promised us you'd come.'

No, I bloody didn't, was my mind's reaction; the version that reached my mouth was a bit politer.

'Then we must come to you,' she countered quickly, sounding flustered. 'It'll mean cancelling a few things . . .'

'Ellen, please. She's got a bad tummy upset, and I want her to rest. We're going to have a quiet Christmas together, just the two of us . . .'

'Well, if the girl's sick, you'll need help in looking after her. And what about her presents? What about . . .'

'Ellen. I don't want you to come.' I said it firmly, despite the fist-sized lump in my throat; feeling like someone withholding a lifebelt from a drowning person's reach. And maybe that was what it felt like from her end, too; her voice was ragged with distress as she tried again.

'Rachel. She's our son's *child*.'

I closed my eyes to stop the tears spilling out. They swelled hotly beneath my lids. *Oh, don't remind me, Ellen. Don't.*

'Listen . . .' I said after a miserable pause. 'We'll come down sometime early in the New Year. All right? Promise.' As if I was in a position to promise. As if we'd ever lead a normal life again.

'You're a cruel, selfish girl, Rachel Young,' her voice came back: brittle with her own dried tears. 'I always knew it. If . . . if Nick knew what –'

The stream of bitter words became a single, toneless buzz as I disconnected. Letting out a shuddering sigh, I set the handset back upon its cradle.

Things between us were as far gone as they'd ever been. The long road back to normal seemed a thousand miles and more. Right now, I couldn't imagine the first step.

'Are all the bridges burned?' asked Razoxane's dry voice.

I sniffed, smeared my eyes, and nodded.

'You'd better get some rest, then,' she advised me. 'No sense in waiting up until the small hours, counting minutes. Watched spiders never move.'

*

It was the fall in temperature that woke me.

Sleep had been long enough coming – kept at bay by the bright fire of worry in my head. But after an hour or two of restless stirring, the fatigue saved up from last night began smothering the flames. The cold blaze withered, and finally went out. I sank into the dark.

And surfaced.

Wide awake as soon as my eyes flickered open, I lay still for a minute – then cautiously raised my head. The room hissed with dead air. There was no sense of presence in it this time; just loneliness and void.

But the cold was razor-keen against my skin.

It had cut its way in through my winter duvet – paring at my toes inside their socks. Sitting up, I felt it pierce my underwear and sweatshirt. Instinctively I looked towards the window, expecting to find it open wide. But it was shut.

I drew up my knees and sat there in the dimness, listening. I'd experienced chills like this before, and knew what they meant. Some unnatural thing was nearby. Maybe roaming my silent flat. Maybe listening itself, on the far side of the door.

Razoxane, I challenged, with my mind: my mouth too parched to voice it. There was no response. It struck me then that I hadn't felt a chill off her before. Phantom or not, she was here in the flesh. So was this . . . something else?

She didn't need sleep, that's what she'd told me. She was in here somewhere, keeping watch. My guardian ghost.

Unless she'd slipped away, under cover of night, and left me to my fate.

The sense of isolation was abruptly overwhelming: like being trapped in the last air pocket of a flooded coal mine. Beyond the reach of help or hope. All I could do was open the door, and let the freezing dark come pouring in.

But what did I have to be afraid of, any more?

Getting up slowly, I crept tight-lipped to the door and curled my fingers round the handle. In the pause that followed – its seconds marked off by the twangy thudding of my heart – I let myself imagine being engulfed. Perhaps the rotting Ragman was poised there, waiting. If so, I'd welcome him with open arms. He'd reunite me with Cathy, after all. Be it one way, or the other.

Clenching my fist on cold metal, I yanked the door towards me.

The passageway beyond was empty.

I hesitated, swaying, on the threshold; then started forward – wading into deep and stagnant shadows. The cold air clung to me, leaching the last warmth from my skin. Gooseflesh stippled my bare legs. The flat was full of a dark, drowned silence. The chill of it grew sharper with each step. Even my core temperature must have started to fall, by the time I groped my way into the kitchen.

Out of the fridge, and into the freezer.

Razoxane was sitting at the table, as I'd left her; but she'd put her hat on now. Its brim masked her downturned face with darkness. The silver circlet glowed with icy moonlight.

'Couldn't sleep?' her sardonic voice enquired.

I just leaned against the doorway, my cheek pressed to the jamb, while my stomach acids sluiced around and settled. I never thought I'd be so pleased to see her.

The feeling didn't last, of course. Puzzlement infused it as I saw that she was dealing out a deck of cards – flipping them casually across the tabletop. And then, as I realized she was distributing them between three empty chairs drawn up around the table, it turned into unease.

'What are you doing?' I murmured.

'Playing a game,' she answered, just as softly. 'It's turned into a long night, after all.'

I straightened up – but not to cross the threshold. The cold was deepest here, in this iceberg light. I shivered suddenly, and hugged myself.

Silence, apart from the faint slap of the cards. Knowing her, they'd be a Tarot pack or something.

'Who with?' I asked, with a dying spark of sarcasm. 'Absent friends?'

'No. Not friends, exactly.' She finished dealing, and picked up her own hand. Spread it to study the cards. Then said: 'Not absent, either.'

I stared uncertainly at her for a moment – then looked round at the unfilled chairs. Five cards were strewn face-down before each place. Their presence there provoked no movement. No unseen hand reached out to turn them over. But suddenly I knew that the players were there, just waiting. Three brooding, shapeless things that sat and watched me.

My hands were already clutching my own shoulders; but now my frightened fingers dug in tight.

'Something I've learned,' said Razoxane slowly, ignoring my gasp. 'About this . . . condition I've achieved. You can see all the ghosts of the people you've killed. They follow your trail: no matter how you try to shake them off. Sometimes at a distance. Sometimes close . . .'

A fresh, more violent shudder built inside me. Bracing myself, I fought it to a standstill: then peeled my lips apart. 'And you can sit here playing *cards* with them?'

She shrugged. 'The game doesn't matter as such. It's recognition that they've come for. A chance to meet their murderer on equal terms.' She turned her own cards down against the tabletop – and looked at me. 'But now that you're here, we can maybe try our hand at something else.'

She said it amiably enough – which didn't augur well.

'Like what?' I asked, warily.

'Divination.'

I gave the scattered cards an unenthusiastic glance. 'Is this one of your Tarot packs, then . . . ?'

Razoxane nodded slowly. 'An original. Elder Arcana. There's much that it can tell us.'

'How?'

She sat back. 'Simple. I've dealt the cards. You pick one from each pile.'

I swallowed hard. 'And . . . what about them?'

Razoxane inclined her head: the moonlight found her smile. 'They can look, but they can't touch.'

I rubbed my tight throat; glanced from chair to empty chair. Their silence seemed a challenge – or a lure. In front of them, the cards. I'd leave no stone unturned to find my angel; but what clinging, crawling life might these reveal?

'Go ahead,' she prompted softly.

I hesitated a moment longer; then sidled over to her, and drew one of her cards. 'Don't look at it,' she warned at once; I almost dropped the thing again.

'Now the next one.'

With exquisite caution, I began to walk around the table. The next seat loomed towards me – the more menacing for its very emptiness. Reaching out to take a card, I fully expected a phantom hand to grasp my wrist and hold me. My stomach surged as I snatched the paste-board clear.

Razoxane had placed both elbows on the table, her mouth against her interlocking fingers; watching from the shadow of her hat-brim. Her compass was still there, I belatedly noticed: equidistant between players. Motion-less and gleaming in the moonlight.

Coming round to the next setting, I was increasingly aware of something else: the atmosphere that overhung the table. It rose from the darkened chairs like respiration: a frigid, baleful sense of *lust*. It made me feel acutely under-dressed.

'Don't worry,' she breathed, as I came up short. 'They can't quite reach you here.'

I hesitated, glancing back; then lifted another card. Gingerly, like a stone from the garden – its underside seething with lice and spiders.

Razoxane nodded me on.

By the time I'd selected the final card, my muscles were

quivering with cold; I had to clench my teeth to stop their chatter. The four rectangles of pasteboard felt soft and gritty in my fingers, as if they'd lain for years in some dank corner. Their texture made me think of the Ragman's book. That was still resting on the living-room table; gathering flies, despite the weather. Or hatching them, between its pulpy pages.

'What now?' I ventured.

'Put them in the middle of the table: faces downward.' I quickly did so. 'And now go back to bed.'

I blinked at her: nonplussed by the anticlimax, for all that its build-up had unnerved me. 'Aren't you going to use them, then?'

'Not before daylight. Just leave them to mature a while.'

'And you expect me to *sleep* now?' I demanded shakily.

'Your body will take what rest it needs: it might surprise you.' Reaching out, she gathered the remaining cards together: embracing the tabletop like a giant bat. I recoiled from the image; but the resonance it struck was even worse. A glimpse of Death's dusty shadow, drawing all men to itself.

My empty room was suddenly inviting.

''Night, then,' I mumbled; and so it was. A bottomless absence of light and warmth. No trace of *good* about it.

Razoxane did not respond. Head bowed beneath her witch's crown, she was slowly shuffling the cards.

Behind me, as I turned towards my bedroom, I sensed the game of ghosts begin again.

Back in my bed, curled up into a ball beneath the duvet, the plunge into sleep was swift and unexpected. As if I'd just stepped backwards off a cliff.

*

'Just *three* shopping days to Christmas . . .' the radio enthused; the voice of the speaker jingle-bright. I cut her off in mid-flow, and brought my coffee over to the table.

Razoxane still sat there, besmirching the daylight; but the three other chairs were truly empty now. I'd edged around them, coming in; but there was no more sense of presence at their places. Two of them had been pushed right back; the other was askew. As if the guests had risen suddenly, and scattered to the winds.

She'd tugged her tattered gloves off, and was massaging her hands; eyes down beneath her hat-brim. The pack of cards had been stowed away, and only the ones I'd drawn were left; two on each side of the dormant compass.

I wavered; then pulled up the chair across from her, and slowly sat. A lingering chill soaked in through the seat of my briefs, and made me squirm. I was still wearing what I'd slept in, with my dressing-gown on over it; the belt had come undone already. I hadn't even bothered to comb my hair, content to swipe it clear of my eyes. It was growing lank again, in need of washing. My body felt stale and sweaty. Give it another day, I thought sourly, and I'd be smelling like Razoxane's coat.

She raised her head, her smile ironic. 'Want to do the honours?'

I shook my own head firmly.

'All right, then.' She finished rubbing her knuckles – and paused for thought. Then: 'A word about these cards, before we begin. They're part of an antique pack – drawn up before the Tarot as we know it now had achieved its final form. Some of its figures were later rejected, or absorbed into others. Explanations vary as to why.

'The traditional Tarot has Greater and Lesser Arcana. Collectively, these lost cards are referred to as the Elder Arcana. Their status is . . .' she gestured for a word.

'Apocryphal?'

'Thank you.' She nodded. 'Yes. Consider your Catholic

Bible as a parallel. Some of its books are apocryphal to Protestants, who hold their provenance in doubt; but *reams* of other writings were discarded or suppressed completely. Psychic visions. Heretical gospels. Tales of myth and magic. Something similar happened with the Tarot pack. After all, they used to call the cards the Devil's Bible.'

I was staring glumly at the musty bits of pasteboard: recalling what I'd learned elsewhere about the Bible's hidden books. Like the Book of Enoch, with its visions of fallen angels . . .

'And as well as these *false* writings . . . as they're called,' she went on softly, 'there are some that were forgotten. Ghost-sources to later works. It's believed that certain Gospels were derived from another document, now lost. But nobody knows what it was . . .'

'Oh, get on with it,' I muttered.

'Just establishing the principle,' she came back mildly – and reached out to turn the first card over.

It was instinct that made me gather my dressing-gown around me and clench it closed; I scarcely noticed that I'd done so.

The picture on the card was scratched and faded, indistinct with age. Reluctant even to lean a little closer, I squinted at the medieval script.

Il Monco.

Razoxane nodded, mainly to herself. 'One of the lost ones. The Maimed Soldier; sometimes called the One-Armed Swordsman. Probably conflated with the Knight of Swords in later packs.'

'And swords . . . are bad fortune, right?'

She nodded again. 'The figure is thought to represent a mercenary: a *soldier* of bad fortune. If drawn immediately after the Devil card, he was called the Left Hand of the Devil.'

'So what does he stand for here?' I ventured.

Razoxane gave a vixenish smile. 'I thought you didn't believe in these things, Rachel.'

'I don't,' I said quickly. 'I was just . . . wondering.'

She shrugged. 'I can't tell, yet. Let's see what the others have to say.'

The next card was in poor condition: the face of the figure worn away. I tried in vain to read the title.

'*Il Becchino*,' she suggested thoughtfully. 'The Grave-Digger.'

'Is that you, then?'

'I don't think so. This is another forgotten card; but it was usually taken to mean burial of a secret. Hiding something from the light . . .'

I thought again of the book in the living room. She herself had said that it seemed to have come from a grave. I swallowed the beginnings of a shudder.

Razoxane turned the third card – and looked up at me. There was something almost avid in her expression. 'You see how it's working? I was dealing from a full pack, carefully shuffled – but you've still picked out the Elder cards.'

I pulled an unhappy face at her.

'This is the *Castigo di Dio*,' she continued smoothly. 'The Scourge of God. A powerful portent. It could have good or evil meanings, depending on context. A cleansing of the land – or its chastisement.'

The crudely-printed figure was hooded like a headsman, but without eye-holes. Perhaps that was meant to represent blind justice. Unsighted: lashing out . . .

The fourth card showed a woman.

'The Priestess,' murmured Razoxane, and lapsed into silence for a minute, staring down at it. I just shifted uncomfortably. The seat of my chair was still unpleasantly cool – like a warm toilet seat in reverse.

'This is a surviving card,' said Razoxane slowly. 'It could stand as a mother-figure, or a guide . . .'

Mention of a mother made me sit up straight.

'. . . but there's a theory that it developed in part from an Elder image; the solitary woman with the wounded soul. The Widow.'

I flinched, despite myself.

'So maybe it means you,' she finished dryly. 'Or maybe not.'

Shaken, I reached for my mug and sipped some coffee. It was cooling already; turning grey.

'I wonder . . .' she mused aloud, 'just what the cards are trying to tell us. Four Elder figures: Mercenary, Grave-Digger, Widow and Scourge. But picturing the past – or the future?'

'Well, you're the expert,' I grumbled.

'Mmm.' She kept on studying them. And studying *her*, I glimpsed a shadow of thought creep across her pallid face.

'Any ideas?' I pressed her, cautiously.

'Nothing I can be sure of,' she answered – sounding evasive.

Whatever clues she might have gleaned, I guessed there'd be no point in prompting her further; she'd give up her secrets in her own good time. Just as she always did. Unable to stomach any more of the scummy coffee, I got up and went to pour it down the sink. A wave of listlessness came over me as I watched it seep away. Apathy foreshadowing despair. I braced my arms against the draining board until the worst of it had passed.

I won't give up on you, my darling. Promise.

I'd drawn up one foot to rub at an itch on my other thigh when Razoxane said: 'We have to leave.'

'What, now?' I said: looking round so fast I almost overbalanced. She was tucking the cards away beneath her coat. I came over quickly, peering down at the open compass – but the dark star hadn't moved at all.

'They haven't stirred yet,' she said, in confirmation.

'We'll have to risk it that they won't. But we need to travel up to London, today. There's something there I have to fetch.'

'What?'

'Instruments,' she answered, just as baldly.

'But if we're out of town, we'll lose them,' I protested. 'Lose their trail. *Razoxane*.' She'd risen, and walked through towards the living room. I followed, my dressing-gown flapping. 'For God's sake . . . we can't just *leave* her . . .'

'Your daughter will be safe enough,' was her curt response. She'd picked up the Book of Martyrs and was leafing carefully through it: pausing here and there to peel its pages apart. Hanging back, I felt my nostrils twitch, as the smell of mould began to spread afresh. 'We can be back by evening,' she went on – and glanced towards the window. 'Besides . . . my familiar will still be around.'

Apprehensively I followed her gaze: half-expecting to find her rook on the outside sill. But seen through a fading mist of condensation, the garden was as empty as the quiet street beyond it.

I looked back at Razoxane. 'You know who they are now – don't you?'

'No, Rachel, I don't.' She closed the book again, and stared down at her hand where it rested on the cover. 'I *am* convinced that the thought-world they're coming from is seventeenth century. The resonances I've picked up are rooted that deep. But the message of the cards can be read in a number of ways . . .'

'Name one,' I insisted.

'All right. It may be that, three centuries ago, an atrocity took place. A martyrdom, perhaps . . .' She tapped the book. 'Part of a struggle between two opposing factions, each as ruthless as the other. The ashes of this evil deed were covered over . . . consigned to darkness. Buried. But now something's digging them up.'

'Something from one of these factions?'

'It's possible, yes.'

'But what has it got to do with *me*?' I almost wailed.

She spread her hands; with the book still clutched in one of them, it made her look like a sinister preacher. 'We need more time to tell that. It could be they're looking for something, and they believe that you might have it. But now that they know I'm with you, they're being more cautious . . .'

I shook my head fiercely. 'I've got nothing they can want . . .'

'Dead things don't listen to reason,' was her flat response. 'And whatever else these are, they come from the *grave*. If I'm going to root them out and burn them, I'll need something to supplement my powers.'

I gazed back at her; then slowly shook my head. 'I don't trust you, Razoxane.'

'Well you're going to have to, aren't you?' she snapped back – so sharply that I flinched away. It seemed she fought to get a grip on herself then; breathing shallowly in before she looked at me again. 'These are implacable enemies, Rachel. I haven't time for your doubts.'

I was still cringing from her unexpected outburst. It had given me a glimpse of rage, behind her calm exterior. The mask was back in place now; but what thoughts did it conceal?

'Can't we be back before dark?' I asked timidly. 'In case they make a move tonight . . .'

She shook her head. 'We need to be there for the dusk.'

I'd crossed my arms defensively against her; now I drew them to my chest to keep from shivering. Since leaving London, I'd gone back once or twice – but always making sure I was on the train home before the daylight died. There were too many memories up there. Too many lurking shadows.

'So why's that, then?' I asked; and Razoxane smiled.

'Because that's when they close the cemeteries,' she said.

*

'Aren't we going up on a ghost-train, then?' I asked sulkily, when I'd bought our tickets.

'Don't joke about such things,' she said.

I gave her a glance – then looked nervously out through the station doors; but the forecourt was empty. Bits of litter on the wind were the only things out there which swooped and scuttled. When the doors hissed open, to admit a pair of backpackers, a gust of cold came with them – nothing more.

They follow my trail, she'd said. But was that only by night? Or could they track her by daylight, too?

Swallowing, I sat down again beside her. She'd taken the Book of Martyrs from her pocket, and was studying its closed front cover.

I moistened my lips. 'This . . . rook-thing of yours. Can it find Cathy?'

'I told you; her name is Vedova.' Razoxane's tone was almost chiding. 'She's an old and venerable spirit: one of the higher ones. Some of her kind were ensnared as crows or jackdaws: the scavengers and thieves. But she was always a seeker – wise enough to dig for her treasure . . .'

The rook feeds on leather-jackets, I thought – and frowned. A piece of useless information learned in primary school: so why did it seem so ominous, just now? Leather-jackets were simply grubs, revealed by fresh-turned soil. My mind flashed up a brief, more literal picture – tall figures in rough, tanned coats – then refocused on the real. Weren't they crane-fly grubs or something? The thought of those flying, flailing spiders was disturbing enough.

I glanced at Razoxane – as ragged and black as a rook herself – and forced my mind clear of that train of thought entirely.

'To answer the question: no,' she said. 'Not on her own. She's chaff-blind. But like any blind person, she can sense them if they move . . .'

Silence fell again between us. The noises of the station couldn't break it. Despite the background bustle, we might as well have been alone.

I sensed that she was working up to something. Holding the book between her palms, she pressed it thoughtfully against her mouth.

'You still have your mindsight, don't you?' she said after a minute. 'You've more than just your faith to help you see in the dark.'

'So what if I have?' I asked, uneasily.

'So it's something we can use. Together . . . if we share our strengths . . . we can journey to other places: other times. Maybe see what's at the root of this.'

I flinched away. 'You leave my mind *alone*.'

'You dream the dreams already,' she persisted. 'With my help, you can steer them; make them show us what we need to know.'

'I don't *want* them, Razoxane. And I sure as hell don't want *you* inside my head.' She'd screwed around in there before, and scarred my mind for years. No way would I sit still for it again.

But Razoxane merely shrugged; and rested that mouldy book against her lips once more.

As we crossed the platform and boarded the London train, I couldn't help glancing above me: studying the gables and guttering – then the trees on the far side of the line. But her grim familiar spirit hadn't come to watch us go.

The coach was commuter stock: all stained upholstery and loose-fitting doors. We slumped into opposite seats.

Bracing my elbow on the window sill, I peered out at the slush-coloured sky.

Oh God, where were they keeping her? A derelict building? Maybe one I could see from here. One I was about to leave behind . . .

Razoxane had bowed her head, as if in meditation; leaving me to stare at the ash-dusted crown of her hat. It struck me then that she might be psyching herself up for the coming journey. London was where she'd nearly been devoured, after all. Perhaps it had its terrors for her too.

I felt the hairs on my nape begin to prickle, and shrugged my collar up around my neck. The slamming of doors had long since stopped. A railwayman paced past the window, checking. A moment later, the whistle blew.

My eyes strayed to the door-latch at my side.

Mummy! Wait for meee!

My muscles spasmed. I swallowed. Two seconds had passed already. Too late now . . .

Next instant, without thinking, I unlatched the door, swung out onto the platform and slammed it hard behind me. Stumbling back, off-balance, I saw Razoxane raise her head as swiftly as a snake – but the train had begun to move already: gaining speed as she started to her feet.

For a moment, resigned, I thought she'd jump down after me – but no. She just stayed there at the door, peering back in my direction, as the train pulled out; her pale face pressed to the glass, without a flicker of expression.

I stared until the train was the size of a toy, its throbbing tail-light dwindling towards the gleam of distant signals. Then a wave of weakness broke inside me. I faltered over to a bench, and sat to get my breath back. Sweat greased my shoulders and my spine. My stomach felt as if it had just been pumped.

Let her ride her bloody ghost-train up to London. Let her face the shadow-city after dark. Forty miles away, but I could feel it: like a looming grey fortress at the end of the line.

God alone knew where I went from here; but right now I felt quite giddy with relief. I was still here for Cathy, whenever she called. I'd missed the train to Hell.

When it was lost to sight completely, I got to my feet and walked back towards the exit.

I kept looking for the rook, but it was nowhere to be seen. As I trudged from street to street, the glowering sky stayed empty.

I waited for a while at the corner, just in case; then hurried across the road with my head down. Coming up to the front door, I felt my heart rise in my chest: but it was too weary to hold on, and sank again.

I rested my aching forehead on the woodwork; then leaned back and pressed the bell. It seemed to echo in emptiness. But after a long, long pause, I heard footsteps approaching; a bolt drawn back. The door was opened a gap and he peered warily out, blinking like a mole even in this dull daylight.

I managed to give him the semblance of a smile.

'Hello, Chris,' I said lamely. 'Let me in?'

6

WATCHERS

It wasn't until I spilled the tea that I came apart completely.

He'd sat me down in the living room while he brewed up a pot. His father's living room, I corrected myself, glancing dolefully around it. The decor did little to raise my spirits; there was dust and clutter everywhere. A couple of framed photos showed the late Mr Jackson – much more vigorous than when I'd known him – with a rifle and the carcass of an animal. He'd been a slaughterman, I remembered; perhaps a hunter, too. It gave me the faintest twinge of guilt, seeing into a patient's private life like this. Even though he was dead and buried now.

'Sugar?' Chris called from the kitchen.

'No, thanks,' I said listlessly. Sweetness from a spoon would be an insult to my daughter. I needed to drink bitterness and gall.

He came through and handed me a plain enamel mug. I cupped my hands around it: sipped its heat. The tang set my teeth on edge, and I was grateful.

'Let me take your coat,' he said again, easing down into an armchair. Like the sofa on which I was huddled forward, it smelled as old as it looked. The hearth was beside him, its ancient gas fire dead and cold.

I shook my head mutely; drank again.

'Rachel,' he went on, with soft insistence. 'You have to tell me what's happened.'

I stared at the shit-brown liquid filling my mug, as if willing myself to drown in it.

'Cathy's gone,' I said in a low, unsteady voice.

He hesitated; I felt his scrutiny. Heard him shift uncertainly in his chair. 'Gone where?' he asked at last.

'I don't know. She's been taken. Bloody *kidnapped*.'

'Rachel . . .' He got to his feet and came towards me; I tried half-heartedly to wave him back. My mug slipped from my fingers, to bounce and spray the carpet with its contents.

'Oh, *fuck*,' I said, with fierce despair – and dissolved into a flood of stinging tears.

He sat down on the sofa and drew me close, wrapping his arms around me as though afraid I'd be swept off on the tide. I squirmed ineffectually for a moment – then clung on for dear life: shuddering in silence as I wept.

He rocked me gently, murmuring against my hair: soothing, incoherent sounds. I felt as if I'd been pulled from a river in spate, and dragged onto the safety of dry land. He held me tight: unperturbed by the smell of my unwashed body, my stale and slept-in clothes. Gradually my sobs became gasps; I let myself relax against him. His fingers combed the lank strings of my hair.

'Have you called the police?' he asked, his voice a whisper. I sniffed, drew back and shook my head.

His eyes had narrowed with concern. 'Why not?'

'I can't,' I came back miserably. 'They'll . . . hurt her.'

'Who's they?'

Oh, Chris. What can I say? Things risen from a graveyard? Brought back to fight some long-forgotten war?

I gave him a helpless shrug, and dropped my gaze.

'So what are you going to do, then?' he persisted.

'I don't know. Wait to hear.' I raised my eyes appealingly. 'What else?'

He stroked my cheek to smear away the tears. I gazed back at him, wide-eyed. His own face was a study of disquiet.

Abruptly he stood, took my trailing hands in his, and drew me firmly to my feet. 'Come on.'

I guessed what he had in mind, and tried to pull free. 'Oh, please, Chris. No, I can't. Not now . . .'

He smiled, and shook his head. 'I know. I don't mean come to bed.' Once more he ran his fingers through my hair. 'You've got days of fear on your skin. You want to wash them all away – feel clean again. So come on: let me bathe you.'

I watched despondently from the bathroom doorway as he got the stiff taps going. The tub looked as old as the house's other fittings – a watermarked enamel shell. The room felt damp and draughty, with a growth of grey along the skirting boards; the dark, tiled floor looked as cold as slate. I was understandably loath to start undressing.

He waited until the rising steam began to warm the air; then turned and hugged me to him. Gently, stitch by stitch, he fumbled and cajoled my clothes off. I was too drained to help him much, still less to hinder him. By the time we were both naked, the tub was almost full.

Stifling a shiver, I slid down into the water; the sudden sharp contrast of cold and heat brought my top half out in goosepimples. He climbed in behind me, slid his arms around my middle, and eased me back to rest against him.

'All right?' he murmured softly; I just nodded.

After a minute, he reached for the soap and got started. Massaging my shoulders with slippery fingers; then reaching round to rub and rinse my breasts. In normal circumstances, I'd have found it quite arousing; but they were anything but normal. I could do no more than slump there, lax in his embrace. Even the care with which he worked at my belly and thighs beneath the surface failed to strike a spark of interest.

He washed my hair as well: shampooed and rinsed it; slicked it back. I just stared ahead, watching the steam rise from the cloudy water: taking heat and comfort with it, by degrees.

'Feel a bit better?' he asked against my ear.

I shrugged; the lump of cold lead in my stomach was certainly still there. But my head felt clearer; the tension in my muscles had eased somewhat. And I didn't smell of fear any more.

I let him ease me deeper, until my breasts were awash in the lingering warmth. I wasn't looking forward to the moment when I'd have to sit up again, and clamber wetly out into the cold.

'Chris . . .' I said, after a while. 'Can I ask you something . . . really strange?'

He gently squeezed my neck, and slid his hands apart. 'Try me.'

I swallowed. 'Do you believe in ghosts?'

His grip grew slightly firmer on my shoulders. I wondered what was showing on his face. But his voice came evenly enough.

'As a matter of fact, Rachel . . . yes, I do.'

He paused there: waiting for the why. I nerved myself to probe a little deeper. 'All right . . . What about witchcraft, then? And spirits?'

Silence for a moment. Then: 'Those too.'

My jaw grew tight; I was afraid I'd already said too much. But even as I wavered, he put two and two together for himself.

'Do you . . . think your daughter's been kidnapped by a coven or something?'

'Oh God, Chris. I don't *know*.' Tears brimmed even as I said it.

'Is that why you're afraid to go to the police?' he persisted mildly. 'In case they don't believe you?'

'Something like that,' I sniffed.

He was silent for a time: fingering my shoulders in a pensive sort of way.

'Do *you* believe me?' I asked querulously, half-turning my head.

'Yes.'

'Even if . . . I told you that it's not just people dabbling in black magic, but . . . dead bodies, brought to life?'

'Shh, Rachel. *Yes*. I believe in the Devil too – and all his works.' He folded his arms around me; I sensed him shake his head, as if in pity. 'God help us: you've had to face all this alone?'

'Yeah . . . sort of.' I pinched my lips into a pout; then yielded to the pressure inside me, and gave up the evil ghost. 'I knew one of them before, and . . . she's come back from her grave to haunt me.'

It was a blessed release to let it all come out – in the arms of someone who accepted it, and cared. I found a moment to wonder at this fresh corner of his character, as he reached over my shoulder to lift the crucifix from my chest, twisting it towards him on its chain.

'Your faith: hasn't that supported you at all?'

I backhanded a tear off my cheek. 'Not enough.'

'You're a Roman, aren't you? Why not go to a priest?'

'I . . . didn't feel I could.'

'So you've told nobody else?'

I shook my head; then let it loll sideways as he nuzzled my neck.

'Oh Chris, what am I going to do?' I whispered.

'Well, first of all,' he said, 'you're going to get some sleep. Regain some strength.'

I made as if to argue; then sighed, and settled back. Keyed-up as I'd been when I came here, a weight of weariness had stolen over me now. Just a couple of hours with my head down, then, I promised myself. While Razoxane was still trying to get back from London . . . and those other things were waiting for the dark . . .

It took effort enough just to stir myself and clamber from the bath. I closed my eyes while he towelled me dry: rubbing warmth through my flesh, while the tiles chilled the soles of my feet. Then, with the bathtowel still wrapped round me, he led me down the passage to a sparsely-furnished bedroom. I laid the towel aside, and let him kiss me. He did so very gently, without lust.

'Don't *worry*, Rachel. You're not on your own any more.'

I managed a wan smile as I climbed between the covers. It had drained away before he left the room.

The bed hadn't been slept in for a while, and needed airing; but the stale sheets were like a welcoming cocoon. I rolled my face into the musty pillow. Before I knew it, I had drifted off to sleep.

Consciousness returned like a bolt from the blue; I found I was sitting upright, my hands pressed to my cheeks. It took me a moment to remember where I was.

The air in the room was grey with twilight: cold and still. A wave of gooseflesh made me draw the counterpane up to my throat and hug it close.

No telling how long I'd been asleep; nor what had woken me. The back of my mind was a dreamless blank, as if I'd just emerged from a void. The room was empty; and though I sat and listened for several minutes, its silence seemed to permeate the house.

At least the lie-down had freshened me a bit. I rolled my head to loosen my stiff neck; then rubbed my fingers through my hair, and found it had dried in matted tangles. Shit.

And the pillow where my head had rested was barely damp now; I felt it, frowning slightly – then shrugged, slid out of bed and padded over to the door. Easing it open, I listened again. The hush of the dusky passageway breathed back at me. The house wasn't centrally-heated;

I felt the chill of stagnant air as I made for the bathroom. Felt sheepish, too, walking nude through an unfamiliar house – for all my intimacy with its new tenant.

'Chris . . . ?' I called from the top of the stairs. There was no reply. The house felt hollow: breathless. It seemed that he'd gone out.

My clothes were still lying where I'd left them; but it occurred to me that to put them back on after my bath would be a waste of his good work. The briefs I had no choice about; but with those in place, I went in search of fresher clothes. I hoped he wouldn't mind.

The room he was using turned out to be just along from mine. Unlike the spartan surroundings that I'd slept in, this one was crowded with bric-a-brac, and laden bookshelves. His father's room, I guessed with some dismay.

The air seemed denser here: as if the gloomy furniture and fittings were absorbing the window's feeble light. An iron-framed bed, draped in a threadbare crimson coverlet, took up most of the floor space. A rumpled sleeping bag was spread upon it. Something about the arrangement bespoke both intimacy and separation. The sight made my heart grow heavy.

Wherever Chris had been on his travels, he was still living out of his suitcase: had slipped back as a squatter, rather than a prodigal son.

Feeling increasingly like an interloper, I picked up a grandad shirt and pulled it on: its unbleached tails reached half-way to my knees.

I was just starting downstairs when I heard the faintest creak of movement from below.

Instinct jammed my heart into my throat. I stopped, and swallowed hard; then went quickly down the rest of the way.

'Chris?'

He didn't answer; the house felt empty again. And it would soon be dark now.

Disheartened, I hugged myself and looked around for a clock. The one above the fireplace said half-past seven, but that had to be wrong: there was still a gleam of daylight left outside. It was only when I found the same time on the clock in the hall that I realized – with a start – what must have happened.

My exhaustion had fed to its heart's content: I'd slept all through the night. It was dawn outside, not dusk.

I swore under my breath; and then again, more fiercely. God knew what might have happened while I'd been snoring in my pit. Razoxane would be back by now – and perhaps in pursuit of Cathy's captors, as they made their move at last. Her aim – she'd *told* me – was to root them out and burn them. If I wasn't there to temper her viciousness, how many innocent people would she kill?

I had a sudden sickening flash of Cathy: tearful, screaming Cathy, encircled by flames. *Mummy*! she'd have pleaded. *Mummeee*! And I'd just slept on, dreamless – deaf to her cries.

I shook the image off before it brought up bile, but was left feeling physically gutted. Standing helplessly there in the draughty dimness, I no longer knew which way to turn. To Chris, in the hope that he could help me? Or to Razoxane again – before she left me behind?

Still chewing on my bitter indecision, I checked the rest of the ground floor. There was no sign of him at all. But why would he have ventured out at this ungodly hour?

There was a wall-mounted metal cabinet in the passage to the kitchen, its narrow doors ajar. I guessed it was a strongbox of some kind – then noticed the lock. A heavy-duty hasp and staple. Somebody had wrenched the thing apart.

I stepped closer with a curious little frown. It looked as if whoever had done it had started off with a crowbar; but then they'd found a quicker way to finish the job. A pair of long-handled bolt cutters was propped carelessly up against the wall. The severed padlock lay discarded on the floor.

The cabinet was empty now; but peering in, I realized what it normally contained. There were upright metal brackets, with lengths of chain attached. The links had been cropped through, and dangled loosely.

My mouth dropped open. *Jesus, Chris*, I thought.

Someone had stolen his father's guns.

For a moment I thought it might have been last night – with me asleep upstairs. But no: I would have heard them. Most likely it had happened while their owner had been with us at St Catherine's.

To take advantage of a dying man like that . . . I felt a brief, disgusted sense of anger. The way of the world these days, perhaps; but still . . .

I looked into the kitchen with fading hope – as if Chris had been in there all along, just brewing me a wake-up cup of tea – but it was as empty as the rest of the house. Ignoring the chill of the cracked, cold lino, I crept over to the back door and checked the bolts. They seemed secure: all but rusted into place. No one had come in by this way for a while. Taking some small comfort from the fact, I turned away – and noticed that another door, beside the cooker, was not quite closed.

Not the entrance to a cellar, surely. The house didn't seem the type of place to have one. But I had to look anyway – just in case it was, and he was down there. Fetching coal. Or something . . .

I eased the panel wider – and as I'd half-expected, found just a cupboard there behind it. Mop and bucket; cleaning things. A few old coats. I sniffed, and dropped my gaze – and saw a metal can of petrol. The smell of it had crept into my nostrils; the cap wasn't properly closed. The thought of those fumes seeping out into the kitchen while Chris was at the cooker made me bite my lip: I felt a surge of sickened fright on his behalf. *You mustn't keep it there, you silly boy*, I thought; hunkered down and reached about me for a rag to wipe the can with. And that was how I came to find the guns.

There were three of them, propped up behind the coats. Two different kinds of rifle, and a pump-action type of shotgun. Their metal parts gleamed coldly in the dimness. The wooden butts looked worn with outdoor use. I sat there on my naked heels, and stared.

They'd been moved here from the cabinet, I realized; not stolen at all. But the things had been much safer where they were. Anyone could use them now. So easy just to fetch one from the kitchen . . .

Were they loaded?

I let my gaze stray back to the petrol can; then up. The nearest coat was long and dark, complete with riding cape. It loomed over me like a hanged figure. A rough-looking coil of rope was draped around its peg.

I felt a growth of fear inside me: it spread like the mould in his bathroom. Slowly I straightened up and shut the door: unable to take my eyes off the guns until the dark had swallowed them again. Then I rubbed my hands instinctively together, as if wiping away a patina of greasy guilt.

I still knew so little about him. I'd looked forward to exploring: delving deeper. Sharing his secrets. Now I felt afraid of what I'd find.

Rifles. Petrol. Rope. What else might he be hiding?

Get dressed, said common sense; *get out*. I didn't need telling twice. Emerging into the cold passageway, I scuttled back upstairs to the bathroom – which felt still colder. Crouching down, I began to sort through my clothes. My woolly winter tights would do to start with . . . *when* I found them.

But they weren't there to be found. I pushed my other togs around the tiles for a minute; then sat back, puzzled: frowning.

Next moment, they'd been wound around my throat.

I gagged with shock; then gurgled as he jerked them taut. The hiss of his breath against my neck seemed to mock my goldfish gawps for air. Then, with clenched fists crossed, he rose, and dragged me upright.

Being hanged must feel like this. My bare feet skidded, and my stretched neck took the strain. My pleas were trapped and flattened in my windpipe; only spittle made it out past my bulging tongue.

I sensed the strength and weight of him behind me; heard his breath rasp out between his gritted teeth. A madman, trying to kill me. Even in the grip of utter horror, I had to know *who*.

Not Chris. Can't be. He wouldn't. Not *me*.

My vision seemed to blur with blood. I kicked and writhed in vain. We stumbled back into the passageway with me groping blindly for his face. I had a fleeting grasp of hair; scratched my nail across his cheek. Was rewarded by a knee in the small of my back. The jolt turned my legs into jelly.

My mind was a smear of panic now. Hypoxia befuddled my brain. My arms flailed out, but found nothing to hang onto. He was bending me back across the brace of his knee. It seemed my spine must snap.

Oh Chris. Please don't. I didn't mean to see . . .

But even my mental voice was thick and slurred; no wonder he didn't get the message. The pressure on my throat was unrelenting.

I squirmed one final time – and wet myself.

The hot rush of release was almost blissful; my body relaxed as my bladder emptied, as if life itself was draining from my loins. It would have shamed and mortified me once; but now it felt like liberation. No need to care or worry any more. Then darkness came, and I closed my eyes and sank.

*

When I finally pieced my sticky thoughts together, I realized I was lying on my face. A rough and matted carpet-pile was pressed against my cheek. My hands were crossed behind me, resting loosely on my back. The wrists were ringed with pressure; I could scarcely feel my fingers.

My squashed throat hadn't quite regained its shape: my windpipe felt too narrow. I couldn't draw enough breath to snuff out the fire still smouldering in my chest. It hurt my neck to try.

I squeezed my eyelids open. Apart from carpet-fluff, close up, there was nothing to see, so I let them close again – and bit my lip till blood came.

I'd never have guessed it could be so frightening: discovering you're still alive.

I was still wearing his baggy cotton shirt. It did little to keep out the draughts that crept around at floor level. My briefs were sodden, my bare thighs sore. I hadn't the strength to register disgust.

Oh God . . . Oh please . . . What happens now?

As if in answer, a hand grasped my shoulder and rolled me over. Belly-up, I squinted through watery daylight – to find Chris kneeling there beside me. His face as motionless as stone.

'So tell me: are you ready to confess?' he said.

When I failed to shape an answer to his cold, insistent questions, he heaved me up off the carpet, slung me over his shoulder and took me back into the bathroom. Without wasting his breath in explanations, he lowered me down into the tub. My head fell back: the icy water closed over my face. I coughed and snorted; tried to struggle up – but with my hands tied fast and trapped beneath me, I was helpless. He let me bubble and squirm for a ghastly moment longer . . . then made a fist in my hair and hauled my head back up. I spat out stagnant water; croaked for air. When he opened his hand, and let my head loll sideways, I nearly drowned again; had to brace my neck just to keep my face awash. My shoulder was stiffly wedged against the side of the tub. I didn't dare move, in case I slipped, and slithered under.

Chris was down on his knees beside the bath, one forearm draped along the rim; his stubbled chin propped thoughtfully upon it. After a moment his free hand reached towards me, and brushed the wet hair from my staring eyes – as gently as he had that time before. I was too paralysed with cold and fright to cringe.

'You can make it easier for yourself,' he told me softly. 'You really can.'

'What do you want?' I whispered.

'To save you, Rachel. I can, you know.' He straightened, kneeling upright: looking down on me like a judge. 'You're in thrall to a witch: you confessed that much yourself. You'll have to give your body up for that. But if you repent, who knows? . . . there may be room in Heaven for your soul.'

His voice was grim and quiet; but those last words had a bitter tang, beyond my comprehension. If the speech seemed to come from another time, his everyday inflection brought it right up to the minute. I could only gape in frozen disbelief.

When I'd prayed that he'd believe me, I'd never meant like this – nor dreamed to see so violent a reaction. My throat was crushed and throbbing. The chill of the water was biting through to my bones.

Chris, who'd been so kind; made love to me so gently. Giving no hint of the violence locked away behind his eyes. Peering up at his personable expression was like seeing the smile of a plaster saint; with a demon curled up, grinning, in the shell.

Still waters, running deep: I'd thought of that before. But not this bottomless: this black . . .

'You don't understand . . .' I protested feebly.

'Oh, but I do. I daresay you fell without meaning to; but that can't be helped now. People like you are so easy for them to use. Being women, you're the weaker sex to start with. But once you start dabbling in the Roman religion, you've got a foot in their domain already . . .'

His hand crept down across my soaked and clinging shirt-front to tease my crucifix, twist it – and snap it viciously from its chain.

'This witch who's snared you: what's her name?'

'Chris, please listen. It's not like that . . .'

His palm slapped the water with a stinging crack. I winced, closing my eyes as droplets splashed my face. The ripples that followed lapped up across my cheeks.

'I asked you what's her *name*?'

'Razoxane,' I said, and swallowed; the reflex scoured my throat. 'She calls herself . . . Razoxane.'

'Is that her real name?'

'God . . . I don't know . . . probably not, no.'

He nodded pensively; inclined his head. 'What do you know of her history?'

I needed a moment just to muster my thoughts. My fear of drowning was at fever-pitch now. It was difficult to think straight with it screaming in my head.

'She . . . *claims* she was born in sixteen hundred and something . . . and used magic to prolong her life. She says . . . believes . . . she's a reincarnated angel. One of the fallen ones. Angel of death.'

'But you said she'd come back from her grave?'

'Last time I knew her . . . she conjured a demon, and trapped herself. Destroyed herself. But now she's come back.'

'In material form?'

'Yes.'

'A mistress of her craft,' he murmured: deceptively mild. Then: 'Has she a familiar spirit?'

'What? Yes . . .' I almost swallowed again, but managed not to. 'Vedova . . . she calls it . . .'

'What form does it take?'

'A rook . . .'

Again he nodded; contemplating my cross. Turning it in his fingers – then flicking it contemptuously away. I glimpsed its fleeting glitter from the corner of my eye. Without it, I felt utterly defenceless.

'And where is she now?' he asked.

'Chris . . .'

'I don't want to make you suffer, Rachel. Where is she now?'

Still so matter-of-fact: so chilling. In terror, I tried again to set the record straight. 'I'm not on her side. Never . . .'

The rest was just a burble as he pressed his palm to my chest and pushed me under. Staring up at him through the silver film of the surface, I could actually believe what he'd just told me. This wasn't what he wanted. His warped, refracted face bore the same expression Nick used to wear when unblocking a drain. Distasteful but determined . . .

I snorted water then: tried frantically to swallow, but it went down the wrong way. As soon as I tried coughing, the rest of the bathwater gushed in. I arched my back in panic; tried to thrash from side to side. My chest was close to bursting when he grasped my hair and hauled me up again.

'Where . . . is . . . she . . . now?'

I retched, and whooped for air, already shivering. The water was as cold as melted ice.

'London!' I gasped, as his fistful of hair grew tighter. 'She went . . . to London . . . Fetching something . . . Focusing her power.'

'I don't suppose she told you what?' he asked politely.

'Oh Jesus, no, she didn't . . .'

He seemed to accept that at face value. His hand

relaxed again: grew gentle. Easing my head back down against the side of the tub.

'What pact have you agreed?' was his next enquiry.

I breathed out hoarsely. 'She said ... she'd get my daughter back.'

Chris shook his head; his smile was almost chiding. 'And you believed her? Took the word of a witch?'

'Oh please ... I had to.'

'No, you didn't. Couldn't you see how she was trying to get her claws in deeper? Joining her coven has already lost you your little girl, Rachel. Don't you *learn*?'

'Cathy's not lost!' I snapped desperately back at him: riding a sudden surge of fear on her behalf. It swamped my own.

'I'm afraid she is.' Again he shook his head – but this time it looked like disbelief. 'You sold your daughter's soul. No mother can be forgiven for such a crime.' I caught a hint of loathing in the words.

It was an argument I couldn't bear to continue. Staring back at him, I just let go a sobbing breath.

'I've met too many of your kind,' he went on flatly. 'Degraded by your own delusions. Too many of her kind, too. She thinks she can squander your pitiful souls – then cheat justice through death and rebirth. Escape from one generation to the next. But I've lived before, as well. I know how old the scores are.'

Oh Jesus, not you too, I thought.

His eyes had lost their focus; now they hardened once again.

'I *knew* about the witch, Rachel. I smelled her on you. Being near you brought all of it back.' He shook his head. 'I hoped to God that I was wrong: that you weren't one of them. But I wasn't wrong: was I?'

I felt my eyes brimming with tears, and struggled to hold them back. Suddenly convinced I could cry enough to raise the water-line, and drown myself.

Once more he stroked my hair – just as he had after washing it yesterday. His voice had grown soft again: not much above a whisper.

'Rachel: listen. A woman infected by witches must be strangled and burned . . . not only to destroy the evil, but to purify her soul. But because I like you, I'll spare you that. You were good to me, in your own blind way. And the Lord be my witness, I never failed to plead the widow's cause.'

I waited: numb with cold and dread.

'Death by water can purify as well,' he murmured: his tone unnervingly persuasive. 'A second baptism. A cleaner end . . .'

'Oh God,' I whimpered, as the memory crammed itself into my head. 'That woman . . . You've done it before . . .' At Elm Hill reservoir. Murder by drowning. *Christ*.

He actually seemed pleased to be reminded. 'I needed to know if I could; if I still had the strength. I do still have it, Rachel.'

'Oh please don't . . .'

He reached across to grasp one of the taps – I tipped my head back fearfully to see – and twist it carefully around. Fresh water dribbled down into the tub.

My heart bulged in my chest. I waited for the stream that would cover my face in moments. But he left it as it was, just slightly open: whining faintly in the cold. Climbing slowly to his feet, he looked down at me with his head to one side.

'Don't struggle, Rachel. Don't try to fight it. Make your peace with God, and let yourself go under. Believe me, it's a blessing.'

Before I could summon the breath to beg, he was gone, closing the stiff door quietly behind him.

The sound of the leaking tap filled the silence of the bathroom. I had to strain my ears to hear above it – and through the solid socking of my heart. But a few minutes later, the front door opened and closed again. I knew it wasn't a ruse: there'd be no reason. This horrid, chilly house was empty. He'd left me alone.

The full weight of my predicament didn't really descend until I tried tentatively to move.

He'd pulled me partway down the tub – like a bride in the bath. I was lying with all my weight on my arms and bound wrists, effectively pinning them beneath me. And the chill of the water didn't feel like ice-melt any more. Rather, it was like being frozen in a solid, glacial block. I couldn't feel my muscles – still less move them.

The drip, drip, dribbling continued, just inches from my ear. The spreading ripples stroked my cheek. My face was only just above the surface as it was.

How long would it take the bath to fill at this rate? How many *hours*?

I opened my mouth to cry for help . . . and found there wasn't the air in my aching lungs. Only a gaspy sigh escaped.

Oh Jesus help me.

Pneumonia would start brewing soon enough; but I wouldn't live to see it. Perhaps hypothermia would claim me sooner. Before I drowned by inches.

From this low angle, the sides of the bath rose up around me like the walls of a canyon. I could see clustered spots of mould on the artexed ceiling overhead.

I wouldn't be missed. I'd covered my tracks too well. Maybe Pat might start wondering, when she phoned to wish me happy Christmas, and got no answer. But by then this tub would be overflowing, with me lying silent at the bottom.

Could Razoxane and her familiar find me? Oh God, perhaps they could. But after I'd ditched her, perhaps she'd be inclined to carry on alone. Settling whatever brutal score she had, without my hindrance . . .

The tap kept trickling, relentless as the sands of time.

I lay in sunken stillness, my teeth chattering uncontrollably. As the water rose gradually higher, my thoughts became divided and confused. Part of my mind was praying, to God and Mum and Mary, for one last revelation. A reassurance that my angel was alive. I thought I might die happy, knowing that.

The rest of me screamed out, in silence, for Razoxane to come.

The two strands had become ensnared, so that I was *praying* for the angel of death to be sent down here to save me, when something jerked my mind to full attention.

I lay there, listening – and heard it again. A sound that came from somewhere downstairs.

I was almost too torpid to react. The thought that Chris had come back to watch the finish couldn't scare me any more than I was already. But the idea that Razoxane might have stealthily gained entry lit a tiny, pallid flame inside me.

The noise came again. I thought of a warped sash window, scraping upwards. The sounds that followed – painful minutes later – seemed to bear that image out. Feet on floorboards, crossing warily towards a door. The hinges creaked.

A low voice muttered something; another answered. The tide of ice snuffed out the flame inside me.

Not Razoxane. Nor Chris. Two other men were in here with me. Quite ignorant of my listening presence – as if I'd already become the house's ghost. As I strained to hear, they began to move around: treading the building's boards like creeping cats. I realized belatedly that I was eavesdropping on a burglary.

Today, of all days. And what would they do if they found me? Tied up and helpless in the tub, my shirt and briefs transparent. My stomach, which had shrunk away inside me, tried to squirm.

But if they *didn't* find me . . . I didn't need to think it further through. Drawing from a well of strength I'd thought was dry, I moistened my lips and managed a faint whimper of distress.

In the stillness that followed, I couldn't tell if they'd heard or not. Perhaps they *thought* they'd heard. Sucking down air, I tried again. My cry was louder this time: high-pitched and pathetic. And then I heard slow footsteps on the stairs.

He came up slowly; paused in the passageway outside. I waited, breathing jerkily. And then the door was cautiously pushed open.

My breath caught in my throat; turned thick as mucus: choked me. If I hadn't wet myself already, I would have then.

His burly figure filled the doorway, bulked out by an unzipped parka. An iron jemmy was half-raised in one hand. Seeing it, and the stone mask of his features, I knew at once he hadn't come to burgle. He'd come for the 'shirt-lifter' who lived here. He'd come to smash his kneecaps – or his skull.

And his lefty girlfriend . . .

Sheer surprise left him blank-faced for a moment; then comprehension came. The tinted glasses couldn't dim the gleam in his eyes as he stared down at my body; nor mask the appetite the sight had whetted. Framed by the handlebar moustache, his lips drew wide and split across his teeth.

'Well hello again, my love,' he crooned grotesquely. 'Just *fancy* meeting you.'

*

For a moment we just stared at each other: in silence, apart from the trickling tap and my gaspy, shivering breaths. Then he lowered his crowbar and came on in. I peered fearfully up as he loomed above me.

'Fallen out with your boyfriend, then?' he asked brightly. 'Didn't we warn you about him, girl? You really should have listened . . .'

The second man appeared in the doorway. Another face I remembered from that evening in the pub. He craned his head in curiously to look – then grinned. 'Fuck *me*,' he muttered.

'Where's lover boy?' the man with the moustache enquired.

'I dunno . . . he's gone . . .' I swallowed painfully. 'Please . . . help me . . .'

The bloke in the doorway was delving in the pocket of his car-coat. As I watched, he dug out a mobile phone and flipped it open. 'Want me to give Dave a call? He'll love this.'

His companion shook his head: still watching me. I felt the weight of his gaze upon my breasts. I'd never felt so wretchedly exposed.

'Leave it,' he said, soft-voiced. 'She's ours: why share her?'

A heartbeat's pause; it felt as if mine had stopped completely. Then the phone was stowed away again. Its owner came to stand at the foot of the tub, trying to get clear sight of my saturated knickers. 'We going to give her one, then?'

'I think we'd better. Just so she know's what she's been missing.'

'Oh, please . . .' I gasped, feeling nausea rise inside me – much colder than the cold. 'You can't . . .'

The man standing over me shook his head, an expression of calm denial on his face. His tone, when he spoke, seemed almost reasonable. 'Oh yes, my girl: we can. You wouldn't really expect us to pass up a chance like this, now would you?'

The second bloke was still trying to peer between my drawn-up thighs. 'Len . . .' he murmured, head inclined.

'Mm?'

The other moistened his lips, and looked across. I saw him hesitate: saw his indecision vie with something darker.

Something vile.

'I heard somewhere . . . that if you . . . if a girl dies while you're screwing her, it really makes you come . . .'

He said it haltingly: as if ashamed of the admission. But excitement was electric in the fixed stare of his eyes.

Len stared back at him, his own face set in thought. After a moment, I realized he was actually giving the ghastly idea his serious consideration. My heart, once sluggish in my chest with cold, was now fighting to get free.

The tinted glasses turned to me. The eyes in the murk behind them looked down from a pitiless distance. He breathed in deeply through his nostrils – and turned back to his companion.

'All right,' he said. 'Let's see if it's true.'

The other licked his lips, with nervous lust. 'Can we . . . get away with it, you reckon?'

Len thought again; and nodded. 'Yes. Yes, I think so. They'll blame him, won't they? He's the one who bloody tied her up.'

'Shall we do it in the bedroom, then?'

'Yeah. Not here. Be a bit *too* wet'n'wild in here. How do you want to do her?'

I just lay there, open-mouthed, while they talked across me, discussing the practicalities of rape and murder. *My* rape. *My* murder. As if I wasn't there. As if I was dead already . . .

'How about . . . putting a plastic bag over her head?' the bloke by my feet suggested. 'Bound to be one in the kitchen . . .'

I gagged in horror. They ignored me.

'Only one of us'll get the benefit of this, you know,' Len pointed out.

His mate dug in the pocket of his jeans, and produced a ten pence piece. 'Toss you for it,' he offered smugly.

'Oh please . . . just let me go . . .' I whimpered.

Len looked down, as if suddenly reminded of my presence – and gave me an affable shrug. 'Nothing personal, my love; but we can't have you telling on us. So that's the way it is: we have to kill you.'

'But the Lord said, thou shalt *not* kill,' exclaimed a cold voice from the doorway.

The explosion that followed was as shocking as a high-street bomb. The bathroom filled with stinking smoke, shot through with sparks and fragments. Len and his mate took the brunt of the blast: it stripped life from their bodies and flesh from their bones. Blood burst in all directions: splashing the walls and spattering the ceiling. A spray of droplets flecked my face, and scalded my cold skin.

'. . . except on Tuesdays,' Razoxane finished dryly.

Len's body toppled forward, as if to join me in the tub. He struck the rim and folded like a sack; his torso slithered down onto my thighs. The displacement effect almost drowned me. I squeaked in panic, struggling to keep my face above the rising water. For a moment it seemed as if the rest of him must follow, pinning me down to choke in his embrace. But the hanging corpse spasmed and stayed there: half in the bath, half out.

The crack of doom had faded to an echo in my ears. The shroud of bitter smoke began to settle. Lying there in its shadow, I felt a creepy, phantom warmth infuse the water. As its glow embraced my frozen flesh, I let tears come at last. Up to my neck in a blood-bath, I sobbed with sheer relief.

Razoxane's shape came forward through the fog. Her form grew distinct as, reaching down, she took hold of

Len's torn coat, and hauled him upwards. I glimpsed an eyeless mask of blood and bonemeal; and then he was off the rim, and flopping to the tiles beside the tub. The water level swirled and sank. I gasped for breath, and let my head slump back.

Razoxane looked down into the bath.

The gun in her hand had the look of a sawn-off musket – cross-bred with a cannon. I recognized it straightaway. The evil blunderbuss she'd carried last time. The thing she called the Devil's Tinderbox.

Lifting it now, she sloped it back across one shoulder, cocked her head to one side – and grinned at me.

'Strange time to take a bath, I would have thought.'

'Never mind the *jokes*,' I spat at her.

With an amiable shrug, she laid her antique scattergun aside, and stooped over the tub. I could only close my eyes against blissful tears as she grasped my sodden shirt, and raised me up from my watery grave.

*

'When can we get out of here?' I asked huskily, as she came back from the kitchen.

'When you're in a fit state,' was her brisk answer. She set a steaming mug in front of me. 'Now drink.'

I peered suspiciously at it: smelled coffee, and something stronger. 'I found this in one of the cupboards,' she confirmed, holding up a small bottle of whisky. The glass was dusty, the label worn and peeling. It made me think of an old turps bottle from yesteryear's repainting.

I was huddled in a chair beside the gas fire, swathed in every musty blanket that my rescuer could find. She'd taken me in hand like a sister indeed; rubbed me down and wrapped me up while I'd just shivered with reaction. Listening to her make coffee in the kitchen, I'd remembered being mollycoddled by my flatmate, years ago, when I had flu; hugging a hotwater bottle on the sofa, while she made a proper fuss of me. The image reacted violently with the hellish here and now: this empty, alien house I'd been lured into. The blood and gutted bodies in the bathroom. The scruffy spectre rooting through the drawers . . .

Razoxane took the chair on the other side of the hearth. With her coat still on, and her hat in her half-gloved hands, she looked intrusive, out of place: like a tramp finding temporary shelter. It was that, as much as anything, which made me realize what it meant to be a ghost. Spirit or flesh, it made no difference. She was out in the cold with the dead.

And for all that, she was smiling – in her sly, ironic way. I took a cautious sip of coffee; then looked warily up again. 'But someone must have heard . . .'

She shook her head. 'I scattered some chaff of my own: broadcast. People will have registered something – but they won't give it much thought.' She glanced towards the ceiling. 'Who were they, by the way?'

I shrugged; it turned into a shudder. 'Dunno. They reckoned they were vigilantes or something.'

'Not vigilant enough. Will there be more?'

I raised the mug again; my teeth rattled briefly on the rim. 'I . . . ran into a gang of them before. I don't know if their mates knew they were here.'

She nodded. 'And what did you do, to anger these admirable men?'

'I was kind to someone,' I muttered.

'I see. Would this be the same someone who tied you up and left you to drown?'

My turn for a miserable nod.

'Such ingratitude,' she said, with mock dismay.

'It's not *funny*,' I snapped back.

'I didn't say it was,' she countered softly: the smile fading back into her taut, anaemic skin. Her shades regarded me in silence, then: like calm black pools. Unnerved, I dropped my gaze.

'Who was he?' she asked at length.

'He ... said his name was Christopher. This is his house; his father's house. He met me at the hospice. He thinks he's lived before – like you. He wants to hunt you down and kill you.'

A pause. Then Razoxane took her shades off, narrowing her bleached-blue eyes against the light.

'Ring any bells?' I asked dully.

'Only funeral ones,' she said, her tone pensive. Then irony crept back in. 'I've walked with death too long to tell one death-knell from another ...'

My heart gave a sudden spasm. 'Listen ... what if this is a trap, if I was bait ...'

She shook her head. 'He's gone, now. Vedova came ahead of me, and found no trace. He left you to die, Rachel. Simple as that.'

I returned my attention to my drink. 'He said you'd just been using me,' I whispered.

'I thought you didn't trust me anyway.'

I gave her a sullen, sidelong glance. 'I don't.'

'Well, then.' And on that casual note, she got up and walked over to the table. The Tinderbox was propped upright on one of the chairs, like a gaunt, unwelcome guest. Ignoring it, she picked up her compass from the tabletop and caressed it gently with her thumb.

I moistened my lips. 'Have they moved yet?'

She shook her head, still brooding on the shut lid.

'Did you ... find the Tinderbox in London?'

A half-smile touched her lips. 'I did; but I still need something more. And your help to retrieve it.'

Oh, God. I winced and took another swallow of heat: grimacing as it seared and tingled through me. 'Not tonight ... I couldn't ...'

'I know,' she agreed, coming over. 'You need to get

your strength back. So yes, we'll wait – though we can ill afford to.' She tucked the compass back into a pocket. 'Until tomorrow.'

It suddenly dawned on me that tomorrow was Christmas Eve. The realization brought no reaction; I felt completely disconnected from the world around me now.

Cathy. A week ago, I'd hoped that she could bring the magic back. All that mattered now was that I found her. Once I had – because I *would* – I'd never want for miracles again.

'What if I get pneumonia, then?' I mumbled to my mug.

'You don't need to worry about that.' She was pulling her gloves off as she said it. I glanced up, frowning: watching her flex her lean, pale fingers.

'What are you doing?' I asked uneasily.

'What I was born to do. Remember me telling you? All this blood on my head; all those shadows on my trail. And all I ever wanted was to *heal*.'

I thought of the bathroom. Two more ghosts to join the crowd. Perhaps the rest had got the house surrounded. Invisible blank faces at the windows, peering in . . . Then, as her meaning finally sank in, I gasped and shrank away. 'Get *off* me.'

She spread her empty hands, as if surrendering. 'I won't hurt you, Rachel.'

I tried to struggle up, but my legs still weren't working properly. In vain I tried to fend her off.

'I'm not going to cast a spell on you,' she insisted, leaning forward. 'You're not even going to rise up and walk. But I can bring your humours back into the balance. Believe me. *Trust* me.'

She was wasting her breath on that score; but I found I had no option but to let her have her way. Stepping round behind my chair, she placed her hands upon my head: her fingertips pressed gently to my skull. I swallowed a sob. Did the electric chair's victim feel like this, as the iron cap was fitted into place? My muscles locked solid – as if the current had already been switched on.

But the jolt that I'd expected never came. She just held my head quite rigid for a moment; then slowly began massaging my scalp. The sensation was oddly soothing; I might have closed my tired eyes, in someone else's hands. After a minute, I felt a small, sporadic tingling: little ripples of warmth in my body and limbs. No change, apart from that. When she finally released her grip, I let myself slump down with mingled feelings: relief and anticlimax intermixed.

'There you are,' she said calmly, walking back over to retrieve her hat. 'You won't get pneumonia now. Not even a cold.'

I stared after her, nonplussed; then ran my own hand through my hair – rubbing the skin through the sticky strands. She smiled at my suspicious look.

'Just psychic energy, Rachel. Nothing sinister. A white charm of my mother's.'

'Pity you didn't stick with that sort of thing,' I said acidly.

She took it on the chin, and didn't blink. 'We make the best of what we're given. In my position, you might have done the same.'

Before I could think up a rejoinder, an eerie warbling noise cut in between us. I jumped, my head snapped round; my nerves growing taut as I failed to find the source. It seemed to come out of the air – insectile and insistent. And then I realized it was leaking downstairs from the bathroom: and knew it was the dead man's mobile phone.

The knowledge didn't bring much comfort. I sat and listened to it ring: unwillingly reminded of what lay heaped behind the door. Razoxane stood motionless, listening too. The warbling tone went on and on.

Mid-afternoon. Perhaps his drinking pals were trying

to raise him – taking a vote on which pub to hit tonight. But what if there was a girlfriend at the end of the line? A worried wife? A daughter . . . ? The thought drew my lips tight shut.

Do you know what he said to me: that bloke you live with? Do you know what he suggested?

Could you bear to imagine where he is right now?

The phone fell silent.

I didn't know that I was holding my breath until it seeped out in a sigh. I looked at Razoxane. 'We've got to get *out* of here.'

'We'd best wait until dark,' she pointed out. 'You can only put motes in so many eyes.'

I glumly returned my attention to my mug – then glanced back up.

'He put his father's rifles in the kitchen cupboard. Chris, I mean. Are they still there?'

She wandered casually out, and returned a minute later – cradling the shotgun. I watched with unease as she weighed it; turning it over in her hands. 'Not really my thing,' she said at last. 'I prefer my guns a little older . . .' She raised her eyes. 'How many were there?'

'Three.'

'Two, now. This one and a bolt-action rifle.'

I swallowed. 'There was one with, like, a lever . . .'

'He's got that one, then.' She sounded almost cheerful, as if relishing the implications.

'Is he part of this?' I asked weakly.

'I don't know. He's not a revenant, I'm sure of that. And I haven't even screwed him.'

Fuck off, I mouthed bitchily back at her.

'Well, you seem to be feeling better,' she grinned – and glanced towards the window. Her pale face grew impassive as I watched. When she looked at me again, her eyes were like an afterglow of the wintry sky outside.

'Just a couple of hours,' she promised softly. 'Dusk

into darkness. Then we can leave.' She caught my pained expression, and smiled again: a sombrely indulgent elder sister. 'The night has its wonders, too. Don't be so downcast. It used to be your element as well.'

*

Her demon rook was waiting at my flat: perched up on the roof like a gargoyle come to life. I glimpsed its shifty movement in the orange-stained gloom, and hung nervously back; but Razoxane just walked in through the gate. I followed more slowly, still peering upward. The bird's hard eyes flashed reflections from the shadows.

'All quiet?' Razoxane called softly, as I fumbled with the keys. The parched response was as grim as the rattle in a dying man's throat. I'd heard a few of those in my time – but none had made my hairs stand up as stiffly. Then the door was open, and I pushed my way inside.

For a moment I felt as if I'd been swallowed. The flat was dungeon-dark and lifeless: steeped in its gloom, unslept-in. The familiar atmosphere just wasn't there. As I hesitated, Razoxane slipped in behind me – and a startling burst of wingbeats filled the hall as her familiar followed with her. I ducked instinctively as it fluttered on into the flat, a blur of shadow in the darkness. The sound of its wings was somehow ancient – like sheets of parchment crackling. It ceased a moment later, as the bird-thing came to rest somewhere. Razoxane shut the door behind us. Breathlessly I clawed for the light-switch.

Revealed again in all its disarray, the flat was barren but unthreatening. With a weary sigh, I dumped the bin-liner I was carrying: worn down by its weight of bloody clothing. I'd never wear those things again. I couldn't help but think of an RTA victim's property bag, the contents soiled and soaking – fit only for the furnace.

Need to get rid of that: before it starts to smell . . .

I turned to Razoxane: watched as she hung her hat on one of the coat-hooks. 'Just make yourself at home,' I muttered, and made for the bathroom.

I'd come here wearing Chris's father's clothes: scavenged with distaste from drawers and wardrobes. They smelled as stale as the bedclothes; the underpants itched unpleasantly. But I hadn't had much choice. No way was I wearing Chris's things. Not even a sock, if it had been against *his* skin.

Stripping hastily off, I turned on the shower, stepped under it – and stayed there for a long, long time. Scrubbing off the taint of warm, pink water. Soaping myself clean between the thighs. Finished at last, I went through to my bedroom, and got dressed.

I sensed Razoxane's presence in the doorway as I pulled my sweater down and into place. Turning my head, I gave her an unsmiling look.

'Let me tell you something,' I said, my voice rock-steady. 'I'm never going to be humiliated like that again. Degraded like I was. Not *ever*.'

'It wasn't your fault,' she said quietly.

'No? I walked right into his bloody parlour.' I stopped, and swallowed. 'And those other blokes: they made me *beg*.' Suddenly my voice was close to cracking.

'Of course they did: why should you be ashamed? They were the ones who chose to be degraded.' She regarded me in silence for a moment; her cold gaze strangely calming. 'You've real strength inside you, Rachel. It's brought you all this way. And it'll lead you to your daughter – if you let me guide your steps . . .'

I shrugged, and let my silence give consent; I couldn't argue. Sitting on the bed, I started pulling on my sneakers.

'. . . and share your dreams,' she added softly.

The words froze my fingers on the laces. My head snapped up. 'I told you, *no*,' I said.

'Two minds are better than one,' she insisted, coming

over. 'Especially now there's someone else against us. He's not one of them; but I reckon there's a linkage somewhere. Some trace that ties him in. If we focus our thoughts together, we might find it.'

I stared up at her, dry-mouthed; struggling not to ask the crucial question. To do so would mean giving that fatal inch – and I knew she'd take much more than just a yard. But whatever inner strength I might be blessed with, it wasn't up to this.

'Will it tell us what *they* want?' I whispered.

'It'll give us an idea.'

I took a deep, uneven breath. Then nodded to myself, and took the plunge.

'So how do you want to do it, then?' I asked.

A candle and a mirror: that was all that she required. Enough to give me sickened second thoughts.

I remembered someone telling me once – in school, or as a student – that if you sat at a mirror with a candle, and said the Lord's Prayer backwards, you could summon up the Devil. I wasn't really sure if I believed it; but nothing on earth would have made me try it out.

'But this isn't the same,' she told me patiently. 'I'm not going to conjure a spirit up for this. Such things are cunning, and can't be trusted. All I'm going to do . . . right . . . is tap into your mind, and use its talents. Weave them with mine. I haven't the power to envision this alone. Not any more . . .'

I was sitting at my dressing-table, gazing nervously into the mirror. She was standing there behind me. Her reflection wore a thin, placating smile.

The candle had come from the box in the kitchen; I still liked candlelight around the flat. With Cathy tucked up safely, I'd relax into its glow; sometimes bathe by it, as well. It made the place feel intimate and holy.

The one at my elbow sat waiting in its wax-encrusted holder. I gave it a glance – and winced as she struck a match beside my ear. Leaning past me, she lit the wick and let the flame grow long. When she went to switch the light off, the greasy glow that filled the room suggested anything but holiness.

Razoxane came and stood at my shoulder: meeting my gaze in the mirror. Reaching into her pocket, she retrieved the Book of Martyrs and laid it on the tabletop before me.

'Put your hand on it,' she said. With the briefest hesitation, I did so, like someone taking an oath. The cover seemed to crawl beneath my palm. The feeling made my flesh creep, all the way to my shoulder.

The dressing-table mirrors held my image like a triptych: an eerie three-piece painting of some martyr being tempted by a demon. Her insect eyes were glinting in the dimness by my ear. My own pale face seemed trapped within the scene.

Razoxane leaned forward, and placed her hand on mine; resting the other on my shoulder. Her face was blank of all expression. 'Now look at the reflection of the flame.'

Swallowing, I did so: obeying her prompting to let my eyes lose focus. The bleary glow grew outward: filled my gaze. She squeezed my shoulder gently; murmured something in my ear. I felt my body loosen up. My head began to swim. Engorged with light, my wide eyes fluttered closed.

I caught myself with a start, as if falling asleep at the wheel of my car. The sudden wave of fright was just the same. My eyes snapped open.

The candle had gone out.

But an eerie light still clung to me, and it came from Razoxane's reflection. She was dressed in purest white now, like the angel of her dreams; but her face looked horribly burned – quite black. And her glasses blazed like headlamps, their bottomless darkness turned blinding bright.

With a jolt I realized that I was seeing things in negative: the white turned black, the black becoming white. But it still shocked me some more to see myself: my own charred face, framed by snow-white hair, with pinpoints of cold brilliance in the centres of my eyes.

Even as I stared at them, the images dissolved. For a moment all was vertigo and void. Then, as my inner eye refocused, a weird black landscape opened out before me – weird because the ground was somehow radiant, like fire without light. The bones of a forest loomed eerily beyond it: luminous white against the solid, murky sky.

I glimpsed movement against the stark shapes of the trees: a white-robed figure at the edge of the wood. It turned to look towards me; then dissolved into the brighter glow within. Too distant to be recognized; but I felt sure it was a woman.

Not Razoxane, though. Somehow I was sure of that as well.

Still out of my body, I struggled to understand. If light and shade had been reversed, then the ground must be covered in snow; the glare through the trees was darkness. And the woman . . .

But other shapes were crossing my field of vision now. Human figures – but faceless and transparent: like ghosts from neighbouring channels on a poorly-tuned TV. They were converging steadily towards the trees, and the point where the woman had disappeared. Their slow, ethereal progress really scared me.

I wrenched my gaze away, swung round – and found a single tree behind me. A bird was perched on a naked branch and peering down: as spotlessly white as the purest dove. But I'd never seen a dove with so vicious a beak – nor heard one croak as hoarsely.

It was Razoxane's rook, of course.

It screeched again, and spread its phosphorescent wings. Before I could even shield myself, it swooped. Gripping my helpless skull between its talons, it craned hungrily forward: plucked out my mind's eyeball, and carried it off.

The ground flashed past beneath me, cinder-black. We crossed it at terrifying speed: the landmarks raced towards us. I glimpsed leaning gibbets, and dug-up churchyards; the glow of open graves. Then a line of ragged bundles, which turned to bodies in the instant before we left them behind – the faces greyish-white against the shimmering black snow.

No chance of looking back; no time to try and work the image out. But the impression I got was of a countryside laid waste: turned over with a medieval spade. My dream swept me across it in a straight, unerring line.

An incandescent shape appeared on the horizon, in ghostly silhouette against the black ice of the sky. My vision sped towards it – fired like a bullet from my brain. As the distance closed, I made out a figure on horseback; he turned in his saddle to watch me come. A heavy-shouldered cloak came clear, a wide-brimmed hat – and then I was heading full-tilt for his face.

The impact never came. The sombre visage disappeared; there was only emptiness behind it. My mind lost its wings, and plunged into oblivion.

Even as I fell, that face came with me. Bleak and haggard, framed by dull, metallic hair. The eyes were depthless pools of oily black.

A fit of sheer panic gripped me – and then I was gripping the table-edge in turn. The dressing-table; mirror-glass: my room. If Razoxane hadn't had me by the shoulder, I'd have slithered from the chair.

The candle was burning again, its flame quite still –

looking for all the world as if it had never gone out. And maybe it hadn't. Maybe . . .

I yanked my hand clear of the musty book, and gasped for breath: engulfed in clammy nausea. Razoxane's fingers dug into my skin. 'Easy now,' she murmured, with surprising softness. 'It's over. Finished now . . .'

Raising my eyes, I met her blanked gaze in the mirror. Her face looked drawn: intent.

'You saw?' I whispered.

'Most of it,' she said.

I swallowed. 'Yellow eyes.'

'What?'

'That last man: yellow eyes. Black in the negative, but . . . yellow real. I've . . . dreamed of him before.'

'Have you, now?' She sounded pensive; looked it, too.

'Who is he?' I insisted.

'I don't know.'

'*Razoxane.*' For a moment I just felt piqued at having gone through that for nothing. And some of those sights had been so unsettling: the scaffolds, and the violated graves. The bodies with bleached, and therefore blackened faces – but whether by fire or decay, I couldn't tell.

'There were things I found familiar,' she admitted slowly. 'Some echoes I picked up. But I haven't seen that face before.'

Irritable, I shrugged my shoulders; she let them go. 'So what was the point?' I muttered.

She gestured. 'Let me think on what we saw. There's . . . something there.'

That moment's hesitation: was it reticence – or unease? I didn't feel quite up to finding out.

'Did you have to bring your bloody bird along?' I asked instead.

'I hadn't planned to. She wasn't prepared. But Vedova feeds on forgotten thoughts. It would've been too hard to keep her out.'

I grimaced, and rubbed my eye. The socket still itched faintly, where I'd dreamed her pecking beak . . .

'You'd better get some sleep,' said Razoxane calmly. 'I'll keep watch.'

I sighed at her, surrendered, and went off to brush my teeth. The things I'd seen kept nagging at the back of my mind. Those ghostly shapes had really struck a chord. Studying my face in the mirror, I remembered my reaction to the haunted glass of Coventry cathedral. One of my earliest memories: how I'd clutched my mother's hand, and shied away, while those eyeless, etched-in figures peered down. *Shh*, she'd said. *They're saints and angels. Look*. But all I could see were skeletons, wrapped up in spider-silk.

Coming back, I met Razoxane in the passageway. An evil grin had spread across her face.

'It isn't wise to gate-crash meditations. The minds of those who do so may never come back. And others will come back changed . . .'

I just frowned at her, perplexed: not knowing what she meant, until she led me through into the living room. And then I stopped short, with a gasp of sheer surprise.

Her rook was perched on the table, staring balefully back at me. But I could have sworn that there was bafflement in its gaze.

From its beak to the tips of its tail-feathers, its plumage had turned immaculate snow-white.

Exhausted though I was by the day's ordeal, I took ages to get fully off to sleep. Small, sporadic noises broke the stillness of the flat. Faint creaks, and muffled rustlings. They brought my thoughts back round to Razoxane: sitting watchfully in the dark beyond the door. And to the blurred white shape of her familiar, as it fluttered from room to room.

Sleep crept over me by inches – and suddenly I was sat bolt upright, gasping: sheened with sweat, and icy cold. It was a while before I got myself together. The sensation had reminded me too much of that slowly-filling bath.

The second time, I forced myself to sink without a struggle. Again, a rush of panic almost roused me: I felt I couldn't breathe. But this time, tired out, I just let go. The darkness opened wide, and sucked me deep. I drowned.

But Nick was there beside me when I opened my eyes.

The room in our new house was summer-warm; the night was over. Rosy daylight filtered through the curtains. Smiling, I kissed his prickly cheek and stroked him; he mumbled something dopey, eyes still closed.

Slipping out of bed, I went sleepily through to get Cathy from her cot; as naked as a babe myself. Eight months old, and quite an armful. She gurgled happily as I brought her back to join us; but the sight of Nick close up made her wary – then fretful.

'Shhh,' I cooed, above her whimpers; cuddling her between us. 'Who's this, then? Who's this?'

She lapsed into a big-eyed silence, peering up at him. He smiled blearily back at her. For a moment I thought she was going to burst out crying, but she kept it back. Brave girl.

'That's Daddy,' I whispered, grinning. 'Isn't it? That's *Daddy*. I'm not surprised you don't recognize him . . . he's been working nights for the past *month*.'

'Oh, go and make us coffee,' Nick murmured.

'You hear that? Daddy's forgotten the Magic Word.'

' . . . *please* . . .'

'That's much more like it.' I leaned carefully across to kiss him.

The sun went out.

All the light and warmth in the world went with it. I found myself alone in utter darkness: a body at the bottom of the sea. They'd been snatched out of my bed, and left no trace. My sweetheart, and my lovely little girl.

I was about to wail in my despair when I sensed a presence at the bedside. A black shape, craning forward. Still more asleep than not, I tried to squirm away – but it stilled me with its grip. Cold, soft fingers squeezed my shoulder.

'Razoxane . . .' I quavered.

No reply.

Something had slipped past her: was crouched in here with me. Before I could begin to struggle, my panicked mind broke surface – and I took a gulp of greyish pre-dawn air.

I was sitting up in bed. The room was empty.

I let out a sobbing sigh, and hung my head. Dark smudges bloomed like rain-spots on the duvet. My cheeks were dripping wet: I wiped them; whimpered softly. I ached inside, like someone waking up from major surgery – and wasn't that the bloody truth? Hadn't part of me been ripped and torn away?

Part of my body. Part of my flesh.

That rosy summer morning seemed a thousand winters past.

I sighed again, and swallowed. Turned around to get my pillows straight. And froze.

When movement returned, a moment later, I clamped my hand over my mouth: not daring to let anything emerge. My other hand flew up to hold it there. Above them, my eyes grew huge.

On the crumpled pillowcase, right next to where my sleeping head had rested, lay a single, long-stemmed flower.

Red carnation.

7

WANDERERS

As soon as we set foot in the graveyard, I knew this was a Christmas-free zone.

A few of my friends declared one every year – rejecting the indulgence of the season. Sometimes I'd even find myself agreeing: worn down by shopping, cooking and compulsory good humour.

But this gloomy place was different altogether. No refuge from the excesses around us; no sense of hope at all. The people still walked in darkness here.

Not that I was feeling Christmassy in any case; far from it. The bright and bustling streets had left me cold – alone in the midst of all those busy shoppers. And had *they* been enjoying themselves? Not really. I'd glimpsed hassle and harassment on every side.

Just three shopping *hours* left to Christmas. A foretaste of frost in the air already. The daylight beginning to fade.

I let my gaze trail off over the gravestones. They were fairly packed together – in sombre solidarity against the living world around them. Lights flickered and glowed through the trees at the cemetery's edge; I could hear the cars stream past on the peripheral roads. Here and there, a glint of Christmas colour: pinpoints sharpened by the cold. But even in the midst of the city, this acre kept its peace.

I shivered, and shrugged deep into my cloak. The nursing cloak I'd had since student days. It had lived in my wardrobe for the past few years; but this morning it had seemed the perfect choice. In practical terms it was heavy and warm; but I'd wrapped it round myself for other reasons. Partly in nostalgia for days long lost; but mainly because it fitted my mood. I was dressed in black today, from jeans to jumper: grimly prepared for whatever Razoxane was planning. The dark cloak set the seal.

But it concealed a blood-red lining. Remembering that brought a prickle of tears, which I hastily sniffed back: not even sure if the surge of inner feeling had been grief – or helpless happiness.

He's come back to wish me well. He's watching now.

I could still scarcely believe it; but the flower was real enough. It hadn't crumbled into dust when I tried to pick it up. I hadn't dreamed it. Gingerly I felt beneath my cloak, to check it was still there; and so it was. Tucked into the second buttonhole of my blouse.

'You're very quiet,' said Razoxane calmly.

'Well it's not the sort of place to do a song and dance routine,' I muttered – defensively aware that she had guessed what I was thinking. I hadn't mentioned my visitor, still less the gift he'd left me; but she must have sensed his presence in the flat. And left us to it. Respected our privacy. Perhaps I should feel grateful, in a way.

A flicker of amusement crossed her face as she dug out her compass. Watching her turn it over in her fingers, I drew my cloak still tighter. The City noise seemed muffled now; its lights like distant campfires. The afternoon sky was losing colour, but the night would fall here first. Just the two of us alone to see it. Widow and witch.

In the midst of life we are in death.

Razoxane flicked the compass open.

'What are we here for?' I asked sullenly; trying to conceal my burgeoning unease. 'You're not . . . going to raise up a spirit or something, are you . . . ?'

'Now what makes you think I'd do that?' she said innocently, glancing over the regimented headstones.

'. . . because if you are, I'm out of here, all right?'

'Don't worry . . .' She paused to pass the compass over the nearest grave; the needle didn't waver. Satisfied, she looked at me again. 'I'm finished with raising ghosts, Rachel. There are enough of us walking this joyless earth already.'

Chewing my lip, I glanced behind myself; then hurried after her as she started down the row.

The same thing happened at every grave. She held the open compass over it – sometimes for a minute or more; then nodded, and moved on to the next. Sidling restlessly in her wake, I kept on looking round; but the place was deserted. Somewhere to avoid, on Christmas Eve.

I hadn't quite got over my London jitters; and nor, in present company, was I likely to. The City still felt like occupied territory. A hostile labyrinth of shadow and stone.

It went back to its anchorhold, or so she'd said; but had it? Could I trust her? What if she was wrong?

On to the next row; then the next. The sky over the buildings to the west was flushed and frosty. A thin dusk rose like mist among the graves.

She finally got a result in the bleakest area of the cemetery. Most of the graves down this end were unmarked – just grassy hummocks. People scraped up off the streets, I reckoned grimly. No fixed abode, no next of kin. No names.

Then the compass needle swung – so suddenly, I jumped.

Razoxane studied the instrument in silence, as if taking a reading from the symbols on its face. Slowly she closed her hand around it: snapped it shut. As I watched, perplexed, she took her hat off, and eased down onto her knees.

What are *you doing?* was the obvious question: but it wasn't one I had the nerve to ask. All I could do was hang warily back and watch. The warmth of my breath was visible now, like smoke.

Hers wasn't.

She didn't speak; just laid the compass on the grass, and bowed her head as if in meditation. Minutes passed. I was beginning to stamp on the spot, in an effort to keep at least the outward chill at bay, when she livened up again, and clambered to her feet.

'Is that it, then?' I asked, in the tone of one forlornly expecting the answer yes.

'No,' she said.

I grimaced, and pulled the collar of my cloak around my throat. 'So now what?'

'Now we make ourselves scarce . . . until they shut the gates.' She nodded her head towards the nearest murky clump of trees. 'Come on.'

There wasn't much indication that the place was closing; just a groundsman walking past along the central pathway, giving the place a perfunctory once-over. I watched from the shadows with wary eyes; aware of Razoxane's patient presence at my side. A short while later, at the edge of my hearing, I caught the squeak and scrape of rusty iron. Hinges. Chains.

She gave it a few minutes longer; then led the way back over to the grave. The air was ashen now, beneath a corpse-coloured sky. The traffic around us hadn't let up; was thicker if anything. People hurrying home to be with families and friends. Nobody with time to spare for this forgotten place.

Razoxane raised her compass to the level of her cheek. It clicked open like a shellfish in her fingers. She stood there for a moment, staring downward; head thoughtfully inclined – as though listening to inaudible music from the mechanism. Then she smiled, and looked at me.

'Ever heard of *resurrectionism* before?'

I groped hopefully for a religious connotation – then remembered what it really meant. 'Yeah . . . Burke and Hare, and people . . .' My mouth dried up as my eyes widened. Then: 'No. *Oh*, no . . .'

'Rachel . . .' She broke off and grasped me by the collar of my cloak as I tried to back away. '*Listen*. There's nothing here that can hurt you.'

'I'm not sticking round here while you desecrate graves,' I hissed at her: still trying ineffectually to get free. 'Just . . . bloody well let me *go* . . .'

'Who said anything about desecration?' she came back flatly. 'This is the paupers' plot; there's nothing sacred here. Just bodies shovelled under without ceremony. And besides . . .' she added, sly smile growing, 'the presence of a *grave* doesn't always signify that there's a body inside . . .'

I stared at her, panting. Her grubby fist still gripped my cloak, but her face was almost friendly: full of confidence. She put it to the test a moment later by releasing her grip; and sure enough, I stood my ground. Not that I'd had anywhere to run to, really. She had me well and truly hooked.

'Going to scratch it up with your nails, then?' I sneered.

'No need,' she answered mildly. 'The grave-digger's just coming.'

I turned my head – and saw two shadowy figures approaching through the twilight, wending their way between the graves. As they drew closer, I saw they were two scruffily-dressed young men. No doubt they'd climbed in over the railings, under cover of the trees. One of them carried a bulky, odd-shaped pack slung over one shoulder.

I eased prudently back as they came up, leaving

communications up to Razoxane. Both men gave me a look: clearly as suspicious of me as I was wary of them. A stale, sweaty smell crossed the hostile gap between us. Together with the state of their clothes, it told me she'd recruited her grave-diggers from London's open streets.

'This the one?' the first bloke said, without preamble. He was wearing an old camouflage jacket: its smeary, drab design contrasting with the patterns on his round Tibetan cap. He was maybe twenty-five, with an older man's goatee beard. Receiving Razoxane's nod, he glanced at me again. 'Who's she?'

'A friend.'

His cool eye looked me up and down. 'She looks like a bloody vampire bat, in that thing.'

'Her tastes are somewhat purer, nonetheless,' said Razoxane dryly – while I just gave a *drop dead* grimace.

Shrugging it off, he returned his attention to her. 'I know you, McCain . . .' he started grimly.

'Of course you do. Why else would you come?'

'. . . and there's whispers enough about the dirt on your hands. So listen. We'll not be involved in Satanism, or any of that shit. We're not that desperate.'

'I told you: it's nothing like that. I just need this one opened. There's something in it that I want.'

There was a pause; and then the other man unslung his burden. I realized it was a battered old guitar case, the seams held together with what seemed like half a roll of masking tape. The handle had clearly given out long since; a leather satchel-strap now acted as a sling to lug it round with.

'In case we run into the Old Bill,' the bearded bloke explained, as his companion laid it out, and got it open. Leaning forward, I could understand his point. Two dossers armed with shovels were just bound to get pulled in.

Instinctively I reached into my cloak: feeling first for Nick's carnation – then for the rosary I'd brought along. The black beads rattled faintly as I drew them out and wrapped them round my fingers. The first grave-digger straightened up from selecting his shovel, and gave me a quizzical look.

'Brought her along to bless us, have you?' Still addressing himself to Razoxane, as if I wasn't even there. Because he'd done his deal with her alone, perhaps. It hurt; but made me realize that he had his pride, as well.

'She prays for the dead,' said Razoxane softly. 'I bury them.'

'Yeah?' He might have meant it to sound sarcastic, but the word came out too cautiously for that. Spitting on his palms, he took a purchase on his shovel, digging in without further ado. I watched, and wondered what he thought about her; what he *knew*. It was clear, despite his coolness, that she gave him the creeps.

The other man wiped matted blond dreadlocks off his forehead, and set to work with his own shovel. The rasp of metal scooping soil seemed indecently loud: disturbing the dusk and all those silent, sleeping graves. I winced, and hunched my shoulders: sickly sure that we'd be somehow overheard. Razoxane, unruffled, walked casually round to the far side of the grave: as if to supervise the excavation – but her attention rested mainly on the compass in her palm.

'I don't like this place,' the blond man said; still digging nonetheless. 'Got too many friends down here . . . or somewhere like it . . .'

Somewhere. I remembered how shocked I'd been to learn that some councils buried the unclaimed poor *en masse* now: using JCBs to dig the graves. It was like the Middle Ages. Like the Plague . . .

The hole grew deeper with the dusk. Despite the chill, the grave-diggers were sweating. The bearded man stripped off his jacket, and dumped it at my feet. Glanced fleetingly at me; then got back to it.

It was a funeral in reverse. Just two mourners present at the graveside. I stared nervously downwards: telling my beads like somebody winding wool.

'You a Catholic?' the bearded man enquired, as if in conversation; tipping off a spadeful of soil.

'Yes,' I said.

'Funny place to find a Catholic girl.'

I raised my eyes to Razoxane's grim smile. 'She reckons she has to balance what she does. With good and evil. Equal shares.'

'And you're good, then?'

I shook my head.

'But the best she's got?'

'Maybe . . .' I swallowed. 'And my name's Rachel Young. What's yours?'

He smiled faintly. 'You can call me Finn. It's been a while, since someone's asked to know.' A pause, while he shovelled up more spoil; then he straightened, rubbed his back and turned to me. 'Don't you Catholics pray for "those who travel"?'

'Sometimes, yeah,' I nodded.

'Well pray for us then, Rachel. We never rest.'

'There's something here,' the other digger said.

Nervously I rubbed my mouth as they set about unearthing it. I wasn't sure quite what I'd expected; but the sight of the small, plain box made my stomach muscles tense. They took stillbirths to mortuaries in boxes just that size.

The man called Finn passed it up to Razoxane, who took and turned it carefully in her hands. 'That it, then?' he asked.

'It is.' Slipping it under her arm, she delved under her coat, and came out with a washleather purse – complete with drawstring. The contents chinked dully as she weighed it.

'Throw in the case and one of the spades as well?' she asked, untying it.

'Why not?' Finn said calmly, shrugging back into his jacket. 'They're not ours, after all.'

Razoxane dug deep into the unlaced purse, and came up with a single coin. It glinted in the last of the daylight – as shiny and cold as a piece of the moon.

'Now this,' she said, 'is an English silver shilling. Dated 1648. It shouldn't take you long to find a buyer, and they'll pay a good price. Or else you can keep it. It'll bring you fortune.'

Finn regarded it shrewdly for a moment. 'Good or bad?' he asked.

Razoxane gestured. 'Who can say?'

After a thoughtful pause, the grave-digger reached out and took it. 'We'll see you, then, McCain,' he murmured dryly – and nodded to me. 'Have yourself a peaceful Yule-tide, Rachel Young.'

With the dusk veiling his face, it was difficult to read his expression; but I guessed he meant it seriously enough. I nodded back.

The two of them slipped off into the dark. I stood staring after them; aware that we'd have to take the railings in our turn. The thought of climbing over them in my cloak didn't promise much amusement. Peering back towards the pit, I saw Razoxane put the one remaining shovel in the case, and latch down the lid. Slipping her arm through the strap, she hoisted it up behind her shoulder, and tucked the wooden box under her arm.

'What is it then?' I asked, unwillingly, as she turned towards the trees.

'Wait and see,' she said, not looking back.

I didn't have the heart to ask again.

*

On the train journey back, as I chewed my thoughts over, I realized I'd have to go home.

We'd managed to find seats on the crowded carriage. I was squeezed in beside the window, staring out into the racing dark, with Razoxane beside me. The guitar case and the box rested precariously on the luggage rack above us.

The train was full: one of the last out of London, before the network began winding down. Another few hours, and the lines would be deserted: shrouded in silence and freezing mist. Given over to the ghost-trains until morning.

Don't joke about such things.

I wasn't, either.

Razoxane's head was bowed, and nodding with the motion of the train. Lost in meditation, I assumed. And as for that object she'd retrieved ... I leaned my head back, peering apprehensively at the box; then returned my gaze to the invisible black fields outside the window.

When we got back, I'd have to go *home*.

I had nothing to remind me of Cathy: no physical trace that I could cling to. No photo, plaything, piece of clothing ... When we'd left the flat this morning, like thieves in the dawn, it was as if I'd locked up the whole of my past, and left it behind.

I tried moistening my lips, but the whole of my mouth was dry.

'Razoxane ... ?'

'What?' came her disembodied voice.

'Listen ...' I swallowed. 'I need to go back to the flat. Collect something.'

'It wouldn't be wise,' she murmured.

'I *need* to.'

There was a pause; then she nudged her hat-brim upward with the tips of her fingers, and looked at me askance.

'I thought I'd made it clear. You have to cross your bridge, and burn it. You have to become a stranger and a wanderer on earth – like me. There's no way back, until this thing is finished.'

She cut herself off from my miserable stare by lowering her hat back into place. I just gazed at the ash-grizzled brim for a moment; then turned my face again towards the window.

I kept silent for the rest of the journey; sulked as we walked through the town. The pubs we passed were packed and glowing. Groups of people trailed between them, laughed and shouted, skittered by. A couple even wished me merry Christmas.

We moved through the festivities like spectres, and found our way to quieter streets. By the time I realized where Razoxane was heading, we were almost at the gate. The town's parish church loomed above us, its spire piercing the night. Staring up, I saw the weathervane's glint against the cloudy, windy orange of the sky.

'They open the crypt for the homeless over Christmas,' said Razoxane beside me. 'It's where we'll stay tonight. Any risk of meeting someone you know?'

I shook my head gloomily. 'I doubt it. C of E.'

She adjusted the burden on her back, and made for the welcoming glow of the doorway. But I stayed where I was.

'I need something of Cathy's,' I told her, as she turned her head. 'Something to take with us. *Please?*'

She hesitated: staring down towards the pavement, as if something there had captured her attention. 'What did your Preacher say?' she mused, at length. 'About putting your hand to the plough, and then looking back . . . ?'

Bitch, I thought. 'I'm not going to run out on you again, if that's what you're thinking.'

She tipped her head back, looked at me direct – and shrugged. 'All right. If you've something to fix your thoughts on, it might help us to track her. But be quick, Rachel.'

I felt like she'd released me from a spell. 'Don't worry. You'll be here?'

'Oh yes. Making sure that there's room at the inn.'

Despite the irony in her voice, the words still carried dispiriting weight: enough to take the wind out of my sails. I was a stranger in my own town now – with just a borrowed floor to sleep on. I watched her turn back towards the promise of warmth; then retraced my nervous steps into the night.

I used to get so excited on Christmas Eve.

At first it had just been Magic Night, with presents in the morning. As I grew up, there'd been the afternoon ritual of helping Mum cook Yule Log and mince pies in our steamed-up kitchen. And when I'd been old enough to stay up late, the walk beneath the stars to Midnight Mass had brought a magic of its own.

Tonight, as I hurried towards home, those memories seemed quite lifeless: like cinders in a cold iron grate.

Black Christmas. Burned black.

I passed quite close to the Catholic church, and glimpsed the knots of people converging towards it. There would be warm golden light in the windows, and friendly greetings at the doors. For a moment I so wanted to go with them . . . but knew I couldn't bear to show my face. The thought sank a pit of loneliness inside me.

Pushing on, I came to the corner of our street and went cautiously down it. Not that I expected my neighbours to be out and about at this hour; but Mr Wheeler had promised to keep an eye on the flat, and the sight of a shadowy figure creeping round might tempt him out to investigate. A great one for neighbourhood watch, was Mr Wheeler.

Fumbling for my keys, I kept glancing up in search of Razoxane's familiar; but the flat had a wholly desolate feel about it. Her Vedova was doubtless occupied elsewhere. Searching. Thieving. Digging . . .

The lock turned. I slipped hastily inside, and shut the door behind me.

The flat was thick with sooty darkness; I breathed it in, and almost coughed it out again. The worst thing was, I couldn't switch the light on. Somebody might see, and start to wonder. *Didn't Rachel say she'd be away for Christmas? She and her daughter . . .*

Blind, I stood there listening, with my back against the door; then cautiously groped forward. Gradually my eyesight grew accustomed; curdling the shadows into vague, familiar shapes. Heart pounding, I went into the living room, past the black and spiky outline of the tree, and over to the mantelpiece. There was a small framed snapshot of her there. Darkness masked the image – but I knew it when it came into my hands. Touching the cool glass with my fingertips, I let my mind fill up with the sunshine of the photo, and the beauty of her face. My daughter, smiling back at me: her unseen eyes on mine. Just because I couldn't see her didn't mean she wasn't there.

A warm, wet pulse of tears rose inside me. Tightening my lips, I forced it back.

A solid wooden *thump* drove through the silence.

I jumped as if the shock had been electric: almost dropping the picture; barely stifling a cry. I knew at once that it had come from the kitchen – as if a gust of wind had blown the back door shut. But of course it had been shut to start with. And locked and bolted too.

For a moment I stood paralysed with fright. Then the sound came again, like a fist on the lid of a coffin – and

I went madly through the darkened flat towards it. It was fatalistic instinct: the need to see how much the door was damaged. How much time I had to flee. A minute or a second, I had to *know*.

My throat closed up as I reached the threshold. The gloom was thicker here, at the back of the house, with only the empty field beyond the windows. The silent field, across which something had come: from the darkness of the woods. Swallowing, I peered into the kitchen.

A splintered, crunching noise came at me. I glimpsed a section of the door staved inwards, dislodging glass, and ducked back with a gasp. It took a moment for the detail to make sense. Something long and smooth and flattened, jutting through. With my back to the wall, I heard it roughly wrested free – to strike again. A screech of tortured wood. The lock was coming loose.

Rifle-butt, I thought in horror: *rifle.*

Another sledgehammer stroke; and as I dodged across the doorway, the bolts came popping out and he was through. I heard the creak of broken hinges as the frosty air flowed in. Which meant he'd hear *me* fumbling with the front door-latch; come after me, and catch me. My screams might rouse the street, but far too late. As a boot crushed broken glass, I dived sideways into Cathy's room, slipped round behind the door, and froze myself as stiff as *rigor mortis*.

He came prowling down the passageway a moment later: his progress smooth and stealthy as a cat's. I could picture the sweep of his levelled gun; the glinting eyes above it. Chris. I knew that it was Chris.

The muscles in my neck grew tense and tender as he paused outside the doorway. My skin was as cold as it had been in his icy bath. Squeezed in behind the door, I pressed Cathy's picture tight against my chest, and struggled not to breathe.

His own respiration stirred the silence. The sound was

hoarse and paper-dry: excited but controlled. As if he'd got psyched up for this – to take the witch's trail.

You *bastard.*

The thought struck echoes in my head: he surely must have heard it. I clapped a hand over my mouth, in case it got out that way. But my mind would not be gagged. Backed into a corner, it started venting fright like filth. You bastard, Chris, you lying sod, you shitty shitty BASTARD . . .

His breathing drifted closer. He looked in.

My fingertips dug deep into my cheek. The air in my lungs had grown stale and scorching – but I had to hold it in, or else he'd hear me. I tried shutting my eyes, just to seal myself off; and found I didn't have the nerve. So it was with a fixed and frantic stare that I suddenly noticed what lay on the carpet, in the midst of Cathy's toys.

The ghostly background light just tinged the details. There, between a picture-book and her beloved panda, I saw an ivory cube on a matchstalk stem; like a spinning-top of sorts.

She was playing with her new little top – so Alice had sobbed. In the chill of the moment, the words had passed me by. But now, as I stared at this unfamiliar thing – and the indistinct black marks upon its faces – I felt a slow collapse begin inside me.

I've found a new toy to play with, Mummy . . . That's what Cathy had said – and I'd shooed her off. Not stopping to wonder. Not wanting to know.

As recognition dawned, the sense of crumbling collapse became a sickening plunge. Cold sweat sprang up across my forehead. I almost wailed into my hand.

I knew that thing, all right: but not because I'd bought it. It came from Razoxane's cold fingers. The ace of spades on every side, like the Devil's loaded die. Her Spinner of Swords.

Chris's wary breaths drew tight, and stopped.

Acutely aware though I was of his presence, just the other side of the door, I couldn't take my eyes off the top. The sign of Swords denoted air in Tarot, so Razoxane had told me; and ill-luck too. No wonder she'd used that spinner to summon demons of the wind.

And somehow it had found its way to Cathy. A pocket ouija board, and she'd been playing *games* with it. I very nearly shuddered in despair. *Keep matches away from children*, sure; but this was a million times worse.

What if she'd called up the Ragman herself?

As the thought swelled in my head, Chris crossed the threshold and moved slowly into view. He was wearing that big, all-weather riding coat: it draped him to the shins. The metal of his rifle glinted dully in the gloom.

He'd seen the spinner too. As I watched, wide-eyed, he stooped to pick it up: turning it curiously by its stalk. He'd found a trace, and clearly guessed as much. A device of wind and witchcraft.

Had Razoxane just left it for my little girl to find? Was she the one who'd set all this in motion? *You bitch*, I thought, with furious fear. *You lying bitch, I'll kill you.*

Chris slipped the thing into his pocket, and quietly withdrew. I listened, sweating, as he moved on through the flat. Cautious though his progress was, he seemed to think the place was empty. Somehow I doubted he'd been home again: so as far as he still knew, I was out of the game. Lying drowned at the bottom of his bath.

He'd come here to root for clues, then. Perhaps midnight on Christmas Eve felt like protected time to him. And he'd be finished soon enough, and gone again. All I had to do was wait and listen. But as the sounds of his random search grew rougher, I felt panic rise and take me by the throat. I managed to keep still until I was sure of his location – in my bedroom, pulling off the sheets – then made a break for safety. Out into the passage and back towards the kitchen, heading blindly for the creaking broken door.

I barged into a chair and knocked it sideways. The sound was an explosion in my ears. At once I felt the atmosphere change: the air becoming tense and charged behind me. And then I heard him coming.

With a whimper of fright I started to run. The familiar interior was suddenly an obstacle course, through which I stumbled and rebounded; but the scent of chilled night air led me back to the kitchen. I squirmed through the gap between sagging door and splintered jamb, and bolted for the sheltering darkness.

The back field opened out around me: a vast, dark space beneath the muddy sky. I could only take my bearings from the lights in other houses; the rest of the horizon was a blur. I felt as if I'd fled into a limitless void. Glancing hastily back, my breathing painful, I saw a shadow emerge from my unlit flat and start across the field in swift pursuit.

Panting, I pushed onward; increasingly hampered by the weight of my cloak. At least it helped me merge into the gloom – but still his eyes were keen enough to spot me. The crack of a gunshot echoed round the field. I felt the bullet zipping pass my ear, like a venomous night insect. I ducked and stumbled, nearly going full-length; my cloak flared out around me. Chris was closing the distance, firing steadily as he came. A series of thuds and rustles stitched the ground; I felt cold soil fleck my face. The flash of his gun licked outward like a live thing, lightning-white.

The invisible wood was suddenly before me: congealing in a grim and ghostly wall. The sight almost stopped me short, despite the hunter at my heels. The dark of the field was unnerving enough – but it was black between the trunks, and deathly silent. The hooked and spindly branches turned each tree into a mantis, poised to spring.

With a raw gasp of despair, I ran between them – fleeing blind into the murk. Something solid blocked my way and bounced me off it; I reeled to get my balance. Chris – I saw – had paused, just short of the edge of the wood. Waiting for me to tread on a twig, and give myself away. I cringed behind a tree-trunk: irrationally afraid that he'd hear my slogging heart, and zero in. There was a pause of many seconds – until I could bear to wait no longer. Muffling myself in my cloak, I peeped cautiously out. His faceless figure hadn't stirred.

He was just resuming his advance when I heard the siren. It came from the far side of the field: wailing up from the centre of town. Another moment and I glimpsed the lights, flashing bright electric blue between the houses.

Chris looked back over his shoulder – then turned his face once more towards the wood.

'Rachel,' he called softly, as if expecting me to answer. 'Listen to me, you stupid, *stupid* girl . . . You should have let the water have you – let it wash your sin away . . . Don't you realize? I'll have to *burn* you now.'

The police car's engine was audible now; the headlights swept a corner of the field as it turned into our road. The fleeting glare behind him made a halo round his head, and threw his figure into black relief.

'Remember that,' he hissed, as the gloom came down again. 'I'm going to have to track you down and *burn you*.'

And with that he took off, loping past me down the edge of the field: a grey, elusive ghost. I breathed a shuddering sigh against my hand as he melted back into the night.

A pounding pause. Then I slid my palm on upwards, across my clammy face: wiping damp hair off my forehead. Cathy's picture was still gripped tight in my other hand.

The cops would have been called to the break-in; but

they'd hear about the shooting soon enough. Someone seen running away, across the field. Before very long there'd be armed police combing this neck of the woods. Loath as I was to start moving, I hadn't any choice.

He's gone now, though. He's gone.

But even if he had, he'd still be out there. Waiting for another chance to catch me alone. To drag me off into the darkness.

To soak me in petrol and set me alight.

A rush of nausea almost made me heave. I sagged against the tree's black trunk, head swimming, and took some cautious sips of air.

The sickness gurgled back into my belly. The fresh air made me feel a little better. But it was a while before I had the strength to creep away.

*

I dug the toe of my boot into Razoxane's ribs. She didn't stir.

Ignoring the comings and goings behind me in the crypt, I tightened my mouth and tried again: using my heel this time – treading down onto her collarbone. But she stayed inert and slumped against the wall, her hat pulled down over her face.

'Don't try and kid me you're asleep,' I hissed. 'You don't *need* sleep – remember?'

Still no response. I pawed at her coat with my ankle-boot, smearing off some of the mud, and squatted down beside her. 'Or are we *meditating* again . . . ?'

As I bent close and grasped her collar, her hand came striking up. A vicious rasp of metal made me jump – and then freeze solid. The switchblade she carried had sprung open like the tongue of a snake. The point was poised to puncture my left eye.

As I crouched there, open-mouthed, she slowly tipped her head back, revealing her cold blue gaze.

'I could, if you'd shut up,' she said flatly.

I eased back, swallowing; she folded the bright blade back into its place. No one else seemed to have noticed.

There was a wrinkled old sleeping bag laid out beside her, with a pair of folded blankets on top. I guessed she'd saved them for me, and wearily sat down, drawing my cloak around my knees. A couple of fan-heaters were humming industriously from the corners, but the place was still unpleasantly cold.

I rested my head against the wall behind me – and realized how hungry I was. Now that the fright of the chase had subsided, my hollow stomach was taking the opportunity to make its presence felt. I'd been too keyed-up to eat anything at lunchtime. And if there'd been a bowl of soup on offer tonight, I'd clearly missed it.

'Chris was at the house,' I said. 'He almost caught me.'

'I told you not to go back,' was her matter-of-fact response.

'He found your spinner-thing. He's got it.'

Her head came round. I met her stare with mine.

'So what the bloody hell was it doing there, then?'

Razoxane glanced down. 'I knew I'd lost it, somewhere round your way. But it creates its own blind spot. I didn't know where.'

'You're always bloody losing it.'

She shrugged. 'It has a knack of finding its way into other hands. That's one of the reasons it's lasted so long . . . and travelled so far.'

'Cathy's been *playing* with the thing.' Suddenly I had to grit my teeth to keep my fierce, frightened voice down.

'It won't have harmed her.'

'It bloody well summoned *something* up.'

Pensively she shook her head. 'I don't think they came in response to that.'

'Why, then?'

'I'm piecing it together. Get some sleep.'

In this draughty room; on this hard floor. With this cold watcher at my side. Making myself comfortable seemed a waste of time. But I did my best – shrugging out of my cloak, and pulling it across me like a quilt. I huddled up beneath it and the blankets, and turned onto my side: away from Razoxane. But after a minute or two listening to the restless silence, I had to twist around again and ask.

'Can he use it to find us? The spinner, I mean.'

'Probably not,' she said.

'Only probably?'

'Not many people know its secrets; I doubt if he does. But then again . . . do we really know who *he* is?'

A lot more than he bloody seemed: I'd learned that much already. I rolled over, to stare miserably into the shadows.

No hope of pleasant dreams with her beside me: and sure enough, they weren't. Maybe she was dreaming too, behind her black glass stare – infecting me with nightmares. Yet the things that crossed my mind that night were more like memories than visions.

I slept shallowly at first, still half-aware of my surroundings – until a deeper current sucked me down. For a long while after that, there was just darkness. Then a sense of sluggish motion, like a river of silt. I heard the scrape of boots on stone and brick. Dozens of boots . . . no, scores. No; hundreds . . .

My mind's eye opened wide.

Daylight; open air. There were burnt-out buildings to left and right. Some were still wreathed in smoke; the afternoon was veiled with dust and ashes. The road my dream-self walked was clogged with people: a ragged, shuffling stream, like refugees. A farm cart just ahead was piled high with worldly goods. And Razoxane was walking at my side.

I didn't recognize her for a moment. Her face was gaunt, her cropped hair scrappy. In place of her shades, she wore dark-lensed goggles; there was an army surplus look about her overcoat and cap. The last was dirty grey, its peak pushed up: like German army issue in the Second World War.

A haversack was slung over her shoulder, dragged down by something heavy. From the weary way she plodded, she might have lugged the thing for days.

There were soldiers at the roadside to watch us go by. Their scuffed, autumnal jackets could have come from any war; but the ugly steel helmets helped me place them. One wore a cap like Razoxane's – emblazoned with a grinning silver skull.

He was the one who stepped suddenly towards us. Spectre though I was, I cringed away. But it was Razoxane he wanted. Grasping her coat, he hauled her out of the line. She stumbled, not resisting. I felt myself drawn in her wake.

I have seen you before, the soldier said: in German, but my mind knew every word.

Razoxane stared back at him, impassive. She didn't even flinch when he tugged off her army cap and tossed it aside; then gazed full into her face. The two blokes with him moved up to look as well.

What's in the rucksack, then? the man went on. My attention was held by his cap-badge; the skull's leering grin looked as if it had been crushed into place.

Razoxane unslung the bag in silence; one of the soldiers snatched it from her grasp. Unfastening the straps, he emptied the contents at her feet. An armful of books hit the stony ground – spines creaking, pages flapping.

As I watched, aloof and invisible, the first man picked one up. Even fifty years into the past, it had an antiquarian look. He opened it at random; then smiled grimly, and raised his gun-metallic eyes.

A book of Jewish writings?

A book of wisdom, said Razoxane softly.

Just paper: like the rest of their past, the soldier said, still smiling. *So easy to burn . . .*

The look on her calm face was almost pitying. *They've four thousand years of history behind them. Be careful, brother: don't step back. You'd fall forever.*

His smile faded. *You are a Jewess, too?*

Razoxane shook her head – and smiled in turn. *Before Abraham was, I* walked.

The soldier struck her hard across the face – wiping the smile clean off. His comrades caught and held her as she staggered back.

This sow needs a lesson in respect. Come on.

They dragged her down an alleyway between two gutted buildings. Helplessly I followed. We came to a courtyard, strewn with rubble. The man with the death's head badge slapped Razoxane again – then punched her in the stomach. Pain twisted her face, but she didn't make a sound.

Why the goggles, bitch? Snatching at the strap, he wrested them off – exposing her eyes to the light. With a hiss of breath, she squeezed her eyelids shut.

A chorus of voices then, all three of them together. *Look, she can't stand the sunlight . . . Nosferatu's fucking daughter . . . Force them open . . . Cut her eyelids off . . .* With both eyes shut, she struggled, but she couldn't hold them back. Her lead tormentor moved in close. Gripping her face, he thumbed her sockets and forced the eyelids up.

Only blobs of glistening whiteness lay behind them.

A cold thrill of revulsion rippled through me, even as

I realized that she'd rolled her eyeballs up into her head. The soldier himself seemed suddenly unnerved – confronted with her blind, unblinking stare.

The shot broke up the tableau like a bomb. The back of the first man's coat blew outward, spattering blood. He staggered clear of Razoxane, revealing the drawn pistol in her hand. His comrades took a whole second to react, and she just squirmed out of their grip – then pivoted to shoot the second, while the first man was still falling. The third soldier backpedalled, seeking room to bring his carbine round to bear. Her blind head turned towards him, along with her gun. Her bullets smashed his chest, and then his face.

The first man lay and gurgled on the ground: doubled up around the pain in his belly. The second was also clinging to life, and trying to crawl away. Razoxane turned again; her awful, corpse-white eyeballs came unerringly to bear. She pointed the pistol almost delicately. Three pulpy holes exploded in the stricken soldier's back.

I gawped at the gun. It was the primitive self-loader that she'd carried since I'd known her. Lowering it to her side, she began to cast around for her goggles, searching for where they'd been dropped.

The surviving soldier yelled – then clenched his teeth.

Razoxane kept walking, like a malevolent blind beggar. Some instinct seemed to lead her to the goggles. She kicked them; hunkered down, and pulled them on and into place.

When she turned back towards her gasping victim, her white stare had reverted to implacable black – and she was grinning.

Slowly she walked over, scuffing bits of shattered brick out of her path, until she was standing right beside him. The pistol angled down towards his head. She flexed her grubby fingers round the grip.

And then she turned her gloating gaze on *me*.

'Shall I or shan't I?'

I stared at her, gobsmacked: punched in the mouth. This was *her* past. I had no business here.

'Shall I kill him, or let him live?' she asked me calmly.

I realized there was no point in pretending I wasn't there. She'd somehow sucked me in to share her flashback. What had started out as memory was suddenly in flux.

'Nothing . . . to do with me,' I offered lamely.

She shook her head. 'It is. It's your decision.'

Feeling horribly trapped, I glanced down at the man on the ground. Below the heaving of his chest, the front of his coat was sodden with blood. I could actually see the scorch-marks, the shot had been so close . . .

'Real time, Rachel,' she persisted.

'God . . .' I said, and groped for an answer. The options met like mill-stones: grinding together in my guts. My instinct recoiled from causing somebody's death; but this man served an *evil* cause. The Devil's cause. I knew what the death's head cap-badge meant . . .

'Well?' Razoxane demanded.

'No, listen . . .'

'No time. He's an SS killer. What's your verdict?'

I stared at her. I'd seen the documentaries – and wept at them. I knew what they had done, all right – to men, women, children, *babies* . . .

'It's really not so hard, when you consider it,' she murmured. 'He's a Nazi, after all . . .' She looked back down the barrel of the gun.

'No,' I blurted.

'No?'

'Leave him . . .'

'Why?'

'I haven't got the *right*.'

Her smile grew tight and taunting. 'He doesn't deserve to live. He's scum. Why save him?'

'Because that's just the way *they* think.'

As I spoke the words, the vision fell apart and left me gasping on the floor: as wide-awake as if someone had just doused me with cold water. The crypt was still: a sink of breathing dimness.

The lowest point of Christmas night – still hours before the morning. Not even the keenest kids would be out of bed yet. I could almost sense the silence of the town outside: its labyrinth of dark and empty streets.

Razoxane was tugging at my shoulder. Squirming round, I found her staring at the compass in her hand. A glint of satisfaction tinged the shadow of her face.

'I think I've got a trace of them,' she said.

8

VOICES

'Rachel . . . ?'

I stared at my porridge as hard as I could, and hoped that he would maybe go away. No chance of that, of course; so after a moment, like a guilty teenager, I slowly raised my head.

It was Graham, all right: his friendly face a study of concern. I knew him from work, just as he knew me. He often visited St Catherine's on business. His dog-collar said he was here on business now.

Oh fuck, I thought – and offered a weak smile.

'Rachel,' he said again: a different kind of question in his tone. I could see him trying to think his way around it: looking for answers other than the obvious. He didn't find them, though. He came up to the table, almost cautious.

I sat there, spoon still poised, and stared at him.

'What's happened?' he asked, voice lowered.

'Um . . .' I let my gaze flick past sideways: deliberately distracted. People were still queuing for their Christmas breakfast. The hall was full and noisy . . . When I looked back at Graham, I still hadn't thought of anything to say.

He pulled up an empty chair and sat down across from me: searching my face. I couldn't have expected any less of him. We got on well together.

'Hi,' I said, belatedly – and glanced over his shoulder.

But this time I'd been genuinely distracted. This time I had reason to feel guilt.

'Rachel, listen,' he murmured, leaning forward: winning my spooked attention back. 'Please say so if I'm talking out of turn . . . but why aren't you at home?'

I swallowed with a dry, stiff throat. 'I'm all right, Graham. It's all in hand. Just . . . let me work things out.'

'Don't tell me you've nowhere to go?'

I gestured helplessly. Thank God he didn't know I had a daughter.

'We've got a spare room: you're welcome to use it. Come back with me after the service, Rachel. I promise we won't ask questions . . .'

'It's really nice of you to offer . . .'

'I mean it: seriously.'

'I'll think about it,' I said – my noncommittal way of saying no. He guessed as much, and sat back with a sigh.

'All right, then. But please, give us a ring if you change your mind. Here . . .' He wrote his phone number down on a sheet torn from his organizer, and handed it across. 'Take care, Rachel. I'll see you later.'

I watched as he made his way across the crowded room; then pushed my spoon back down into the porridge, and stirred the stuff dejectedly around.

Razoxane slid into the seat he'd just vacated. Her smile was sly; enquiring. 'Friend of yours?'

I glanced towards the door, making sure he was gone; then fixed my gaze on her. With her hat slung carelessly behind her neck, her short-cropped hair and scruffy clothes marked her down as a travelling type. No one here would pay her much attention. My nursing cloak looked much more out of place.

'The curate,' I said. 'I know him from St Catherine's.'

She digested that in silence, watching me.

'Why haven't we got *moving*?' I insisted.

Razoxane had her elbows on the table, her gloved

hands interlocked. The naked trigger fingers resting steepled on her lips. She tilted them towards me, smiling grimly.

'I got the faintest trace last night: like seeing someone blink. Nothing else stirred before daybreak. Hard to place it . . . but I'd guess at woodland to the north.'

I took another spoonful of porridge, and swallowed with an effort. It was a mechanical operation, like refuelling. Taste didn't matter; just warmth and weight. The church hall buzzed and bustled in my ears.

'So . . . they're still there, then?'

'Some of them, at least. I don't know if they've split their force.'

'And . . . Cathy?'

She shook her head. 'No trace. But that doesn't mean she's not still with them.'

'So what're we going to do?' I mumbled.

'Well . . . once you've finished your breakfast . . . I think we'd better go and look.'

I stirred the sticky remnants of my porridge.

'How well do you know the countryside round here?' she asked.

'Hardly at all.'

'Farmland, for the most part. Some woods and copses. Country lanes. It hasn't changed much, these past few hundred years. You could map it from an Anglo-Saxon charter . . .' She grinned at my enquiring frown. 'Oh, yes: I've been here before. I was born . . . *re*born, I should say . . . just a dozen miles from here.'

'And this was . . . in sixteen hundred and whatever.'

'And whatever; I forget.'

Trust me to come and live *here*, of all places. As if I'd sensed her roots – and let them draw me. Like that weird fellow-feeling that you sometimes get with twins.

Discomfited, I shook the image off.

'Local history your strong point?'

I shook my head.

'No matter. I doubt you'd find this rumour in a book. It's probably died out by now . . . but it was connected to Lickfield Wood, just east of what was then the village. I remember hearing a fragment when I was very young: some veiled account of burnings and hasty burials, in the years after the Civil War. The place still had an evil reputation a hundred years later, when I passed this way again. Now I'd imagine it's just a neat piece of green on the parish map. Not even the name would give you pause.'

'And . . . should it?'

'*Lych-field* was the older form: the field of corpses. A burial place. Connotations of plague.'

Oh, wonderful, I thought. 'But what about this rumour, then? You think it's a clue?'

'It's possible, yes. I don't know how exactly. But there's a man who might.'

'Who?'

'An acquaintance. We'll visit him tonight. In the meantime, we can scout around . . . and see what we can find.'

We left the hall, and walked round to the church door. I expected a return to the crypt, to fetch her things; she'd doubtless put some spell on them, to keep them safe. But instead she went on through into the body of the church, and sat in one of the back pews.

Puzzled, I took a seat beside her. The place was all set for Christmas morning service; tree and crib and candles in their places. Yet its silence now was curiously unsettling. In less than an hour it would be filled with families, and old familiar carols. But until the people came, and gave it life, it was just an empty building: dim and draughty.

Razoxane reached under the pew in front, as if feeling

for a hassock – and retrieved the box we'd recently dug up. I gave it a distasteful glance, and almost slid away along the pew.

'What's it doing *there*?'

'I put it there. Last night, while the supplicants were otherwise engaged. I had to let it cool: in a psychic sense . . .' She picked it up, and placed it on her lap. Studied the dirty lid for a moment; then carefully prised it open.

Even as I felt my skin turn prickly-cold, I couldn't stop myself from looking. I'd already half-convinced myself the thing was full of body-parts – or bones.

And I'd been right, I realized numbly; but not in quite the way I'd feared.

The stripped, dissected object revealed by the lid was in pieces of metal and wood: interlocked with all the neatness of a jigsaw. It took me a moment to get them sorted out. But then I saw a trigger, with an ornate guard around it, and knew that I was looking at a gun.

Razoxane glanced casually over her shoulder, and lifted out the stock. Nervously I checked behind us too. There was no one here to see.

The wood was stained and weathered: she ran her naked fingers down its length. The breach-lock was black iron, as ugly as the beak of her familiar. She cupped her palm around it; eased it back. It clicked.

'This is a *church*,' I hissed at her – still staring.

'So was this thing, once,' she answered dryly.

That threw me; I just frowned.

'A long time ago,' she went on, leaning back. 'A church that was destroyed. But someone raised this engine from the ashes.

'They used wood from a broken pew to make the stock. The barrels were cast from cut-down organ pipes . . .' She lifted these out – half a dozen in a cluster – and locked the central axle into place. A thumbscrew tightened here, a fixing there – and suddenly, once more, it was a weapon. An evil, mechanical sawn-off shotgun.

I gawped at it. *Oh, God.*

With a sidelong little smile, she retrieved a handle like an Allen key, and fitted it to a socket above the trigger. Bracing the butt against her thigh, she gave it a couple of turns – like the windlass of a medieval crossbow. The cluster of barrels rotated in sync.

'A little stiff,' she murmured; 'but I reckon it still works.'

'How long has it been buried, then?'

She gestured with her lowered head. 'Who knows? Arcane weaponry like this was custom-made – and utterly suppressed. You can count the surviving examples on the fingers of one hand. They're put away in secret places: available to those with the need and the knowledge. Like the Tinderbox, remember?'

I remembered right enough. The first time she'd retrieved it, the thing had been hidden up the chimney of a derelict house. She'd ditched it at the end of her mission – and an unknown hand had hidden it again.

'Like the Tinderbox, it uses ash for powder. Sanctified ash this time, though – so there's a limited supply . . .' Cradling the gun, she lifted a flask from inside the box and weighed it in her hand. The thing was made of stiff, cracked leather; its oddly-funnelled metal cap giving it the shape of an oast-house. I caught a glimpse of what looked like rosary beds, coiled up – then realized they were balls of shot, strung together on a thread.

'. . . and lead from the old church roof was melted down for shot. It fires nothing else.'

'Got a name, has it?' I mumbled.

Razoxane smiled faintly. 'In Germany, where it was made, I hear that it was nicknamed *Todesorgel*. The Death Organ. But by other accounts, it's simply the *Machina Maleficarum*.'

'And what does that mean?' I had to ask, when no further translation was forthcoming.

'The Witches' Machine,' she murmured; and allowed herself a grave-digger's grin.

My stomach soured. I looked away. After a minute I bowed my head, and interlocked my hands against my mouth. Trying to shape a prayer. But nothing came.

*

The afternoon was overcast and still. Past the southern edge of town, the countryside spread out towards the skyline: a drab expanse of undulating fields. Naked trees stood singly or in clumps, with denser woodland looming in the distance.

'Something's been this way,' said Razoxane slowly: staring down at her compass. 'But they've covered their tracks with care . . .'

It didn't feel at all like Christmas Day. Glancing back towards the nearest houses, I saw the glow of their living-room windows: pale yellow squares in the dishwater daylight. People would be slumped in front of TV sets, replete and sleepy. Not interested in us. Not dreaming what might have passed them by, while their windows were still dark . . .

The sound of a growling engine made me turn – to see a Landrover come jouncing up the track. At last, a sign of life in this dreary landscape; but it came as no relief. Watching it close the distance, bearing down on us both, my sense of isolation was suddenly redoubled.

'We're not trespassing, are we?' I asked, glancing back.

Razoxane closed the compass between fingers and thumb. 'Depends on your point of view,' she said.

The Landrover came squeaking to a stop; the driver clambered out at once. He was in his thirties, with a strong face and unruly hair. His green waxed jacket hung unfastened over sweater and jeans. His expression was bleakly hostile.

'Piss off out of it,' he said.

I blinked at him – then bridled. 'Sorry, did I miss something then?'

'Go on, get off my land. I've had it up to here with you lot.'

'Which lot?' Razoxane asked mildly, coming up.

The farmer breathed out through his teeth. 'I'm not going to bandy words with sodding hippies. If you're not out of here in five minutes flat, all right, I'm going back to fetch the dogs . . .'

Razoxane's switchblade sprouted from her grasp: all six malicious inches of it. She raised it almost casually; both he and I could only stare as it moved towards his face. Abruptly the point was picking his nose: he gave a snort of scared surprise, and tried to flinch away – but the bulk of his own vehicle blocked him. Wide-eyed, he tried to focus on the knife that teased his nostril: bending back across the bonnet in his effort to escape.

'Wrong answer, peasant,' said Razoxane softly. 'Try again.'

The farmer gasped for breath: his previous healthy colour had turned leaden. I bit back a cry of my own – part shock, part protest – and found my knuckle wedged between my teeth.

Razoxane kept him teetering at arm's length. The hint of a smile hooked the corner of her tight-lipped mouth. 'So who else has been wandering on your land?' she asked.

'Dunno . . .'

'Why object to us two passing through, then?'

'Please . . . I've got a wife and kid . . .'

'Do you want to see them again, or not?'

'Oh, God . . . Someone's been creeping around at night.

Frightening my animals. They tried to get into the stables: almost sent the horses mad . . .'

'See anything?'

'Nothing, only . . . tracks in the mud next day. Three of the bastards, last time. The police've been up, but what can they do, there's horses gone from two farms already, and one been ripped . . .' I saw a spasm of panic close his throat. 'I'll not tell them about *you*, I swear to God . . .'

He would, of course: as soon as he got home. Instinct urged a hasty retreat – the coward's way of pleading innocence. But I knew I couldn't turn my back on this.

'What else?' asked Razoxane, lifting her chin enquiringly; her blade as well.

He tipped his head back further; I wondered dimly if the knife under his nose was going to make him sneeze. 'There've been . . . travelling types around. I thought . . . they'd be camped out somewhere. I looked around. One copse, the dogs just wouldn't go into. Refused point-blank. There was . . . this weird silence over it. No birds singing. Not even crows. So I knew there was somebody in there.'

'And you went in after them?'

Carefully – very carefully – he shook his head. 'Not on my own. No way. They'd probably have jumped me . . .'

It was a reasonable reaction; yet even through the mask of his present fear, I sensed a deeper-felt unease that had kept him out.

And maybe saved his life.

'Which copse?' Razoxane breathed.

'The one . . . by Furze Barrow.'

'When?'

'Tuesday, afternoon. I went back yesterday with a couple of the lads, but they'd gone. The dogs went in, no trouble . . . we didn't find any trace. Not even a campfire . . .'

'Anything else you've seen?'

'No, just . . .' He hesitated.

'Yes?'

'Just that . . . my little lad called to me to say that the scarecrow from the high field was walking. Yesterday evening, dusk. He was watching from the top of the house. But when I went upstairs to look . . . it was out there on its post as always. Of course,' he added shakily.

'Of course,' Razoxane agreed – and withdrew the knife: so suddenly that the farmer lost his tiptoe balance and slid down into the mud.

'I'd get back to the bosom of your family, if I were you,' she told him. 'And forget our faces. Or I'll take yours clean off.'

Dismissively she turned away, and continued up the track. With a winded feeling in my chest, I followed. There was silence from behind us for a minute; then a scuff and squelch as he struggled up. The door of the Landrover slammed. He fired the ignition several times before he got the engine started. I didn't look back.

'Enjoy that, did you?' I muttered, as we breasted the hill.

'A diversion,' she allowed.

'Haven't you killed enough people yet?'

Razoxane smiled grimly. 'What makes you think I've got a choice?'

'He's bound to call the cops, you know.'

'That doesn't matter. We just need a little more time.' She paused to survey the fields around us, then looked at me again. 'They're cunning ones, these shadows – and they know this countryside. But so do I. There's a watchman they might just have overlooked.'

'There was always a scarecrow on Northolt Hill,' she said.

The stubble-field rose up towards the skyline: its gradient steep enough to make my weary ankles ache. The scarecrow stood its ground and watched us come.

From this low angle, it seemed to loom above us: in gaunt silhouette against the thickening sky. The breeze stirred the tails of its tatty old coat, and tugged at the brim of its hat. The closer we got, the slower my pace became – and not just because of the slope and crumbly soil. There was something palpably ominous about that solitary shape. Negative connotations crowded in. A hill-top gibbet, from some half-forgotten film. A man impaled, and left to decompose. A crucifixion . . .

I thought of that statue of Jesus, on the mountain above Rio de Janeiro: arms stretched wide in welcome to the world. Here on this windswept hill, a rag-and-bone parody mimicked the pose. Calling us up to be with it for ever . . .

The impression stopped me dead in my tracks.

Razoxane turned her head; still walking. 'Come on. There's nothing to be scared of.'

Wasn't there? I drew my cloak still tighter round my shoulders – and cast a wary glance towards the wood on our right. It was crammed along the far edge of the field: its upper layers stripped by wind and winter, but the trunks beneath still husbanding the gloom. Whatever the farmer's son had seen, it must have emerged from there – and gone back in.

The Ragman was here.

There were maybe fifty yards of open ground between us and the treeline. If something broke cover right now and ran towards us, that was all the leeway we would get. The sense of exposure was unnerving. I squinted my eyes towards the wood – but the only stirrings I saw were caused by the fitful wind. Scrappy branches wavered in the breeze, leaving tatters and holes in the slow grey sky beyond them; giving glimpses of gunmetal blue.

Razoxane had reached the scarecrow, and was waiting

for me to catch up. I let my gaze swing round to check behind me – the other fields we'd crossed were still deserted – then trudged reluctantly up to join her.

Closer to, I saw that the figure had a face on its cloth-wrapped head. Worn though it was by years of weather, I could still make out the features. An empty, stitched-up smile – and two void eyes.

The silence of the field was no surprise; not with this thing at its centre. The gloom of its presence pervaded the air, as insidious as bad body odour. No wonder it scared the crows off; and more than crows, perhaps.

From the corner of my eye, I glimpsed a white shape winging towards us: moving against the backdrop of bruised clouds, like a snowflake on slate. For a moment I just thought it was a seagull – or even a dove. But then it was close enough for me to see its shaggy-feathered outline, and the splay-tipped wings it spread to settle down; and the beak that split into a cry as it landed, like an insult, on the scarecrow's leering head.

I stared up in distaste as it peered around from its perch. The creature's pristine whiteness was unsettlingly bizarre. Not just for its albino weirdness, but for the way it turned impressions upside-down. The purity was only plumage-deep; the heart still black and cunning.

Razoxane acknowledged its arrival with a lazy grin – and then walked slowly round the scarecrow; like an officer inspecting a soldier on parade. I waited sullenly, feeling the breeze stir my cloak. We were high up here, with a view over the countryside around. Behind me, the town spilled out across the middle distance. Lights glowed amid its grey roofs, like a fallen constellation.

'I remember . . .' said Razoxane thoughtfully, 'the crow-scarer that stood here in the 1660s. It didn't look so different. And it stood in just the same place.'

I'd long since ceased to doubt the truth of it: but the fact of her longevity was still difficult to cope with. What

I'd read of in history books, she'd seen with her eyes. Sometimes I thought I'd strain my mind – trying to grasp the distance hers had spanned.

'A century or so ago, the figure had changed; but not its position. In medieval times there would probably have been another on this spot. There's more than just tradition working here . . .'

The rook made a death-rattle sound.

'You're right, Vedova,' said Razoxane, preoccupied. 'There's something about this field . . . there really is.'

I shivered, and looked towards the wood again.

'And I suppose I've always sensed it. But . . .' She paused, then turned to face the scarecrow. 'Who knows what might have happened here, and been forgotten?'

The solemn way she said it made me wonder for myself. Unpleasant possibilities came to mind: like ancient rituals of sacrifice. Perhaps such things could stain the earth for ever. Or maybe this had been a different field of blood. A place where the bodies were buried . . . I'd been scuffing the soil with the toe of my boot, but that thought made me stop.

The scarecrow stood between us like a silent witness. 'So why don't you ask *him*, then?' I muttered.

'I'm going to,' she said.

I frowned at her, not following.

'The things we're after are using chaff, to screen their movements from mindsight . . . but they haven't thought of this. A watcher on the heights that sees everything that moves below it. Whatever's in this ground, it may have transpired into a thing that's rooted in it. So it's possible this figure will have registered their passing.'

I looked from her to the stained cloth face. Just an old sack, stuffed with straw . . . surely. The eyes just empty holes. They stared over my shoulder, towards town. But of course a scarecrow couldn't see; still less remember.

I took an instinctive step backwards then – to be clear of its wide-stretched arms.

'The farmer said his son saw something moving around here,' said Razoxane amiably. 'So let's see what.'

She went and stood behind the figure, resting her hands on its bony shoulders: the frame on which the ragged coat hung loose. She stood there for a moment, in meditative pose – then raised her head.

'Piss off, Vedova – you're blocking my concentration.'

The bird obediently fluttered down, to scratch at the soil a dozen yards away. Perhaps it was hoping to turn some bones up. I felt my lips purse tighter at the thought.

Razoxane dipped her head in close to the rag-bag, as if to nuzzle it. Stepping back another yard, repulsed, I had the grotesque impression of *two* scarecrows, consorting; the one being seduced by the other.

I saw her lips move; heard her whisper sour nothings in its ear. Perhaps her eyes were closed now, but her shades were round and staring – as unblinking as the eyes of her double.

Around us there was silence, apart from the scrunch and rustle of the wind. Like crepitations through a stethoscope: the sound of a sick man's lungs.

Abruptly Razoxane raised her face. 'I see them now,' she said.

I swung around – but the farmland was deserted. Looking back at Razoxane, I saw the twisted smile around her mouth.

'It's dark,' she went on softly. 'But I can just make out . . . their shapes. They're moving.' She peered past me like a blind woman. 'Crossing the field, down there . . .'

I felt adrenaline rush through me. 'What, now?'

Marginally she moved her head: the smallest shake. Her smile and eyeless stare stayed fixed. 'These are after-images; hours old. Or days, perhaps. But they've been this way all right.'

Chewing my lip, I surveyed the empty field: imagining what had crossed it under cover of darkness. Half-expecting to see traces in the dirt. The light had turned foul since lunchtime, and the air was getting raw. From the look of the clouds across the valley, there might well be snow on the way: too late for Christmas, but catching up.

Razoxane broke contact with a grunt, and straightened up. I turned, to see her squeeze the scarecrow's shoulder – as if taking leave of a friend. Then she looked at me.

'I counted eleven of them,' she said.

I took a breath. 'And Cathy?'

'One of the shapes was binary . . . a lesser one cocooned within it. I imagine she's being carried.'

'She's alive, though, isn't she?' I scarcely dared to frame it as a question.

'Yes. Not conscious . . . but alive.'

My shoulders sagged. 'How long ago was this?'

'I'd wager on last night. One of them was scouting ahead – probably the one the boy saw. The rest were in single file, with the drag bringing up the rear. And there was one ranging out on the flank. Covering dead ground.'

'So . . . what are they?'

She shrugged. 'When I said after-images, that's as clearly as I could make them out: just moving blobs of light. Except that this time the light was black.'

Darkness visible, I thought.

'Four of them, I think, are mounted; the rest on foot. They were headed in that direction . . .' She pointed westward. There was more woodland over there, immersed in low visibility. 'They may have gone to ground; there's a disused railway tunnel down that way.'

'It's been bricked up, though . . .' I pointed out, dry-mouthed. Having passed it on a walk with Cathy once,

I knew that the approach was choked with brambles, too: the cutting overgrown.

Why have they builded a wall there, Mummy?

To stop people going in, poppet.

Why? (Always *why?*)

Because it's dark, and full of creepy-crawlies, and people might get hurt.

She'd absorbed that in silence; then tugged at my hand. Anxious to be away, in case the things behind the wall broke free. In case the dark got out. She'd had bad dreams that night, and kept me up. It served me right for such a thoughtless explanation.

Oh God, they haven't taken her in *there*.

'Are we going after them, then?' I ventured.

She shook her head. 'We need more information first . . . don't we, Vedova? An idea who they really are. A clue to what they want.'

'You know who they are, already, don't you?' Voicing the challenge, I wasn't really sure – but it vented my frustration. And I wouldn't have put it past her, anyway.

Again she shook her head, with inscrutable calm. 'No, I don't. Not yet.'

'A faction from this feud you talked about – isn't that what you think?'

'I only suspect; I don't know. It looked like an old military deployment . . . but that still doesn't tell us why they've singled you out.'

The Scourge of God, I thought. *The Left Hand of the Devil.*

'Which one of them?' I asked.

She stared off across the field for a moment; then looked at me. Her face, for all its paleness, was as sombre as the livid sky behind her. When she spoke, her soft tone drew my muscles tight, until I fairly ached with apprehension.

'Believe me, Rachel. If I've read the cards right, it

doesn't really matter which side has got your daughter. It doesn't really matter at all.'

*

'It's really kind of you,' I said. 'I'm sorry I was a bit, you know . . . this morning.'

'Think nothing of it,' said Graham – or rather, Graham's voice. I tried picturing his pleasant face at the end of the line; but Razoxane's grin, a foot away, was much too off-putting for that. She'd squeezed into the phone box alongside me, as if to relish my discomfort. I couldn't help but glower as I spoke.

'When can we expect you . . . ?'

'Um . . . I may be quite late – if that's all right with you?'

'That's fine,' he assured me. 'You're welcome any time, I mean that. But don't stay out too long. They're forecasting snow tonight.'

'I'll be there as soon as I can,' I promised. 'I've just got something to attend to first. There's someone I need to see.'

The house was detached in the fullest sense – standing back from the road and apart from its neighbours; the next bend took you out of town completely. Three bedrooms, perhaps; the brickwork overgrown with climbing ivy. Apart from a stain of lamplight against one of the curtained upper windows, its rooms were filled with darkness.

'I have been here before,' murmured Razoxane beside me – and smiled, as at some ugly private joke.

'Who lives here, then?' I asked uncertainly.

'His given name is Virgil Crown.'

'*Virgil*?'

'A pseudonym. Dante's guide through the world of the dead. Mr Crown styles himself a *spiritualist.*' She spoke the word with wry contempt. 'He called me once before, when I was drifting . . . not realizing what he did. That's how I came to be haunting home ground. But half a mile behind his house is Lickfield Wood, where those burnings and burials were rumoured . . . dating back to Civil War times. So I'm wondering what else he might have roused.'

'Like . . . some kind of evil spirit?'

She nodded. 'Raising the dead is his business. He talks to them. And some things answer. Not loved ones, though. Things incapable of love . . .' She lapsed into silence; then gave a faint grunt of amusement. 'You should have seen his face, when I came up from the basement. I could have melted away through the wall and left him sweating – but I'd been called from my walk for no reason, so I gave him a taste of despair. Fused all the lights, and stalked him from room to room. He was a gibbering wreck by the time I'd finished. But you can see he hasn't learned.'

I peered up at the smudge of lamplight. 'Is he having a séance or something?'

'That's what it feels like. Him and a few friends. People who think it's a perfect after-dinner party game for Christmas night.' She shook her head . . . and hefted the shovel she'd got from Finn. 'Come on.'

I hesitated. 'So . . . are we going to gatecrash it, or what?'

Razoxane grinned, and rested the implement across her shoulder. 'Not really; there's an open invitation, after all. *Come, and speak*. He's had enough sham spirits darkening his door. It's time he had a visit from the Queen of Spades.'

*

An automatic floodlamp came silently on as we walked towards the door; the suddenness made me jump, and shield my face. Razoxane kept striding, staring forward – and the stark white light went fizzling out again.

Gloom closed in as my eyes adjusted. The unlit house rose up and overhung us, like a cliff against the clouds – with just that one dim window to relieve its dark façade. Apart from a few stray flakes, the snow had held back thus far; but the orange sky was bulging with its weight.

I pictured the scene in the upper room: people sat around a table with the light turned low. Holding hands, or touching fingers; expectant and hushed. *Is anyone there? Please knock, if there's someone there* . . .

Razoxane gripped her shovel in both hands and took an overarm swipe at the door.

The sound of the impact went ricocheting off along the hall: a heavy, crunching *slam* that made me flinch. The wreath that hung from a nail above the knocker was jolted loose, and tumbled at our feet.

The reverberations faded; there was absolute silence from upstairs. Razoxane took a calm step back, and struck the door again.

This time the solid blow awoke a different kind of echo: the stiff and timid squeaking of an upstairs window sash. We both looked up to where the light was; I glimpsed a nervous face peer out between the drapes.

'Who's there . . . ?' a man's voice faltered.

'Your grave-digger,' called Razoxane, with audible relish.

The face disappeared at once; there was consternation from within. I caught a whiff of their panic, and recognized its cause. Something had come in answer to their call – and nobody knew how to banish it again.

Razoxane renewed her assault on the door. She might have had the scrawny physique of a street girl in her twenties, but there was real, brutal strength behind the blows. The panel protested, rattling on its hinges. A sharp, metallic screech came from the lock.

I stood and watched in awful fascination – drawing the collar of my cloak around my mouth. A change had come over her, I sensed it: the methodical attack was growing frenzied. I couldn't see her face in the dimness, but could tell that its humour had drained away, to leave just a merciless mask.

The shattered door gave way, and shuddered open. Razoxane kicked it wide. There was somebody cowering in the darkened hall beyond . . . and she stepped aside to let him out. It was a youngish man, fair-haired. He stumbled past her, eyes fixed on the blade of her shovel – then glimpsed me in my sombre cloak, and took off with a yelp.

I just turned my head to stare, as he ran into the road and pelted down it. Then Razoxane was entering the house, and calling me to follow.

Gritting my teeth, I did so – almost treading on her heels. Another person blundered past us both, and made it to the doorway. We found a well-dressed woman whimpering in the lounge. Razoxane hissed at her like a rabid cat, and sent her scurrying for safety.

A light from the first-floor landing tinged the stairs, and showed us the man who crouched on them in terror. As Razoxane moved back into the hall, he tried to clamber to his feet; she placed the shovel's edge against his chest and forced him down again. Her voice, when she spoke, was slimed with irony.

'Good evening, Virgil Crown . . . but not for you.'

'For pity's sake, begone,' he gabbled. 'Please, just leave me . . .'

'Not yet. You called on us to speak. So come and listen.' Taking hold of his collar she hauled him upright, and made for the back of the house with him staggering in tow. The shovel in her free hand swung carelessly at her side; I heard it banging and scraping on walls and door-posts, and hurried in pursuit of the sound.

Out through the back door and into a spacious garden, I came across her prodding him backwards, levelling the shovel like a spear. In the reflected orange gloom, I saw a man in his forties, with patrician features and dark, receding hair. His eyes were wide and staring.

As he opened his mouth to renew his pleas, Razoxane clouted him round the head with the shovel.

I winced as he spun around and fell, to sprawl face-down across the lawn. It took him a numbed, befuddled moment to piece himself together and begin to struggle up. Razoxane stepped forward, stooping slightly – as if suddenly concerned. Then, as he raised his bleary eyes, she kicked him in the chest with all her strength.

The spiritualist flipped over with a squawk, and lay where he had landed, gasping. Razoxane herself was breathing hard, as if fighting to keep herself in check. She took another step towards him; waited for him to try and clamber up – then kicked him again, pivoting all of her slim weight behind the upswing of her boot.

My hands went to my face; but my eyes stayed unprotected. I could only stare in horror as he slumped back to the grass. The wheezing cry she'd driven from his lungs made me think of an old accordion, stamped on; but my training offered up a far more clinical assessment. The rasping of his breath bespoke chest injuries; contusions: the sort of thing sustained by road-crash drivers. I'd treated enough of them in my days as a Casualty nurse. But I'd never seen those injuries inflicted while I *watched*.

Razoxane stood over him, her own breaths deep and ragged.

'Remember the last time you convoked the *friendly spirits?*' she asked, with pitiless emphasis. 'Well I wasn't one then . . . and I'm not now.'

And on that note she kicked him flat once more.

'Razoxane . . .' I protested sickly.

'Be *quiet*,' she snapped back, and returned her attention to her victim. 'Now it's your turn, Virgil Crown. Rise up and speak.'

The man dragged himself up on one elbow, feeling tentatively for his face. Perhaps he was afraid he'd find some of it missing. Blood coated one torn cheek with oily blackness.

A hoarse croaking sound came from somewhere above us. I jumped, and craned my neck: saw the rook's ghostly shape peering down from the eaves.

'You hear?' said Razoxane dryly. 'Vedova's pleased to see you too.'

'Hence . . . horrible shadow . . .' the man mumbled, in the tone of one clutching at straws.

She jabbed the spade into his ribs. 'Something's crawled out of Lickfield Wood. It's walking around out there. Perhaps you called it, Virgil Crown. Perhaps you know what it might be?'

'For God's sake . . . *no*.' He cowered as she aimed her shovel, bracing his arm across his face. 'I thought he was the Devil,' he gasped out.

Razoxane looked at me; then back at him, ignoring my disgust.

'Who?' she hissed.

'His eyes. His eyes were yellow . . .'

'Who . . . was . . . he?'

'I don't *know*. The room was dark, he was sitting in the chair. I didn't even see him . . . till he turned his head. Only . . . when he leaned forward, I got a look at his eyes . . .'

'So what did he say?'

'*The martyrs have come home . . . to be revenged.* He smiled, and told me that. So calm, he was . . . so cold. *The martyrs have come home. And we shall have the widow's child.*'

I gasped against my fingers.

'I didn't go upstairs again for three days . . .' the spiritualist mumbled. 'I slept in the front room . . . washed in the kitchen. But he must have slipped away that same night . . .'

I was still caught up in picturing the figure he'd encountered: the thing in the chair.The shadow which had stolen my daughter.

This fractured account, and my own fleeting glimpse, were all I had to go on – but enough to make my skin go cold with loathing. Every mother shares the nightmare of the Man in the Bushes, with his greasy smile and pocketful of sweets; but the shape in my head was from a different league. Wrapped up in an old fur cloak, as he'd been in my vision; the wide-brimmed hat overshadowing his face. I could imagine the dark head turning, like a turret. Bringing those uncanny eyes to bear.

The martyrs have come home.

'There's a local legend about that wood,' said Razoxane tersely. 'Going back to the seventeenth century. You know of it? Tell me what you know.'

'I've read a version . . . something about people who meddled with arcane *devices* . . . and were consumed . . .'

Razoxane considered that with a frown: clearly it was a new part of the puzzle – not familiar. 'Anything else?' she asked at length.

'Lord, no . . .'

Razoxane stared down at him, still thoughtful; then shook her head. 'And after his visitation, and mine, you still call up the spirits, don't you? Still reach into the dark. *Why hast thou disturbed our rest, that we should be brought up?*' I felt my nerves begin to tingle as her breathing quickened. Something was rising up within her, like an icy liquid coming to the boil. The hapless Mr Crown seemed to sense it too, and cringed away – but with nowhere to crawl.

Sudden rage suffused her features. She swung her shovel down against his head. The audible crunch made my stomach roll: I felt my mouth turn bitter. Crown slumped back into the grass – but she didn't let him lie. Again the shovel thudded down; again. I whimpered against my muffling palm – and Razoxane straightened up and turned towards me.

'What do you call a man with a spade in his head?' she asked, abruptly cheerful once again. The mood-swing left me reeling; but so did the sight of the shovel, now lodged in her victim's skull: the haft sticking up at an angle. One look at that, and a spasm of nausea gripped me.

'Doug,' she answered smugly, and jerked it loose.

I was too busy being sick into a rose-bush to respond.

Not that I had much in my stomach to be sick with. After a strung-out minute of spittle and sobbing breaths, I raised my aching head – to find myself alone in the garden. The corpse lay sprawled where she had left it, belly-up towards the gloomy orange sky; the shovel at its side. The rest was stillness. I was just beginning to panic (*really* panic) when Razoxane re-emerged from the black chasm of the doorway, walked over to the body, and dropped the wreath from the front door casually on top of it.

Then she looked towards me once again – and grinned.

'I don't know how you can *live* with yourself,' I muttered thickly.

She picked the shovel up, still smiling. 'I no longer find that a problem, Rachel.'

'You know what I mean.'

'He was probably the first cause of it, you realize? Whatever they are, he gave them a focus . . . and summoned them back into the flesh.'

The rook fluttered down to land on the medium's shattered skull. Perched there, it began to dig. I turned my face aside.

'And you heard what he said,' went on Razoxane calmly. 'What the apparition told him. *We shall have the widow's child.*'

'But *why*?' I blurted out. 'For God's sake . . .'

'To take revenge for something, it would seem.' She dug the shovel into the turf, and rested one boot on the blade. 'Some kind of martyrdom.'

'But . . .' I began again, with a glance at the dark, disfigured body. The rook's beak scraped on bone, and broke my thread. I gulped to get my breath back. 'He said . . . they'd been punished for meddling with occultish things themselves . . . or something. The people in the woods. The ones who burned.'

'Martyrdom is usually in the eye of the victim,' she pointed out dryly.

'So these *are* witches, then?'

'Vedova – don't gobble your food.'

'*Razoxane*.'

'Perhaps they are,' she allowed.

'So what have they got to do with *Cathy*?'

She shrugged. 'Maybe any widow's child would have done: for whatever it is they have in mind.'

I felt my skin turn clammy.

Razoxane hefted her shovel. 'Listen to me. The best thing you can do now is go to your curate friend, and try and get some rest. You'll need it. I'll move around tonight, and see what I can turn up.'

Desperate as I was to get closer to Cathy, I didn't envy Razoxane the prospect. The thought of venturing out alone into the unlit countryside, with its empty fields and contorted clumps of trees, sent a fresh chill through me.

I wouldn't get much sleep tonight, no matter how comfortable the bed might be; and not just because my heart was with my daughter. Another, covert look at the murdered man's body drew my stomach muscles tight.

Tonight had been a revelation; an apocalypse indeed.

Razoxane had come unhinged back there – as savage and psychotic as when she'd still been alive. Whatever state she'd managed to achieve, she'd brought her madness with her . . .

When I looked at her again, she was staring off into the distance: strangely vacant. 'Can't you hear them?' she asked softly. 'Can't you hear the voices in the wind?'

I wavered for a moment, still revolted; then followed her gaze into the deepest dark: the open countryside behind the house. But it wasn't voices that I heard; nor even whispers. Somewhere out there, at the very limits of perception, a faint and ghostly music teased my ears.

I stood there like a statue, frozen still, until the chimes dissolved – like snowflakes when you clutch them – and the music box was silent in the night.

*

'Are you sure you don't want anything else, Rachel?' the curate's wife asked kindly.

Reality crisis. Staring down at my picked-at plate, in the comfort of their dining room, I felt like someone shaken from a dream. But which was real: the present or the past? The warmth and hospitality in here, or the gulf beyond the curtains?

I swallowed, and raised my eyes. Ruth peered at me, concerned. 'No, thanks,' I told her meekly.

She took me at my word, and reached politely for my plate. I sat back, hands folded; apology in my pallid smile. I'd managed to get some soup into my sour, empty stomach, but the salad had defeated me. Cold turkey, from their Christmas lunch. The first clammy mouthful had pitched me back into the spiritualist's garden. I'd almost choked on the memory – covering my distress with a coughing fit.

'You're sure you don't want to talk?' Graham asked

softly, as Ruth carried the plate into the kitchen.

I nodded firmly. 'It's all right . . . really. I'll have things sorted out in a few days . . .'

'I'm worried about you, that's all. Not having a home to go to – today of all days. I mean, surely to God there must be *somewhere* . . .'

'Graham, just leave it, okay? Please? There are reasons, and I don't want to go into them.' I said it as darkly as I could, and let him draw his own conclusions. A row with my husband would be the likeliest bet (I'd glimpsed him looking at my ring). I was sure he didn't know my real status.

He lapsed into a pensive silence. I rested my elbows on the table, and my chin in my hands. Drawers rattled in the kitchen.

The sound of a crying baby made my fine hairs stand on end.

'I'll go, love,' called Graham, getting up. 'The joys of parenthood,' he murmured to me, with a theatrical roll of the eyes; but I could read the pride and pleasure on his face. That, and a faint relief at being able to get out from under the cloud which had settled on the room.

Left alone, I felt a stinging weight of tears begin to build, and sniffed them back. The sound of his cajolings carried clearly from upstairs; the baby's cries tailed off, replaced by more contented gurgles. I could picture it being gently lifted up and dandled.

Poor Nick had never had the knack. I remembered how baffled he'd been, discovering that our bawling little bundle wouldn't follow the rules.

I've bloody well fed her; what more does she want? And what are you *grinning at . . . ?*

'Do you want some coffee, Rachel?' Ruth called from the kitchen.

I swallowed; the sound was wet and squelchy in my throat. 'No, thanks.'

Graham came downstairs to introduce me to the baby. 'Now, this is Rachel Young,' he told it softly, as if trusting it with a secret; then beamed at me. 'Rachel . . . this is Jennifer.'

I cleared my throat. 'She's lovely. How old is she?'

'Nearly one.'

She was pink and chubby, curly-haired; her eyes like saucers as she looked me over. I had to pinch my smile into place. My insides felt ravaged and raw, as if I'd just digested something sharp.

Ruth came in to complete the Holy Family; giving her daughter a finger to play with, before looking happily at me. 'She's learned to crawl now, so I have to keep an eye on her all day; don't know what mischief she'd be getting herself into otherwise . . . And before long she'll be walking, and talking . . . getting picky about her food . . .'

'It's true,' I nodded, 'they grow up before you know it.' I glimpsed a quizzical flicker cross her face, and realized how much feeling I'd let slip into the words. 'That's what they say,' I added lamely.

'I'll just get her put back to bed,' Graham said. 'Why don't you go into the living room, Rachel . . . make yourself comfortable. There's something by Alan Bennett on BBC2 that looks quite good . . . Or whatever you'd like to watch . . .'

I shook my head. 'I'll be okay with a book in my room; just reading. Really.' I saw the protests taking shape, and struggled on. 'It's about time you two had some time to yourselves. You've earned it . . .'

'Rachel,' Ruth said worriedly. 'You really don't want to hide yourself away. We're happy to have you here . . .'

'I know,' I nodded, 'you've been terrific, and I'm ever so grateful. But I'd . . . rather be alone for a bit.'

'You're sure?' insisted Graham from the doorway. Baby Jennifer was playing with his ear. 'It might help, just to be with someone . . . even if you don't want to talk.'

'Yes,' I said. 'I'm sure.' I could feel my smile beginning to come unstuck.

'All right then,' Ruth agreed, relenting; still probing me with anxious eyes. 'By all means, have a bath if you'd like one. And there's plenty to read in the spare room, as you probably saw. I'll look in a bit later . . . just to make sure you're okay.'

'Thanks,' I said, with a gratitude that was genuine enough. Following Graham upstairs, I stepped carefully past as he carried Jennifer back into her room – her eyes caught mine over his shoulder – and went quickly on down the passageway to my own door. Those last few paces felt like a morning-sickness dash to the bathroom; but this time it was a race against tears. I managed to shut myself safely in before the upsurge overflowed. Then I slumped down across the bed, and let them come. More endurable than vomit; less defiling. But just as bitter. Just as hot.

I'd wiped the evidence away by the time Ruth knocked gently on the door; but I could tell that she suspected. Curled up on the bed now, with a paperback held open at my elbow, I smiled innocently up at her, hoping my eyes weren't as red as they were sore.

'Would you like a hot drink or something?' she asked.

'No thanks. I think I'll get to bed. I'm pretty tired . . .'

She'd brought a clean towel and one of her nighties. 'Take your time in the morning . . . there'll be breakfast for you whenever you want it.'

My indebtedness made me feel awkward: the grief almost got out again. Forcing it down, I said goodnight; and she was gone.

Rolling onto my back, I reached up under my sweater

and brought the dead carnation out. *His* carnation: Nick's. It was crushed and flattened now – but still physical between my fingers. The nightmare was reality; but so was the dream.

I stared at it for quite a while; then closed my eyes and pressed it to my chest.

Can you hear me, sweetheart? Do you know what happens now?

But the room around me kept its peace. The only sound was my heartbeat, and the snuffling of the wind against the window. At length I sat back upright: dislodging a last stray tear which trickled coolly down my cheek. I sniffed, and wiped it off with my sleeve.

I guessed this room was frequently in use; a little too claustrophobic to be cosy, but well enough aired. The tartan bedspread lent some brightness – enriched beneath the smoky yellow bulb. Getting up, I tucked the book into one of the well-filled shelves; and then went over to the window. Inching the curtains open, I squinted out – but with condensation formed already on the inside of the glass, and frost encrusting the exterior, I could only see a smeary lake of darkness.

Listlessly I changed into the nightie, switched the light off and climbed blind between the sheets.

Exhaustion quickly claimed me; my mind sank into sleep. And when my spirits had reached their lowest ebb, the visionary inside me started stirring in her cell.

What followed was all my own; I didn't need Razoxane to bring it into being. My clouded inner eye was suddenly clear, and I found myself alone in a landscape of mist and mud. At the foot of an open grave.

It was shallow and scraped-out, like an archaeological find. Something ancient and long lost. The sight of the skeleton laid out there made my inner self recoil.

Its bones were brown and yellow, still semi-clad in threadbare rags of skin. The face was a featureless mask upon the skull, with holes instead of eyes. But that fixed and baleful gaze seemed to focus all the emptiness behind it.

And something was still moving in its chest.

The ribs were mostly bare; but a flap of skin had quivered while I watched. And then again, a few moments later. I felt myself come out in gooseflesh. I thought it was a rat.

The withered face stared up at me; a resentful set to its bared, discoloured teeth. I glanced at it, and quickly looked away – but knew it was still watching, like a stranger in a crowd. It made me think of the spying scarecrow.

A noose of rotten rope had been pulled tight around the neck.

The skin twitched again, like the feeblest pulse. I glimpsed a stirring in the cavity below. I wanted to turn and run, but I was hooked already. No choice but to creep forward, as the nightmare reeled me in.

I caught a flash of liquid brightness in the shadows of its chest. Puzzled, I craned in closer . . . and found a heart of silver nestled there. Unbelievably, the thing was beating: the gleaming shape contracting like a mercury blob. Each slow pulse widely-spaced, like the heartrate of a thing in hibernation.

It's alive, I thought; and the rib-cage split wide open.

The suddenness would have made me squeal with shock, if I'd only been awake. The ghastly sight might well have made me heave. The ribs on each side parted and peeled back, revealing the shining heart in all its wonder. The sound of the unlocking was thick and sticky.

I stood there, shaken; staring down. The wide-splayed bones curved skyward, like the fingers of two dead hands. They reminded me of something else as well, but I didn't pause to wonder what. In opening, they'd exposed their treasure. The silver heart was there for me to take.

It was a beautiful thing; a miracle of living metal. Purity preserved inside corruption. An urge to touch and hold it grew inside me. Steeling my nerves, I stepped down into the grave.

The faceless sockets gazed at me between the sharp, spread-eagled ribs. Again I had a sense of the *void* beyond them: much more than just the vault of the skull. Apprehension gripped me tighter, but by now I was committed. Bending forward, I reached out for the heart.

An instant before my fingers touched it, I realized what those jagged ribs had almost made me think of. Some vile Venus Fly-trap – just waiting to be sprung.

Too late: I brushed the surface. It was pure burning cold. And in that fraction of a second, I heard the trap begin to close. Heard uncanny sinews creaking as they started to contract. As if, with a gun to my head, I *heard* its spring uncoiling as the trigger was squeezed back . . .

'Mummmyyyy!'

The wailing cry was Cathy's, and it snatched my spirit up. The shallow grave dissolved into the darkness. Even as I floundered like a drowning swimmer, I knew the interruption had saved my life. If I'd still been in the dream when those ribs had snapped closed, I'd never have come up for air again.

But I did so now: shocked awake in my strange bed. Sitting up with a gasp, I squirmed back against the pillows, my arms wrapped tight around myself. There was a chilly film of sweat on my bare shoulders; Ruth's nightie clinging damply to my back.

The air in the room was dense with cold; I caught a glimpse of my breath as I heaved a shaky sigh. The light of a frosty dawn filtered in through the curtains.

A fading after-echo seemed to tingle in my ears.

Her cry. Her cry was real. That's why it woke me up.

With an urgent little whimper I sprang out of bed and darted to the window. It was fogged like a bathroom mirror; I rubbed a hole in it. The outside of the glass was scaled with rime, but I could see the slope behind the house.

The snow had come. The ground was whipped-cream white. There were no tracks to mar it. But then, at the very limits of my hearing, her cry came again. More sensed than heard – like a trick of the wind. The wind and my own tormented mind.

But those weren't possibilities that I could cope with. It had to be her. It had to be my poor little Cathy.

Pulling off the nightie, I began hurriedly to dress.

9

MURDERERS

The house was silent as I sneaked downstairs. No sound from Graham and Ruth's room; not a peep from the baby. Just the ticking of a clock in the lounge. I tiptoed to the hall in my stockinged feet; past the poster on the door of Graham's study. *Peace Be to All Who Enter Here.* Biting my lip, I pulled my boots on.

Come on, girl, hurry up . . .

I realized how quickly I was breathing, and tried to slow it down. My stomach felt tight and hollow. It occurred to me that I should scribble them a note or something: say I'd slipped out to get some air. But I couldn't spare that many seconds. Retrieving my cloak from the hooks by the door, I slung it round my shoulders and gathered it close; then let myself quietly out into the snowy hush.

The dawn chill settled on my cheeks, and dug in tiny claws.

The streetlamps were still on: bright yellow-orange blobs against the backdrop of the sky. I hurried to the end of the street, the dry snow crunching underfoot, and turned down a lane that seemed to go in the right direction. Sure enough, out past the back gardens, it led me onto open ground: rising up towards a black wood on the crest.

If there was a footpath, it was blanketed and lost. I just hiked upwards, slipping and stumbling, my breath coming in clouds. At the top I glanced guiltily backward; but no lights were on in the house I'd left – nor in any of its neighbours.

My forehead and cheeks felt raw now. Pulling my cloak tighter, I peered into the copse. Again, no tracks to see; just bluish shadows pooled between the trunks. I stood quite still and listened – but she didn't call again.

Skirting round the straggle of trees, I found a field spread out before me: dipping away, then rising to another, longer wood. With a growing sense of desperation, I started out across it. The snow wasn't too thick – patches of frozen soil still showed through here and there – and I was able to keep a slow but steady pace. The urge to call her name took hold of me at one point, but it died on my lips. The bleakness of the fields was too imposing. And the silence would have swallowed it whole.

The wood ahead was dark and dense, looming larger as I struggled up towards it. I felt unpleasantly exposed, approaching over open ground; but with no real sense of being watched. By the time I reached the wood's edge, I was panting, and had to lean my shoulder up against a tree.

I stared until my eyes ached, but couldn't penetrate the weave of trunks and branches. Just layers of grey, receding into gloom. If there *was* a trace in there, I wouldn't find it just by standing here. Taking a breath, I ventured forward, in between the trees.

The twilight deepened. My breaths drifted through it in quivering plumes. I could feel my spirits dwindle as the emptiness of the wood became apparent. An awful disappointment overcame me; sky-high hopes brought plunging down to earth.

For Christ's sake, God, I thought, with raw frustration; then felt a little sheepish.

A brittle rustling sound came from somewhere ahead.

I was pretty much frozen already; but now I went as stiff as a board.

Stillness again. I stood there with my heart doing double-time; but as the silence persisted, the grip of fright grew looser. I guessed it had just been an animal, going about its early-morning business. At length I swallowed, and eased forward again. There looked to be a clearing up ahead, like a bald patch on the crown of the hill. As the trees thinned out, I picked up my pace.

If my mind hadn't been full of Cathy's face, I might have remembered the last time I'd looked for her in a wood that seemed deserted. Remembered, and retreated. As it was, I kept on going, and we reached the top together: me and the iron horseman.

For a moment I looked right through him, horse and all: their greyness blended with the trees, the wintry light. But then he moved, and sprang up there before me, fully-formed. The flanks of his mount were pallid under days of dirt; his long, withered coat revealed a breastplate of rusting iron. He wore an iron helmet, too, with a jutting peak, and bars to guard the face – if face he had. For when his head turned sharply round in my direction, I saw only a mask of rags, with ill-matched holes for eyes.

The chill in the air was nothing compared to what I felt inside me then.

The rider sat there watching for an endless second longer, in the rising wreath of his horse's breath. Then he gathered the reins in his gauntleted fists, and turned the animal's head towards me. The rag-mask face kept staring. Incapable of expression, right enough; but ghastly in its promise.

With a muffled shriek, I spun away and ran: he came after me at once. Pelting headlong through the trees, I heard the horse's hooves behind me – unable to overtake me yet, but keeping pace.

Oh God, oh God, I've dreamed this.

And so I had. My sleeping mind had tried in vain to warn me. I remembered the snow; the clawing twigs. The weight and panting breaths of my pursuer. The trees were hampering his progress, and could have helped me to elude him; but I was too panicked to do anything but flee. Horror rode that horse – something evil and old which belonged in the ground. I had to get *away*.

Branches scratched at me like cats and stung my face. Sobbing for breath, I blundered through them. I sensed he'd found a path through the trunks behind me; was coming faster now, and catching up. The hooves beat the earth at my heels. I swerved downslope, and skidded, and went down on one knee. Something snagged at my cloak, revealing the scarlet lining like a flap of flayed skin. Hauling myself up, I limped onwards. The horse crashed through the bushes in my wake.

The edge of the wood was coming up: another field beyond it. Once out of the trees I'd have nowhere to hide, but I hadn't any choice: he was driving me ahead of him. Gasping and whimpering, I burst into the open, and fled towards the far side of the field.

After a dozen breathless yards, I swung around to see where he had got to – to find that he'd halted just clear of the trees. In better light he was no more prepossessing: a vision in mouldy grey. Still staring after me, he raised a wooden baton in one hand. The upper end was bulbous, wrapped in cloth. It spontaneously ignited as I watched – flickering pale blue, then flaring yellow. Bearing the flaming torch aloft, he spurred his mount towards me once again.

I tried to keep my lead, but it was useless; the snorting horse closed the distance in a matter of moments. As it loomed above me I threw myself aside, and the downswing of the torch just missed my head.

The rider reined in at the far side of the field, and came thundering back while I was only half-way to my feet.

My cloak was dusted with snow; my left cheek caked. Helplessly I watched him come, knowing I couldn't make my move until the very last second. But then I noticed something that quite froze me to the spot.

The horse was blind. Its eyes had been gouged out. Black sockets glared towards me like a skull's.

I was so shaken that he almost ran me down – blocking off the sky before I knew it. A glancing, jolting impact knocked me sideways; horse or horseman's boot, it *hurt*. Winded, I rolled in snow. He wrenched his mount around and came again, leaning down from his saddle to flail me with the torch. I ducked, and felt it singe my hair, sparks trailing past and fading. The horse overshot and he gave it its head, galloping back to the far end of the field.

Sobbing, I scrambled up and took off at a tangent, though the gradient was against me; instinct rebelled against the prospect of him chasing me downhill. My bruised side ached: each breath was like a lungful of broken glass. The crest of the slope seemed impossibly distant; smeared and shaky. And then I saw the scarecrow on the skyline, its tattered arms spread wide.

Come to me . . .

A bitter, barking sound escaped my throat. We were back on Northolt Hill; the symmetry was almost mocking. Since yesterday I'd come full circle. And now that gloating thing would be a witness to my fate.

I stumbled up towards it; there was nowhere else to go. Behind, the horse was coming at the canter.

The scarecrow wobbled closer: as stark as a charred tree amid the whiteness. Its head had sagged forward, like someone dead on a cross.

I slipped in the snow, and went down on hands and knees.

The scarecrow raised its empty eyes to see.

Razoxane's smile was there beneath the hat-brim. Even as I gawped, her outstretched arms came back together, and brought that multi-barrelled shotgun to her shoulder. It blasted once, laying high-pitched echoes and a streamer of smoke across the field. I rolled onto my back to see my nemesis fall from his saddle, bouncing clangorously off the frozen earth. His horse galloped off to one side, its stirrups flying; quite lost without its rider's eyes.

The fallen body twitched and stirred – and suddenly erupted into flames. As I watched in horrified relief, it scrabbled for the sky like a dying insect, the convulsions dwindling as it was inexorably consumed. The fire was greasy orange; I could feel its heat from here. Within a few fierce moments, the corpse had been reduced to a shrivelled wreck, its arms drawn up like the forelegs of a mantis; enclosed in a shell of scorched iron.

Only then did I breathe again – and turn my head.

Razoxane had straightened up from the scarecrow's post – the T-shaped frame on which she'd been reclining; the butt of the shotgun braced against her ribs. For some reason she seemed wickedly amused.

'You really do walk into these things, don't you?' she said cheerfully.

I sat up in the snow, too drained to stand, and curled my lip at her; then looked reluctantly back at the burned rider.

'So what . . . the hell was *that*?' I asked weakly.

'Something that was buried a long time back,' was her meditative answer. 'Dust to dust. But this one didn't turn.'

I was staring at the helmet. 'It looked like . . . a Roundhead.'

She nodded. 'Ironside. I knew the trace was from that period . . .'

'And that's what's taken Cathy, then?' I whispered. 'Eleven of *those*?' At last I could see what she'd dreamed – and screamed – about. The Ragman. The rotting thing which had walked into our flat. No wonder poor Alice had been scared shitless . . .

'That's right. Their hostage to misfortune. But it doesn't tell us why.'

What if there wasn't a *why*? What if the risen dead, like their living counterparts, could terrorize at random – beyond reason?

And we shall have the widow's child . . .

The stray horse interrupted that desolating thought. It whinnied pitifully, demanding my attention. Turning, I saw it move in aimless circles, sniffing at the wind.

'The bastards blinded it,' I murmured. 'Poor thing . . .'

'Ensuring its obedience,' Razoxane said, reaching under her coat. 'The mount and the rider are *one* . . .' I saw that old automatic in her hand. Still looking at me, she extended her arm off sideways, towards the bewildered horse; smiled benignly and squeezed the trigger.

That was the bit I had to glance away from.

'Well, aren't you fortunate that I was here?' she went on briskly, tucking the gun away wherever it lived. She didn't even bother to confirm her hit; but I couldn't stop myself from doing so. The hapless mound of horseflesh had subsided, and was still.

'All right . . .' I said, still short of breath; still sitting. 'Why *are* you here, then?'

'I told you there was something about this field. Some power. It drew me back . . .' She walked off to one side; and turning, I saw the scarecrow where she'd dumped it in the snow, as shapeless as a heap of old clothing. The guitar case lay beside it. She stowed away the shotgun, and came trudging back with the shovel. There was still dried blood on the blade.

I climbed unsteadily to my feet, and looked around us; but the open fields were empty. No black flies were crawling on the counterpane of white. The grungy mass of town in the middle distance lay undisturbed, hemmed in by snow and silence. The echoes of Razoxane's shots would have carried that far; but this was farmland, and I guessed they'd go unquestioned.

'I . . . thought I heard Cathy,' I murmured; already doubting my own ears.

She shook her head. 'Not her. Nothing else is close. You picked up a phantom echo, I'd say . . . still lingering in the wind. You'd be surprised what mothers can sometimes hear.' She smiled thinly. 'Or perhaps you wouldn't.'

But the wind was empty now; as bleak as a series of dying breaths. The only sound was a faint, metallic ticking from somewhere close by. Irregular sounds: uncanny yet familiar. It took me a moment to trace them to the corpse's blackened armour, slowly cooling in the snow.

Razoxane was scraping the tip of her shovel over frozen soil: describing a slow circle round the scarecrow's prop.

'*Now* what are you doing?' I asked; ineffectually dusting down my cloak.

'I think there's something down here,' she replied: teeth clenched in concentration; etching on. 'Entrusted to the watcher . . . a long time ago.' With the circle completed, she knelt to run her fingers through the powdery snow; the shovel braced beside her.

'What sort of something?' I asked warily; remembering her speculations last time.

'I don't know; artefacts, perhaps. *Arcana*. There's a definite signature now.' She paused, while I stamped the snow; then glanced at me. Her grin was eeriely engaging. 'You know what a pulsar sounds like, Rachel? Sort of a cold static . . . from the edge of the universe. This registers like that.' Straightening up, she stepped away.

Strange how they unsettled me: her cosmic insights. Much spookier than the ramblings of astrology. While others got hung up on the zodiac and planets, she'd already seen much further: into the coldest depths.

Perhaps she heard the pulsars for herself; those ghostly unseen objects at the back of beyond . . .

'I'd step back a little way if I were you,' she said pointedly. I came back to myself, and hastily complied.

Razoxane brandished her shovel like a sorcerer's staff. She spat out a word. The T-shaped prop caught fire.

I flinched back even further, feeling the heat on my frosted cheeks. The flames spread out along the crossbar, clinging – a Ku-Klux version of the primitive Cross. Yellow light flickered and stained the snow. The ground began to sizzle.

Razoxane looked on, impassive; the fire reflecting from her shades. I forced my gaze away and looked back towards town, sure that this beacon would draw attention. But a moment later it had guttered and gone out – as completely as a snuffed candle.

A haze of smoke hung around the blackened spars. Below, the earth within the circle had grown pulpy and soft: thawed through. Razoxane grasped the smouldering wood between her gloves, and dragged the post clear. Then picked up her shovel again, and began to dig.

I watched her, rubbing at my mouth. Not sure whether I wanted to stick around and see what she turned up. The way she'd uprooted that sharp-tipped post . . . It made me think of someone pulling a stake from out of a vampire's heart.

I glanced again at the burnt-out corpse. Its own heat had left it sunk into the soil. Another fall of snow might even cover it up. I looked back towards the carcass of the horse. There wasn't much chance of *that* going undiscovered.

Once more I turned my gaze towards its rider.

'You're making me nervous, Rachel,' said Razoxane dryly, looking up from her labours.

'Sorry. I . . . keep expecting him to move.'

'Does he *look* as if he's going to get up again?'

'Well he was dead to start with, wasn't he?' I pointed out, defensively.

'True enough; but he's finished now. *Deus ex Machina*, you might say. And perhaps it gives them peace, after a fashion . . .' Shrugging, she drove her shovel in again.

I wondered what the police would make of this. A horse attacked and blinded; shot. Civil War relics that had somehow been unearthed. And human remains which would send forensics haywire . . .

'There's something *here*,' she said.

I maintained my prudent distance as she crouched, ploughing her hands into the soggy hole she'd dug. As she started sifting the dark soil, I turned away in a slow circle, scanning the fields . . . but the loneliness up here was unrelieved. Grey air, and ghostly whiteness. I wrapped up tight, and shivered.

When I looked back at Razoxane, she was examining a fragment of mouldy cloth; or so I thought. Only when she murmured as much did I realize it was paper: a page out of some decomposing book.

'There's more . . .' she told me thoughtfully; still trying to read it. 'A whole word-hoard. But all just crammed together: pulped. As if someone just stuffed it down to rot and be forgotten . . .' A strange new note had crept into her voice, I noticed: a perplexity of sorts. A *why*?

'Maybe they had good reasons,' I suggested grimly.

The page disintegrated as I spoke. She wiped its film off her gloves, still staring down into the hole.

'There was *wisdom* in those books. There's still a matrix of power in the pages. But scrambled now. All spoiled.' She sounded almost offended; still frowning as she glanced my way again.

'Did that Book of Martyrs come from here?' I asked, in a tentative sort of way.

She looked pensively back towards her case, and shook

her head. 'I don't believe so, no. Not here. But somewhere like it.'

On that crisp final note she straightened up. 'Come on.'

I felt my heart sink. 'Where?'

'There must have been something more down there: a seal of some kind. Whoever buried those pages . . . didn't want them found again.' She finished packing the hole with cold earth, and went back to put the shovel in its case before resuming. 'My guess is, there was an artefact turned up by someone else. While ploughing this field perhaps. They probably thought nothing of it. Some quaint little relic to keep on the mantelpiece . . .'

I just stared at her. 'From the farm down the track, you mean?'

She nodded. 'Perhaps it only recently worked its way to the surface. Or maybe it's been in the family for generations . . .'

'Sorry,' I broke in sarcastically, 'this is the farmer whose nose you nearly cut off yesterday, is it?'

She grinned. 'I imagine so.'

'So . . . are we just going to turn up on his doorstep, then?'

'Well . . .'

' "Hi, remember us? We're actually from the *Antiques Roadshow* . . ." '

'Rachel . . .'

'What?' I snapped.

'Why don't you just shut up for a minute?'

I looked sulkily away.

There'd been a chill in the way that she'd said that; but right then I was feeling too pissed off to care. The memory of her madness failed to move me. And when she spoke again, a moment later, the dust of dry amusement had slipped back into her voice.

'I'm sure we'll think of some more plausible excuse. But first, we'll scout around.' She hoisted the black case up behind her shoulder, and nodded towards the naked hedge. 'Let's go.'

*

As we moved down towards the buildings in the hollow of the hill, her familiar came winging towards us, like a ghost across the snow.

I stepped away to one side as it fluttered down to land, coming to rest on Razoxane's upraised fist. She studied it with something like indulgence: smiling faintly. It peered back into her face, its eyes as hard and glassy as her shades.

'What news, Intelligencer?' she asked dryly.

It retched a reply; but perhaps it was those eyes which bore its message. Razoxane's face grew pensive. She glanced at me.

'She says the house is empty.'

Staring at her, I felt my forehead crease. 'What . . . this early?' I lifted my wrist to look – and realized I'd left my watch behind. It would still be curled up on the bedside table, for Ruth to look in and discover; along with the crumpled nightie and the unmade bed. God, she'd be so worried . . .

'The message is clear enough,' said Razoxane – and launched the bird-thing back into the air. 'Keep looking,' she told it flatly, and watched it climb obediently away, its wingbeats stiff and leathery in the cold air.

In the stillness that followed, I heard the clamour of crows: their scraping cries adrift above the farmland. I could see the roof of the farmhouse now, and the trees around it. There were nests among the branches, like inauspicious shadows on an X-ray of the lungs.

Razoxane pushed onward; I reluctantly kept pace. A few minutes later, we reached the crest of the slope overlooking the yard.

The house was stone, and of decent size; its tiled roof mantled with white, like the icing on a cake. A number of outbuildings were ranged about it, their angles of brick and corrugated iron likewise softened by the snow. The yard they framed was open and deserted; and here the snow was churned in patches. Dirtied. So someone had been up and about.

Some of the house's curtains were still drawn. No light showed at any of the windows. Staring down, I felt a stirring in my stomach – and apprehension reared its ugly head inside me.

The crows were still heckling in the background, but the buildings before us were steeped in silence: as if they'd lain derelict for weeks. Even the animal sheds seemed empty. I could just see the nose of a tractor, poking out from the entrance of its shelter. A cartload of what looked like winter feed was parked nearby. An air of sudden abandonment hung over them both.

I blew a long stream of breath, and glanced at Razoxane. 'What do you reckon?'

'Something's been,' she said.

'And gone?'

She produced her compass and flicked it open: studying the pentagram points. 'There are background traces of chaff . . .' she murmured after a moment. 'But I'm picking nothing up from here . . .'

She dropped the thing, and let it dangle from her fingers by its chain; then bounced it back into her palm like a yo-yo. The click of the closing lid was like a small bone snapping. I winced.

And then, just as I'd feared, she smiled and jerked her head. 'Let's take a look.'

Slowly we descended the slope; digging our wary boots into the snow; drifting gradually apart. The empty, unlit windows watched us come. At the bottom I just waited, while she wandered to the centre of the yard; turning on her heel there, to look back the way we'd come. I noticed she'd unbuttoned her greatcoat now. Her free right hand was hanging at her side.

The crow-calls floated on the breeze, like flakes of rust. The birds were back in the trees now, watching. Had something only recently stirred them up?

Razoxane nodded me on towards the house.

The door was closed, but only on the latch. She eased it open, glancing back as I came crunching up to join her; then stepped inside. With a last look round at the empty yard . . . the slope beyond . . . I followed.

The interior was as cold as the open air: I could still see my smoking breaths. The whitewashed walls seemed to reflect and magnify the chill. All it needed was the smell of disinfectant; it already felt exactly like a morgue.

A toddler's toy was sitting in the hall. A bug-eyed telephone on wheels. Gritting my teeth, I stepped carefully around it: fixing my attention on Razoxane's back.

There was an open fireplace in the first room we looked into, but apart from a few fragments of calcified wood, there were only ashes in the grate. The bright cards on the mantelpiece above were almost mocking; colour without warmth. A bushy Christmas tree was squeezed into the corner. Home-grown, perhaps; I smelled its sap. Saw crumpled bits of gift-wrap strewn around it . . .

Razoxane backed out, and crossed the draughty hall into the kitchen. Following, I found that the stained-pine table was still laid: two places set, and plates with cold food on them. There was a vat of solid stew on the kitchen range.

The sense of desolation was redoubled. I thought of the *Marie Celeste*. But that was a page from the history books. *This* was as immediate as the nausea in my stomach.

Razoxane unshouldered her burden, and placed it flat on the tabletop. Carefully she unfastened the catches, but didn't raise the lid. Instead she cast a pensive look towards the ceiling.

'Oh, God, what's happened?' I whispered – and even that seemed too loud amid this silence.

'Let's check upstairs,' she came back, just as quietly. Reaching under her coat, she came out with her pistol and caressed it with her ungloved thumb. It clicked.

I stepped back again, and let her take the lead. The staircase was steep and creaky; the stairwell claustrophobic. A right-angled turn half way up left us blind to whatever might be waiting. She craned around the corner, pistol raised; then relaxed marginally, and kept on climbing. I followed, my footsteps leaden; silently cursing each rasp and squeak of wood. My heart-sounds seemed to echo in my chest.

The door to the child's bedroom was at the near end of the passage. *Lee's Room* read the nameplate. Turning towards it, my sick sense of foreboding became a physical thing. My fingers crept unbidden to my lips as Razoxane nudged it open to peer inside.

Drawing back, she shook her head. 'No sign,' she murmured softly. I wasn't sure if I should feel relieved.

We went on down the passage, past the empty bathroom, towards the facing door. The carpeted boards creaked dryly underfoot. I felt my gorge begin to rise again as Razoxane reached down to grasp the handle, turned it – then gave the door a gentle push.

A sudden, icy draught swirled out to meet us. It brushed by my leg like an unseen dog escaping, and I stepped back with a gasp. A silent chill set in behind it: sharp enough to sting my cheeks. Then, over Razoxane's shoulder, I saw that the window in the room beyond was open.

She had paused on the threshold, staring in. Now she took a slow step forward, and gave me a sight of the bed.

It was a pine-framed double bed, its counterpane drawn

down and crumpled at its foot. Something lumpy lay upon it – covered up with a single sheet.

The sight made me think at once of a shrouded body on a hospital bed: wrapped in a sheet and ready for the porters. My heart sank like a stone.

Razoxane stepped cautiously towards it, and reached for a corner of the sheet; leaning back as she did so, her levelled pistol close against her side. A tingling pause while she took a purchase on the cotton, finger by finger – then she jerked the sheet off the bed, as violently as a tablecloth in a party trick.

For a moment, I thought the black thing it revealed was just a charred lump of wood . . . Then I realized that it *was* just a charred lump of wood. A statue of some kind. Eyes widening, I went inside to join her.

'Now what do you make of this?' she asked.

Moving gingerly to the foot of the bed, I stared down at it. The carbonized shape contrasted starkly with the pristine sheet beneath it – like a victim of spontaneous combustion. It was a statue all right, maybe four foot high. The details were hard to make out: the wood burned black, and cracked. But after a moment, the image came together in my head.

'Oh, Jesus . . .' I breathed.

It had once been a statue of the Virgin and Child: taken from a church somewhere, and burned . . . then brought here and left. Like a message. As if someone had expected us to come . . .

Swallowing, I glanced at Razoxane. From the look on her face, she'd reached the same conclusion.

A mother and child, together: burned. Looking back to the statue, I suddenly remembered that ghastly account of a fire-storm, and its victims. The infant here seemed fused to its mother's breast: cremated as it clung there. For just a moment I imagined its screaming – and had to grasp the bed-frame to keep my balance.

Mother and baby. *Burned.*

'Chris . . .' I whispered: all my weight on my arms.

'Maybe,' said Razoxane thoughtfully.

Even if it had been those Ironsides instead, the message was the same – for me and Cathy. The parallel showed no pity.The Virgin Mary was a widow, too.

Head down, I sensed Razoxane push her gun under her coat, and retrieve the compass from a pocket. She tapped it on the window frame, as if to check that it was working; then opened it up and placed it on the sill.

'So he . . . or they . . . came here last night?' I asked dully.

'I'd guess so. The family just fled, most likely. The Landrover's not here.' She smiled, half to herself. 'They must have been really afraid, not to have called the police in yet . . . or ventured back. Perhaps they're still driving now.'

Something cold pierced the blanket of shock: something I should have thought about sooner. I straightened up so quickly, my upset stomach almost overspilled. 'Listen, if he left . . . me . . . this message: what if he's still around?'

'I don't think he is,' was her calm reply. 'Vedova would have sensed him. He couldn't have known you'd come here, anyway. Perhaps this is a ritual thing, more than a message . . .'

I let my shoulders slump into a sigh. 'And the Ironsides . . . ?'

She glanced at the compass, and shook her head. 'Still nothing stirring. Dead ground in all directions. I think they've been here, though.'

'What for?'

'Maybe the reason *we* came. Trying to find more clues about that word-hoard.'

I looked miserably back towards the statue, and tried to think it through. Books of magic, buried in an English field. The past had come to claim them – and gutted this unsuspecting home. So what other secrets might be under the snow, I wondered. What other unmarked graves . . . ?

'So we're presumably too late, then?' I prompted, hopefully: more than ready to be gone.

'It's still worth looking round,' she said.

I was just opening my mouth to protest when something registered at the back of my mind, and put me right off my stroke. For a moment I couldn't pin it down, although my nape was cold and tingling already. And then it dawned, like a rising winter sun.

'Razoxane . . .' I whispered.

'What?'

'The crows . . .'

She only frowned.

'The crows have stopped,' I said.

The silence that fell between us then was as pure as the driven snow outside – and just as cold. Not one croak snagged the hush. After a dozen muffled heartbeats, I heard a distant, disembodied moaning sound that made my flesh shrink tight. Then I realized it was the wind in one of the chimney flues, and nothing more.

I thought of the wood near the hospice; my first close encounter with an Ironside. The crows had flown that time, as well. Cleared out, and left us to it.

Razoxane drew her pistol out; head cocked, as if to listen. Her eyes were unreadable behind their shades. I swallowed hard, and glanced round at the window sill.

The points of the needle were beginning, oh so stealthily, to move.

'Oh God, look . . .' I almost mouthed.

'I know,' she said.

'The family . . . coming back . . . ?' I wondered desperately. *Or even Chris?*

She moved her head left-right. 'It isn't calibrated for living men.'

I looked out through the window: not daring to venture

closer. From here I could only see a corner of the yard, and the slope down which we'd come – our tracks cutting across it. The snow was otherwise unmarked. One of the curtains bellied out in a snatch of wind, momentarily obscuring the view; then settled to hang limp again.

'We need windows on the other directions,' said Razoxane. 'Come on.'

It fell to me to check the bathroom; but the frosted glass in the window left me none the wiser. I thought about shoving up the sash, and decided against it. The wooden frame looked stiff and warped, and the noise of my efforts would carry. I didn't want to think about what might be waiting below by the time I got it open.

I sighed a pale cloud of dejection, and went after Razoxane. She was just emerging from the boy's room. 'They're out of sight,' she said, grim-faced, as I came up. 'Somewhere . . .'

'What's the range of that thing?' I asked hoarsely.

'Miles and *millennia*,' was her curt response. 'But these readings are from within an acre . . .'

'So what do we do?' The house was feeling more oppressive by the second: closing round us.

'Downstairs,' she said, and led the way. The front door was still ajar; she went down the hall and closed it, pistol poised. I watched as she pushed the corroded bolts across – then glanced at me.

'I'm going to have a look out the back. You stay here, all right?'

I didn't quite know how to respond to that: not wanting to be left on my own. Not wanting to stick my nose outside either.

'Do you know how many there are?' I asked instead.

'Maybe three,' she said – and flashed me a mercurial grin. 'Which could be two too many.'

'It's all bloody right for you,' I snapped back at her. 'They can't kill *you*.'

The grin died to an ember. 'Can't they now?' she asked softly – and walked past towards the back of the house.

I stared after her, nonplussed; then turned back to the closed door. It looked solid enough – oak braced with iron – but succeeded in making me feel more shut-in than safe. God knew what might be creeping across the yard beyond it, hidden from my gaze. I moved into the kitchen, and went cautiously to the window. My heart flipped over as I put my nose to the scaly glass; but there was nothing to see. Just snow and stillness. The naked trees around the farm barely wavered in the breeze. Outside in the crisp clear air, they'd stood out stark as slashes in the whiteness. From inside, they were blurred by the frost. I couldn't tell if the crows had flown their nests, or were simply sitting silent. Waiting.

I stepped away, turned round – and found myself confronted with Razoxane's sinister guitar case. Dumped there on the table, in the midst of the domestic remains, it looked as ominous as a coffin.

Chewing my lip, I walked round it, and returned to the hall. There was silence from the rear of the house. I looked unhappily back up the narrow staircase, then went through into the living room. Where someone promptly grabbed me from behind.

Christ help me.

The words surged to my throat – to be stifled by the hand across my mouth. I squirmed and snorted, unable to break free. Back we went into the corner, my boot-heels scraping on carpeted stone. And then a shape came round into my frantic field of vision – and I stiffened up and froze.

The wolfish grin was gone, now; but the eyes had that animal's hunger. The bearded jaw was set and stern. He carried a baseball bat in both gloved hands.

The leader of the local vigilantes was clearly done with pussyfooting around.

I whimpered something stifled. 'Shut up, you slag,' my captor hissed in my ear.

'Hello, you lefty bitch,' the bearded man said calmly – and jabbed me in the stomach with his bat. Not forcibly enough for lasting damage; just hard enough to really hurt. My reflex was to double up and retch, but the other bloke's arms kept me forcibly upright. All I could do was close my eyes and gurgle, forcing spittle through his fingers. My pelvic-floor muscles almost let me down again, but I managed just to keep them in check.

As the burst of pain contracted to a throb, I forced my eyelids open. He'd come very much closer. The tone of his voice had been deceptive; his face was almost bloodless with choked-back rage.

'Do you know what your fucking boyfriend did?' he asked, still frighteningly soft-spoken. 'Blew up two of our mates with a nail-bomb. In his own fucking house. Know anything about that, do you? Know where he might be now?'

Oh, I hope you run right into him, I thought.

Using his bat, he parted my cloak – holding one side out to study the lining. Then shook his head with what seemed like genuine disgust.

'Call yourself a fucking nurse?' he muttered; and laid the bat against my aching belly.

Razoxane, please, I screamed inside: *where are you?* But she'd still be scratching round out back – unaware that the intruders had already gained entry. Not rot and iron but flesh and blood. The compass had misled her.

'Know how we found you?' the vigilante hissed into my face. 'Bloke who lives here gave us a ring. He's been onto us before about the hippies on his land; we see 'em off for him, y'see. The cops are a waste of time.' He raised the bat to nudge my chin up higher. 'But yesterday the poor sod got assaulted . . . and one of the bitches who did it was wearing an old nurse's cloak. Just like yours.

And then this *morning*, he calls me up from his brother's house in fucking *Farnham* . . . and says he's not coming back until the whole countryside's been cleared. You and your pals have really scared the shit out of him, you know that? Him, and his wife, and his little lad too . . .'

He breathed out through his nose, as if relieving pent-up pressure in his chest; then nodded to his mate. 'Okay, let's hear her squeal. If she tries to scream, just pinch her windpipe, right?'

The other man took his black-gloved hand away: smearing my own spit off across my cheek. I gasped for breath, almost gagging as his fingers settled down around my unprotected throat.

'All right then, *nursie*. Your girlfriend's out the back . . . who else is around?'

'No one,' I croaked. 'Just us two . . .'

'And where's your long-haired lover-boy?'

'I don't know . . . Anywhere . . . *God* . . .' This last as his blunt wooden bat renewed its pressure.

He stared at me for a moment; then stepped back. 'I'm just going to check upstairs . . . and then I'll come down and ask you again. God help you if you don't give me some answers.' He looked at his companion. 'Make sure you get the other one when she comes back in. Tony said she's vicious, so give her a clout first off. Break her arm. Then we can chat to them both.'

He went out. A pause while he listened for Razoxane; then the stairs began to creak as he ascended. My captor loosened his embrace, and let me breathe – then grasped me by the collar of my cloak.

'Come on, then, let's go through.'

I could get a look at him at last: hard face and lank fair hair. Like his mate he wore a zipped-up leather jacket, muffler, gloves; but the hair was tucked away beneath a roll-up balaclava. I was suddenly sure that if he pulled it down, there would be eye-holes, and a frayed slit for the mouth. There was nothing amateurish about these blokes. They came on like a paramilitary punishment squad.

'We're going to teach you a proper lesson, girl,' he promised bleakly, as I was steered towards the door. 'That poor sodding animal out there ... You're bloody sick, you people. Sick ...'

I missed his meaning, and suddenly that seemed important. 'What animal?'

'The bloody horse, of course ... standing there in the cold. So which of your sick friends gouged its bloody eyes out, eh ... ?'

An icy tide surged through me. I tried to wriggle free – but he jerked my collar tight and almost choked me. Back we went towards the kitchen, so fast I nearly fell over my feet. Crossing the hall, he looked towards the shadowy back of the house; but of Razoxane there was no sign.

He propelled me on across the threshold, towards the guitar case; still trying to get a grip on his anger. 'The gypos and the scroungers are bad enough ... but it's perverts like you who really need mopping up. People who get off on things like *that* ...' He shoved me forward. 'You cold-blooded, vicious little cow.'

He broke off then – too suddenly – and turned to look behind him.

'I never said I wasn't,' said Razoxane equably; and hit him in the face with her shovel.

I staggered back against the chimney-piece while she finished him off. She did it brutally, in silence: digging deep, with her boot on the blade, to divide his spasming throat. His gasps became a gargle. Blood splurted out and slicked the flagstones: steaming.

I pressed my fist against my lips and looked away.

Razoxane rubbed her own mouth with her sleeve, like

a half-remembered reflex; staring down at the corpse without expression. Then she was on the move again, coming over to lay the shovel on the table, and opening up the case. Liquid scarlet pooled across the pine, and began to worm its way between the settings. I turned to watch it, shaking. My forehead must have looked like chalk. It felt like sweating cheese.

She withdrew the Devil's Tinderbox; unshrouded it. The barrel glinted dully in the dead light. Her thumb hooked the hammer, and levered it back.

'*The Ironsides are here*,' I hissed at her, my voice hysteria-pitched.

'I know they are,' she came back, stony calm.

There was the brittle creak of floorboards from upstairs. The boy's room, at a guess. Like us, the other man had started there.

The next set of noises came a moment later: from the other end of the silent upper storey.

I raised my eyes, appalled. The cracked white plaster of the ceiling gave no clues. But that had definitely been the sound of something moving.

'Oh shit,' I whispered through my fingers.

Razoxane was looking upward too, her lips drawn tight.

The vigilante trod on another loose board, somewhere over the living room. The footfall that followed was directly overhead: as if the one was shadowing the other. I thought of a spider. A rag and iron spider, creeping up on its prey . . .

The ceiling spread above me like a vast, blank wall. I half-expected it to quiver: imperceptibly subside. But the only movements came from the cobwebs in the corners . . . stirring gently in the draught.

He must have climbed in via the outhouse: up its gently-sloping roof and in through a window. We were cooped up here with something dead, in search of its revenge . . .

The boards above us creaked again.

Razoxane brought the Tinderbox to her shoulder, swung it steeply up and fired. The blast was deafening – driving my eardrums in against my brain. Smoke and plaster mingled in a dusty burst of fog. Gaping holes fanned out in all directions; the ceiling positively sagged. Even with my ears full of pain and pressure, I heard a squawking cry, and the thunder of a ponderous collapse.

'Well, he got his come-uppance,' said Razoxane dryly.

The suffocating cloud came down around us, along with half the ceiling, and suddenly I couldn't stand it any more – it was like being boxed-up, buried and cremated all at once. Dodging past her, I fled for the front door. I heard her follow, shouting something, as I wrenched the rusty bolts aside; but before she could catch me up, the door was open. Fresh air flooded inward, razor-keen against my cheeks. Filling my lungs, I stumbled out onto the step.

The Ironside waiting in the yard reacted almost at once; in retrospect, he seemed to take an age. My widening eyes recorded every detail: the wide-brimmed hat, and cloth-masked face; the leather coat that draped him to the shins. But most of all, the bulky rifle he was aiming from the shoulder – the muzzle gaping right towards my face.

Then his shape was blotted out by a shimmering cloud that rolled across the dirty snow towards me; the coughing gunblast echoed round the yard. I cringed from the bullet I thought was coming – then gasped in horror as the fog became fire.

It came at me like a giant grill igniting: a ghostly burst of gas-devouring flame. The chill on my cheeks was replaced by a furnace breath. I threw myself backwards, slumping down into the hall, my arms across my seared and stinging face. The cloud was consumed just before it reached the doorway. Its oily yellow flare turned sullen orange, and blackened into smoke – a filthy, toxic pall that almost choked me.

Razoxane came wading through it, kicked the door shut, and dragged me back into the kitchen. I came without resistance. I felt as if I was coughing up my lungs.

'I said, don't go *outside*,' she snarled exasperatedly.

'Oh God . . .' I gasped. 'He's got a bloody *flame-thrower* . . .' I broke off to retch again.

'Fire-lock.'

'. . . what . . . ?'

'Fire-lock,' she repeated, as I mopped my mouth. 'Reprisal weapon. Fuel-air ignition . . .' She glanced at the window. 'It projects a cloud of inflammable gas, and then sets light to it. Quite ingenious, for the seventeenth century . . .'

I squinted up at her in disbelief. 'I never knew . . .'

'Few people do. They were called the Devil's weapons. Like the *Machina*, and the Tinderbox here . . .'

'Reprisal . . . against witches?' I quavered: talking to keep myself calm now.

She nodded. 'Fire against fire.'

'And you'd know all about that, wouldn't you?' I muttered.

Razoxane ignored the barb. Getting to her feet, she went over to the window, her pistol ready in her hand. Smoke was still drifting past outside: darkening the room like the shadows of passing clouds.

'He's gone,' she murmured, peering out. 'He's changed position . . .'

The floor above us was silent. I wondered briefly where my vigilante friend had got to. Doubtless he'd shut himself in the little boy's bedroom: scared rigid by the turn that things had taken. His turn to do some sweating for a change. I allowed myself the briefest, sourest smile.

Something heavy slammed against the back door of the house. My smile dropped off and smashed.

'Don't worry: it's locked and bolted,' said Razoxane, glancing back.

I wasn't reassured. The sombre, solid impact came again, and echoed through the farmhouse. Something unspeakably grim was demanding admission. I pictured the butt of an antique musket being struck against the door, with force enough to jar it in its frame.

Even Razoxane seemed to have her doubts. She came across to peer into the hall. The muffled blows kept coming, with a ponderous persistence. I thought I heard the crack of splitting wood.

The kitchen window shattered.

Back on my feet again, I swung around – to see the barrel of a gun come poking through. It belched a ghostly cloud into the room; the confined space filled in seconds. In the instant before it lit, I grabbed hold of Razoxane and shoved her forward, clear of the doorway. Together we lurched out into the hall. Behind me, the kitchen was suddenly an oven. A smell of scorched wood and blistered paint assailed my nostrils, as if the room had just been stripped by giant blow-lamps.

Blazing gas flared after us, and died. Razoxane ducked back in through the doorway to retrieve her case. Flames were digging in already, tooth and claw – I glimpsed them through the smoke – but she managed to drag it out unscathed. The effort left her crippled for a moment, slumping back against the wall: hawking to clear those black fumes from her lungs.

The back window of the living room crashed inwards.

Her face came round towards me, bleached pale beneath its grime. 'Get out of the way,' she hissed at me. 'Upstairs!'

I did as I was told: trying to outrun the rising pall of smoke. Behind me, I heard the front door creaking open; a draught got in, and eddied through the cloud. I realized that Razoxane was going *outside*.

Half-way up, I stopped and turned to stare – but the hall was a sea of murk. The fear of being abandoned overwhelmed me; but after a moment I sobbed and kept on climbing. I didn't really have a lot of choice.

An acrid haze already blurred the landing. The door to the child's bedroom was firmly closed, which was fine by me. I hurried by – towards the door to the main bedroom at the end of the passage. Ajar, just as we'd left it. I came up short.

The Ironside had been in there. She'd shot him through the floor. And killed him? Could such a thing be killed?

The corpse hadn't caught fire. A withered fog was drifting from the room, but that would be from the kitchen underneath. From here, I could see perhaps a yard of floor. No body lay across it.

I hovered, undecided: then started to retreat. Step by cautious step. As I passed the open doorway of the bathroom, the Ironside lunged.

I glimpsed him from the corner of my eye, and squirmed aside: he crashed against the facing wall, and slithered down it – between me and the stairs. Still stumbling back, I lost my balance, and we both ended up on the floorboards. Belly-up and gasping, I began to crawl away; his helmet-head turned rustily towards me. Behind the bars, his face was muffled by a scarf; just a dark gap for the eyes. The smell of him washed over me: a shroud of rotting clothes – and something worse. Something I'd smelled down in Casualty once, and never quite forgotten. The reek of half-cooked flesh . . .

His gauntleted hand shot out, and seized my ankle. I squealed, and kicked it clear, thrashing back along the passage. He dragged himself in pursuit; riddled with Razoxane's shot, but far from finished. I drew my legs in sharply, and began to clamber up. He struggled to follow suit. Helplessly I backed into the bedroom.

The air was growing thicker: hot and sour. The open

windows couldn't clear it all. Smoke rose from the floor like a noxious mist, coming up through the tattered carpet and the shredded boards beneath. The latter creaked in protest as my heel came down. I swore in fright, and scuttled to the wall; then side-stepped down past the pattern of holes. Glancing back, I saw the Ironside fill the doorway.

He had me trapped. He knew it. So did I.

Smoke wreathed the bed and the burned Madonna. It crept into my lungs, and set me coughing. Eyes watering, I watched him come.

There was a sword at his belt, but he made no move to draw it. Just spread his mildewed gloves in ghastly greeting. As panic rose inside me, my frantic gaze jerked back towards the bed.

Mother Mary.

The thought was a prayer, a desperate plea – and inspiration came as if in answer. Biting my lip, I moved away from the wall: keeping the bed between us. An eerie calm overtook me then. I stopped, and simply waited.

He spoke as he stalked forward, the words distorted by his scarf. His voice was hoarse and croaking, as if coming from a throat baked dry. But in my hyped-up state, I heard him all too clearly. I even sensed the relish in his tone.

'Thou shalt be burned and buried, papist *whore* . . . and who will pray for *thee*?'

On which note the splintered boards gave way, and down he plunged – crashing through into the furnace of the kitchen.

'Not you, mate,' I said.

A gust of heat surged upward from below, and sent me lurching backwards. The glimpse I had of the kitchen was like seeing into the heart of a hot coal fire: a weird, white chamber, fiercely aglow. Then the jagged edges of the hole began to char. The hanging rags of carpet flickered and caught. Suddenly the room was dense with smoke.

I flailed my way to the window, and leaned out to clear my lungs. The cold air hit my scorching face – more stinging than a slap. I gasped for breath, hanging half-way out across the sill.

Razoxane was standing in the yard, and staring up; the Tinderbox raised and ready. The snow was scuffed around her. Bootprints were clustered beneath the glaring kitchen window. But of the second Ironside there was no sign.

Where did he go? her expression asked.

'*I* don't bloody know!' I shouted down at her.

The heat on my back was beginning to sink its talons in. I gazed at the snow, one storey below me. It didn't look thick enough to break my fall. The thought of jumping made my nerve-ends shrivel in revolt.

In desperation, I raised my eyes again – and caught a flicker of movement, away to my left. I looked that way, and glimpsed a figure in the tractor shed: ghost-grey against the shadows.

'Over there!' I called, voice cracking.

Razoxane spun around and fired: flame flared and burst like a bubble from her gun. The tractor blew apart as if in sympathy.

Something must have touched off the petrol tank: a fragment of winking shot. Perhaps a near miss had been enough, from so malefic a weapon. They were right: it *was* the Devil's.

All this as a cloud of burning fuel billowed outward, engulfing the shed. It rose and darkened, from yellow to red and orange, and finally an oil-black pall above the fiery wreckage. Bits of debris curled across the yard, trailing misty condensation and streamers of smoke.

A blackened helmet bounced and came to rest, steaming grimly in the snow.

Stunned though I was, I could wait no longer. My cloak smelled like it was starting to singe. Taking a deep, cold breath, I drew the collar up around my mouth and nose, and turned my face into the dark.

The air was a thick and scalding soup; the gloom barely lit by the glowing depths. I slithered along the wall – the paper was already peeling – in the general direction of the door. My eyes stung with tears until I could barely keep them open; but after what seemed a suffocating *age*, I made out a paler blur, and plunged towards it. Out in the passageway – oh thank you, God – I stumbled back towards the top of the stairs; coughing my way through wreaths of smoke. Reaching the landing, I had to peer out through the window there, and see what was happening outside.

The first thing I saw was the Ironside who'd fired at me. Up on the roof of an outbuilding, now – and Razoxane, below, was in his sights. Before I could scream a warning through the glass, his fire-lock had discharged.

She sensed it, swung around – and dived aside. The congealing cloud of gas burst into vivid flame, melting a swathe of snow across the yard, but it just licked her heels as she tumbled over and out of its path. She rose out of her roll, and found her feet; the empty Tinderbox discarded, and her pistol jumping back into her hand.

The Ironside was already fumbling with his bandolier. Razoxane crossed the yard towards him, firing the pistol more rapidly than I'd have thought a gun that age could manage; aiming single-handed – then with both. He flinched and jerked with every hit: and suddenly he was toppling forward, falling onto the load of winter feed below. The fodder-heap ignited in a rush. A vicious ball of flame consumed the trailer.

I teetered back from the window, as if pushed; then turned towards the stairs.

A furious, frightened face was there behind me.

Before I could react, the bearded vigilante had seized hold of me: twisting me around with his arm across my throat. Pinioned, I tried kicking at his shins; he promptly slammed his fist into my kidneys. Half-crippled, I wheezed with pain.

'We're getting out of here,' he snarled in my ear. 'All right?'

I wasn't going to argue. He shoved me forward, then manhandled me downstairs. The hall was dim with smoke. The door to the kitchen was closed, and blackening almost as I watched; the smell of burning wood was overwhelming. The front door loomed before us. Seeing his way to it unbarred, he slung me bodily aside and yanked it open.

Razoxane was waiting on the doorstep – a grim black scarecrow framed against the snow. A fierce, exultant yell came tearing from her lips, and the vigilante screamed as loud in sheer terror. He cowered back as she came in across the threshold: still funnelling her fury through her throat, and focusing it on him. And as she passed me, a surge of basic instinct made me fling myself against her and wrestle her up against the wall. I felt a spasm go through her, as if she'd retched – or come. A gob of something ectoplasmic sizzled into the wallpaper.

'*Run!*' I yelled at the stupefied man. 'As fast as you can!'

He just gawped at me for a moment; then bolted past us, and fled across the yard – skidding and stumbling in panic. I stared after him until he was out of sight behind the buildings; then realized I was still holding onto Razoxane: clutching her bony shoulders through her threadbare coat. With a shaky gasp, I let her go, and went out into the mercifully cold, clear air.

I walked to the middle of the yard before stopping to fill my aching lungs. Gradually my breathing eased, my heartbeat winding down. Standing in a cloud of my own breath, I stared at the snow . . . then the pale blue sky . . . before turning to look back at the farmhouse.

The building was well ablaze, now: flames ebbed and gushed from the kitchen and bedroom windows. A cumulus of smoke was building up above the rooftop. The sickening snap and crackle filled my ears.

Razoxane had followed unhurriedly. I gave her a wary glance.

'Don't ask,' I muttered. 'He was a sod, that bloke, he *hurt* me . . . but I couldn't hurt him back. Or let someone do it for me . . .' I shook my head then; confused by my own instincts.

'I wouldn't worry,' she came back dryly. 'Mercy takes a lot more strength than murder.' Leaving me to chew that over, she went to retrieve her Tinderbox. Dusting it off, she looked at me again. 'And besides . . . you did me a service. I've got enough ghosts on my trail as it is.'

I kicked morosely at the snow, and glanced around me. The wreck of the tractor was blazing fiercely, and the flames had spread to the adjacent buildings; but from their silence, I guessed they were storehouses. The animal sheds were across the yard, with hopefully enough of a firebreak between them and the main house. The feed-cart against the wall had burned itself out: reduced to a smouldering black mass.

'The fire-lock was always a volatile weapon,' Razoxane muttered, following my gaze. 'Sometimes they blew up in the user's face. Or the charge just combusted on contact with the air. All I had to do was knock him down. The whole bandolier ignited . . .'

And what a localized inferno that had generated. I took a few steps nearer, and just made out the Ironside's remains. There wasn't much left: just the breastplate – like a rust-corroded bonnet from an old scrapped car – and the skull: as featureless and frail as papier-mâché.

'So . . . you can't just shoot them, then?' I said.

Hunkered down beside her case, she shook her head. 'Things like this must be burned: broken down to dust and ashes . . .' She paused; what followed sounded pensive. 'But there's some kind of fire inside them, Rachel. A memory of it. The *Machina* can obviously release it. Maybe bullets can, as well – if you hit them hard enough . . .'

Something had caught my eye, and drew me closer. The holes punched in its breastplate by her shots. They were grouped on the left-hand side. After a moment, I realized the cluster formed a crude heart shape.

'Oh, you *show-off*,' I muttered.

The sharp cry of a rook cut through the crackle of flames. Turning, I saw the white bird settling on the cowshed roof.

'And where the bloody hell were you, then?' Razoxane called.

Undaunted, her familiar croaked again. Its hoarse cries left me none the wiser; but the pair of them were doubtless communing on a much more fundamental level. Razoxane drew out her pistol as she listened, and extracted the used magazine.

'Vedova's found the rest of them,' she said, once the bird-thing had relapsed into a watchful silence. 'In a wood three miles away.'

I swallowed. 'Cathy too?'

She shrugged. 'They were cloaked with chaff: just a blind spot on the map. But she'll be with them.'

Oh God. With things like these. I shuddered, and folded myself deeper into my cloak. It still smelled scorched.

Razoxane flexed her jaw. There was an introspective air about her now, like someone working a piece of food from between her teeth. Her throat spasmed as I watched; she craned forward and spat into her hand. My eyes grew wide as I saw that she'd produced a bullet.

It lay there, glistening dully in her palm. She looked up from it to me, and grinned.

'My condition has its advantages, sometimes.' So saying, she slotted the round into the magazine, and set about working up the next one.

All I could was stare, with a mix of fascination and repulsion, as she methodically reloaded. 'Are we going after them, then?' I asked at length.

'In our own good time, Rachel.' Finished, she hawked and gobbed into the snow, and snapped the magazine into its place. 'But we'd best be getting out of here. This comedy is bound to have attracted the wrong kind of attention.'

Walking over to where she'd left her case, she paused at the Ironside helmet which the explosion had thrown out. Picking it up by its face-bars, she gazed at it like a skull in a soliloquy.

'A few minutes' pain for an eternity of peace,' she murmured softly. 'I'll wager you said that to all the girls. All the women that you *burned*.'

'There's no need to gloat,' I muttered piously.

'Why not? Gloating is one of life's little pleasures.' Tossing the hunk of iron away, she gave me a grimy grin and went on to retrieve the guitar case. This comedy – as she'd called it – was clearly to her taste.

Well I'm glad she's having a good time, God. Because I'm not.

She looked back once, as we crested the rise. I saw the fire reflected in her shades, and looked as well. The roof of the house had fallen in, and giant yellow flames were grasping upward.

Razoxane set her face forward, and strode on.

'People will see our *tracks*, though . . .' I panted, slogging after her. The local police might seem part of a different world – but there'd still be a *lot* of explaining to do, if they managed to catch us up.

'They're not as easy to follow as they look,' was her unperturbed response.

I had to take her word on that – so I did. One last glance towards the funeral pyre; and then I got moving. Treading in her bootprints, as she'd told me. Following the flight of the rook.

*

'Remember what the spiritualist said?' I asked.

'About what?'

'The legend of Lickfield Wood. People who were destroyed by *arcane devices* . . . That was their fire-locks, wasn't it?'

We'd paused in the cover of a small copse. I was sitting on a fallen tree: still short of breath, and feeling sick and hollowed-out inside. Delayed shock, I supposed. But the cold was weighing heavily as well.

'Probably,' she said: still looking thoughtful. Gazing out across the fields we had to cross.

'And the way their faces are covered up . . . as if they've been burned themselves . . .' My voice trailed off in helpless trepidation. Being a nurse had made it easier, but not by much: I still found few sights more ominous than a head completely bandaged, with just two mournful holes for eyes. Worse than the scars behind it, in a way.

'There's more to it than that, though,' Razoxane said. 'A fire-lock accident would be viewed as divine retribution, yes; the victims would get a quick, unholy burial. But something happened to keep bodies and souls together in the soil. And their leader doesn't *seem* to have rotted at all; nor burned . . .'

Her turn to lapse into silence. I breathed a stream of condensation. The countryside around us was graveyard-still.

We'd heard the commotion behind us earlier: sirens,

faint with distance. Hopes of a quiet Boxing Day being thoroughly dashed. There wouldn't be much of the Ironsides left; but they'd find other remains, much more recently dead, in the ashes of the burnt-out farmhouse.

Another family Christmas screwed up? What really bothered me was that I couldn't find it in myself to care.

It was afternoon now, and the day was closing in; but no one had come after us. Looking back the way we'd come, I realized why. Our tracks had melted back into the snow, like a well-healed scar. Close examination might have found them; but to a casual glance, the whiteness was unmarked.

'What I don't understand,' said Razoxane slowly, while I marvelled at her magic, 'is why they're trying to kill you. They sprang an elaborate trap back there . . . but not to take you alive. They meant to kill you. As if that's all they're after . . .'

'He called me a papist whore,' I murmured; with the smallest spark of satisfaction at what had happened to him then. 'He said I'd be burned and buried.'

She grunted. 'His kind saw sorcerers and Catholics as much the same thing. Impurities to be purged. It doesn't explain why they've singled you out, though, does it?'

'Do you know who they are?' I asked.

'I think so, now. I keep thinking of those soldiers I remember . . . from way back. This would have been near the end of Cromwell's rule. The witch-craze was burning itself out – and those last fires were the fiercest of all. You could smell the ashes in the smoke, that winter. It was like another civil war; one with bitter magic on both sides. A lot of what happened was repressed by living memory; just fragments survived, in the folk tales; the place names . . .' She paused. 'War's the wrong word, though. There were no battle-lines; no armies. Just footloose factions; fire-skeins; cells. Fighting as they found, through the fields and woodland. The country areas had it worst. A lot of ancient ways were lost. In some of the towns it was the same. The Black Physicians, for example, were almost totally destroyed. But they took a few souls with them . . .'

She broke off then. I sensed her tensing up.

'Look,' she said. I turned my head, and saw.

The sky to the east was dense with the promise of snow – but a sudden darker flurry rose before it, like a weird black blizzard. Birds, I realized after a moment. Crows. Taking wing from a gloomy wood, a half-mile distant.

Whatever had roused them, they didn't return to their branches. I watched them drifting in a cloud towards a neighbouring clump – as if anxious to shun the shadows of their previous roost.

Shadows. I looked back towards the mass of trees, and felt my gut grow tighter. A premature darkness had congealed there, only adding to its sinister aspect. It was an ugly-looking wood in any case: all straggling and contorted. Like something that had tried to crawl across country, and come to rest, exhausted, on its belly.

'Let's get closer,' said Razoxane softly.

'They'll see us,' I objected, breathless.

'Not if we go that way . . .' She pointed to the lane running down past our copse: half-clogged with snow, and framed by frosted hedgerows. It dipped and veered between the fields, passing very close to the lower edge of the wood. So close, it was overhung by trailing trees. Even from this distance, their limbs seemed poised to snatch at passers-by.

I bit my dry, cracked lip, and tasted blood.

Razoxane adjusted the strap of her guitar case: confirming the weight of two shotguns and a shovel. Companions on the road. She glanced at me then, and offered an icy smile. 'Come on. It'll be dark before too long.'

She moved out onto the slope, and side-stepped down towards the lane. I followed, crouching low; my cloak brushing the snow. Once in the lane, only the topmost branches of the wood were visible above the hedge and rising ground. The hedgerow itself had a fairytale aspect, silver with frost; but the treetops beyond were an altogether grimmer grey – like bones against the backdrop of the sky.

We made slow progress; the snow had drifted ankle-deep. Crow-calls carried faintly across the silent farmland, but the wood ahead was frozen still. Step by step, it loomed towards us, like a slowly brewing storm.

Half-way there, Vedova overtook us, and flew on into the trees. By the time we reached the bend, in the shadow of the wood, it was perched on a branch in patient vigil.

Razoxane struck upslope, and reached the treeline. I stared after her, feeling desperately uncertain. But Cathy was close now; alone with the ghosts of this frost-withered place. How could I not keep going?

Her strong hand grasped my own as I scrambled up, and hauled me the rest of the way. I skidded, caught myself, and joined her in the cover of the trees. The silence of the wood wrapped round me like a blanket.

'Are they here?' I husked, from the bottom of my throat.

Razoxane nodded; staring off into the depths. I followed her gaze, but the gaps between the trees seemed spun with cobwebs: sheets of clinging grey. I thought of giant wolf-spiders, prowling the wood. My cold skin rippled in revulsion.

Above us, Vedova shifted restlessly – then took flight with a sudden clatter, swooping off between the trees. That was more than enough to make me jump. Razoxane, impassive, watched it go; then followed. Treading carefully. I followed her as if on eggshells.

At least I knew what I was looking for this time; which almost made it worse. Fear of the unknown was daunting enough – but the fright of that first Ironside was still with me. I could feel it resounding dully in my chest. Every tree seemed about to transform itself into a horse and rotting rider.

The snap of frozen twigs came like a whipcrack through the hush. We both stopped dead. Razoxane eased down into a crouch, and gestured me back. I complied, heart beating hard; glancing down to check that I was stepping on snow. Slipping behind a tree-trunk, I pressed myself against it: felt the thudding of my breast against the bark. Then, with a grim little swallow, I peered warily out.

A bulky shape was moving through the wood. A horseman. I shrank back into my cover, as if to see must mean being seen; then risked one wide eye to follow their slow-paced progress. All I got were glimpses, between the trees and twisted branches. The Ironside sat hunched in his saddle, picking a path for his sightless mount: his peaked iron helmet like a bird of prey in profile. I moved around the trunk to keep track of him; saw the ugly rifle braced against his thigh. Wasn't *arquebus* the word for one like that? So ancient, it looked almost futuristic.

I held my breath, and the Ironside passed on. No other rider came behind him. Letting my lungs deflate, I crept forward to where Razoxane crouched.

Somewhere ahead of us, Vedova rasped a warning.

'Lead rider,' she whispered, taking hold of my shoulder to keep me there beside her. 'Others following . . .'

The next sound of stepped-on twigs came from directly behind us.

Oh God. I drew my shoulders up around my neck, in fear of being struck. Razoxane's hand pressed harder: held me still. On our knees together, heads bowed low, we held the pose like praying pilgrims as the horseman crossed our trail. From the corner of my eye I saw him tower above us; mouldering hat pulled low, and a scarf that looked to have been tie-dyed with human blood concealing his face. His horse snorted smoky plumes that drifted down around us; I smelled its heat. And then he too was past, and moving on through the undergrowth. My muscles loosened up and let me sag. I leaned against Razoxane, drained of breath.

'Over-watcher,' she muttered, still gazing after him. 'The rest of them will be in file, behind the first. Let's shadow them.' She squeezed my shoulder; a kind of cold excitement in her smile. I couldn't share it; but it lifted my own confidence a bit.

Rising cautiously to our feet, we moved forward: converging with the path the first had taken. More cracklings were coming from the heart of the wood. Hooves and boots on snowy, shrivelled leaves. I felt my chest compressing like a screwed-down vice as the Ironsides took shape out of the gloom.

They were coming in shambling single file; a couple were two abreast. One more of them was mounted, but the others moved on foot. I took in tattered coats, and rusty armour. Hats and helmets. Rifles borne on shoulders, as overlong and heavy as machine-guns. And all through a filter of thick grey light, like a filthy, frosted window.

No faces. Scarecrow faces. Save for one.

I recognized him straightaway: that rider in the middle of the line. His features pale and haggard, framed by shoulder-length grey hair. In the shadow of his broad-brimmed hat, his eyes were hooded; but I already knew their colour – and their coldness.

He was swathed in his cloak of shaggy fur: the garment gathered close around a bundle on his lap. Muffling it against him as he rode.

Something silent, small and very still . . .

'Don't even think of it,' breathed Razoxane beside me.

I watched, with open mouth, as the horse paced past; but my throat had closed up tight. I couldn't breathe. The Ironside leader dipped his head; I saw the crust of snow around the crown of his hat. Flakes grizzled his cloak like frosty dandruff. But the shape against his stomach was too well wrapped. I stared and stared, but got no glimpse of gold.

I felt her, though. My heart cried out in anguish as she passed. After so many dreadful days of separation, my little girl was there within my reach.

And all I could do was stand there, while the current bore her off. No help for it. No hope. Gazing after the receding horseman, I felt like a medieval woman being martyred: *pressed* to death.

Razoxane's hand was back on my shoulder. Reassurance or restraint; I felt too sick to be sure.

The last footsoldier had the chaff-drag at his heels. I saw it was a coffin, caked with mud. A Y-shaped piece of rope had been fastened to the handles, and the Ironside was towing it behind him, hunching his shoulder against the weight. Benumbed, I watched it scrape and slither by.

'Come on,' said Razoxane, already moving: 'let's follow.'

We kept pace: slipping from tree to tree. More than once we lost sight of them, and had to follow the disembodied snap of branches up ahead; but then the coffin came in sight again, the Ironside half-glancing back as he corrected its bumpy course.

'What's in that thing?' I whispered.

'The Devil only knows,' she muttered back, and sounded like she meant it. I pulled a face, and didn't ask again.

We followed them as far as the edge of the wood. The sky had grown more solid in the meantime, and the light was fading fast. Creeping up behind a fallen tree, we watched them straggle out onto a farm-track.

'We can't go any further,' Razoxane said.

Relief and raw frustration clashed inside me. Keeping those stealthy shapes in sight had been like contemplating spiders: too hair-raising for words. But I couldn't bear the thought of leaving Cathy.

'Dusk's coming down,' she pointed out: reading my mixed emotions off my face. 'There's more snow on the way. We should be getting back.'

'But we'll lose them again,' I complained; still following their leader with my gaze. He'd already begun to melt into the gloom.

'Vedova'll keep track. They're redeploying, but they won't go far. We cut them deep today, Rachel. We made them bleed – as much as corpses can. They'll be wary; but they will come again.'

And again, I echoed bleakly. *And again*. Until they killed me. Or until she burned them all – and saved my daughter.

Watching that last figure drag his grisly coffin off across the snow, I couldn't say which outcome was more likely.

We watched until they'd faded in the deepening dusk; then started back towards town. Robbed of our impetus, we trudged in weary silence. By the time we'd reached the outskirts, my head felt light as air; my legs like lead. Once or twice back there, in the freezing twilight, I'd thought that I might faint.

'I'll take my leave of you here,' said Razoxane dryly, as the soft white flakes began to fall around us. 'Let you make your peace with your curate friend. And don't go wandering off on your own next time. I'll come and fetch you – right?'

'Right,' I said.

I looked behind us one more time. The sky was dense and greenish-grey; it tinged the sickly pallor of the snow. And everywhere the trees were black, as if a fire had charred them.

*

Graham and Ruth were understandably hurt, and didn't stint in showing it. Where *were* you? We were *worried*. At the end of a cold, cruel day, I could have done with a warmer welcome; but of course they weren't to know. And besides, their annoyance was refreshing in a way. Saints, as that Nun's Prayer says, can be so hard to live with . . .

So I swallowed their reproach like a penance: volunteering to help wash up as proof of my contrition. Graham had adjourned to the study to work on next Sunday's sermon, and Ruth and I did the dishes in silence. It seemed to grate between us at first; but gradually its edges softened.

'Sorry if we snapped,' she said at length; giving me a rueful smile. 'But waking up like that, to find you gone . . .'

'I'm the one who should be apologizing,' I put in hastily. 'I . . . needed to go somewhere. But I should have said . . .'

'Rachel . . . is there something we can help with?'

I dropped my gaze to the plate I was wiping. It was dry already, but I turned it over and towelled it again. 'It's all right: really,' I said after a pause. 'Nothing I won't have sorted . . . in a couple of days.'

She didn't want to push me, but needed to know more. I sensed the conflict. Even with my eyes down, I could tell.

Snow flurried briefly against the steamed-up window. Glancing round, I could just see it, faintly falling, where the light pushed back the darkness. It hadn't slackened for an hour.

'I don't like to think of you wandering the streets in weather like this,' Ruth murmured: coming in from a different angle. 'Don't, for Heaven's sake, feel obliged to get out from under our feet. You're welcome to stay indoors for as long as you want. Until your problem's sorted . . .'

I thought of what lay out there, beyond the light. Fields being buried deeper by the minute. Woodland shrouded; lanes stopped up. And where was Cathy in that wilderness? How would she keep *warm*?

The tracks would be covered. Come daylight, we'd be starting from scratch . . .

I sensed Ruth beside me, her hand on my arm. 'Oh Rachel, love: *what is it?*'

'Oh . . . nothing.' My eyes were brimming with betrayal, but I kept it back. Sniffed once, and forced a smile. It felt as fragile as bone china. 'I appreciate your asking, really I do . . . but I have to see this through on my own.'

With a last squeeze of my arm, she relented; reluctantly concluding I had reasons. She turned back to the worktop – I quickly rubbed my sleeve over my eyes – and checked the water in the kettle. 'Coffee?' she asked over her shoulder; accepting that this was the only question I'd be answering tonight.

'Please,' I said.

'How's it going?' I asked Graham from the doorway.

He gave me a glance; then sat back from his desk, and stretched. 'Slowly,' he admitted. 'There are times when you know you've got to make mention of something . . . but you don't know how.'

'Vicar's block, eh?'

He gave a dry snort of amusement; it faded in the gloom beyond the desklamp. With one shoulder on the door-jamb, I sipped my coffee: waiting.

'You've heard what's been happening, these past few days?' he asked. 'No, sorry . . . you wouldn't have, would you? Would you believe there've been *four* people murdered here this week? This week of all times. We're going on about peace, goodwill to all men . . . and look what's happening in the world.'

'I suppose Christmas is just another day, for some people,' I said neutrally.

'You're right there, I'm afraid. One of these murders was last night, can you believe that? Christmas night. The poor man was beaten to death in his own back garden, for no apparent reason. That's the worst thing, isn't it . . . ?'

I nodded urgently. *Only yesterday?* It seemed I'd come so very far since then.

'Then someone sets fire to a farmhouse, early this morning, and reports say a body was found in the wreckage . . .' He shook his head; then looked apologetically towards me. 'So you see why we were worried about you, Rachel? Even a quiet town like this can fly off the handle sometimes.'

'In some wars there's never a Christmas truce,' I murmured; eyes steady in the knowledge that he couldn't see the frozen depths behind them.

He tapped the end of his pen on his desktop, and grinned at me. 'I like the sound of that. D'you mind if I put it in my sermon?'

'Be my guest,' I said.

10

LOVERS

The bedroom window was covered by a cataract of frost; but with my nose pressed up against it, I could see the flakes still falling, straight and slow.

I drew back, and pulled the curtains closed. What shelter had the others found, I wondered? The depths of a wood, perhaps; a derelict house. They couldn't still be moving round in this.

Please God, they had my daughter somewhere warm.

It was cold enough in here – cutting in through my flimsy nightie. With a shiver, I went over to my clothes: delved among them, and brought out the photo I'd retrieved from the flat. Clutching it, I clambered into bed; then sat back against the pillows and just stared at her picture. After a minute, I passed my fingertips across her face; or rather the cool, smooth surface that lay over it. That summed it up so bleakly: the hard, invisible barrier between us.

I remembered what I'd dreamed last night, in this same bed. That corpse with a heart of silver – and gin-trap ribs. It was the first chance I'd had to reflect upon it. I still had no idea what it might mean.

It occurred to me then, as I circled Cathy's features with a slow and yearning finger, that perhaps I could use the picture as we'd used the Book of Martyrs. If I concentrated wholly on her image, my inner eye might give me clearer sight. Of where she was; where we could find her. Of what I'd have to do to get her back.

I gazed at her smile for many minutes. It was like meditating with an icon: using it to channel my prayers. But it brought my childhood back to me, as well. The way I'd cram my mind with happy thoughts, in the hope – so often vain – of pleasant dreams . . .

At length I reached out for the bedside light, and clicked it off. Then curled up in the dimness and waited for sleep; my daughter's smile pressed coldly to my breasts.

A part of me had doubted: convinced it couldn't work – or afraid that it would. But when sleep sucked me down, I seemed to go on sinking, as if the bottom had dropped out of my bed.

The void beneath engulfed me: growing colder and more stifling by the moment. Panic began to flutter like a small, blind bird inside me. I *clenched* my mind, and halted my descent; then started groping around. The sensation was of swimming beneath a frozen lake: limitless dark on every side, and an icy roof above me. I'd taken the plunge of my own free will, and trapped myself below it. I had to find another hole, before breath ran out completely.

The wings inside my chest were beating harder. My fear of drowning gripped me by the throat. I cast around; flailed upward. But there was no way back now.

Then I glimpsed a fuzzy glow ahead: pallid and blurred, like a full moon through fog. Renewing my mental strength, I swam towards it. The closer I got, the clearer it became – focusing into a face. A spasm snatched at my heart as I realized it was Cathy's.

Her eyes were closed. She looked so very tired.

I could see no further detail: couldn't make out where she was. This was a tunnel vision, and her face was the light at the end. Her expression was pinched, as if she were sleeping off a sulk; her golden hair was tarnished and awry. But she was still alive: still breathing. Her upturned brow just waiting for my goodnight kiss.

A great black claw moved into sight above it.

I must have cried aloud, but the sound was just an echo in my ears. I tried to struggle forward – but the dark solidified around me. The ragged claw hung poised above my angel. Her forehead creased as if, from deep within her dreams, she sensed it: that shadow on her moon-pale skin . . .

Then the claw drew back, and turned aside: palm upward. A second set of talons came from out of the murk, and clasped it; started tugging off its skin. And then I realized, gasping, that the claw was just a glove.

The hand that it revealed was long and lean, with fine-boned fingers. Slowly they reached down and touched my daughter's forehead; stroked it. Smoothing the frown away, along with her fringe.

As I looked on, petrified, my mind's eye grew accustomed to the dimness, and drew back to show me more. I could make his arm out, now; his shoulder; the matted, mangy cloak which made him loom like a bear. And then, as he craned forward, I caught sight of his face.

It was the first time I'd seen him clearly; bare-headed, in repose. His hair was an iron mane, tinged silver by the moon – but I was startled to see how young he looked. Not much older than me, perhaps. The face was as severe as I remembered, like flint beneath flesh . . . but the expression on it threw me altogether. No sneer of satisfaction; not a glimmer of lust. Instead, I glimpsed a kind of sombre longing. A wistfulness that went beyond words.

It was the shadow of a look I'd seen before – on Nick's face. A father's look. A father's spellbound love.

My mind recoiled in shock – and the bowed head came up sharply. It turned my way, as if in guilty reflex. That haunted look had hardened once again; its tenderness scabbed over.

'Rachel . . . ?' he asked softly.

I floated in darkness, frozen solid to the core. But this was *my* vision; he surely couldn't see me . . .

'I *know* thee, Rachel,' he murmured, as if mocking my assurance. 'I know that thou art come.'

With a thin smile he returned his gaze to Cathy; slid bony fingers back into her hair. Suddenly I found I couldn't help myself.

'Leave her *alone*,' I hissed.

He glanced again towards me, smile still faint; his eyes like yellow glimmers in the gloom. 'Thou fearest for thy daughter, Rachel Young?'

I'd given myself away now. There was no longer any point in containing my fright – or my fury.

'Of course I bloody do. Of course . . .' I bit down hard on my mind's sharp tongue, before it could spit out worse. It might be that I'd crack his calm – and what might leak out then?

His fingers were a spider in her hair. Long and leathery: feeling their way. I watched them start to creep across her scalp.

'It is not my wish that she be harmed,' he said.

'What do you *want*?' I whispered.

'A meeting such as this,' he answered dryly. 'Thy dark companion stands between us; but neglects to bar the windows of thy mind.'

I almost choked on the words in my throat, but managed to bring them up: be rid of them. 'You want me, you can have me . . . Right? Just let my little girl go free.'

He tipped his head backward, a glint of grim indulgence on his face. 'And what shall we do with thee?'

I remembered my dream: being dragged towards a funeral pyre. I felt my skin shrink tight.

'I don't *care* . . . Whatever you want . . . just let her go.'

He glanced down at Cathy; took a lock of her lank hair between his finger and thumb. His voice, when he spoke, was low and pensive.

'With thy child in my hands . . . I can make thee to do anything I please, is this not so?'

I swallowed. 'Yes . . . It is.'

He released her hair, and drew back his hand. 'I would rather it were otherwise. What I have to ask of thee should be done in faith, not fear.'

'I'll come to you,' I breathed. 'I promise . . .'

He shook his head. 'I do not seek thy life.'

I tried and failed to register relief. 'Then . . . what?'

The Ironside's fingers interlocked: the first two steeple-stiff against his chin. He regarded me in silence for a moment; then let a pallid smile brush his lips.

'I want the witch thy sister to come settle things with me,' he said.

I simply stared: struck dumb with disbelief.

The grey young man leaned forward, eyes intense. 'Hear thou my name. My name is *Warwick*. A fitting name to bear in a war against the witches.'

'You're after *her*?' I whispered.

'We are. We have followed her trace through town and country; beyond our graves – and hers.'

I cringed beneath his stare. It gave me just a glimpse of what his steely calm enclosed: a flaring at the windows of a furnace. I saw zeal beyond reason there. A hate that even death had not destroyed.

'She was safe from our wrath behind the prison-bars of Hell. But at the end, her hunger brought her back. Her greed for power. She took flesh again, to walk in her old ways.'

A *witchfinder*, I thought – still catching up. A thrill of dread went through me.

'And once we have her trapped in human guise, we can truly put her soul to death – for ever.'

'Why drag me into this?' I gasped. 'For Christ's sake, why my *daughter*?'

'Thou art bound to thy dark sister,' he replied. 'She bids thee place thy trust in her alone. Thy love for this child will be thy strength against temptation.'

'She's not my *sister*,' I burst out desperately.

'Not by blood, perhaps. But in spirit, ye are as faces of a coin.'

My gaze was drawn to Cathy once again. Her small, pale, sleeping face. *Oh God, please give her back, I WANT her . . .*

'Deliver her to us, and thou shalt be free – and thy daughter.'

He sat back, then; let me weigh that up in silence. I did so, feeling sick and bruised with shock.

'Does she know?' I asked, after a pause.

He nodded once. 'She knows. She has not forgotten all the debts that still have to be paid.'

Razoxane. You bitch. You could have told me.

Which didn't make me loathe *him* any less. Baby-snatcher. Gloating ghoul. My mind was thick with fear and disgust.

'Thou owest *nothing*,' he persisted. 'Not to her. She spreads death and perdition wherever she goes. Be not deceived: a woman she is no longer. She is death's device: a swift, infernal *engine*, with no soul. She comes to thee because she has no choice – her magic demands innocence to feed its malice. She will seek to profit from it, if she can.'

Absurd that I should hesitate at all; and yet the thought of giving in to him was utterly revolting. Razoxane was evil, and I'd known that from the start – but her twisted goal had always been salvation. Whatever she was up to this time, I couldn't just condemn her out of hand.

But *Cathy* . . .

'Thou art her plaything,' Warwick said. 'She will consume thee. Just as my daughter was consumed.'

I stared at him; and saw that shadow cross his face again. The dim, regretful ghost of something *human*.

'Your daughter?'

'Aye, lady. I had a daughter once.' He gazed at me in silence for moment. 'The Devil took her: twisted her around. She was devoured. For this, the witch will pay.'

I looked at Cathy, huddled in his lap. Asleep in the arms of the bear.

He showed his teeth. 'Why hesitate? Why doubt? Thou knowest she is damned – and now her judgment is upon her. Her wandering spirit will be laid to rest at last. It will trouble thy peace no longer.'

Cathy. Oh my angel. I had to have her back.

'Thy word upon it, Rachel Young: that thou shalt render up the witch. And thy daughter shall return to thee unharmed.'

I opened my mouth: not quite sure, even then, what words would fill it. But before I could begin, something plunged into our midst, and the glacial dark was suddenly in ferment.

The vision broke apart before my eyes: wiped out like the reflection in a pool. Cathy's face was swallowed by the void. I tried to scream – and felt a presence close beside me. A mouthless, urgent shadow in the night.

'Nick . . .' I whimpered faintly, and reached out. But when I clawed my way back up through the hole in the ice, it was Razoxane I found waiting at my bedside.

'Pleasant dreams?' she asked me dryly.

I wrapped my arms around my drawn-up knees, and glanced aside; not deigning to reply. Not daring. Behind the sullen mask I'd just put on, my mind was bright with fear. I felt as if my guilty face was glowing in the dark.

Had she dipped into my thoughts just then? Had I murmured them aloud? Did she know who I'd been speaking with, behind her back . . . ?

A rustle in the dimness brought my head back round – to see the white blur of Vedova at the foot of my bed, furling its wings like fragments of the snowy night outside. Perched on the bedpost, it fixed me with a beady, knowing stare.

I was suddenly aware that a strap of my nightie had come adrift. I hastily pulled it back up, and drew my legs in closer.

Real snow caked Razoxane's hat-brim; a dusting flecked the shoulders of her coat. However they'd got in, they'd brought the bitterness of winter with them. It scoured the room. I felt it start to gnaw my naked shoulders.

As I watched, lips bitten closed, Razoxane pushed my clothes off the single chair, and took a seat. She slouched comfortably back on it, her smile showing palely through the gloom; but the shades made her stare as void as two round holes.

The way I'd just reacted must have kindled her suspicions. Stifling a shriek against the palm of my hand, I'd kicked the duvet off and recoiled against the pillows. A shock to find her standing there, of course; but there'd been more than rude awakening in my horrified stare.

Oh Jesus, did she *know*?

'Your lover's ghost been visiting again?' her calm voice asked.

A pause while I searched for pitfalls: double meanings. Then I mutely shook my head.

Razoxane took her hat off, and brushed snow onto the carpet; then tipped her head towards me once again. 'You'd do better to let him rest, you know,' she murmured.

I stared, as if she'd slapped me in the face. Then: '*He* came back to *me.*'

She nodded, once. 'Because you called. You're crying out to him, inside; he answers. He can't rest until you let him.'

For a moment I just sat there, open-mouthed – while defensive denial met a gutting surge of guilt. Had I disturbed my darling's peace? Dragged him back from the comfort of the grave?

'I love him, Razoxane,' I whispered. 'He's part of my *life.*'

Razoxane made a small, sardonic gesture. 'A man, a story.' Summation and dismissal, just like that.

'And what would *you* know about it, then?' I hissed – too loudly for this quiet house.

'Not much,' was her soft admission. 'My mother warned me what I'd find if I followed her way. Nights without love, she promised. People without faces. Roads without end . . .' Her voice grew fainter as she spoke, as memory caught her up. Her thin smile faded with it.

'Cathy's his daughter, too . . .' I muttered.

'Sorry?'

'Nothing.' I raised my eyes. 'And what the hell do you want, anyway?'

'To talk about tomorrow,' she said calmly.

'How did you get *in* here?' I persisted: a vain attempt to put the subject off.

'With difficulty. Now listen.' She leaned forward. 'Before we can get your daughter back, there's something we have to do.'

Isn't there always? I let my shoulders slump. 'Like what?'

'Isolate their chaff-drag, and destroy it.'

I remembered that sinister coffin, and almost shuddered. I didn't want to think what might be under its nailed-down lid.

'We don't have a choice,' she murmured. 'For as long as they have it, it masks their movements. I can't keep track of them, except by sight. If we're going to get in close . . . maybe deep in woodland . . . it makes it too easy for one of them to take me from behind.'

And that's what they're after, isn't it? The chance to cut you *down.*

I rested my chin on my drawn-up knees. 'But . . . it's right in with them, isn't it?' *So we can't get close to it – can we?*

'At the moment it is. But I'm just thinking what new tactics they might use. A fire-lock troop like that . . . they used to call them fire-skeins: burning their way cross-country in loose formation. But on more hostile ground, they'd divide into cells: move independently of one another. If they do that tomorrow, we can go after the one with the drag. They won't expect that.'

'Might Cathy be with that one too?' I ventured.

Razoxane shook her head. 'They'll still be *caput* and *cauda*: the head and the tail. Their leader will ride with the other cell – and keep his hostage with him.'

Warwick's face rose up, like a reminder: still sealed within the shadows of my mind.

I swallowed: almost gagged. 'Where are they now?'

'It's hard to keep focus in weather like this . . . but there's a cloak of chaff round an empty house just west of town – so my intelligencer says . . .'

She tipped the rook a wry, indulgent glance. It rasped a response. The sound could have carried over miles of open field; in this restricted space, it was explosive. I winced and hunched my shoulders; gestured frantically for quiet. Too late. After a pause, the creak of a mattress came from Ruth and Graham's room.

Hands to my mouth, I heard one of them murmur something: half-asleep. Trying to decide whose turn it was, I hoped. Roused suddenly, they'd think it was the baby. Except that the house was quiet again: snow-still.

Razoxane smiled.

Her familiar was preening itself, unruffled. I glared towards it, willing it to silence; daring it to make another sound. *I'll wring your scrawny neck*, I promised, impotently – knowing I'd never have the nerve to try. Not against that barbed-wire bundle of beak and claws.

The door down the passageway clicked open. I heard feet on the floorboards outside my room; a yawn half-stifled. I guessed that it was Graham.

Just past my door, the stillness seemed to register. He stopped.

Razoxane had dropped her gaze, as if to listen; her blank shades staring into the darkness. A smile still snagged the corner of her mouth.

Vedova turned around upon the bedpost, like an eerie chimney-cowl. I bit down on my lip with my two front teeth – just waiting for the outcry that would give us away.

Then the baby really started, like a siren. I heard her crank up her wail, and felt something collapse inside me. Relief at the distraction, to be sure; but a surge of pain came with it. The call was still unbearably familiar. It put a hook into my heart, and *pulled*.

Razoxane held her pensive pose. I gave her a glance, then lowered my face onto my knees: listening while Graham cuddled and quietened his daughter.

At length – the nappy changed – he went trudging back to his room. I waited until the stirred-up silence had settled back into its place, before raising my damp eyes.

Razoxane was watching: waiting. I felt a cold contraction round my heart. Again I asked myself the question: does she know?

I couldn't read the answer off her pale and patient face. Was she biding her time? Simply playing me along? I knew I couldn't trust her; but what if she decided that she couldn't trust *me*?

I swallowed miserably, and sat up straight.

'I'll see you in the morning,' said Razoxane softly. 'Make sure you have yourself a hearty breakfast. It's as cold as the grave out there.'

*

'Rachel,' Ruth said gently: almost humouring. 'You don't want to go out in *this*.'

A glance through the kitchen window, and I had to agree: I didn't want to. The snow had stopped, but the sky was low and livid; the daylight had a used, reflected look. It might have been another world out there.

I turned back to Ruth, and shrugged. 'There's someone I need to see.' I crunched into another slice of toast, pre-empting further argument. It tasted cardboard-dry, and just as difficult to swallow.

She stared at me, then shrugged in turn. I sensed a touch of *please yourself* about it, and guessed her patience was wearing thin. I couldn't blame her really: I felt wretchedly ungrateful. When I'd met her on the landing in my borrowed bathrobe, she'd urged me to lie in for as long as I liked; but here I was now, fully-dressed, and clearly anxious to be gone.

Ruth hesitated; tried one more time. 'At least . . . if you have to go out . . . take one of my coats. Wrap up warm.'

But I couldn't even take her up on that. My cloak was something special, almost magic: a part of my past – enfolding me in memories as much as warmth. I'd still been a student when I first put it on . . .

'Thanks; but I'm okay.'

'I can't understand you, Rachel,' she said frankly. 'Why do you have to keep us at arm's length? We're here, and we can help, if only you let us.'

'You sound like my mum,' I murmured. Tagging a weak smile onto the end – but it wasn't a compliment in the context, and she knew it. With a short, defeated sigh, she went on out.

Listening to her slapping cushions around in the living room, I heaved a sigh of my own; then washed down the last dry shreds of toast with the dregs of my black coffee.

Vedova picked me up soon after I'd left the house: weaving and circling ahead of me like a will o' the wisp, starkly outlined in the odd light. I plodded after it down silent streets. There was patchy evidence of gritting on the roads themselves, like raw black grazes in the whiteness; but the pavements were still ankle-deep.

Razoxane was waiting at the edge of town: sitting perched on a stile behind some houses. Beyond the hedge of naked thorns, the woods looked very close: as pregnant with shadow as the clouds were with snow.

She smiled to see me coming: like somebody at ease in this dead white wilderness. Dropping lightly down, she dusted herself off; but her black gaze didn't waver for a moment.

Snow-blind, I thought, and shivered.

The guitar case was propped up against the frosted wooden framework. She slung it over her shoulder; tugged at the ends of her moth-eaten scarf. 'Ready?'

'Where are they?' I asked dully.

'They've split, just as I thought they might. One cell's been moving since just before dawn: creeping round the southern fringe of town. The other one's static. The chaff-drag's with that one, for concealment.'

'And . . . Cathy's with the first one?'

'Yes.'

'With . . . the leader?' I dared not shape his name inside my head: she'd glimpse it.

She nodded, watching my face. I felt a sudden stinging in my cheeks, as blood rose to my cold skin.

'Can't we just go for that one, then? One against four, you . . . could manage that. Couldn't you?' I glanced pointedly down towards the case. She followed my gaze; then looked back towards me.

'It's not so easy. They've got a sower with them, scattering chaff. Their tracks are blurred.'

As ours had been before them. Craft against craft. I stared past her, into the trees; not wanting her to meet my naked eyes.

'There's an old tithe-barn a quarter-mile from here,' Razoxane went on calmly. 'Completely screened from mindsight. Vedova's been to spy it out. We think they've got it there.'

I felt like a mouse in the paws of a cat: feeling the shapes of her cold, sheathed claws. She knew. She had to know. She was a *spirit*.

Swallowing, I forced my thoughts to take the other path. She wasn't infallible, she'd admitted that much. She'd taken on flesh again – with all its weakness. Perhaps she saw no further than my cowed exterior; the meekness of her sacrificial lamb.

And if she *didn't* know . . .

I shook my head instinctively: afraid to think it any further through. Not while she was so close.

Razoxane climbed the stile, and set off towards the woods; I followed. Staring at the back of her head, above the battered, jouncing bulk of the guitar case, I risked a Judas thought.

I sell my skin dearly: that's what she'd said. But Cathy was a pearl beyond price. To give one for the other would be a fair exchange . . .

Razoxane looked back; my heart leaped up inside me. But all she did was wait, until I'd joined her by the treeline.

'There's a track through the wood,' she said. 'An old hollow way. It leads to the site of a lost village. The barn's the only building left.'

Vedova fluttered in to land above us, dislodging snow from a branch. I gave it an unwelcoming glance.

'It may have been plague that wiped it out,' continued Razoxane, sounding thoughtful. 'Or perhaps it just dried up from slow decay. But you get strange echoes from places like that. Ghosts call out for ghosts.'

On which eerie note, she set off into the trees. Following, I found myself reminded of some allegorical tale I'd heard in Sunday school. It struck a real resonance, right now. The pilgrimage of Much-Afraid – and her two companions Sorrow and Suffering.

The barn was long and low-walled, with a steeply pitched roof. It lay on the far side of a field, looking all the more isolated by that carpet of white. From where we crouched at the wood's edge, I could just make out the roofs of more modern farm buildings through the straggly trees beyond it.

There weren't any tracks in the snow. I glanced at Razoxane. 'You're sure?'

'Can't you feel them?' she murmured back.

I peered again through the mesh of frozen twigs, towards the barn. The ridge of the roof looked lumpy and uneven, like a knobbled spine. It made me think of a stony beast, crouched down beneath a mantle of snow.

I could feel them, all right.

'You reckon there's four, then?' I asked.

'Probably four.' She'd produced a matchstick, and was nibbling thoughtfully at the end.

I waited, fighting the urge to get up and stamp around. It had been chilly enough while we'd been moving; but now that we were motionless, the frost in the air was beginning to show its teeth.

'So now what?' I prompted, when nothing further was forthcoming.

'I'm thinking about it.'

Pulling a face – my cold skin seemed to creak – I lowered my chin onto my drawn-up knee, and gathered my warm cloak closer. After a minute I tried again. 'Do you want to wait until they move again . . . or what?'

'We can't afford to wait,' she said; still picking at her teeth.

'Why not?'

'Because we're being followed . . . aren't we, Vedova?'

She said it so casually – with an amiable glance at her familiar – that the meaning took a moment to sink in. Then I twisted awkwardly around. Our trail of scuffs and slithers stood out crisply, fading back into the shadows of the wood. Whatever spell she might be using to cover our tracks, it wasn't acting quickly enough.

I gathered both legs under me, ready to go. 'What . . . The others coming back?'

She shook her head, not stirring from her crouch. 'This one has a different signature; unscreened. One man coming after us on foot. I'd guess it's your witch-hunting friend.'

God, I thought, and almost gave myself away right then; then realized who she meant.

'Chris?'

She nodded. 'Perfect timing.'

I stared at her.

'We can play both ends against the middle,' she explained after a moment. 'Set him against them. Then, while they're distracted, we can do what we came to do.'

I looked again towards the brooding barn. 'How?'

'Simple. I draw those Ironsides out, and over here – and you lead your friend right into them.'

There was a pause.

'You *what?*' I said, in a *sod off* sort of way.

'You've proved your courage, Rachel. You can do it.'

The rook croaked something raucous, as if agreeing.

'And you can shut up as well,' I told it.

'I know how close you got to him,' said Razoxane quietly. 'And how close he got to you. There's leverage in that link, which you can use.'

'He wants to bloody *kill* me,' I protested.

'I thought you said it was me he was after,' she countered evenly. 'So why not take him up on that? Make him an offer. Tell him that you want to sell me out.'

She *knows*.

Picking my wary way between the trees, I couldn't help but pause and look behind me. Straining my ears: as if I might hear them whispering, back there.

She was playing me along. A sick conviction said so. Giving me this task to do would suit her sense of humour. Even if I managed to draw Chris in, the ambush she was planning might be set to catch me too.

Horror at the prospect hemmed me in; I groped for a way out. It wasn't as if I'd given in to Warwick. I'd never meant to raise him in the first place. She'd understand that, surely.

If she knew.

I shuddered, and crept forward: through the silent, snowy half-light of the wood. Things could be quite the other way around. She might have sent me back because she thought that she could trust me.

Still hunched around my acid indecision, I reached the hollow way. It flowed through the wood like a still, white river: its trough half-filled again with snow. The trees on either side arched over it, their branches interweaving; the daylight here was shredded and dispersed.

Easing down into a crouch on the bank above it, I listened again; then leaned cautiously out to look. There was more light to the left. The shaded track grew brighter as it neared the outside world.

There was a solitary figure coming up it: a silhouette against the background glow. I made out his long dark coat – and the rifle he held close against his chest. His head kept turning: moving like a snake's. Checking every slope and cleft for signs of passage.

'Chris . . .' I called. The word fell from my dry mouth like a stone.

He swung towards me: gaze and gun together. My every nerve-end tingled with the urge to duck away – but I stiffened my muscles and stood my ground. The height advantage helped; along with the reassuring thickness of the tree beside me.

Staring up at me, he seemed to waver; the rifle still half-raised. I glimpsed a hunted shadow cross his face. It went to ground at once, and left me guessing; but it took another moment for composure to return.

'Rachel,' he said, and licked his lips: an almost cautious gesture. 'You want me to make it quick for you? I can.'

I shook my head; almost gritting my teeth as my nerves sang out again. If he snapped his rifle up right now, and shot, could I dodge behind the tree in time?

'I want to talk,' I called down hoarsely.

'There's nothing to say,' he answered back; a hint of resignation in his tone. 'All I can offer is to shrive you and shoot you dead. You won't feel the flames: I promise . . .'

'Don't you want Razoxane, then?' I asked.

His eyes grew narrow. 'How do you mean?'

'I can show you where she is – right now. You can kill her *now*. And . . . maybe I'll be saved, so long as you kill her.'

He considered that in silence, his eyes on mine. Even in this raw cold, I felt perspiration oozing through my skin.

'Come down from there,' he told me finally.

My legs refused to move for a moment – and then I was out in the open, and descending carefully towards him: committing myself before second thoughts set in.

As I reached the bed of the track, he brought the rifle to his shoulder, aiming right at my chest. The telescopic sight was an overkill absurdity, this close. I felt my heart shrink tight.

'My father used this gun to slaughter bulls,' he said, with studied calm. 'Forty-four magnum. Fires a bullet of one hundred and fifty grains . . .'

Grains of sand? I wondered numbly. *Grains of salt?* Whatever, he was rubbing them in with relish.

I raised my gloved hands as far as my shoulders – an instinctive gesture of surrender. It parted my cloak, unfurling the scarlet lining on this bleak and bloodless setting. But I wasn't going to cower: not to him. Despite the heavy-duty thumping in my chest, I found the strength to glare through the wisps of my fringe. The effort set my teeth on edge.

'Have you ever seen a butchered carcass, Rachel?' he asked, still aiming. 'I've seen dozens. One twitch of my finger, and I'd make you just like them.'

Oh, you bastard, I thought fiercely, trying hard not to cringe. 'I said I'd show you her,' I hissed.

He lowered the gun to chest height – still pointing it towards me.

'Where is she?'

I swallowed. 'There's the site of an old village . . . just the other side of the wood. She's hiding there.'

'And why should I trust you, Rachel?' He asked it reasonably enough; but the muzzle of the rifle didn't waver, any more than his stare. Any second could bring its shattering blast. I might just have time to jump with shock, before the bullet hit me . . .

'Because I want to be *free* of her,' I said; not needing to fake the desperation in my tone.

'Do you, though?'

With cold deliberation, I crossed myself. 'Name of the Father, and of the Son and of the Holy Ghost.'

Unholy Ghost, more like.

I sensed that his instincts were pulling him two ways. Mistrust of me on the one hand; his desire to trap Razoxane on the other. Perhaps it was the cross that tipped the balance. If so, I had no qualms.

He gestured with the rifle. 'All right then, Rachel. Lead the way. But bear this in mind. If you put a foot wrong, I'll blast you inside-out.'

Grimacing, I wrapped my cloak back round myself and turned away. He followed me up the slope; scrambling where I stumbled: keeping close. I paused to get my bearings at the top, and heard him breathing evenly behind me.

The wood was suffused in a kind of gloomy glow: the light trapped, like bad air, beneath the branches and the clouds. I could see my tracks in the snow, weaving back towards the barn – and what was in it. What Razoxane was luring, even now, in this direction.

No sign of them yet. Just silence, like a blanket: even thicker than the snow.

'I'm waiting,' he said softly in my ear.

I glanced miserably back at him, feeling very small and alone. The sanity of normal life was far behind me, on the other side of that stile. I was caught here in a wilderness, in the hands of a murderer, being driven towards an ambush of cadavers.

Oh God, don't let her blame me. Please make her get this right.

Lowering my head, I started forward again; my backbone fairly buzzing with the closeness of his gun.

'You really look the part,' he murmured after a minute.

Widow or witch? I wondered sourly, and looked back. His face was stiff, unreadable; but what was going on behind it? A hunter like him should have been happy with this stillness – and yet he'd had to break it. Had to talk.

'I'm no servant of hers,' I muttered back. 'I told you.'

'Not of your own free will, perhaps . . .' he allowed. The words were dryly-spoken, but they gave me room to breathe. A grudging inch or two. Turning to stare forward again, I suddenly – belatedly – knew why. I'd caught him with a snare of my own.

God help me, I'd *bewitched* him. Even walking here, on tenterhooks at gunpoint, I very nearly giggled at the thought.

'I might not be able to save you, Rachel,' he went on – like someone weighing up the pros and cons. 'It's the sentence of God, you know that . . .'

I hesitated before answering; listening ahead. Still nothing.

'I don't believe it,' I said flatly.

He snorted. 'Your kind never do . . . until it's too late.'

'How can Christians be happy while souls burn in Hell?' I asked over my shoulder; straining to keep my tone level.

Something flickered on his face. Doubt? Or derision? 'It's the punishment they deserve,' he said.

'*Nobody* deserves that.' It was the same line I'd pursued at our Women's Group, three endless weeks ago; grist to the mill of our liberal gathering. But I knew that Chris would take the bait, bite hard – and be distracted.

'It's *judgment*,' he insisted grimly.

'And who's judging?' I ducked a bough. 'Do you know what it is, to be a parent? Do you think he won't bend *every* rule, to get his children home?'

'Be careful, Rachel. You don't know what you're saying.'

I side-stepped a tree, peering nervously ahead. A screen of frozen holly blocked my view. He kept on speaking sternly at my back, but I hardly heard him. The Ironsides were surely getting nearer. Each step I took closed whatever distance lay between us.

You heard that, God? Just get me home. *And Cathy with me . . .*

A brittle, thorny crackling, away to the left. I swung my gaze that way: saw bushes stirring. Glimpsed something ponderous beyond them, coming through. Height and hat: a faceless shape. I came up short; the figure paused. But now something else was moving in the shadows up ahead.

I eased myself aside, to let Chris see – then dodged away, and broke into a run.

He fired almost at once; the gun-crack stung my ears. I flinched in expectation of its brutal blow – but the bullet had buried itself already, spreading powdered snow and splinters in a cloud. A glimpse of the gouged tree-trunk as I skidded past it; then I swerved, lost balance and went down on hands and knees. His second bullet slashed above my head.

Keep going, girl, keep going!

Panting for breath, I scrambled onward. The rifle's rasp-and-clink came after me; then another searing shot. An exclamation-mark of snow leaped upward. Then I was over the lip of a hollow, and rolling down: entangled in my cloak. Even as I slithered to a stop, my mind flashed up an image of myself: face blank and white, and entrails steaming scarlet – ripped open like a savaged sheep. I gagged, and kept on going.

Razoxane rose up without warning – the snow sloughing off her murky coat. Even her shades were encrusted: she looked like a polar explorer. Teeth bared in a fierce grin, she grasped hold of my trailing cloak and dragged me with her.

Stumbling up, I twisted round to see; but nobody was there above us. Just snaps and rustles, drifting through the trees. The sounds of grim things prowling forward. The next shot wasn't aimed in my direction.

'That was well done, Rachel,' she hissed in my ear. 'He's up against all four of them. Let's *go*.'

As if I needed any further prompting. We made for the edge of the wood as fast as the snow would let us; flailing our way through thorns and brambles. More shots rang out behind us: as sharp and sporadic as wood cracking up in a fire. Maybe Chris was tasting fear this time. His turn to be outnumbered and alone.

Whose judgment now? I thought.

The barn came in sight through the outermost trees – and then we were out in the open and crossing the field towards it. The pristine white we'd seen before was broken up by tracks, like suture-scars: weaving past us to the dark mass of the wood. I was glad I hadn't been there to see them made.

The building loomed sombrely up; we slowed our pace. In the silence, I could almost hear it creaking: weighed down by the shroud of snow on its great canopy of a roof. The Ironsides might have left it, but their aftersmell remained. Each shuttered aperture seemed to hide its secrets. And the coffin was still inside there: the evil thing we'd come for. Its presence turned the barn into a barrow. A burial-mound.

I turned to look behind me – but nothing had followed us across the field. I was just in time to glimpse a flare in the trees: a sudden gout of bright, voracious flame.

Had they got him? Was he burning as he'd planned to burn me? I hadn't time to wonder. Razoxane was already moving to the door.

Pushing it open, she paused – then beckoned me in

behind her. With a last glance back towards the wood, I followed.

The interior was cavernous and dim, and smelled of damp. Our shadows went before us, stretching out along the central aisle as bitter light seeped in. Razoxane unslung her case and laid it carefully aside; then started to advance. Reluctant though I was, I matched her pace.

The chaff-drag lay waiting at the far end of the barn; resting on two trestles. Its weathered wood was plastered with black mud. As it took shape out of the shadows, I felt my nerves begin to fray.

'It's safe,' Razoxane murmured. 'So long as we're careful, it can't hurt us . . .' She moved up to stand beside it; motioned me round to the other side. We faced each other across the slimy lid.

'Now what?' I whispered: like somebody afraid to wake a sleeper. Which I was.

Razoxane rested her palms on the coffin-lid, and leaned towards me. 'Feel it,' she urged softly. 'Feel its *power*.'

I hesitated; then lowered my own hands towards the wood. The lightest touch sent ghostly pins and needles through my fingers. Even through my gloves, I could feel the subliminal vibration of what lay beneath the lid.

Then a briefer, much more solid sense of movement. A stirring in sleep. I flinched away; stared back at her in horror. She was grinning like a ghoul.

Quickly she produced a drawstring bag from under her coat – like the purse in which she carried her coins. But this one hung slack and shapeless; and when she upended it over the coffin, only smoky ash spilled out.

She trailed the grey dust down the length of the lid, murmuring weirdly to herself. I backed away still further. Then she was finished, and tossing the empty bag aside.

'All right, now: let's get going.'

We made quickly for the doorway; I didn't dare look back. Outside, the snowfield was still empty, but

Razoxane started to run. I floundered in the wake of her flying coat-tails – away from the wood and the way we'd come. There was a five-barred gate in the field hedge, and she made straight for it; tossing the case over it, and scrambling after. I followed suit, encumbered by my cloak. Dropping to the ground, I saw she had the matchstick in her fingers again. Her gaze was focused on the barn.

'*Fiat lux*,' she murmured – and closed her fingers to a fist. The match flared, hissing, into life.

The barn exploded.

Snow and stone could not contain the blast: the place went up like a liquid oxygen tank igniting. A ball of flame soared upward, seared my eyes – then shrivelled into smoke. Fragments of tiles dropped down and bounced towards us. A thin gruel of snow blew after them, and flecked our faces.

'Fuck . . .' I murmured numbly, through my fingers.

'Shame about the architecture,' Razoxane said. 'But still . . .'

I took a shaky step backwards, still staring at the ruin. Apart from some burning bits of wood, the fireball had snuffed itself out, as suddenly as it had erupted. Only the cloak of smoke was left, brooding black over the field.

The shooting in the wood had stopped. Shocked silence thickened in the air.

'A lot of dark matter in that coffin,' Razoxane murmured. 'A *wealth* of black gold . . .' She clapped her hand to my shoulder, making me jump. 'But it's lost to them now. Come on; let's get well clear.'

There was more smoke in the trees: a fainter, greyer smudge, creeping upward in the cold. Closer to the ground, I glimpsed the crackle of flames. The fire-locks had set a tree alight. Apart from that winking dance of orange, the depth of the wood lay dark and still. I sensed Razoxane turn away; but couldn't force myself to follow until the bushes at the edge of the trees began to rustle and stir.

That was enough. I was off and stumbling in her relentless wake before the Ironsides emerged. I didn't want to see them coming. Even from here, I could feel their icy rage.

*

'I thought we wouldn't shake him off so easily,' Razoxane said.

There was a trace of wry amusement in her tone; but the back of my neck began to prickle at once – before I'd even turned my head to see.

We were being followed by a lean and hungry figure. Even at this distance – perhaps a quarter-mile or so – I knew it was Chris. He was up on the skyline, keeping pace.

'Shit.' I looked around for something we could put between us and him; but we were down on a farm-track, with sparsely straggling hedges on either side, and just isolated trees along the way. This time he had the advantage of height; I reckoned he might try to pick us off.

'Don't worry,' Razoxane said, still strolling. 'He can't touch us from there.'

'He's got a telescopic *sight* on that rifle,' I pointed out nervously, glancing back at him again.

'It won't do him any good, though. I can refract the light between us . . . just enough. He'll know that.'

I could only envy her unconcern. 'Well, he's giving me the creeps up there.'

'A wolf isn't easy to lose. Let's just live with him for a while.'

'It's just . . . I need to rest. We've been walking for bloody hours.'

After the destruction of the chaff-drag, I was hoping

she'd head back into town; but instead she'd led me out into the countryside. Even before Chris picked up our trail, I'd been challenging the sense of that. We'd surely be much safer among streets and buildings. Besides which, the cold and heavy going were beginning to wear me down.

But their shroud's been blown away, she'd argued back. *Out here my mind can see them.*

Well, maybe it could. But they could see us, too. And maybe cut us off, so that we couldn't make it back before nightfall. Come dark, we could be trapped out here. And then they'd split us up – and hunt us down.

Come dark . . .

Razoxane paused, and adjusted the sling of her case. I glimpsed the grim set of her face, and vaguely wondered if she felt fatigue. Did revenants grow weary of their wanderings? I guessed they might.

We slogged on down the track, to where the next tree waited: a gaunt silhouette against the afternoon sky. The countryside was deathly silent. Whatever we'd stirred up by destroying the barn, it hadn't spread this far. I'd been nervous about police helicopters, at first – but perhaps they'd all been grounded by the weather. Vedova, circling watchfully above us, was the only thing that moved.

The next time I looked back, Chris was coming downslope. His intention was clear: to join the track and follow in our footsteps. A hummock of ground concealed him from my sight.

Vedova found a perch in the tree ahead, and furled its wings.

Razoxane glanced backwards – then at me. 'Hungry?' she asked casually, as if our pursuer had been no more than a distraction.

'*Yes.*'

I was ravenous, in fact; but with Vedova brooding over us, it wasn't a word I could bring myself to use.

Razoxane had stopped in her tracks. I followed her fixed gaze towards the hedge. Every twig was frozen stiff. There was nothing to see.

'What?' I said.

She touched her finger to her lips, still staring.

Spooked, I glanced behind us. Away down the track, still keeping his distance, Chris had crept back into view.

Razoxane dropped abruptly to a crouch; the blast of her pistol made me spring aside with shock. Time seemed to freeze as solid as the landscape. And then she straightened up again, unfazed, and grinned at me.

Awash with adrenaline, I gazed stupidly back. The echoes of her shot were still scraping round the skyline, and after a moment I turned round to check on Chris. He'd come to a wary halt back there.

Razoxane ignored him, walking over to the hedge. With my heart still doing double-time, I watched her tuck her gun away, and stoop to rummage in the roots. When she turned back towards me, there was a dripping, dangling rabbit in her grasp. She raised it by its ears, beside a smile of cold conceit.

'Bloody *hell*, Razoxane,' I burst out.

'You do eat meat, I take it,' she said.

I started to nod; then realized what she meant, and stopped.

'No need to look like that about it,' she murmured, trudging back. 'I learned this skill a long time ago, but it still holds good. Now let's find ourselves a sheltered spot, and get you fed. You need it.'

Watching it roast on its makeshift spit, with a warm smoky smell in my nostrils, I had to admit to a growing anticipation. I'd burned up breakfast long ago, and my stomach was cold and empty.

We were sat by a small – almost smokeless – fire of

twigs, in the lee of a lonely copse. The ground was higher here, away from the track, and we could keep an eye on the approaches. I could see Chris whenever I raised my gaze; his dark shape waiting, hunkered down, two hundred yards away. He hadn't tried approaching any closer.

Razoxane leaned forward, prodding the scorched meat with the tip of her switchblade. She'd butchered and skinned the thing with grisly swiftness, barely staining her gloves. I'd seen too much to be disturbed by that; and any qualms of distaste had been eclipsed by pangs of hunger.

'Nearly done,' she murmured – and followed my stare. 'Perhaps we should invite him over for a taste.'

I gave her a sidelong look. Somehow it wasn't as sharp as I'd intended.

The fire popped and crackled – tingeing my cheeks with its fitful warmth; gilding her face with its glow. I shrugged deeper into my cloak . . . and let my gaze slide back to Chris again. He seemed to be making himself comfortable; still watching us. Still waiting.

'Who is he, Razoxane?' I almost whispered. 'Who is he really?'

'I was wondering that myself: what role he's come to play. Here . . .' She cut a slice of meat, and proffered it. I took a cautious bite. It seemed the richest thing I'd ever tasted.

'Feel like finding out?' she went on casually.

For a moment I stopped chewing; then slowly resumed, and swallowed. 'What . . . you mean raise another vision?'

'It might give us an idea, with him so close.'

The prospect sank like lead into my stomach: crushing my appetite completely. I was sure these spirit-journeys must be risking my sanity. But I only hesitated for a moment.

'Let's do it, then,' I said.

* * *

She dropped more twigs onto the fire, and fanned it. The glow grew brighter. I sat and watched it, biting on my lip. I'd managed to eat a bit more meat; the greasy after-taste still lingered there.

'Relax,' Razoxane murmured, rocking back on her heels. 'Just focus on the flames, like you did with the candle. Concentrate your mind. Leave the rest of it to me.'

I remembered gazing, rapt, into a fire: the coal fire that we used to have at home. In the glowing, flameless depths of its cracks and hollows, I'd fancy I could see another world.

A child's illusion; but she could make it real. And now I remembered something much more recent: my encounter with Warwick. Perhaps his whispered thoughts were still around me: still travelling their ghostly wavelengths. Perhaps, in my trance, I'd tune back in – to him, and all his torment.

Another world, in flames. Might it be Hell?

I shook off the thought, and looked for Chris again. He hadn't stirred. 'What if he makes a move, though?' I asked.

'Vedova'll let us know.'

I could put it off no longer. Swallowing, I turned back towards the fire. Whatever we might glean from this, I felt no anticipation. Rather, the resignation of someone with a wound to be re-dressed and cleaned, who knows that they'll feel better when it's done.

The small, hot flames danced up like sprites: an oasis of life in this desolate white landscape. I let my gaze melt into them. The world turned fiery red.

Dimly – like the last thing you feel before going under for an op – I sensed Razoxane's hand upon my shoulder.

Then Warwick turned his head, and looked at me.

I tried to cower away, and couldn't. He was there before me, close enough to *kiss*. And I was seeing things in negative again, but this time coloured by the flames: red highlights, yellow shadows. Blood and gold.

The moment held – then broke. He looked away, across the burning fields. His grim expression hadn't flickered. This time he couldn't see me.

Adrift in the stream of consciousness that followed, I realized why. I was seeing into the past again: the period that the Ironsides had come from. Images overlapped, like flashbacks from a dozen different minds. Helmeted horsemen, and musketeers on foot; people stabbed, shot down or set on fire. And the fire was spreading everywhere: to buildings, fields and hayricks. Charring them yellow in its phantom scarlet flames.

And I was in the midst, with no escape. I couldn't even close my staring eyes. A horseman rode towards me as if galloping underwater, his riding cloak billowing behind him. I saw him through a bath of boiling blood. Helmetless, with hair in his eyes; a carbine in one hand. A glimpse of a young-old face, drawn tight with desperation – and he was past.

A spasm of nausea almost broke me free. As it was, my grip began to loosen. I realized I was starting to wake up.

An Ironside toppled from his saddle, arms outspread: a gaping hole blown in his breastplate. People were being hanged from trees. They swung in the wind, like washing. Warwick was there on horseback, directing operations. Bodies burned on pyres.

I could feel her fingers on my shoulder now; the vision was starting to dissolve – becoming blood and water. Someone else was being dragged towards a waiting noose, and I thought I recognized that cloaked rider. His aquiline face was clenched but calm; his deep-set eyes were steady. But his features rang no bells with me.

Not even death-knells . . .

Warwick himself put the rope around his neck.

I came to with a start.

The surge of shuddery reaction was the same as ever; Razoxane grasped my shoulders until it was past. Despite the warmth of the fire, I could feel cold sweat on my forehead; wisps of damp hair were sticking to my skin. The weight of what I'd seen made my stomach ache to be emptied. It was all I could do to keep my makeshift meal down.

'All right?' Razoxane asked.

I nodded jerkily – and looked down towards the track.

Chris wasn't there.

'Oh, God . . .' I whispered.

'He's come no closer,' she assured me grimly. 'He's moved off east. Vedova's gone to look.'

'He's not given up though, has he?'

'Unlikely,' she agreed.

I rubbed my forehead. 'So . . . what did you make of that lot, then?'

She took a twig, and prodded at the fire. 'Warwick's war. His last campaign. At least one hamlet in this area was simply razed to the ground. History may not record it; but the memories still linger – in the air and in the earth.'

'So how did he lose it?'

She shrugged, still stirring embers. 'I don't know. It wasn't just a weapons misfire, though. You can be sure of that.'

I thought of the first vision we'd shared; that woman disappearing in the woods – pursued by ghosts. I'd been sure it wasn't Razoxane; and yet . . .

'Did you . . . have anything to do with it?' I ventured.

She gave me a glance; then smiled thinly, and shook her head. 'I'd barely been reborn, Rachel. I was only a child when these events took place. No older than your daughter . . .'

I studied her face, without speaking. Searching for a

subtext. Looking for lies. But it was no use. As well as I thought I knew her, I still couldn't see behind the mask.

'We'll start heading back to town before long,' she said after a minute. 'Both cells have gone to ground. They know that I can track them now.'

'And Chris?'

'He'll keep his distance.'

But keep on coming. I looked around me, but the open fields were empty. It seemed he too had found his foxhole in the snow. The coppice behind us blocked our view – just gashes of white between the darkness of the trunks – but I assumed Vedova had that direction covered. No way could he have crept that close; maybe close enough to listen . . .

'I'm going to have a long, hot bath tonight,' I muttered, like a promise to myself. I was just wondering what evasions I should have ready for Ruth and Graham, when Razoxane quietly said: 'You can't go back.'

I blinked at her. 'Why not?'

'Because we're going to end this thing tomorrow, and you need to be prepared.'

End. The simple word bounced off my brain, its meaning too enormous to be grasped. This nightmare was a part of reality now. It was going to last forever . . .

Then comprehension blossomed, like a bruise. Would I see my little girl again *tomorrow*? Get her back? Or die in the attempt?

'End it how?' I asked cautiously.

'Without the coffin, we can meet them on our own terms.'

'And what . . . do a deal?'

Sombrely she shook her head. 'You couldn't bargain: not with such as these . . .'

I glanced down into the fire.

'What we need tonight is a stronghold,' she went on smoothly. 'An empty house. A defensive position, should it come to that. They might risk raiding into town, if they can find you . . .'

'So . . . my friends will be safe, if I don't go back to them?'

She nodded. 'Best to keep them out of it, I think – don't you?'

I had to agree. Since getting involved with her, I'd seen too many people suffer just for being my friends. Sometimes – after all these years – they still came back to haunt me.

'All right,' I muttered. 'What kind of preparations?'

'A vigil. You need to focus your strength; summon every ounce of feeling for your daughter. There'll be no quarter tomorrow – this thing won't be over until I destroy everyone. I'll need to draw a portion of your spirit, to sustain me. I need to feel *alive*.'

*

'Rachel,' Ruth's distant voice said sharply in my ear. 'Couldn't you have the grace to tell us to our faces?'

I cringed against the glass side of the phone box; rubbed my other hand into my hair. 'I'm sorry, Ruth . . . all right? You've both been really wonderful – I mean that. But I felt I was taking advantage, and . . . I thought I should find somewhere else . . .'

'We *told* you you were welcome. Honestly, Rachel . . . my best friend's teenage *daughter* behaves like this. I mean, I'm sorry to scold but . . . we *care* about you. Right?'

And I care about you too, I thought. *That's why I can't come back.*

'You're not in some squat or something, are you?'

'No . . . nothing like that . . .'

In point of fact it was exactly like that: a high, narrow house at the end of the street. Twisting round, I could see it from here – boarded up, and left to brood. Its pinnacle standing out against the flushed, unhealthy-looking evening sky.

The gritted street was empty; the snow along the pavements tinged with pink. Razoxane was loitering outside the phone box, looking off towards the corner. I couldn't help but follow her gaze.

'Please, Rachel. Don't stay out in the cold . . .'

No sign of Chris now. He'd picked us up again as we started back towards town: dogging our tracks through the gathering dusk. But we'd shaken him off in one of the peripheral estates. At least, I hoped we had.

'. . . still there?'

'Sorry, Ruth, I'm out of change. I'll speak to you soon, all right?'

'Rachel . . .'

''Bye,' I said, as brightly as I could, and hung up. Another severed lifeline fell away. Now it was just the two of us again.

Razoxane jerked her head. 'Come on; I'll get us in the back way.'

I looked across the street, towards the house. She'd spoken of finding a stronghold, and this place fitted the bill. With its height, and dirty brick, and barricaded windows, it looked as imposing as a fortress. After the briefest hesitation, I went crunching across the road towards it.

The chipboard screen blocking access to the kitchen didn't pose her ghostly magic any problems. She coaxed the nails out smoothly, one by one. I hovered at her shoulder, glancing nervously up the back wall of the building. Rusty gutters dangled overhead, weighed down with snow. The high-walled little garden was several inches deep in whiteness.

With the board laid aside, she sprang the lock and let us in. The old house opened to us like a black and smelly hole. Razoxane struck a match to stain the darkness, and led the way towards the stairs.

With no light coming in from outside, the gloom had had months to mature. It pressed against us now, as if resenting our intrusion. As the spark of her match passed on, any details that I'd glimpsed just melted in, and left me blinking. Only eerie shifts in the sense of space and depth made me aware of open rooms, as we crept by them.

'Are there ... ghosts here?' I asked, as we creaked cautiously upwards. I really didn't want to know; but the airless hush was preying on my nerves.

'None except the ones we've brought ourselves,' she answered calmly.

The ceiling of the stairwell flickered; the match flame made it look too low. Claustrophobia started rising up my throat. I did my best to swallow it back down.

We turned left onto a landing, smearing the light of her match across dirty wallpaper and foul graffiti. The far end of the passage seemed to yawn like a tunnel. It was almost a relief when she paused at the nearest door, and eased it open.

I crept through at her heels. The match had burned slowly, and brought us this far; but now the flame was cooling – turning blue. Unruffled, she moved forward through the darkness. Before the glimmer died completely, she'd kindled a handful of sparks along the base of the far wall.

A diffuse and dusky glow crept upward – revealing a monstrous shape that loomed from skirting board to ceiling. I stepped back in apprehension: staring. A giant figure was painted on the wall. Its face, framed by a cowl, was scratched and faded; but the eyes stood out, and saw me.

I gazed helplessly back across the cold bare room. My gorge rose in revulsion. I thought it was the Devil.

Then realized that it wasn't.

'Oh Mary mother of God,' I whispered faintly.

Razoxane smiled through the dimness. 'I thought you'd be impressed.'

Slowly I crossed towards it, and came up short. It was the last thing I'd expected to find at the heart of this dead house. Through the darkness of decay, past the glimpsed, obscene graffiti, she'd brought me to a shrine.

Someone had made it months ago, or years. The paint had peeled, grown dark with damp, and been defaced. But it was still recognizably a mother and child. Even when fresh, the image had been blunt, and boldly-drawn: it gave no easy comfort. Like the stern, austere icons of the Third World Church. Someone homeless and poor had painted this.

I looked down at the night-lights, spaced out to illuminate the wall. How long had they lain cold, before we came here?

'You'd best make yourself comfortable,' said Razoxane dryly, scuffing at the floorboards with her boot. 'It's going to be a long watch.'

I gave her a sidelong glance. 'Listen . . . you're not going to . . . drain my energy or something, are you?'

She tipped her head back, grinning. 'What do you think I am, a vampire?'

'I *know* what you are, Razoxane.'

Still nursing her amusement, she went over to the corner and retrieved a tattered old blanket; dragged it across, and dumped it at my feet. I wavered; then carefully sat down, drawing my cloak around me: putting my back against the mouldy wall.

She let herself slide down to sit beside me.

'All I need . . .' she said, 'is for you to concentrate your mind. Fix all your thoughts on tomorrow, and your daughter. You'll sink a well of power we can share, and I can draw from. But remember this: you mustn't look back. You can't let anything distract you. You've got to be prepared to give *everything* up, if you're going to win her back.'

'Everything,' I said; and glanced at her. 'You mean . . . including my life?'

Her upper face was shadow, but her mouth was smiling faintly. 'Easy to say, isn't it?'

'No. No . . . I mean it.'

'Being a Christian, I suppose death's not a word that really scares you, is it?'

I swallowed, and shook my head. 'Not my death, no . . .'

'Is *disfigurement* a word that scares you, Rachel?' she asked softly.

I stared at her – and felt my hand betray me. It crept to my cheek, and touched it. My skin was soft and smooth against my fingers.

'How can that be worse?' she said. 'It only goes skin deep. But it *is* worse . . . isn't it?'

I nodded mutely; ashamed of the admission – and afraid.

'Everything, Rachel,' she murmured. 'Including your life. Including your *face*.'

Shaken, I cupped my fingers round my mouth: my eyes fixed on the scarred Madonna.

'The monastics call it the "little death",' she said, after a pause. 'The vigil before they take their vows. That's what you've got ahead of you tonight.'

I looked at her sidelong, and moistened my lips. 'I'd rather be alone, if it's all right by you.'

'What, in this old hulk? With candles for company?'

I turned up my nose at her sarcasm, and nodded towards the dark shape on the wall. 'And her.'

She shrugged, and clambered to her feet. 'All right,'

she said, still lightly mocking. 'I'll find some darker corner, then.' She paused at the door, tapping pensively on the jamb; then looked at me again. 'Perhaps this was a visionary's cell, one time. A place where they tried hiding from the world. But you can't turn your back on the things out there. In the end, you have to turn again, and face them.

'You say your prayers, Rachel . . . and I'll say mine.'

She went out into the passageway, and left me alone. I listened to the fading creak of floorboards, still watching the dim face across the room. Then slowly, almost guiltily, I drew out Cathy's photo, and stared down into her smile.

*

The night went by so slowly, it seemed not to pass at all; but I marked it by the dying of the lights. One by one, with painful slowness, they were beginning to go out. The dimness thickened: drawing a veil over the Widow Mary's face. But her pale eyes watched me still.

The hush inside the house was even thicker. Listening to it, I recalled another monastic term: one that covered the empty hours between compline and matins. The Great Silence.

I looked at Cathy's face again, and touched it with my finger; traced its outline with my nail. *Won't be long, my darling. Soon be home.* I felt a trembling in my throat, but couldn't cry. I'd been sucked dry of tears.

I raised my eyes to the icon of shadows, still looking for a gleam of inspiration. The Madonna seemed to stare at me with infinite sadness. *She*'d been obedient; prepared to give all that she had. But she hadn't known then that her child would be required of her too. The baby she still cradled in her arms.

Oh God, I thought in sudden fright. *Oh no. You can't ask that.*

Everything, so Razoxane had said. You have to be prepared to give *everything* up . . .

Who for?

A horrid doubt began to squirm inside me: a worm I could crush no longer. She'd promised to get my daughter back; I hadn't any choice but to believe it. But what was in all this for *her*? There was some age-old feud involved; unfinished business with Warwick. Being Razoxane, she'd want to pay her debts.

What if there was a wider plan at work?

I felt my skin turn clammy as I pictured them together: the black queen, and her brooding rook. Plotting their next move – prepared to win this evil game, whatever it might cost. Manoeuvre. Gambit. *Sacrifice* . . .

Something jerked me back to full attention. I thought I'd felt the briefest sense of movement: stirring the gloom like dust. I waited, heart in mouth, for it to settle. When it had, the silence was as empty as before.

I stared into the corner for another creeping minute; then swallowed hard, and dropped my gaze again.

I'll hear you, Cathy, love. I'll come like the wind. Even my own shadow won't be able to keep up . . .

Except that she would. Oh, yes.

The shapeless sense of movement came again.

I drew my legs up sharply; glanced around. The air was dense now. The few surviving night-lights glowed like sparks.

Warily I climbed to my feet. My joints felt stiff and creaky. Moving sideways to the door, I eased it open.

The passageway beyond seemed to bulge with blackness: my instincts almost slammed the door against it, before it flooded in to drown the room. Steeling myself, I leaned out into the dark.

'Razoxane . . . ?' I couldn't pitch my voice above a whisper.

There was no response. The house felt unnervingly empty. Draughts crept around like rats.

Oh Lord, I thought: *she hasn't gone and left me . . . ?*

No way was I going to venture further out. Closing the door with care – as if the house was full of sleepers I might waken – I slumped down onto my heels against it, and rested Cathy's smile against my mouth.

Even my own shadow won't be able to keep up . . .

Another glimmer died. I heaved a deep, tired sigh.

And then I realized Nick was in here with me.

There was nothing I could grasp. Nothing as real as that solitary flower. But I could feel him: close. Within this room. Perhaps at touching distance . . .

'Oh, why did you come back?' I whispered. 'I didn't mean to wake you . . .'

There was no response. His presence crept no closer. But the pieces of an answer came together in my head. Somehow, in my fear and grief, I'd forged a link with him. Bereavement *burns*, but it had brought us back together. Like nuclear fusion: stronger than the sun . . .

I was spine-tinglingly aware that he'd come to tell me something – but try as I might, I couldn't hear his voice. Perhaps it only reached me in my dreams. Was he here to give me strength? Or trying desperately to warn me? I didn't *know*.

'Oh, Nick,' I breathed: 'I don't know what to do.'

The photo was still gripped tight between my fingers. I could summon Warwick up, just like before. All I had to do was agree to his terms, and our daughter would be safe. As for Razoxane . . . well that was a temptation in itself. To do it to her before she did it to me.

Besides: what did I owe her? The witchfinder was right.

I raised my face again, and searched the darkness – but whichever way Nick wanted me to go, he still couldn't get through. This was a decision I would have to make myself.

The thought of raising Warwick made me hesitate again. I'd already got too close to his twisted mind, and felt its radiant hate. But Cathy and I were just caught in the crossfire; it was Razoxane he wanted. This wasn't my quarrel. I should let it take its course.

He had a daughter to avenge. Could I deny him?

I shifted uncomfortably against the door. The sod was using Cathy as a lever. Something inside me balked at giving in.

I don't trust either of them, Nick. I'm his pawn, and I'm hers.

But Warwick had been a father, too. The man knew what it was, to lose a child. I remembered his face, as he'd stroked my daughter's hair. He wouldn't play me false. He'd let her go.

My heart began to wallop as I felt the choice being made. A part of me still kept its options open: I could question him again, and then decide. But deeper down, I knew this was the point of no return – and I'd just passed it.

I fixed my gaze on Cathy's photo, until every detail was absorbed; then closed my eyes, and rested my head against the woodwork. Willing my heart to quieten. Letting my mind drift.

And suddenly the walls were gone, letting stark, cold light come bursting in. It washed away the dimness of the room, and left me stranded in the open: adrift in a vast, white silence.

Snow and milky sky had blurred together, as if I'd been wrapped up in cotton wool; but it felt as sharp and cold as crystal shards. The only breaks in the blankness came from glimpses of tree-bark, here and there; but most of the gnarled shapes were completely covered. I thought of tortured skeletons, imprisoned. I thought of Hell, frozen over.

This was Warwick's thought-world, sure enough. The bleak and barren wilderness he came from.

I began to cast about me: very aware of how I must stand out, so darkly-dressed amid this landscape. Like a fly in the ointment: struggling not to sink.

The chimes began at the very edge of silence: ghost-noises in my inner ear. I swung round, but there was nothing to see. Just unrelieved white: as soft and thick and smothering as fog.

The music rose, and fell away – as if snatched by a wind I couldn't feel. But I recognized the tune. A twisted, tinny parody, but I knew it all too well.

I ran towards it, and it faded: receding before me like a rainbow's end. Then it was behind me, distorted and off-key. I spun on my heel, but couldn't get a fix. The sound was everywhere, and nowhere. For a horrid moment I thought it only existed in my head.

Then it seemed to focus, over in the direction of some trees. I plunged towards them, panting – but by the time I got there the chimes were over my head, and drifting away on the breeze.

The pretty tune that Cathy loved was slurred, decaying now. The box's mechanism was running down. I was suddenly and dreadfully convinced that her life was fading with it: that the silence following the final chime would be the stillness of her death. Unless I found the box, and wound it up again.

In rising panic, I started running in circles: floundering through the slough of whiteness. The music was gone, now – the cacophony was tuneless in my ears. But it didn't fade away; it *lingered*. Every last note being wrung from the box's works: eked out as if to mock me.

I sobbed and stumbled; flailed and fell. And at last, down on my knees, I just pressed my hands against my ears and screamed for mercy.

A shadow fell across me. Something vast and dark was

at my shoulder. I dropped my hands, and squirmed around in fright.

They towered above me: horse and rider, one foul flesh. The animal's head dipped close to sniff my cloak, its empty sockets glaring. Warwick, gazing down, seemed as high as the sky itself, wrapped up in shaggy grey. His face was masked with shadow.

He held Cathy's music box in one gloved hand. As I watched, my arm half-raised, he snapped it closed, and killed the chimes stone dead.

Something stabbed me in the heart. I gasped, and let myself slump back.

Warwick tipped his head, and let the wan light ooze across his face. His features were as expressionless as stone.

'So, Rachel Young,' he observed after a moment. 'Thou art come to us again.'

'Where's Cathy? Have you hurt her? *Have you?*'

'Thy daughter sleeps, as thou doest. Wilt thou see her waken? Then give us the witch.'

I forced myself to struggle to my feet; found strength to glower up into his face. 'I want to see her first,' I hissed.

His mount moved skittishly; he tightened its rein. I thought at first my voice was what had spooked it – then felt the sombre presences myself.

There were other shapes advancing in the whiteness: a gathering of scarecrows from the snowfields all around. And I was in the middle. They'd caught my dreaming mind, and cut it off.

These Ironsides were on foot. Wherever I looked, they were closing in: their faces masked or muffled beneath the hats and helmets. I thought again of burns victims, bandaged up; felt the baleful stare of unseen eyes, and cringed.

Warwick took them in with a sweep of his arm: his eyes still fixed on me.

'Behold the evil deeds she must atone for. These were

my soldiers, sister. These were brave and godly men. Cooper, Langshank, Nickolas . . . All burned in the fire of Hell – by the Devil's servant.'

The soldiers stopped. I glanced fearfully around; then back to Warwick as I sensed him leaning forward.

'What faces are here? Wilt thou look upon these faces?'

Shuddering, I shook my head.

'Then see what we have seen,' he rasped – and locked his gaze to mine.

It felt like icy water being funnelled through my eyes. A sharp ache pierced my forehead. The figures around me faded, grew transparent: once more becoming ghosts in cathedral glass. Then everything spun away – and came round different.

I was moving through a winter wood. My vision was in the negative again: black snow, and bleached white trees. Pale shapes were keeping pace to left and right. And up ahead, a glowing figure walked.

We have her now, said Warwick in my head.

I was only getting glimpses through the thickening trees, but I knew this was the woman I'd seen before. The woman dressed in black.

There were Ironsides advancing with me: picking up speed, like dogs who've seen the fox. They seemed not to have noticed what had registered with me: the sense of isolation hanging over the wood.

We're in too deep, I thought – and felt a sudden, sick foreboding.

But this was still the past, and no one heard me. The beaters were beginning to spread out. I felt I was a ghost at Warwick's shoulder, riding high on his horse. It was from that vantage point that I saw the hunted figure turn and face us.

Go back, she called. *For mercy's sake. Suffer me and mine to live in peace.*

Her voice was hoarse and desperate. God knew how

long they'd harried her. But Warwick merely gestured – directing his men in for the kill.

And suddenly the winter turned to autumn.

The blaze was so bright that – for that first instant – I saw it in its true colours: the bare trees engulfed in orange and gold, like a mass of burning leaves. Then vision was reversed again: dark flames, and glowing smoke.

I scarcely saw what happened to the men. A howling in the haze; a glimpse of someone flailing past, half-smothered in black fire. But time seemed fragmented; bits of memory were missing. I guessed his mind had managed to suppress them.

We were down in the snow: thrown off by his bolting horse. The screams had stopped. The wood was silent, except for the crackling of flames in the fog.

The woman stood before us. I gazed towards her: no less afraid because I wasn't *there*.

She looked about my age, and much older than her years. Her shadow-face was drawn and drained; disgusted. Her eyes glowed black, as Warwick's had – which meant they must be pale. Purer than his. A perfect blue, perhaps . . .

Turn again, she whispered. *I will not see thee dead.*

I stared at her in fascinated horror. It wasn't Razoxane, of course; but those pale eyes were horribly familiar.

Then the moment fled away, and Warwick was there before me: his image grey with deep, remembered pain. I stumbled backwards, blinking, in the unaccustomed light. The shapes of his men moved restlessly around us. I sensed they were reliving their own fate.

The witchfinder leaned forward in his saddle.

'Now doest thou see? The widow tricked us: lured us to our doom. She took my daughter from me. Now I will slaughter hers – and she shall *know it.*'

It took a moment for his meaning to hit home. When it did, the impact made me gasp.

'Razoxane's her *daughter*?'

'Thy companion is a witch, and spawned of witches. The sins of her mother shall be visited on her. We shall be revenged for what we lost.'

Still shaken up inside by what I'd seen, I found an inconsistency to cling to. 'But she just said . . . she didn't want to kill you.'

'She spared my life: for my daughter's sake, she said. Such mockery as that I could not bear. I put my pistol to my brain, and made an end . . .'

I stood before him, huddled in my cloak. It hadn't sounded mocking, what she'd said. More of a plea for all this horror to be over. But Warwick hadn't heard it.

'We hanged the widow's hireling close to here. We'll bury her daughter's bones in the same field.'

I thought of the hanging I'd visualized before – then shied away, as Warwick's horse moved closer. Bending down, he extended Cathy's music box towards me.

'Give us the witch,' he said again. 'And save thy daughter's life.'

I instinctively reached out for it – and then drew back.

'Take it,' Warwick urged. 'She waits for you.'

I stared at it with dreadful indecision; then slowly, tentatively, began to reach for it again.

And suddenly I felt a hand seize mine and drag me clear. The dream relinquished me like water; the glaring snowscape vanished in the dark. I found myself sprawled, panting, on the floorboards of the shrine, with Razoxane bent over me. Still gripping my hand, as if she'd just saved me from drowning.

'He almost had you,' she breathed. 'Almost . . .'

I tried to struggle clear; to squirm away. She used her other hand to hold me down.

'Rachel. It's all right. He can't reach you any more.'

'He's still got Cathy, though,' I blurted; then stopped

to stare at her. The half-smile on her lips. 'You knew about us?' It sounded so absurd. As if we'd just been lovers – not conspirators to kill her.

She shook her head. 'I didn't. That surprise you? But your husband's spirit warned me. He couldn't get through to you about the danger, so he had to come to me.'

Oh Nick, I thought, *I'm sorry. I'm so sorry.* I could picture his face behind a soundproofed window: screaming to be heard.

I looked at Razoxane again, and swallowed. 'His name's Warwick. He wants revenge for the death of his daughter. He blames your mother for that.'

'He *burned* his daughter, Rachel. He loved her, and he burned her alive.'

I gaped at her. She nodded.

'My mother told me so: years later. This man who'd had a daughter, the apple of his eye. But he came to believe that the girl was infected by witchcraft – so he put her on a pyre. She was fourteen years old.'

I pressed my hands against my mouth – just stifling a whimper. If he'd done that to his daughter, what hope did Cathy have?

'It turned him grey with grief. It made him mad. He became obsessed with hunting – killing – witches. My mother was a healer, but he blamed her just the same. The widow, in her cottage. One of *them* . . .'

I shrugged her off, and clambered to my feet; she rose with me. 'She killed his men, though, didn't she?'

She gestured, looking sombre. 'I guessed that she had. She never spoke of it. She never told me how.'

'I *saw* her, Razoxane – through his eyes. She begged them to turn back. She didn't want to kill them.'

'I told you, she was a healer. She raised me in white ways . . .'

'But she knew the black ones too,' I said. 'Enough to burn her enemies alive.'

I remembered the vision: my sense of her despair and self-disgust. She'd used destructive magic as her very last resort – to save her own life, and her daughter's.

Razoxane. I stared at her, and slowly shook my head.

'She buried her books in that field,' I realized aloud. 'Under the scarecrow. She thought she could forget the past: protect her daughter that way. It's bloody ironic, isn't it? You chose the road yourself. You set out to be a healer and you ended up a killer. The disease and not the cure . . .'

Razoxane slapped me then, across the face – in a perfunctory sort of way. Just hard enough to knock me back against the wall. I caught myself, and glared at her. 'It's *true.*'

She came forward and caught hold of my cloak. Pinning me there, against the mouldy plaster. Leaning close.

'Do you know how much it cost me, to come back? Do you know how much it *hurts*?' She breathed through her bared teeth. 'I've risked my afterlife for you. What sacrifice are you going to make for me?'

'It's *you* they want,' I spat at her in fury. 'This whole thing was a trap they set for you. You *knew* that – all along . . .'

She allowed herself a twisted little smile. 'I wasn't sure. I hoped my guess was wrong. But I remembered his eyes. His skein was the one I watched go past our cottage. We thought they'd let us be . . .'

A pause, while she reflected. I took the chance to ponder for myself. Just as her grip grew looser, so I found my rage replaced by puzzlement.

'And you came back. You *still* came back.'

She snorted without humour. 'Would you have believed me, if I'd told you the truth?'

'What truth?'

'That I couldn't leave you facing him alone. Disbelieve it if you want, but we're still sisters.'

I studied her face, and found no trace of falsehood. This close, I didn't think that she could hide it. Not from me.

'You . . . came back just for me?' I whispered.

'Yes. Even if you really were the bait, it didn't matter. I *owe* you this.'

'Witch's promise?' I asked shakily.

'Angel's honour,' was her soft response.

Numbed, as if she'd punched me, I let myself slump back against the wall.

'Oh, how can we save Cathy?' I asked her – on the very brink of unexpected tears.

'By putting the Ironsides back into their graves,' she said.

'And . . . can you do that?'

She chewed on it; then nodded. 'Yes.'

So saying, she eased back. I straightened up. The room was almost fully dark now.

'While you were communing with Warwick . . . did you have any kind of sight of where they were?'

I shook my head. 'No; there was just wilderness . . . and the wood where it happened. But . . .' I turned my frown on her. 'He said something – about your mother's *hireling*. That man we saw being hanged. He's buried somewhere close, he said.'

She absorbed that in thoughtful silence. 'I don't remember him; but he must have played his part. His grave's as good a meeting-place as any.'

She smiled to herself; then nodded towards the door. 'Come on.'

'Where?'

'The attic.'

I cast an apprehensive glance towards the ceiling. 'So what's up there, then?'

'Vedova's roost. I've one last task for her.'

She struck another match, and led me up the creaking

stairs. A fluttering in the dark made my hackles rise; but then, as we reached the landing, the white shape of the rook came towards us, and settled on Razoxane's welcoming fist.

The match went out; but the faintest luminescence still remained – seeping in through the open skylight overhead. Razoxane was a silhouette below it as she stroked her pale familiar. After a minute, she glanced at me.

'Remember the story of Noah? He sent out a raven and a dove from the top of his Ark, to scour the wastes. Vedova's both in one . . .' She paused; and then continued in a strangely wistful tone. 'The shadow flew back and forth endlessly, and found no rest . . . but the shining one found her way home.'

She brooded on the thought a moment longer; then raised her head, and lifted up the rook.

'Intelligencer: find me a grave.'

11

RECKONERS

The sky was still dark when we emerged from the house. The lamps lit an empty street; a spectral hush. Snow glowed rusty orange in their light.

'She's calling us,' said Razoxane. 'This way.'

There was no wind, still less a voice upon it; but I didn't doubt that she could hear the summons.

'How far?'

'About a mile. Just out of town. A churchyard.'

I glanced up and down the street; looked back towards the phone box that I'd used last night. The light in it still burned, through a filter of frost: summing up the town's abandoned feel.

I thought of other people, keeping watch. The night staff at St Catherine's shared this moment; along with the girls on the hospital wards, a half-mile further out. Instinctively my thoughts reached out to them – but went astray: losing themselves in the haunted gloom beyond the lights.

Warwick was waiting in those frozen fields; my angel in his arms.

We set off through the silence. At this ungodly hour, the cold was crushing. Even with gloves on, I had to push my hands into my armpits: hugging myself beneath my cloak.

'What time is it?' I muttered, between grittings of my teeth.

'The last watch of the night,' she said. 'You know which morning?'

I didn't. I'd lost count.

'The twenty-eighth day of December. Remember the Feast?'

I stopped in my tracks – my stomach turning colder than my skin. 'Oh, *Jesus*.'

Holy Innocents' Day. So soon after Christmas, a memorial for murdered children. I stared helplessly at Razoxane. She smiled to see my horror.

'Remember this,' she said after a moment. 'There's one sure way to stop a slaughter of the innocents.'

I swallowed against the thudding in my throat. 'What's that?'

She tugged at the strap of her guitar case – still nurturing the grim ghost of a smile.

'A slaughter of the guilty,' she explained.

The road to the church lay beyond the reach of street-lamps. We passed the last one, and there was just a sickly ribbon up ahead, offset by murky hedges, and the gloomy sky above.

'Good place for an ambush,' I pointed out; coming to a wary halt.

'Not on this road. The way's still clear. But we need to be there for the dawn.'

I looked around us; listened to the hush. The stillness of the town had been unnatural. Out here, the quiet was positively stifling.

'Do you know which church it is?' I asked: pushing on along the pale, ungritted lane.

'Vaguely.' She left it at that for the next few yards, then raised her head. 'Rumour said the soldiers had it as their barracks when they were fighting in this district. Warwick would have slept there, the night before he met his fate. Perhaps that's why the place has never flourished . . .'

The lane was growing sunken; the hedges looming up

to left and right. We came to a corner, rounded it – and saw the church's outline up ahead. I stopped again; and this time so did she.

There were a couple of cottages nearby, but no lights showed in them. I strained my ears for sounds of life: the muffled thud of hooves, the creak of saddles. But I only heard the blood in my own head.

Razoxane resumed her slow advance. For all my doubts, I followed close behind her.

A dim, weird light was growing round the church. The building loomed in silhouette against it. Yew trees brooded in the churchyard, great blobs of inky shadow.

We left the lane, as if climbing from a chin-deep stream, and went in through the lych-gate. The crisp snow gave, and crumbled round our ankles. The graves were blanketed: just shapes under shrouds.

Razoxane slowed to fumble out her compass, and halted to thumb back the lid. It was still too dark for me to see the reading; but after a moment she nodded to herself.

I sidled up. 'The Ironsides?'

'No movement. But they're watching.'

I shivered, and heard my teeth click in my head. Beyond the churchyard, a field lay in hazy half-light, sloping down towards the black wall of a wood. A look behind me was no more reassuring. The cottages we'd passed still lay in darkness, cut off by the sunken lane.

Even the church's gargoyles seemed to gloat, peering down from the frozen eaves.

'There's a void under here,' said Razoxane suddenly, wading forward; already unslinging her burden. With a last glance back towards the lych-gate, I followed her across to an open patch of snow. She laid her case on top of a tomb, and retrieved her shovel. Dipping my chin inside the collar of my tight-wrapped cloak, I watched her start to scrape the snow away. Almost at once, she struck wood; and with more of the covering cleared, we found what looked to be a house-door lying flat upon the earth. Razoxane knelt, prised it up with her shovel, and lifted it half-way – to reveal a sagging layer of tarpaulin. The sheet was anchored all around with bricks; I turned one up with the toe of my boot.

A freshly-dug grave – just waiting for its tenant.

Shrugging, she let the door thud down, and used her spade to push herself back upright.

A hoarse croak scraped the silence. Wincing, I turned my head, and saw Vedova waiting for us, perched upon a solitary headstone. We shambled over to see what it had found.

The grave looked very old. The stone had developed a list, as if the earth had not been quiet. Its face was crusted thick with frosty lichen. It stood over in the corner, apart from its neighbours; very close to the unkempt hedge.

Razoxane went down on one knee, and began to scrape it clean with her glove. Peering over her shoulder, I had the vague impression of a face growing out of the dimness: taking shape beneath her palm. A glimpse of its shadowed grin made me feel queasy. Then the hollow eyes came clear, and I saw it was the face of a skull; revealed by moss that sloughed off like a skin.

Razoxane fished inside her coat, produced one of her matches, and struck it on the stone. The flare threw the image into stark relief: deepening its sockets to a scowl. She leaned closer to study the inscription underneath.

'Can't read the date . . .' she said after a moment. 'But I'd say three centuries old, and more. No wonder it's been worn to a shadow . . . The epitaph's still there, though. *Hodie Mihi – Cras Tibi.*'

I'd seen that carved on stones before, and idly wondered. This time I had to know. 'Meaning?'

She smiled, and snuffed the match out. 'Today it's me . . . tomorrow you.'

Vedova lifted off with a clatter of wings, and took up position in the nearest yew.

'Who's down there, Razoxane?' I whispered.

'Touch, and see,' she answered, just as quietly.

I stared at her – then at the stone. Its sombre, weathered surface was inscrutable, and yet . . . I had a sense of *threshold* here; far more than from that doorway in the snow.

Again I glanced around us. The graveyard and the ground beyond still lay in empty silence.

'Take your glove off,' Razoxane said; already tugging at her own.

I swallowed, and complied. No time for hesitation now. The cold air clasped my fingers, and began to squeeze them numb.

'They might try sneaking up on us . . .' I muttered.

'Don't worry; it should only take a moment.' She gestured for me to lay my hand upon the stone. After a heartbeat's pause, I did so. It was freezing. Then she placed her ungloved hand on mine.

I felt the past flow through me like a sharp electric shock. However long the dreaming moment lasted, my mind had time to soak up every detail. It was suddenly bright day, and I was stood at Warwick's shoulder – watching him place a noose around another man's neck.

It was a scene I'd glimpsed before, in the flames of our campfire: the haggard horseman, dragged towards his fate. But even with the rope in place, his face stayed calm: disdainful. His hard brown eyes met Warwick's gaze full-on.

Other Ironsides were ranged around us, on horseback or on foot. Their faces were uncovered here – and all too human. One helmeted man was red-cheeked, like a farmer. Another rubbed his jaw, his grey gaze thoughtful. A beardless youth was chewing on a piece of straw . . .

Warwick's own face was dark with blood and stubble; but the lines of its rage were carved much deeper. The hatred was ingrained. Stepping back from his victim, he spoke through gritted teeth.

'The fire is a *mercy*; thou knowest this. The soul is made pure by the burning of the flesh.' He gave his head a slow, grim shake. 'No such mercy shall be afforded thee. Thou shalt be buried with the wages of thy sin, to rot for ever.'

I noticed three earthenware jars at the feet of the youth. He was guarding them with studied nonchalance, rolling the shaft of straw between his teeth. His coat and wide-brimmed hat seemed oversized; but judging by his smoke-grimed cheeks, he'd done his part in the skirmish they'd just won . . .

'Three thousand silver pieces,' continued Warwick. 'A Judas price one hundredfold; enough to keep thee down till Judgment Day. And when thou art buried, we shall hunt the woman down, and burn her.'

The condemned man turned his head against the tension of the rope. 'She has renounced the old ways. She lives for her infant only. She has *no part* of this.'

Warwick snorted his contempt. 'What truth shall we hear from *thy* lips, traitor?'

'The Lord be my witness,' the man said, almost mildly: 'I never failed to plead the widow's cause.'

Warwick merely gestured to the men who held the rope. They took the strain at once: hauled it tight across the bough. The doomed man rose up, kicking . . .

And the vision flickered out, as contact broke; my hand was yanked clear of the power source of stone. Razoxane – thank God – had had the strength to intervene. She steadied me now, as I groped to get my balance. Back in the dark – and horribly enlightened.

'Chris . . .' I whispered hoarsely. 'That was *Chris*.'

'How do you know?'

'He said that to me, one time. About pleading the widow's cause. He said it just like that.' I frowned then, in confusion. 'But the face, the voice . . . All different.'

'What was it he told you, about himself?'

'He said he'd lived before, like . . . you did.'

'Perhaps he was right, at that. Perhaps his mind's far older than his body.'

'Warwick called him a traitor . . .'

'A mercenary, I'd guess. Fighting for the outcasts.' She gave a small, tight smile of comprehension. '*Il Monco.* Didn't the cards predict as much?'

The Mercenary, I remembered; the soldier of misfortune.

The Left Hand of the Devil.

'But he's hunting you . . . ?' I asked.

'He wants peace. If they buried his body with all that silver on its chest, his soul will just keep wandering; going through the cycle again and again. But now its memories have been uncovered . . . perhaps by *my* return. Maybe he's realized that there's something he has to do.

'Three thousand silver coins. He'll have to earn as much again, to pay his debt. To break the circle. And three thousand shillings was the price on my head, once . . .'

Her words melted into the background. I stepped away from the grave, my gaze fixed on the headstone. The carved skull seemed to watch me: as dim as a thumbprint on the shadowy stone.

His mind, in Chris's body. The ancient corpse down there had shared my *bed.*

Then Razoxane touched my shoulder, and I jumped.

'Look,' she said. I did, and caught my breath.

A shrouded shape had emerged from the wood, and was crossing the field towards us – crawling like a moth across the ghost-white carpet. A horse and rider, coming at the walk.

Warwick.

My heart leaped inside me. I took a step forward, squinting my eyes against the twilight.

Razoxane stood and watched a moment longer; then moved over to the tomb where she'd left her case. I stumbled across to join her as she threw it open.

'For God's sake, don't just shoot ... he might have Cathy with him.'

'I know ... but let's be careful.' Selecting the organ-shotgun, she slotted its windlass handle into place, and tested the mechanism's rotation. Its sounds were dry and brittle on the freezing air. All I could do was give her room – and watch the ugly weapon.

The horseman's shaggy shape was drawing closer.

Razoxane closed the lid on the waiting Tinderbox, and slung the case again; then took the *Todesorgel* up once more. I looked back at Warwick. He'd come alone – but was he bringing Cathy? Perhaps he still believed we had a deal.

Razoxane stood motionless beside me; the shotgun's barrels angled at the sky. The tomb was like a rampart we were guarding. I used the thought to help me stand my ground.

Still in the field, Warwick turned his mount aside and reined it in. He sat and stared towards us, like a cardinal in stone: a stern grey eminence against the faintly-glowing snow.

'Hast thou made thy choice then, Rachel Young?' he called.

I had, but didn't quite know how to say so.

'Then thou shalt die,' he said, with grim assurance. 'And thy sister. And the child for whom it seems thou carest nothing: she as well.'

'*No*,' I shouted back, and heard the fissure in my voice.

Razoxane broke silence then, her own voice hard and clear. 'Your quarrel is with *me*, brother Warwick. Let Rachel and her daughter walk away.'

He shook his head; a cold smile stirred the shadow of his face. 'Thy mother's evil must be rooted out. Thy sister's soul is stained already. Her daughter's, too, perhaps ...' It seemed he hesitated then, for just a moment. But before I could think of a way in, he'd lifted Cathy's music box on high.

From the corner of my eye, I glimpsed a stirring in the snow. Despite myself, I had to turn and look. A dozen yards away, it came again: a shift of pallid light among the graves. The drifted white was suddenly disturbed.

An Ironside rose up through it.

'*Shit*,' I yelped, recoiling. Up on one knee, the dark shape swung towards us: his shroud disintegrating into dandruff. The bastard had a fire-lock, and was bringing it to bear.

A soft, rustling sound from away to the left. Another buried figure sat bolt upright, displacing snow; a ghastly parody of resurrection. And more of them were rising – from their cover amid the gravestones, or their foxholes in the field. God help us, they'd been waiting all along.

We ducked behind the tomb, just before a wave of heat washed over us. I heard the hiss and sizzle of melting snow. The discharge filled my nose a moment later; its acrid taste went scorching down my throat.

Razoxane grasped my cloak, hauled me up and pulled me backwards. I stumbled with her, coughing. Smoke screened us from the Ironsides, like a vile photochemical smog. She glimpsed one of them moving, and fired at him one-handed: single shot. The blast struck broken echoes off the fields.

It wasn't for several seconds – those muffled sounds still ringing in my ears – that I realized they were fast approaching hoofbeats.

The smoke spread apart on the windless air, and showed two riders galloping towards us. Neither of them was Warwick, who'd spurred his own mount off towards the left. The last of his horsemen had been kept back in the wood, awaiting this final charge.

'Stay clear,' Razoxane snapped, and started forward: the *Todesorgel* jammed against her hip. As the leading rider reached the hedge, she squeezed the trigger, and began to crank the handle. The barrels turned and belched in jerky sequence, kicking up spouts of snow. The plunging horse pitched forward, and the Ironside tumbled clear. The second horseman sheered away. Razoxane tried to track him with her aim, but the scattering of shots became the *click* of empty barrels. She swore, and threw the smoking gun aside.

The fallen rider was struggling up: trying to prime an antique-looking pistol. Razoxane turned towards him. With unearthly calm – my heart beat double-time on her behalf – she unslung her case, dragged the Tinderbox out and fired it from her shoulder. Its vomitus of lead and iron knocked the target over backwards. He came apart in flames.

The crack of a different gun made me drop full-length; but the premature sunrise never came. Something far more dismal swept above me, like a murder of unseen crows: whirring, chirping, and pecking the snow into plumes.

Rolling over, I saw Razoxane was down as well, in the shelter of a headstone. She'd hauled her automatic out from under her coat.

'Shot-flint,' she smiled across at me. 'A good old-fashioned peppercorn gun. Makes a real mess at close range . . . but takes an *age* to reload.' And with that she took off like a sprinter, skidding and swerving through the gravestones and trees – towards the tomb where we'd been standing. She opened fire on the run, pouring shots from her pistol at the Ironside's position. I heard one bullet ricochet off stone; another rang on metal. Then she'd reached the tomb, sprung onto it, and thrown herself aside: still shooting as she fell. A burst of flame and filthy smoke engulfed her.

I rose up on one knee, horrified – and Razoxane rolled clear. A flicker of flame had caught her coat, and was chewing like a dog. She rolled over once again, to crush it out; then pushed herself up, and came scampering back towards me.

Behind her, the Ironside burned; but others were moving up, to left and right. I waited, shaking, for her to skid back into cover next to me.

She snapped the magazine out of her pistol; panting softly. 'Seen how many there are?'

I shook my head.

'Nor me. That should make it interesting.' Putting her back against the stone, she was still for just a moment, like someone on the very point of vomiting – then shuddered, and began to spit up bullets.

Still prone, I leaned out sideways. Apart from a wraith of smoke, there was nothing stirring. In this twilight world of snow and stone, the grey shapes of our attackers were invisibly still.

How long before one crept – or scuttled – forward?

Razoxane kept reloading; slotting in one bullet, with the next already held between her teeth. She thumbed them down and down into her pistol's magazine; her fingers strung and sticky with an ectoplasmic phlegm.

'You need the shotgun back?' I asked under my breath. I already knew and dreaded how she'd answer; but I had to do my part of this as well.

She nodded, and I moved at once: outstripping second thoughts. On my hands and knees I crawled to where she'd dropped the case. It wasn't fully shut. The powder flask and rosaries of shot were still inside; she'd need those too. Fear took my throat like a strangler's hand as I heard a rustling noise close by – but I forced myself to lie there on my stomach, fumbling at the catch with my gloved, numbed fingers, until I'd got it closed.

The organ-shotgun was just beyond it, steaming hotly in the snow. I sat up, glanced around – then made a lunge for it, clutched the case's strap as well, and went floundering back to where Razoxane was waiting.

A shot-flint fired towards me: its blast sounding dry as sand, and sharp as gravel. A foul cloud of smoke swelled through the twilight. Something tugged at my cloak and seared my thigh; then I tumbled into cover at her side.

'Thanks,' she breathed, and set about reloading that gun too; her pistol laid out ready on a hunk of frozen snow. After a moment's hesitation, I reached under my cloak, and felt towards the numbness on my leg. There was a rip in my jeans; and when I brought my hand back out, the tips of my gloves were warm and wet. After fifteen years of nursing, the sight still made me sick with apprehension. I could only hope to God it was a flesh-wound.

Razoxane tamped the last load down, and glanced at me. 'Okay?'

I nodded. 'I'll survive.'

'There should be only three or four left. I'm going to have to winkle them out. Shot by shot.' She pulled out the windlass and tossed it away. 'Just stay here: keep your head down.'

I half-wanted to protest. Just like before, it felt much more scary just to sit and wait. And this was *my* fight too: to save my daughter. But if I followed her around I'd only get in the way . . .

I watched her creeping off, like a shadow over snow. Without thinking, I rubbed my mouth – and grimaced at the salty taste of blood. I dug my rosary out instead: clasping my hands around it, as if the cross could keep them warm.

Razoxane had crawled a dozen yards. The churchyard kept its silence. The smoky ghosts of the Ironsides she'd finished were beginning to drift away.

Then I glimpsed a movement, to her left. An Ironside stealing forward from the shadow of a yew. Blood or no blood, I pressed my fists against my mouth. He'd spotted her; she hadn't spotted him.

No time to shout. I started to my feet, and lurched towards him. The masked face swung towards me; then the gun. Fire-lock or shot-flint, its muzzle seemed to gape like a maw. I let my stiffening leg give way, and flopped into the snow. The gun exploded – I glimpsed the flying shot amid the smoke. Most of it went overhead, and none of it quite hit me – though my cloak took on a moth-eaten look. Panting with reaction, I scrambled up again.

Thou shalt be burned and buried, papist whore . . .

I stared at the Ironside – and dangled my rosary before him. My Catholic cross. 'Come on, then! Take it off me!'

He lunged towards me, hefting the heavy musket like a club. I dodged away, stumbling off to the side. He followed, striding quickly. I let him see the crucifix again; gasping the Hail Mary as I fought to stay ahead – provocation and genuine prayer.

'Holy Mary . . . mother of God . . . Pray for us sinners . . . *now*.'

Razoxane shot him, and rolled aside. The Ironside fell heavily to the snow, and smouldered there. Razoxane came to rest on one knee, and fired again into the body. This time the *Machina* worked its magic, exploding the corpse into flames.

I slumped against a gravestone to steady myself. '. . . And at the hour of our death, *amen*.'

'Nicely done,' she muttered. 'Let's get ready for the next one.'

She jerked her head; I looked in that direction. Two and two came together right away. Together we crawled and scrambled back, and started digging in the snow. The next bit took some effort. Glancing up from my labours, I saw a hunched grey shape go scuttling from one headstone to the next.

The cry of the rook broke the silence. I looked, but couldn't see it.

Ducking my head, I got on with the job.

Vedova called again: the sound was as harsh as a football rattle – but I sensed an urgency about it. An *insistence*.

'Your friend's getting worked up about something,' I

said uneasily, still scooping chunks of snow back into place.

'So she is.' Razoxane glanced upwards; I glimpsed the rook perched high on the church tower.

'Something's spooked her . . . but I'm not sure what.' She paused; then touched my shoulder. 'A couple more handfuls, then get up and run.'

I nodded, staring downward; then filled my cupped hands one last time. Snowflakes clung like sugar to my gloves. The cold had reached my bones.

I pushed myself up, and ran in a limping crouch towards the lych-gate. Glancing back, I saw the Ironside break cover and come pounding in pursuit. He reached the place where we'd just been crouching – and there the ground beneath him just gave way. The tarpaulin sagged, and slithered inward: dragging chunks of snow down with him as he dropped into the grave.

Razoxane stepped up quickly, and fired down into the hole. A burst of flame lit her features from below.

I realized I was grinning, like a naughty little girl. I paused for a moment longer to get my breath back; then turned again to look towards the gate.

An Ironside was blocking my way.

I nearly squealed with shock: the only, doomed reaction I had time for. *Silly little girlie*, said my mind.

Then a shot pierced the stillness and spun him away, the musket still unfired. The *clang* of ruptured iron carried clearly. He crashed against the gatepost, and clutched at it to save himself from falling. The impact dislodged snow from the steeply-pitched roof.

I dived into cover, my body soaked with instant sweat. A two-tone metal scraping came from somewhere very close. I looked around – and saw that it was Chris.

He stood six yards away, his rifle aimed. From where I crouched, it seemed a frozen moment: his finger on the trigger, the sight within an inch of his cold, wide eye. The whipcrack of the gunshot stung my ears. One hundred and fifty grains of bullet: enough to punch through armour – and break a spirit's grip on burning bones. The Ironside in the lych-gate went up like a torch.

As the fireball swelled beneath the roof, Chris worked the rifle's lever once again. I watched the cartridge fall – and saw what waited at his feet. Two plastic flasks of petrol, tied together by a string. *Oh Christ*, I thought, *he's come to burn us both*.

Even as I cringed away, he turned, saw Razoxane and loosed a shot at her. She ducked behind a gravestone; the bullet took a chunk off it, scattering snow. She flitted onward, shadow-swift, and reached the wall of the church: putting a buttress between them. Chris changed his position, brought the carbine smoothly to his shoulder – and staggered as I flung myself against him. The gun went off; I glimpsed a spurt of snowflakes. Before he could get his balance I grabbed at his hair; got a grip on his waxy coat. Trying to haul him backwards – drag him down.

He snarled, and shook me off. I lost my footing, and landed on my back. Chris turned on me: brought the rifle round to bear. With nowhere to roll, I reacted without thinking – scooping up a snowball to pelt him in the face. Bull's-eye; he stumbled back, shaking his head with animal confusion.

I gathered my legs beneath me, scrambled up – and he was ready. The butt of his gun sank deep into my midriff. With an anguished whoop, I doubled up and dropped.

He stood over me, breathing hard. I could sense the carbine pointing down like an accusing finger. I heard him swallow.

'You lost your daughter's soul, as well as yours. Take that thought to your grave.'

Still gasping painfully for air, I turned my head. The muzzle of his gun was very close. My mind, shocked cold, could almost feel the bullet: a hideous hammer, poised over my skull. Lights-out at the twitch of a finger. But it couldn't finish here. Not *now*.

I opened my mouth to say as much – but he cut me off with a gurgle of surprise. I sensed his body twist and thresh. The rifle fell aside into the snow.

Seizing my chance, I squirmed away; then rolled onto my back to stare. Chris was still on his feet, but in no position to pursue. There was a noose round his neck, drawn tight, and he was struggling not to choke. I looked along the length of rope, and found an Ironside at the end: the last of Warwick's horsemen. He sat and watched his victim for a moment – with his face in shadow, the helmet looked quite empty – then turned away, and set his blind mount walking.

The sagging rope grew taut, and Chris went stumbling in his wake. Then, as the horse picked up its pace, he slipped and fell. The rider's helmet didn't turn. He kept on across the field, relentless, towards the trees. Dragging his captive bodily behind him. Ploughing a ragged furrow through the snow.

Even as I got myself together – sweaty and numb with shock – I felt a thrill of horror at the image. Like a spider hauling something away; crawling back to a dark corner of its lair. It wasn't sympathy I felt; but empathy, perhaps. Enough to make me sick.

'Rachel!' Razoxane called – but it was Warwick who came in answer.

He'd crept forward through the graves without us seeing; using up his men to get in close. Now he was up and charging. I yelled a warning as he loped across the snow; but she was already swinging round to meet the threat. He was brandishing a sabre, notched and rusting. It scythed towards her face, and would have sliced it if she hadn't tossed her head. The evasive action cost her her balance, and she let herself slump back against the stonework.

Warwick closed with her, and thrust. The butt of her shotgun turned the point, but the impact jarred the weapon from her hands. She threw herself aside, rolled clear. His blade struck sparks from the old church wall as he swung again, and missed.

I pelted over to where she'd left her case; but there was only one thing left of any use. Grasping her shovel, I threw it into her path as she scrambled out from under his sword. She seized it, squirmed around and fairly powered to her feet.

Now they were more evenly matched: circling like duellists in the dirty, trampled snow. All I could do was stand well clear, and watch.

Warwick slashed with his sword; she parried with the shovel – holding it out stiff-armed to block the blow. He followed through; she ducked, and stumbled back. He pressed home his advantage like a prowling, grisly bear – but Razoxane moved as quickly as a cat. She sprang away, spun round to gain momentum, and swung the shovel hard against his ribs.

Warwick's turn to stagger, and lose ground.

Razoxane moved round him, breathing hard. He glowered at her, brandishing his sword. Two baleful spectres in the dawn: death-black, and dismal grey.

He feinted: came again. She knocked his blow aside. Warwick's sword went flying from his grasp.

'*Yes*,' I almost yelped, as he retreated. Razoxane strode forward, readying her swing. I didn't understand why Warwick's face was so exultant – until he drew a pistol from under his cloak.

'Take this to thy heart,' he snarled, and shot her.

The gun discharged a gout of dirty smoke – but I clearly saw its bullet strike her chest. It blew a hole in her coat the size of a fifty-pence piece. The sudden, brutal impact arched her spine, and threw her backwards, arms flung wide. She teetered on her boot-heels for a moment, then fell back into the snow.

Frozen with shock, I waited for her to struggle up again; but all she could do was twitch, like someone fitting. And then her body slumped, and she was still.

'Razoxane . . .' I mouthed, my eyes like saucers. Even as Warwick turned and moved towards me, I couldn't stop staring; couldn't turn and run. Another moment and I'd lost my chance. Seizing me by my shoulder and my hair, he dragged me round, and over to the church.

'Come thou with me,' he grated in my ear. 'Be purified.'

The wooden doors weren't locked. Kicking them wide, he hauled me through and down the aisle – towards the carved stone font.

Oh no, I thought, *not water – not again.*

He couldn't do this: I'd been through it once already. Not even fate played games like that.

I tried to wriggle free; he jerked my head back – hard. Grimacing with pain, I veered into a pew, rebounded off, and almost lost my balance. But his grip on my hair and arm stayed firm, and held me upright. I stumbled as he shoved me on before him, forcing the pace with his grim, relentless strides. The cupola of stone loomed closer. *Closer.*

'Oh God,' I gasped: vainly digging in my heels against the flagstones. 'You've got her now. Leave me . . .'

'This must be done,' was his implacable response. 'Suffer it for the good of thy soul.'

We lurched against the font, with a jolt that emptied my lungs. Pinioned by his weight, I threshed against it – but he was much too strong. I couldn't resist the pressure bearing down on my skull. Inch by painful inch, he forced my face towards the water. My final plea raised ripples on its cool black surface.

'Jesus, please, just let me see my daughter . . .'

'Ask that of thy God, not me,' he said: and pushed me under.

Holy water felt no different from the stuff you get from taps: as cold as the contents of Chris's bath – and just as horrible to drown in. I squirmed in panic; and Warwick dragged my dripping head back up.

'I baptize thee, Rachel Young . . . in the name of the

Father . . .' he ducked me again; I came up coughing water '. . . and of the Son . . .' I scrabbled to get a grip on the crumbled rim, but couldn't find one. Down I went once more '. . . and of the Holy *Ghost*.'

A shattering *bang* split the stillness of the church, and pelted every cranny with its echoes. But something much more solid hit the font's stone rim, and glanced off with an upflung plume of dust.

Warwick flinched away, and lost his hold. I slithered, panting hoarsely, to my knees. With one damp cheek still pressed against the stone, I looked towards the doors.

Razoxane was standing just inside them.

Bathed in a spill of pallid twilight, she stood out in dark relief. Her pistol was levelled in one hand; the smoke from her shot spreading palely through the gloom, like incense. Her other held the shovel at her side.

I felt an icy tingle through the wet hairs on my nape.

A muffled oath from Warwick. I heard him stepping back. Razoxane stood her ground a moment longer. Then, slow as a mourner, she started down the aisle towards us.

My stomach cringed away, against my spine. There was no glint of fellow-feeling on her cold, pale face. He'd shot her down out there. Destroyed her. And now her corpse had come for its revenge.

Suddenly Warwick's mildewed glove was in my hair again. He clenched his fist, and dragged me back against him.

'Get thee gone!' he barked into the settling hush. 'Go to thy grave, in the name of Jesus Christ!'

Razoxane kept advancing. The muzzle of her weapon didn't waver. Her trailing shovel scraped across the stones, like a rusty counterpoint to her slow and measured steps.

I drew my legs up under me, boots skidding for a purchase. Warwick yanked me back off-balance. My mouth opened wide in a silent scream as my hair took all my weight.

There was a small black book in his free hand; I glimpsed it out of smarting eyes. He brandished it at Razoxane now.

'Come no closer. Thou hast no power here. This is God's house.' His voice was low and fierce: a dark blaze of conviction. But Razoxane's slow footsteps didn't falter.

I could smell her now. The bloodless hole over her heart shed an ancient, musty odour of decay.

'I bid thee *go*,' snarled Warwick. 'In the name of Jesus *Christ*.' Hearing that invocation on *his* lips distressed me beyond words.

Razoxane was very close now. Warwick extended his Bible or prayer-book at arm's length; I thought I saw it tremble, very slightly.

'Jesus Christ,' he repeated, gravel-breathed.

Razoxane halted then; inclined her head: a half-indulgent gesture. She raised her antique pistol with a flourish – and tossed it aside. Its clatter on the flagstones filled the church.

Then she snatched her shovel in a two-fisted grip, and swung it at his head.

Warwick ducked away, but not quite fast enough. I felt a jolt go through him as his frame absorbed the blow. He lurched off sideways, and let me fall. His devotional black book took flight, and crashed to earth, its withered pages fluttering like wings.

I scrambled round, to see him slump against a pillar. The blow must have split his collarbone, at least. He began to slither downward, helpless to resist as Razoxane stepped forward.

'No fire in *your* bones, Warwick,' she snarled through her teeth. 'But once the brains are out, the thing is done . . .'

'No, *wait*!' I blurted out, and struggled up. 'Where's Cathy? Ask him that.'

Razoxane looked round, her shovel poised. That thin, familiar smile touched her features like a frost. Cold as it was, it was something I could cling to. It was *her*.

'All right then, Rachel,' she said dryly. 'Go ahead.'

I swallowed, and looked to Warwick. His baleful eyes glared up from where he crouched.

'Thy daughter lives,' he spat, before I could open my mouth. 'She sleeps at the wood's edge. Pray for her soul, that the sins of her mother be not visited on her.'

I felt a moment's giddiness, and almost swayed. 'You haven't hurt her, then?' I ventured hoarsely.

'Not a hair of her head,' was his harsh retort; but the sneer felt like a mask – disguising deeper feelings. 'Go, take her – and be damned.'

'After you,' said Razoxane, and aimed her blow.

'Your mother spared his life,' I said suddenly.

Her expression didn't flicker – but she paused. I felt my throat grow tighter as the moment lengthened. The words had come from nowhere: the thought that lay behind them still half-formed. Oh God, I wasn't sure if I had meant it.

Razoxane gave me an interrogating glance. I hesitated. Then, flicking wet hair from my eyes, I sidled closer. The idea was growing clearer with each step, like the day coming up outside.

Warwick watched with loathing from the shadows.

'She was a healer-woman, wasn't she?' I said, ignoring him. 'She wanted you to follow *her* way.'

A smile with no humour crossed her face, and faded. 'I tried, Rachel. You know I did. But my destiny was otherwise. You know that too.'

'Change it, then,' I murmured. 'Change it now.'

Her nostrils flared with grim amusement; but the pale skin had grown tight across her cheekbones. 'You think it's that easy?'

'If you're strong enough, perhaps.' I moistened my lips. 'Didn't you say that mercy takes a lot more strength than murder?'

Now I could read the struggle in her face – and so

could Warwick. With his good arm still half-raised, he was watching our exchange with an uncomprehending scowl.

'I ask no mercy from the likes of thee,' he muttered.

'Oh, just shut up, you bloody *Puritan*,' I snapped at him. It took an effort of my own to quell the outburst. I was still half-breathless from his pitiless attempt to drown me; could still taste bitter water at the back of my throat . . .

Razoxane shifted at my side. I took hold of her sleeve, still glowering at Warwick.

'I know what you did to your daughter,' I went on grimly. 'I know you can't forget that. My Cathy reminds you of her – doesn't she? So my little girl's life can cancel your debt – all right? If you'll just leave us in peace . . .'

Warwick's face was carved in stone; I still couldn't see what feelings lay behind it. Razoxane, beside me, was as rigid as a statue herself. I realized my fingers had locked tight around her arm.

And then, quite suddenly, she lowered her shovel – as if weary of its weight. Like someone laying down a cross. Her shoulders slumped, relaxing. So did mine.

Stillness for many seconds. Then Warwick gave a slow shake of his head.

'No. This cannot be. If thou sparest my life, then I must needs be damned.'

'You can keep your soul,' I said. 'We give this free. Now go. Now *leave us*.'

He just stared at me, perplexed; then clambered slowly to his feet. The rustle of his cloak, the creak of leather: those were the only noises in the silent church. We moved to either side to let him pass. My skin prickled nervously as he drew level: I was well within reach. But he just gave me a sidelong look, and kept on walking. Even in retreat, the set of that shadowed face gave me the shivers.

He looked at Razoxane as well – she'd kept a prudent

hold on the haft of her shovel – and dismissed her just as mutely. We watched him go: down the aisle, and out into the dawn. A shadow into daylight. He didn't look back once.

An ache in my chest reminded me to breathe: I took a gasp of air, and sighed it out.

'Is it finished now?' I whispered: still staring towards the empty doorway.

'You offered him a way out, and he took it,' said Razoxane thoughtfully. 'I think perhaps it is.'

I looked at her then – and down at the hole in her coat. The noxious odour of decay made me wrinkle my nose.

'Oh God,' I said, still whispering. 'What's happened to you now?'

She gazed back at me for a moment; then opened the coat, delved into it . . . and came out with her Tarot pack. With a saturnine grin, she held it up for me to see. The end card showed the scythe and skeleton of Death. A soggy pit was sunk into its centre.

'*Razoxane*,' I said, with miffed relief.

The cards had been compressed into a single pulpy wad; the smell of centuries squeezed out of them, like rancid juice. But now, as her fingertips increased their pressure, they began to peel away and tumble to the floor. I stood and watched them streaming from her hand, each card with a hole blown through its ancient image. They scattered round my feet like bits of old, wet cardboard.

Warwick's shot had got two thirds of the way through the pack. I glimpsed it suddenly, a rough black ball – and Razoxane's free hand caught it as it fell. She closed her grip on the remaining cards, and turned them to see which one had stopped the shot. '*Il Becchino*,' she murmured softly; as if it were no more than she'd expected. *The Grave-Digger*. She slipped the undamaged cards into her pocket; then raised her head, and nodded towards the doors. 'So come on, then. Let's dig up a grave.'

Nervousness welled up as we emerged – but nobody

was waiting in ambush. I turned on my heel, looking warily around . . . but Warwick was nowhere to be seen. The bodies of his men lay cindered where they'd fallen: sunk in slush.

There were lights on now in the homes across the lane: the windows butter-bright against the monochrome landscape. The last act of her comedy had woken up an audience. But none had had the nerve to venture out.

Razoxane gestured towards the mercenary's grave, and led the way towards it. 'This one.'

I thought of Chris being hauled away: a fly on the spider's strand. I bit my lip.

'But why? If he's dead now?'

With a surge of effort, she drove her shovel down into the frozen earth – then glanced at me. 'His body is, perhaps. But whatever they've just done to him . . .' (I didn't want to think about that) '. . . his spirit will keep on travelling. Until we lay that to rest, there'll be no peace for either of us.'

'So how do we do that?'

'Get the coin-hoard out of the grave, and scatter it.'

I looked down at the snow. The ground would be rock-hard – and six feet solid. It might take us all day.

'All right . . . but we have to find Cathy first. She's all alone out there. And there's one of Warwick's men still left, remember . . .'

'We've been making some noise, in case you hadn't noticed,' she countered dryly, nodding off towards the houses. 'There'll be people here to see, and soon. We have to hurry.'

'It'll take us bloody *ages*,' I protested.

'Will it, now?' She gripped the shovel's handle, and bowed her head; then let it go again, and stepped away. Taking hold of my cloak, she tugged me backwards, leaving the shovel planted like a strange, gaunt tree. 'Come on, let's find some cover.'

Not quite sure what to expect, I withdrew across the

churchyard: picking my way between the jumbled graves. She gestured me down into a crouch behind a tombstone, and joined me in its shadow.

A jittery pause. Then the grave erupted in a burst of mouldy earth, like a septic tank exploding. It stank like one, as well: a slurry-stench that filled my nose, and made my stomach heave.

Razoxane bounded up while the fall-out was still settling; I raised my head more slowly. There was a pit of raw soil where the grave had been, surrounded by spatters of filthy snow. The headstone was in pieces.

'One blasting-rod's as good as any other,' she murmured, sounding pleased with herself; and beckoned me up and on towards the brink.

Lingering dusk had drained into the crater, making it seem deeper than it was; but the dim shapes at the bottom were five feet down at least. Muffling my mouth and nose against the dreadful smell, I tried to make them out. Three ill-defined grey lumps amid the churned-up soil. With all manner of gruesome possibilities on offer, it took me a moment to realize what they were.

'Any idea how much that hoard would fetch today?' mused Razoxane dryly.

One of the jars had split full-length. A dull, caked mass of silver coins gleamed faintly through the mud.

I shook my head. 'I wouldn't touch them with a bloody *barge-pole*.'

'Very wise. But you are going to have to climb down and fetch them out.'

Like hell, I thought, looking up from the hole. 'Oh I am, am I? What about you, then?'

She made a mock-apologetic gesture. 'They're the price on my head too, remember. I can't get near them. He'll sense me, if I get too close.'

I hesitated. 'Who will?'

She nodded downward. I looked again.

At first – for just an instant – I thought there were

worms down there: wriggling fitfully between the jars. Then, with a freezing flush, I realized they were long, grey fingers, poking up through the mire: feeling blindly for the light. Still linked to rotting hands beneath the surface; hands that had been clasped on a dead man's chest.

'Oh my God,' I whispered.

'There's no need to worry. Not if you're quick. He's got no claim on you.'

I shivered, and stepped right back from the edge. 'I am *not* climbing down in there.'

'You have to,' she said equably.

'Listen, wait . . . How can he be down there . . . and in Chris too?'

'His soul has wandered, but some of his instincts linger in the flesh: that's all. It might be I'd trigger them off . . .'

'And what if *I* do?'

'Rachel,' she grinned. 'Don't you trust me yet?'

'Good God, no,' I muttered.

Her expression sobered. 'We have to get the silver out of the grave, to lay his ghost. I can't lay hands on it. You have to.'

I glanced down again at those maggoty grey stirrings, and felt nausea rise within me. I remembered that dream I'd had: the corpse-trap with a bait of living silver; the rib-cage snapping closed. That had to be a warning. Had to be . . .

'Mummy . . .' said a tiny voice behind us.

Oh Jesus.

My body had reacted before my brain could take it in. My legs almost went from under me; an upsurge of emotion filled my chest.

Oh Jesus: make this real.

I swung around – and gasped in utter horror.

Cathy was there, peering miserably towards me. Hoisted up in Chris's arm; held close against his shoulder.

His free hand held a pistol on us both.

12

MARTYRS

He'd burned the Ironside that had snared him – I realized that at once. His coat had singed; his face was grimed with smoke.

Cathy's angel-face was just as dirty.

She was watching me with big, scared eyes; unable to understand how the nightmare could continue when she'd woken up at last. Just waiting for me to come and take her home.

It wasn't the gun that stopped me running forward. The threat of a mere bullet didn't faze me for a moment. But the tableau was as frozen as the snow around us; I was afraid to break it. Afraid of what might follow.

Chris looked me in the eye, expressionless; then switched his gaze to Razoxane. I felt her tensing up beside me – and saw a flicker on his face. A glint of satisfaction through the grime.

He renewed his steady purchase on the pistol's grip.

'My father used to use this for finishing jobs,' he said into the silence. 'One bullet, in the brain-pan. It takes more than that for these *things* you've summoned up. You have to fire, and fire, and fire again. But in the end, they burn.' His voice was slightly breathless, as if he'd just run the race of his life. And won it.

Cathy's eyes: imploring. She couldn't understand why I just stood there.

'You want peace? We can give it,' said Razoxane softly.

'Spoken like a witch,' was his sneered response. 'A temptress to the last.'

'She's right,' I joined in: biting down the quaver in my voice. 'All we have to do . . . is get the silver out of the grave. You'll be free then. You can rest . . .'

'You really think I'm stupid, don't you?' he said calmly.

'*No*. Please . . .' I swallowed, and spread my hands. 'I know about your past now – just as you told me. The man you were before is buried here. You don't have to earn the silver; just carry it away. That's *all*.' My desperation made the subtext clear: *Just give me back my daughter. Let her go.*

All this was way above her poor little head. She clung to Chris's coat like a limpet: he'd saved her from the Ragman, after all – and the ground was a long way down. But she knew she wasn't safe outside my arms. I could see it written clearly on her face.

Oh *Cathy*.

Razoxane took a wary sideways step. I glanced nervously towards her. Her weapons had been scattered round the churchyard, but God knew what powers she might still have up her sleeve. Powers to blind and to burn. But she couldn't use them; not with Cathy there.

She *couldn't*.

'I made common cause with your kind, once,' Chris said – still addressing us both. 'I've suffered for that so *much*. So don't waste your breath in lying to me now . . .'

'For God's sake, Chris,' I hissed, beside myself. 'Warwick made his peace with us. Can't you?'

Cathy began grizzling then, against his shoulder. He jogged her irritably, but the tears kept flowing, pearl-bright against her grubby cheeks.

'Sshhh, poppet,' I called, close to tears of my own. 'It's all right. It's going to be all right . . .'

'Of course it will,' said Chris; and squeezed the trigger.

The sudden blast made me physically jump; Cathy's voice rose in a wail. And Razoxane spun and fell into the snow.

I swung around – and knew at once she wasn't faking

this time. He'd hit her in the shoulder; the arm was twisted, crippled. Her face, already pale, was bleached with shock. She lay where she had landed, on her back: wheezing urgently for breath. With hat and glasses shaken off, she looked younger and more vulnerable than I'd ever seen her.

Cathy was developing hysterics, her face crimson and contorted. I was just starting forward when Chris shrugged her off and dumped her in the snow. The shock stemmed the flow for a moment; then redoubled it. Ignoring the poised revolver, the smoke that hung like breath, I rushed towards her, skidded to my knees and scooped her up. Crushed her warmth against me, her wet face to my cheek, and rocked her crying body in my arms.

Cathy. Cathy. Cathy.

Beside me, Chris shot Razoxane again.

'*Mummy . . .*' Cathy mewled in my ear. Still rocking her, I turned my head to see.

Razoxane had been trying to rise; he'd flattened her. But she wasn't finished yet. Grimacing with pain, she squirmed and arched her spine; then opened her mouth in a silent yell. Even if she had kept power back, she wasn't in a state to use it now.

I looked at Chris. He was smiling down with dreadful satisfaction.

'When people are executed by firing squad . . .' he said, to one or both of us, 'the sentence is, that they'll be "shot to death". That implies a process. It takes *time*.'

Again he fired. Razoxane doubled up as if he'd stamped on her stomach.

'Leave her,' I blurted. 'You don't need to do this.'

He gave me a glance; and renewed his aim at her.

'Please . . .'

He pulled the trigger. The pistol just went *click*.

'Don't look, poppet,' I whispered to Cathy. Setting her down, I clambered to my feet and made for Chris. This would be the only chance I'd get.

He'd swung the cylinder out already, spilling empty cartridges across the snow. Still rummaging in his pocket, he looked towards me.

'Stay *away*.'

The sudden flash of venom made me falter. My stomach spasmed. I'd lured him into one death-trap already: we both remembered that.

'Please, Chris. No tricks this time. Just leave us now. It's over.'

He snorted; fished up the first bullet, and plugged it into the gun.

I risked a look at Razoxane. She lay exhausted, panting; her pale eyes screwed half-shut. Trapped in her body – and everything she'd risked was in the balance. Spirit. Soul. *Survival.*

She'd come back here to help me. I couldn't leave her now.

'*Listen* to me,' I said; not sure what I could say if he did.

He left off his reloading to look at me again. Stared for a moment; then shook his head. 'I really fancied you, Rachel, you know that?' He sounded almost aggrieved.

Then he kicked me hard in the stomach.

Caught completely unawares, I folded forward, retching. The snow came up and hit me in the face. Bleating for breath, I rolled over and lay writhing.

'Mummy!' Cathy squealed, sounding very far away. Silly little girl: of course she'd looked.

'It has to be this way,' said Chris's voice, much closer. 'Bludgeon her to death, then burn her. Don't worry, you'll have it quicker. And your daughter won't suffer, I promise you that.'

With pain filling my belly like broken glass, that last bit took a moment to sink in. When it had, I didn't dare to believe it. Still helpless, I looked up at him in horror.

'. . . what . . . ?'

He shook his head. 'I can't leave you alive, Rachel.'

I didn't give a damn about me. 'But . . . Cathy . . .'

He looked past me towards her. 'You'll have poisoned her between you. It's the kindest thing to do.'

'*No!*' I tried struggling up, but couldn't make it past my knees. The pain was so acute, it felt as if my seven-year-old appendix scar had opened up again.

The revolver was full: he snapped it back together. I followed his gaze to where Razoxane had fallen. She was trying to crawl away.

He took aim and put a bullet in her path: kicked snow into her face. She looked round with a snarl – still defiant. A rabid bitch about to be put down. Her features were livid with pain and hate. But the passion was merely human now, without power to damage her tormentor.

I squirmed around. 'Cathy, run away! Go, *now*!'

Crouched down by a gravestone, she shook her head. 'I'm *scared*, Mummy . . .'

'For Christ's sake, *run*!'

She moved, then – but in the wrong direction: scuttling up to cower next to me. I tried impotently to fend her off; then held her close, and kissed her unwashed hair. It crossed my mind to pick her up and carry her – but I felt so weak and winded, I couldn't even make it on my *own*. He'd shoot me down before I reached the gate.

Chris started to advance on Razoxane: still deciding where to put his next bullet. I looked towards the houses and their warm, lit windows. Everyday life, just fifty yards away. The violence out here had kept the occupants indoors. But if I cried for help, might someone come?

Perhaps; and they'd get killed. Besides, I didn't even have the breath.

My helpless gaze came round again – and stopped half-way. For a moment I just stared at what I'd seen. And then the impulse: hideous, overwhelming. An icy spasm racked my aching stomach. Fighting it, and the nausea it brought with it, I glanced at Chris's back; then heaved Cathy up and turned her round towards the church.

'I want you to be very brave now,' I whispered hoarsely

in her ear. 'Run and hide in the church. Right inside. And *don't come out*. Whatever you hear . . . don't look outside, until good people have come inside to fetch you. Will you promise?'

Pouting with pent-up sobs, she nodded. I tugged a strand of her hair: lank straw between my fingers. Everything was focused on this moment. Even my frightened heartbeat seemed to slow.

'Remember Mummy loves you very much,' I told her, as my own tears reached the brim. 'And I'll see you again, all right? One day we'll all be home again, together.' I gave her a little push. 'Now off you go, sweet. *Run*.'

She took her first, faltering steps; then looked back one more time, her face perplexed and pale.

'But Mummy . . . where are *you* going?'

'I'm going to be with Daddy, love,' I said.

Chris fired at Razoxane again. Her body seemed to bounce against the snow. But even that close, he wasn't shooting to kill. Just maiming her, limb by limb.

I blinked to clear my stinging eyes, and turned back to check that Cathy was safe inside the church. She wouldn't peek this time; I'd made her promise. She was big enough to know what that meant.

Please God, don't let her see.

As soon as I rose upright, my heart began to hammer at my sternum: as if it knew what had to happen, and was desperate to get out. I felt a lurch in my stomach; my bone-dry throat was abruptly slick with bile.

It took appalling effort to make that first step forward. But once my muscles had unlocked and I was moving, I couldn't have stopped again if I had tried.

'Chris,' I called, as his gun turned down once more.

He looked around; smiled thinly. 'You want to believe she's safe in there? All right, believe it . . .'

Still walking, I raised my hands, feeling my cloak spread

heavily to left and right. 'You can have me, Chris – all right? I mean, *really* have me . . . if you just let Cathy go.'

'I can have you anyway, Rachel,' he said softly.

'Not without a fight, mate . . .' I swallowed, almost gagging on the taste. 'But just let her go, and I'm yours. I'll do anything you want.'

He brought his revolver round. 'No closer.'

I hesitated: my palms still spread, to show I was no threat. We were close to the edge of the gouged-out grave; the stench of mouldy soil filled my nostrils.

'Didn't you say you fancied me?' I said.

Sour amusement lit his face. 'This wouldn't be just a ploy to distract me, until someone interrupts us?' He glanced back at Razoxane; then sneered at me again. 'Think I'll lay off her to give you a quick one in the snow?'

'I'll come away with you,' I said.

He seemed to think it over – for a second or two. Then gave me his answer: a husk of a smile, without humour.

'No one can follow me where I'm going.'

God, but my heart had almost punched me breathless. I wiped wet hair from my streaming eyes. His own gaze flicked down towards the outline of my breasts. I felt them swell and sink as I took a gulpy breath.

'I'll let you put your hands on me,' I whispered. 'Then shoot me, I don't care. Just let her live.'

He stared at me for an awful, dragging moment. The hollow smile still rested on his features; but his eyes gave a glimpse of what was going on behind it. A conflict of doubt and desire.

I was hardly in a state to give him any come-ons; but maybe the wet and waifish look might tip the balance. He had a thing about water, after all; and drowning women . . .

Please . . . I begged him; shaping the word in silence with my lips.

He wavered . . . then stepped cautiously towards me: levelling his pistol at my belly. A backward glance showed him Razoxane still twitching in the snow. His head came round. The haunted amber eyes stared into mine.

Instinct urged me to back away before him, but I couldn't, I was rooted to the spot. My skin was wet and freezing with a sheen of perspiration. My heart jerked like a puppet by its strings.

Even at the last, at point-blank range, he seemed to change his mind. 'I promised I'd make it quick for you,' he murmured – and began to squeeze the trigger . . . then let it slacken, and reached out with his free hand to caress my dripping cheek . . .

He never saw it coming in my glazed and wretched stare; my lunge took him completely by surprise. I knocked his gun-hand sideways and just threw myself against him. He skidded, lost his balance and fell backwards; I landed on his chest, entangling him in the folds of my sodden cloak as we struggled for the gun. The pistol was between us; I went for it with all my nails. And as I clawed at his grasp like a spitting cat, I glimpsed the realization reach his face. It wasn't Holy Water that dripped from my clothes and hair and made my wide eyes weep. It was petrol. I'd emptied his jerrycans over myself.

His fierce face grew frantic. He tried with all his strength to fight me off. But I had only one purpose left in the world – and one sure way to do it. Forcing my finger through the trigger-guard, I pressed his knuckle down.

The gun went off with an ear-splitting crack. The burst from the muzzle lit the fumes that wreathed us both. I had one instant left to think of Cathy before the soaking petrol flashed to blinding flame.

*

When I finally opened my eyes, it was to find Razoxane crouched beside me, her face still drawn with pain.

My first, half-dazed assumption was that both of us were dead. Rising from our bodies now, and ready to move on. Thank God it was all over. Thank Christ it had been quick . . .

But the soggy feel of snow was too intrusive; much too real. I could feel my arms and legs; my hooked, claw-fingers. And if this was death, then why was she still hurting? Why was I?

A sense of utter horror flooded through me. I realized I was somehow still alive.

'Oh Jesus, no . . .' I whimpered. Dousing myself in petrol, I'd hoped and prayed to die outright; not linger. Not *survive*.

The skin of my face was sore and stinging, like a foretaste of the agony to come. I reached up for Razoxane then, to beg for her to kill me . . . and saw that my glove was barely singed.

I stared at it for a moment, quite nonplussed; then brought it slowly down to touch my cheek. The flesh was cool and smooth: unscarred. I looked at my other hand. The joints felt stiff, but that one was all right too.

It must have been the look on my face that made Razoxane grin.

'It's true, Rachel. Don't ask me how. The power of what you did for us, perhaps. A little bit of magic of your own.'

No reason to dispute the fact. I swallowed hard. 'And him . . . ?'

'Look,' she said.

I looked. Chris's body was slumped a dozen yards away. It seemed to have sucked in the flames through every pore; had burned so fiercely that it now appeared fused to the headstone against which it sagged. A charred and gutted shell: quite black, apart from the blind milky whites of the eyes. And still he smouldered.

'But is he really dead?' I asked in a small voice.

'Yes,' she murmured, just as softly. 'This time he really is.'

*

I didn't look back until we'd reached the cover of the trees. The snow dragged at my boots, but scarcely hindered my progress. Cathy clung to me in silence, resting her head against my shoulder.

Razoxane trailed behind us like a shadow, her guitar-case laden and slung. I was vaguely surprised that she was still walking. Chris had forced her to the edge, but he hadn't pushed her over. As soon as he'd stopped shooting, she'd begun clawing her way back. Clearly, in her present state, she could take enormous punishment.

But had she been punished enough?

When at last I turned my head, there were distant stirrings in the churchyard: people creeping out to look. Maybe the police had forced their way through at last.

I wondered what they'd make of the mess we'd left behind us. Long-dead bodies, burned twice over. Ancient bits and pieces scattered round. In the absence of a credible explanation, would such things be covered up? Perhaps they could.

'They'll follow our tracks . . .' I said suddenly; but Razoxane shook her head. Peering back across the field, I realized why. Once more, one final time, the scars were healing.

Cathy stirred against me. Hoisting her up a little higher, I touched my forehead to hers, and briefly closed my eyes. We were both beyond tears now.

'Want to go *home* . . .' she whimpered.

'Shh, now: soon be there,' I murmured, gently rocking her. 'Soon be home, my darling. I'm sorry I took so long.'

She snuggled closer, her grubby, tear-streaked face unsmiling. I patted her hair; then looked past her to where Razoxane was standing.

'It's over *now*?'

As if by way of answer, she dug in her greatcoat pocket – and fished up her spinner. The ivory cube was barely scorched, though she must have taken it off his body. She studied it for a thoughtful moment; then crushed it in her tattered leather glove, and looked at me.

'All over now. All done.'

I swallowed. 'Please, don't take this personally . . . but I don't *ever* want to see you again.'

It sounded hard: I knew that even as I said it. She'd risked so much – even though she'd owed me to begin with. But death followed Razoxane wherever she went. I'd sooner ask a plague victim to baby-sit than let her near my daughter.

There was grim determination in my voice; it lingered in my stare. But Razoxane just gave a rueful smile.

'I understand, Rachel. I've roads of my own to travel; bridges to cross. And who knows . . . maybe this time, I'll find my way home.'

Up in the branches of the nearest tree, her familiar cawed a rusty interruption. Razoxane glanced up at it; then shook her head.

'I know, Vedova,' she said softly. 'Still a long, long way to go.'

She paused for a moment's reflection; then glanced at me again. Still smiling faintly.

'Good fortune on your road, Rachel Young: wherever it leads you. I hope your journey's not as long as mine.'

I nodded dumbly, and watched her turn away. Vedova took wing from its perch, and flew ahead like a pathfinder. Still soothing Cathy, I watched them drift between the trees, and vanish. I kept on staring for several minutes longer, but the snowy wood was still.

Madwoman. Murderess. Revenant. Witch. Fading out of my life at last, like a shadow at the rising of the sun.

It was strange, how lonely I was left feeling.

*

So I carried Cathy home: skirting the wood, and joining the westbound road back into town. I barely noticed the ache in my arms and back, nor the sting of the cold on my drying cheeks. Cathy stayed quiet, but I had a growing sense of her contentment. Muffled warmly in a fold of my cloak, she slipped gently into sleep.

And Nick was somehow there as well – just as I'd promised her he would be. Not a sense of presence; much more intimate than that. I felt his reassurance, like a secret in my heart. *Morning's come. It always will. You won't be alone any more.*

I'd only been away from home three nights, but the flat seemed practically derelict when we got there. Still balancing Cathy, I hooked the keys from the pocket of my jeans, and let us in. There was a note to ring the police station lying there on the doormat, letting me know there'd been a break-in while I'd been away. No doubt they'd boarded up the broken door.

Walking through, my eye was caught by the picture in the hall: the optical illusion. I stopped in front of it and stared, but couldn't see the crows. There were only the doves, in wing-to-wing formation: flying west into the twilight, to their rest.

Cathy stirred sleepily against me. 'Are we home yet, Mummy?' she asked.

'Yes,' I said, and kissed her. 'Home at last.'